She paused at a store window, pulling her scarf over her head as a sharp gust of wind hit her. She glanced up the street out of the corner of her eye, and her breath caught. She spun around, convinced she'd made a mistake, but she hadn't.

Jack stood at the entrance to her building.

Susanna didn't move. His dark eyes were on her. He had on his white cowboy hat, a suede jacket, jeans and cowboy boots, and she thought he was the sexiest man on the planet.

But she fought a visceral, inexplicable urge to bolt. Not that she'd get far if her husband meant to talk to her, but this was her office, her city, her space. His presence felt like an invasion—yet it was what she'd wanted. For months, she'd dreamed of him coming to Boston, telling her he wanted her back in his life. She wanted to know she mattered to him. She wanted him to tell her. She wanted him to ask her to tell him all her secrets, one by one, to understand all of them. To admit his own fears and secrets, finally, she thought. To talk.

"When it comes to romance, adventure and suspense, nobody delivers like Carla Neggers."
—Jayne Ann Krentz

CARLA NEGGERS

THE CABIN

MIRA®

ISBN 1-55166-845-9

THE CABIN

Copyright © 2002 by Carla Neggers.

All rights reserved. Except for use in any review, the reproduction or
utilization of this work in whole or in part in any form by any electronic,
mechanical or other means, now known or hereafter invented, including
xerography, photocopying and recording, or in any information storage or
retrieval system, is forbidden without the written permission of the publisher,
MIRA Books, 225 Duncan Mill Road, Don Mills, Ontario, Canada M3B 3K9.

All characters in this book have no existence outside the imagination of the
author and have no relation whatsoever to anyone bearing the same name
or names. They are not even distantly inspired by any individual known or
unknown to the author, and all incidents are pure invention.

MIRA and the Star Colophon are trademarks used under license and registered
in Australia, New Zealand, Philippines, United States Patent and Trademark
Office and in other countries.

Visit us at www.mirabooks.com

Printed in U.S.A.

ACKNOWLEDGMENT

One of the great pleasures in finishing a book is getting the chance to express my gratitude to the many generous, knowledgeable people who took time from their own busy schedules to answer my questions. Christine Wenger not only answered every question I put to her—she made calls for me, read me penal codes, fact-checked and was an all-around pal who never told me to go away. (Well, she did, but I didn't take her seriously!) My wonderful friend Dorice Nelson and her husband, Shel Damsky, opened their gorgeous home to me and showed me the history and landscape of the Andirondacks as I've never seen them before—incredible!

I'm also grateful to Kathy Lynn and Sandy Emerson, Gretchen Neggers, Joe Rebello, Maggie Price, Sandi Kitt, Julie Kistler and two incredibly courteous and knowledgeable Texas Rangers for answering law-enforcement questions. Many thanks also to Meena Cheng for talking money with me. Blythe Jewell Gander, Jo-Ann Power, Mary Lynn and Len Baxter and all my family and many friends in Texas—thanks for everything.

Finally, I want to thank everyone at MIRA Books—especially Valerie Gray, Amy Moore-Benson and Dianne Moggy—and Meg Ruley, my amiable and wonderful agent.

Of course, any mistakes I've made and liberties I've taken are my doing. This is a story of pure fiction, straight out of my imagination, and I couldn't have had more fun writing it. Watch for Sam Temple's story next!

Carla Neggers P.O. Box 826
Quechee, Vermont 05059
www.carlaneggers.com

To Kate Jewell of central Vermont,
Elizabeth Cesarini of middle Tennessee,
Mikisha Doop of west Tennessee and Nicole Carbrera of
southeast Texas...who all came together on that frightening
July 4th weekend in western Massachusetts,
and made it through. You're an inspiration.

Love you all,
Mom/Carla

One

Susanna Galway sipped her margarita and watched the countdown to midnight on the television above the bar at Jim's Place, the small, dark pub just down the street from where she lived with her grandmother and twin teenage daughters. It had been a fixture in the neighborhood for as long as Susanna could remember.

An hour to go. There'd be fireworks, a new year to celebrate. It was a clear, dark, very cold night in Boston, with temperatures barely in the teens, but thousands had still gone out to enjoy the many First Night festivities.

Jim Haviland, the pub's owner, eyed Susanna with open suspicion. He made no secret that he thought she should have gone back to her husband in Texas months ago. And Susanna didn't disagree. But, still, she hadn't gone home.

Jim laid a sparkling white bar towel on one of his powerful shoulders. "You're feeling sorry for yourself," he told her.

She licked salt off her glass. It was warm in the

bar, and she wished she hadn't opted for cashmere. Silk would have been better. She'd been determined to feel a little bit elegant tonight. But Jim had already told her she looked like the Wicked Witch of the East coming in there in her black skirt, sweater and boots, with her long black hair—apparently only her very green eyes saved her. Her coat was black, too, but she'd hung it up and tucked her black leather gloves in her pocket before sliding onto her stool. She hadn't bothered with a hat since the bar was only a few doors down from Gran's house.

"I never feel sorry for myself," she said. "I looked at all my choices for the evening and decided I'd like nothing better than to ring in the New Year with one of my father's oldest friends."

Jim snorted. "I know bullshit when I hear it."

Susanna smiled at him, unrepentant. "You make a pretty good margarita for a Yankee." She set her glass down. "Why don't you make me another?"

"Okay, but two's your limit. You're not passing out in my bar. I'm not calling your Texas Ranger husband and telling him I let his wife fall off one of my bar stools and hit her head—"

"Such drama. I'm not getting myself drunk, and you'd call Gran, not Jack, because Gran's just up the street, and Jack's in San Antonio. And I know you're not the least bit intimidated because he's a Texas Ranger."

Jim Haviland gave her a half smile. "Sixty-eight degrees in San Antonio."

Susanna refused to let him get to her. He was the father of her best friend in Boston, her own father's boyhood friend and a surrogate uncle to her these past fourteen months since she'd been on her own up north. He was opinionated, solid and predictable. "Are you going to make me that margarita?" she asked.

"You should be in Texas with your family."

"I had Maggie and Ellen for Thanksgiving. Jack has them for Christmas and New Year's."

Jim scowled. "Sounds like you're divvying up dibs on the neighborhood snowblower."

"It doesn't snow in San Antonio," Susanna said with an easy smile. She'd put an imaginary, protective shield around her to get her through the night, and she was determined nothing would penetrate it—not guilt, not fear, not thoughts of the only man she'd ever loved. She and Jack had done the holidays together last year. That hadn't worked out very well. Their emotions were still too raw, neither ready to talk. Not that her husband was *ever* ready to talk.

"You know," Jim said, "if I were Jack—"

"If you were Jack, you'd be investigating serial killers instead of making me margaritas. What fun would that be?" She pushed her glass across the bar toward him. "Come on. A nice, fresh margarita. You can reuse my glass. Hold the salt this time if you want."

"I'll hold the liquor before I hold the salt, and I'm not reusing your glass. Health laws."

"There are six other bars within walking distance," Susanna said. "I have on my wool socks. I can find somebody to serve me another margarita."

"They all use mixes."

But Jim Haviland didn't call her bluff. He snatched up her empty glass and set it on a tray, then grabbed a fresh glass. His bar was impeccably clean. He offered one nightly dinner special and kept an eye on his customers, running his bar in strict accordance with Massachusetts law. People didn't come to Jim's Place to get drunk—it was a true neighborhood pub, as old-fashioned as its owner. Susanna had always felt safe there, welcomed even when Jim was on her case and she wasn't at her nicest herself.

"I shipped Iris and her pals up a gallon of chili," he said. "How do you like that? Even your eighty-two-year-old grandmother's having more fun on New Year's than you are."

"They're playing mahjong until five minutes after midnight. Then they're calling it quits and going to bed."

Jim eyed her again, less critically. He was a big, powerfully built man in his early sixties who treated Susanna like an honorary niece, if a wayward one. "You went home last New Year's," he pointed out softly.

And she'd meant for her and Jack to settle whatever was going on between them, but the one time they were alone, on New Year's Eve, they'd ended up in bed together. They hadn't settled anything.

Exactly one year ago, she'd been making love to her husband.

Two margaritas weren't going to do the trick. She could get herself rip-roaring drunk, but it wouldn't stop her from thinking about where she'd been last year at this time and where she was now. Nothing had changed. Not one damn thing.

Fourteen months and counting, and she and Jack were still in limbo, a kind of marital paralysis that she knew couldn't last. Maggie and Ellen were seniors in high school now, applying to colleges, almost grown up. They'd called a couple of hours ago, and Susanna had assured them she was ringing in the New Year in style. No mahjong with Gran and her pals. She didn't want her daughters thinking she was pitiful.

She hadn't talked to Jack.

"There's nobody here, Jim," she said. "Why don't you close up the place? We can go up on the roof and catch the fireworks."

He looked up from the margarita he was reluctantly fixing for her. His movements were careful, deliberate. And his blue eyes were serious. "Susanna, what's wrong?"

"I bought a cabin in the Adirondacks," she blurted. "But that's good. It's a great cabin. It's in a gorgeous spot. Three bedrooms, stone fireplace, seven acres right on Blackwater Lake."

"The Adirondacks are way the hell up in New York."

She nodded. "The largest wilderness area in the lower forty-eight states. Six million acres. Gran grew up on Blackwater Lake, you know. Her family used to own the local inn—"

"Susanna. For God's sake." Jim Haviland shook his head heavily, as if this new development—a cabin in the Adirondacks—was beyond his comprehension. "You should buy a place in Texas, not in the boonies of upstate New York. What were you thinking? Jesus, when did this happen?"

"Last week. I went up to Lake Placid for a few days on my own—I don't know, it seemed like a positive thing to do. I needed to clear my head. I saw this cabin. It's not all that far from my parents' summer place on Lake Champlain. I couldn't resist. I figured if not now, when?''

"You and clearing your head. I've been listening to that line for months. The only thing that's going to clear your damn head is marching your ass back to Texas and sorting things out with your husband. Not buying cabins in the freaking woods.''

Susanna pretended not to hear him. "Gran's practically a legend in the Adirondacks, did you know that? She was a guide in her teens and early twenties, before she and my dad moved to Boston. He was just a little tyke—I'm sure he doesn't remember. Gran seemed a little shocked when I told her I'd bought a place right on Blackwater Lake.''

Jim shoved the fresh margarita in front of her, his jaw set hard. He didn't say a word.

She picked up the heavy glass, picturing herself standing on the porch of the cabin, staring out at the ice and snow on the lakes and surrounding mountains. "Something happened to me when I was up there—I don't know if I can explain it. It's as if this cabin was just meant to be. As if I was supposed to buy it.''

"Moved by invisible forces?''

She ignored his sarcasm. "Yes." She sipped her drink, which she noticed was not as strong as her first one. "My roots are there.''

"Roots, my ass. Iris and your dad haven't lived in the Adirondacks in, what, sixty years?''

He shook his head, plainly mystified by this latest move of hers. He hadn't liked it when she'd set up her office in Boston with Tess, his daughter who was a graphic artist, then stayed on her own after Tess had moved up to her nineteenth-century carriage house on the north shore with her new family. Office space implied a permanence Jim Haviland didn't want Susanna to establish in Boston. He wanted her back with her husband. It was the way his world worked.

Hers, too, but life wasn't always that simple.

Plus, she knew Jim liked Lieutenant Jack Galway, Texas Ranger. No surprise there. They were both men who saw most things in terms of black and white.

Jim wiped down the bar with his white towel, putting muscle into the effort, as if somehow it might relieve his frustrations with her and make him understand why she'd bought a cabin. "The Adirondacks are what, a five, six-hour drive?"

"About that." Susanna drank more of her margarita. "I got my pilot's license this fall. Jack doesn't know. Maybe I'll buy a plane. There's a nice little airport in Lake Placid."

Jim stared at her, assessing. "A cabin in the mountains, a plane, black cashmere—how much damn money do you have?"

Her stomach twisted into an instantaneous knot.

She had ten million as of the first of October. It was a milestone. People knew she was doing well, but few had any idea how well—not even her own husband. She just didn't talk about it. She didn't want money clouding anyone's opinion of her. Of themselves. She didn't want it to change her life, except maybe it already had. ''I've made some lucky investments,'' she told Jim.

''Ha. I'll bet luck had nothing to do with it. You're smart, Susanna Dunning Galway. You're smart, and you're tough, and—'' He paused for air, which he sucked in, then heaved out in a despairing sigh. ''Damn it, Susanna, you have no goddamn business buying a cabin in the Adirondacks. Jack doesn't know?''

''You don't give up, do you?''

''That means, no, Jack doesn't know. What are you doing, trying to piss him off to the point he gives up on you—or comes up here to fetch you?''

''He's not coming up here to fetch me.''

''Don't count on it.''

A young couple wandered in and sat at one of the tables, hanging on to each other, not bothering with First Night festivities, Susanna thought, for very different reasons than hers. Jim greeted them warmly and went around the bar to take their order, but he stopped to glower back at her. ''Did you tell Iris you were buying a place in her old stomping grounds, give her a chance to weigh in?'' He didn't wait for her to answer. ''No, you didn't, because you're bull-headed and do what you damn well want to do.''

''I'm not selfish—''

''I didn't say you were selfish. You're one of the kindest, most generous people I know. I said you're bullheaded.''

Her head spun. Maybe she should have consulted Jack. His name wasn't on the deed but they were still married. She planned to get around to telling him— it wasn't like her cabin was a secret. Not really.

When she was on Blackwater Lake, her husband and her marriage weren't the issue. The cabin was about her, her life, her roots. She couldn't explain. She'd almost felt as if she'd been destined to go up there, see the lake on her own, that somehow it would help her make sense of the past fourteen months.

Jim took the couple's order and headed back behind the bar. Before she said another word, he dipped her up a bowl of steaming chili and set it in front of her. "You need something in your stomach."

"I really want another margarita."

"Not a chance."

"I live up the street." She stared at the chili, spicy and hot on a very cold Boston night. But she wasn't hungry. "If I pass out in a ditch, somebody will find me before I freeze to death."

Jim refrained from answering. Davey Ahearn had come into the bar, easing onto his favorite stool just down from Susanna. Susanna could feel the cold still coming off him. He shook his head at her. "Pain in the ass you are, Suzie, I wouldn't count on it. We all might leave you in the damn ditch, hope the cold'll jump-start your brain and you'll go back to Texas."

"The cold weather doesn't bother me."

Of course, the cold wasn't Davey's point at all, and she knew it. He was a big man, a plumber with a huge handlebar mustache and at least two ex-wives. He was another of her father's boyhood friends, godfather to Jim Haviland's daughter, Tess, and a constant thorn in Susanna's side. Tess said it was best not to encourage Davey Ahearn by trying to argue with him, but Susanna seldom could resist—and neither could Tess.

He ordered a beer and a bowl of chili with saltines, and Susanna made an exaggerated face. "Saltines and chili? That's disgusting."

"What're you doing here, anyway?" Davey shivered, as if still shaking off the frigid temperatures. Boston had been in the grips of a bitter cold snap for days, and even the natives had had enough. "Go play mahjong with Iris and her pals. A million years old, and they know how to party."

"You're right," Susanna said. "It's not a good sign, me sitting in a Somerville bar drinking margaritas and eating chili with a cranky plumber."

Davey grinned at her. "I eat chili with a fork."

She bit back an unwilling laugh. "That's really bad, Davey. I mean, *really* bad."

"Made you smile." His beer and nightly special arrived, and he unwrapped three packets of saltine crackers and crumbled them onto his chili, paying no attention to Susanna's groan. "Jimmy, how long before we can stick a fork in this year?"

"Twenty-five minutes," Jim said. "I thought you had a date."

"I did. She got mad and went home."

Although she wasn't hungry, Susanna tried some of her chili. "Davey Ahearn annoying a woman? I can't imagine."

"Was that sarcasm, Mrs. Jack Galway?"

Jim intervened. "All right, you two. I'm opening a bottle of bubbly at midnight. It's on the house. What do we have, a half-dozen people in here?"

He lined up the glasses on the bar. Susanna

watched him work, the chili burning in her mouth, the two margaritas she'd consumed on an empty stomach making her a little woozy. "Do you think I had kids too young?" Susanna asked abruptly, without thinking. It had to be the margaritas. "I don't. I think it was just what happened. I was twenty-two, and all of a sudden, I'm pregnant with twins."

"I bet it wasn't all of a sudden," Davey said.

She pretended not to hear him. "And here I am with this man—this independent, hardheaded Texan who wants to be a Texas Ranger never mind that he went to Harvard. We met when he was a student—"

"We remember," Jim said gently.

"They were cute babies, Maggie and Ellen. Adorable. They're fraternal twins—they're not identical."

But Jim and Davey already knew that, too. Her chest hurt, and she fought a sudden urge to cry. What was wrong with her? Margaritas, New Year's Eve, a cabin in the mountains. Not being with Jack.

Jim Haviland checked each champagne glass to make sure it was clean. "They were damn cute babies," he concurred.

"That's right, you'd see them when we were up visiting Gran. Her place was always my anchor as a kid—we moved around all the time. It's no wonder I came here when push came to shove with Jack and me."

She shut her eyes, willing herself to stop talking. When she opened them again, the room was spinning a little, and she cleared her throat. If she did pass out and hit her head, Jim Haviland and Davey Ahearn would seize the moment and call Jack. No question in her mind. Then Jack would tell them a concussion served her right.

Susanna's heart raced. "This is only the second time Maggie and Ellen have flown alone." She narrowed her eyes to help steady the room, imagining Jack there with one of his amused half smiles. She couldn't remember when she'd had two margaritas in a row. He'd take credit. Say she was lonely. Missed him in bed. She gave herself a mental shake. "I was a nervous wreck the first time they flew alone."

"Doesn't look like you're doing much better this time," Davey said.

She had to admit that a third margarita would put her over the edge. She was hanging by her fingernails as it was. That was why Jim Haviland had glowered and chatted with her and served her up the chili—not just to give her a hard time, but to keep her from freefalling.

"What if Maggie and Ellen end up going to college in Texas?" She gulped for air, looking over at Davey. "What if I stay up here? My God, I'll never see them. And Jack—"

Davey drank some of his beer, wiping the foam off his mustache. "Are there colleges in Texas?"

His wisecrack cut through her crazy mood. "That's not funny. What if Texans came up here and made stupid assumptions about northerners?"

"What, like we're all rude and talk too fast? Maggie and Ellen tell me that all the time. Some of us also eat saltines with our chili." He winked at her, knowing he'd made his point. "And you're a northerner, you know, Suzie-cue. I don't care how many times you moved as a kid. Your dad grew up right here on this street. When Iris can't keep up with her place anymore, he and your mom will move in with her. They'll board up the gallery in Austin before you know it.''

"That's the plan," Susanna admitted.

"A plumber, a bartender and an artist." Davey shook his head in amazement. "Who'd have thought it? Although Kevin always was good with the graffiti.''

Susanna smiled. Both her parents were artists, her mother also an expert in antique quilts. They'd surprised everyone seven years ago when they opened a successful gallery in Austin and started restoring a 1930s home, a project seemingly without end. But they still spent summers on the New York shore of Lake Champlain. When Susanna was growing up, they'd moved from place to place to teach, work, open and close galleries and otherwise indulge their wanderlust. They'd been a little shocked when Susanna had gone into financial planning and married a Texas Ranger, but she'd always gotten along well with her parents and had liked having them close by in Austin. They didn't interfere with her relationship with Jack, but she knew Kevin and Eva Dunning didn't understand why their daughter was living with Gran. Their response to both Susanna and Jack had been the same: they'd come to their senses soon enough.

Jim examined a frosty bottle of champagne and said idly, as if reading Susanna's mind, "You've never explained what it was that made you come up here. Did you and Jack have a big fight, or did you just wake up one day and decide you needed to hear a Boston accent?''

"Maggie and Ellen had already planned to spend a semester up here—"

"Like it's Paris or London," Davey said. "Their semester abroad."

"Their semester with Gran," Susanna corrected.

"Yeah, now it's a year," Jim said, "and it doesn't explain you."

"There was a stalker." The words were out before she could stop them. "I suppose technically he wasn't a stalker—he turned up where I was a couple of times, but I can't prove he followed me. I didn't even know who he was until he showed up in my kitchen. He said things."

Davey Ahearn swore under his breath. Jim stared at her, grim-faced, neither man kidding now. "What did you do?" Jim asked.

Susanna blinked rapidly. What was wrong with her? She'd never told anyone this. No one. Not a soul. *This* was a secret, she thought. "I tried not to provoke him. He wanted me to talk to Jack on his behalf. He said his piece and left."

Jim looked tense. "Then what?"

"Then…nothing. I decided to come up here with Maggie and Ellen. Stay a few weeks." She almost smiled. "Clear my head."

Jim Haviland held his champagne bottle to one side and studied her closely while she ate more of her chili, barely tasting it now. Finally, he shook his head. "Jesus. You didn't tell Jack about this bastard in your kitchen."

"I know it sounds irrational." She set her fork

down and sniffled, picking up her margarita glass, noticing the slight tremble in her hand. "I mean, Jack's a Texas Ranger. *You'd* tell him if you had a stalker, right?"

"Goddamn right. It's one thing not to tell Jack about buying a cabin in the mountains, but a stalker—"

"It seemed to make sense at the time."

Jim inhaled sharply, then breathed out. "Tell him now. You can use the phone in back. Call him *right now* and tell him."

"It's too late. It wouldn't make any difference."

"This guy's in jail?"

She shook her head.

Jim narrowed his gaze on her. "Dead?"

"No, he's never been charged with anything. He's a free man."

"Because you never told anyone he was stalking you—"

"No, no one would be interested in my stalking story. He'd just explain it away. Coincidence, misunderstanding, desperation. The authorities would never touch it, now or then." She sipped her margarita, the melting ice diluting the alcohol. "They wanted this guy for a much bigger crime than spooking me."

This got Davey Ahearn's attention. "Yeah? Like what? What else did he do? Kill his wife?"

"Yes, as a matter of fact, Davey, that's exactly what he did." Susanna stared up at the television and watched the clock tick down to midnight. Four minutes to go. Three minutes and fifty-nine seconds. Happy New Year. "He killed his wife."

Two

Jack Galway woke on New Year's Day to an empty bed, a raging headache and dark thoughts about his wife. Push was coming to shove between the two of them. He didn't know when or how, but it would. Soon. He was tired of waking up alone in bed. He was tired of being pissed off about the things she hadn't told him. Susanna and her secrets.

He'd celebrated last night with his daughters and about a million of their friends. No alcohol. They were under twenty-one, and he had to drive a bunch of them home. He was in bed by one. Alone.

Last year was better. Maggie and Ellen had gone to a friend's house, and he and his slim, dark-haired, green-eyed wife had headed straight for the bedroom. He supposed they should have worked on some of their "issues" then. But they hadn't. The emotions between them—the anger and frustration—were still too volatile. They were locked into their silence, stubborn. And it had been too many weeks without making love.

Jack gritted his teeth. There was no point in dwelling on last year, but the truth was, he'd thought a night in bed with him would at least keep his wife from going back up to Boston. Wrong.

Steeling himself against his pounding head, he rolled out of bed and pulled on jeans and an ancient sweatshirt. With Susanna in Boston making her damn gazillions, he tended to keep his jeans and sweats in a heap on the floor. What the hell difference did it make?

He headed down to the kitchen for aspirin. Maggie and Ellen, wide awake and dressed, whirled around him, pots and bowls out, the mixer, eggs, milk, lemons, a five-pound bag of sugar. Then he remembered their New Year's Day Jane Austen fest. Tea, scones, lemon curd, clotted cream, watercress sandwiches and one Jane Austen movie after another. It was an all-day event. They'd invited friends.

Jack stifled a groan and gulped down two aspirin. He could feel his headache spreading into his eyes.

Ellen pushed past him with the scone bowl and set it in the sink. She was athletic and pretty with chestnut hair that was so like Iris Dunning's before hers had turned white. Ellen's eyes were dark like his, and she was better-tempered than either parent, a people person and a rugby player with a perpetual array of bruises on her legs.

She turned on the water into the bowl. "We've decided to start with the Laurence Olivier and Greer Garson *Pride and Prejudice*. That makes sense, don't you think, Dad?"

Jack nodded. "Sure."

"You can watch it with us if you want—"

"*Ellen.*" Maggie swung around from the stove.

She was dark-haired and willowy like her mother, hardheaded like both parents, but, somehow, she'd managed to inherit Kevin and Eva Dunning's artistic streak. She, too, had her father's dark eyes. "Dad is *not* invited. Remember? You know what he's like. He'll make comments."

Ellen bit her lower lip. "Oh, yeah. What was I thinking? Dad, you're not invited."

"Good," he said. "I'll go for a run and make myself scarce."

He headed back to his bedroom and changed into his sweats, drawing on years of training and self-discipline not to fall back onto his bed and dream about his wife. He could hear East Coast tones slipping into Maggie and Ellen's speech. At least they'd done Jane Austen fests and high teas before they'd moved north. He hadn't objected to a semester in Boston, a chance for them to live with their great-grandmother and really get to know her. Iris Dunning was a special lady. But he did object to Susanna heading up there—not that he'd asked her to stay or come back. Not explicitly. But she knew what he wanted.

He hadn't expected Susanna to last past the first hard frost. She was used to life in south Texas. It was home. She knew she belonged here, but she was just fighting it, hanging in up in Boston, because it was easier than fighting him. Easier than admitting to her fears, dealing with them.

Easier than coming clean with him.

He knew he'd contributed to the impasse between them. He'd tried to deny it for months, but now he couldn't. He was still contributing by not talking to

her, not telling her what he knew. What he feared—
not that he was supposed to be afraid of anything.
He definitely had his own sorting out to do.

He pushed thoughts of his wife to the back of his
mind. Maybe some action was called for on his part,
but he didn't know what. The status quo was aggra-
vating, but doing something stupid and losing Susanna altogether—that was unthinkable.

He slipped out into the bright, warm San Antonio
morning, breathing in the slightly humid air and
making himself hear the birds singing. He started on
his ten-mile route through the pleasant suburban
neighborhood where he and Susanna had raised their
twin daughters. Everything about his home said
"family man." Husband, father. Their house had a
big family room, a nice laundry room, pictures of
sunflowers and chickens in the kitchen. He remembered teaching the girls how to ride bikes on this very
street. Maggie hadn't wanted any help whatsoever.
Ellen had accepted all help but still managed to bust
herself up a few times.

He hated to see them fly back to Boston in a couple of days. He knew he could go with them. He was
due some time off.

His headache dissipated after the first agonizing
mile of his run. Then he went into a kind of zone,
jogging easily, not thinking, just putting one foot in
front of the other. That was what he'd done in every
area of his life for the past fourteen months. Put one
foot in front of the other. Steady if not patient, pushing ahead but always coming back to where he
started, never getting anywhere.

"*Damn* it, Susanna."

He wasn't waking up next New Year's without his wife. Hell, he didn't want to wake up *tomorrow* without her.

Probably he should tell her as much.

He came home sweating, breathing hard, purged of his bad night and recharged to enjoy his last two days with his daughters. He peeked in the family room, where Maggie and Ellen and two friends had set up their Jane Austen fest. They all held crumpled tissues and had tears in their eyes. Jack smiled. They'd be running the world in a few years, but right now they were crying over Darcy. Maggie shot him a warning look. He winked at her and retreated to his bedroom.

He showered, put his jeans back on and turned on a football game. If he could make it to the kitchen and back without someone offering him a watercress sandwich, he'd fetch himself a beer.

Ellen knocked on his door and told him they'd voted to invite him to tea, after all. "We all agreed we want to see you try lemon curd."

"I went to Harvard," he said. "I've tried lemon curd."

"Come on, Dad. We feel terrible having tea without you."

There was no way out of it. He'd had two perfect weeks with his daughters. He'd taken time off and did whatever they wanted. Shopping, visiting colleges, going to movies, tossing a rugby ball around the yard—it didn't matter. They'd spent Christmas Day in Austin with his in-laws. Kevin and Eva didn't understand what was going with their daughter's marriage, but they determinedly stayed out of it.

"Do you want Earl Grey or English Breakfast?" Ellen asked.

"There's a difference?"

He was kidding, but she took his question seriously, as if her father couldn't possibly know tea. "English Breakfast is more like regular tea. Earl Grey has a smoky flavor—"

"English Breakfast."

They had the good china set up on the coffee table in the family room, with Susanna's favorite cloth napkins, small china platters of crustless sandwiches and warm scones, little bowls of clotted cream, lemon curd and strawberry jam. There were two teapots, one with Earl Grey, one with English Breakfast. Very elegant, except the girls were in jeans, jerseys and sneakers, all but Maggie, who favored what she called vintage clothing and had on a housedress Donna Reed might have worn. She was on the floor, her back against the couch, studiously avoiding looking at her father. Her nose was red. Ellen would cry at movies in front of him, but not Maggie.

The Emma Thompson *Sense and Sensibility* was playing. Susanna had dragged him to it when it first came out. One of the sisters was in bed sick. The sensibility one, as Jack recalled.

"You've all seen this movie a dozen times," he said. "How can you still cry?"

All four girls waved him quiet. "Shut *up,* Dad," Maggie said.

It was the sort of "shut up" he could let go because he'd asked for it and she wasn't three anymore. But her time up north had sharpened her tongue. He was convinced of it.

Ellen handed him a china cup and saucer and a plate with a scone, lemon curd and a tiny watercress sandwich. "You know, Dad, you should rent some Jane Austen movies for yourself. You might learn how to be more romantic."

"I know how to be romantic."

Both daughters rolled their eyes. He drank some of his tea. The watercress sandwich was bearable, probably because it was so small. The scones were okay. The lemon curd had lumps that he didn't mention.

"What about me isn't romantic?" he asked.

"Everything," his daughters and their two friends said in unison.

He was spared further analysis of his romantic nature by the arrival of Sam Temple. Maggie and Ellen liked to pretend they didn't notice him, but every woman in Texas noticed Sam. He was in his mid-thirties, a Texas Ranger for the past three years, and he was unmarried, good-looking and smart.

He sauntered into the family room and glanced at the television. "Isn't that the guy from *Die Hard?* He's something. Remember when he shot that coke-head weasel?"

Maggie snatched up the remote, hit the pause button and glared coolly at the two men. "There ought to be a law against Texas Rangers watching Jane Austen movies."

Sam grinned at her. "I thought you wanted to be a Texas Ranger."

"That was when I was eleven."

She eased onto her feet, elegant even in her quirky Donna Reed dress and black sneakers. Jack glanced at Sam, who was wisely showing no indication of noticing that Maggie Galway wasn't eleven anymore. She put her hands on her hips. "Why don't you two get all your comments out of your system? Then we can finish watching our movie in peace."

"What comments?" Sam asked, pretending not to understand. "That's the guy from *Die Hard,* isn't it?"

Ellen started refilling teacups. Their friends weren't about to say anything. "Dad and Sam actually want to watch Jane Austen movies with us, Maggie, but they're afraid they might cry."

Sam's grin only broadened. "Hey, I read Jane Austen in high school. What's the one with Darcy? I remember that name. Holy cow. Darcy. Can you imagine? It's a girl's name now."

Maggie exhaled loudly and refused to respond. Ellen fixed her dark eyes on Sam. "You're referring to *Pride and Prejudice.* We have the 1940 version with Laurence Olivier and Greer Garson and the 1995 miniseries with Jennifer Ehle and Colin Firth, if you're interested."

"Oh, man. You girls are tougher than I am."

He grabbed a couple of watercress sandwiches and headed for the kitchen. Jack went with him. Sam hadn't stopped by just to rib his daughters.

Sam pulled open the refrigerator. "I need something to wash down these lousy sandwiches." He glanced back at Jack, grimacing. "What was that, parsley?"

"Watercress."

"Jesus." Sam took out a pitcher of tea, poured himself a glass without ice and took a long drink.

Then he settled back against the counter and looked seriously at Jack. "Alice Parker got out of prison yesterday."

"Happy New Year."

"She's renting a room in town."

"Job lined up?"

"Not yet."

Jack stared out at his shaded patio, remembering how petite, blond Alice Parker had pleaded with him to look the other way when he'd come to arrest her just over a year ago. She was convinced Beau McGarrity had killed his wife—she just couldn't prove it. McGarrity was a prominent south Texas real estate developer with political aspirations. Alice was the small-town police officer who answered the anonymous call to check out the McGarrity ranch and found Rachel McGarrity dead in her own drive-way, shot in the back after she got out of her car, presumably to open the garage door. The automatic opener was broken.

She and Beau had been married for seventy-nine days. They'd known each other less than five months.

Jack could understand how Alice Parker might have panicked coming upon her first homicide. It was late at night, she was alone, and she was young and inexperienced. But she didn't just make ordinary mistakes that night—she completely mucked up everything. Instead of immediately securing the crime scene and calling in an investigative team, she took matters into her own hands and contaminated evidence to the point that virtually nothing was of any use to investigators, never mind being able to stand up in court. The classic overzealous, incompetent loose cannon.

But before anyone fully realized the damage she'd done, Alice Parker tried to make up for her mistakes by committing a crime herself. She produced an eyewitness, a drifter who did odd jobs and claimed he'd seen Beau McGarrity crouch in the azaleas and shoot his wife.

That was when her chief of police got suspicious and asked the Texas Rangers to investigate. Jack unraveled Alice's story within a week. She'd found her drifter, paid him, then coached, threatened and cajoled him into lying.

Jack refused to look the other way. Alice reluctantly admitted to fabricating a witness and plea-bargained herself from a third-degree felony to a Class A misdemeanor, then settled into state prison to serve her full one-year sentence.

As a result of her official misconduct—and incompetence—the murder of Rachel McGarrity remained an open, if cold, case. Jack was convinced there was more to Alice Parker's story, but she'd kept silent all these months. And now she'd served her time and was a free woman.

A week after he'd finished the Alice Parker investigation, Susanna had headed for Boston. Jack didn't believe it was a coincidence.

"She's not on parole," Sam reminded him. "She can go anywhere, do anything, so long as she doesn't break the law."

Jack nodded. "Let's hope she puts her life back together."

"She wanted to be a Ranger. That won't happen now."

But they both knew it wouldn't have happened anyway. The Texas Rangers were an elite investigative unit within the state's Department of Public Safety. There were just over a hundred in the entire state, generally drawn from other DPS divisions, not small-town police departments.

Jack turned away from the patio doors, hearing the closing music to *Sense and Sensibility* coming from the family room. "Alice Parker was in over her head as a patrol officer."

"Maybe not as much as we think. Maybe little Alice wanted us to believe she's incompetent. Maybe she did it—maybe she killed Rachel McGarrity herself." Sam drank more of his cold tea, obviously giving this idea serious thought. "A year in prison on a plea bargain beats the hell out of a lethal injection for premeditated murder. Admit to incompetence and produce a phony witness, draw attention away from what you really did—shoot a woman in the back in her own driveway."

Jack shook his head. "No motive, no evidence, and I don't think it's what happened. Alice knew the victim. She knew the husband. That's one of the hazards of small-town police work. She had the whole case figured out in her own head and thought she could make it all come together, put Beau McGarrity in prison and maybe get a little recognition for herself."

"Didn't work out that way, did it? Dreams die hard, Jack." Sam set his tea glass in the sink. "Watch your back."

Jack knew this was the real reason Sam had come to his house on New Year's Day, not to rehash the Alice Parker investigation, but to communicate his misgivings about what Alice Parker might do now that she was free. Sam Temple had good instincts. He'd graduated from the University of Texas and joined the Department of Public Safety, earning his master's degree in criminal justice on the side. He was tough-minded, decisive and naturally suspicious, but also fair. People liked Sam—they'd probably make him governor of Texas one day, if he ever decided to leave law enforcement.

He was frowning at the kitchen counter. "What the hell is that?"

Jack followed his gaze. "An espresso machine. The girls gave it to me for Christmas."

"You're kidding."

"Come on, Sam, you know what an espresso machine is."

He grinned. "You start drinking lattes, Lieutenant Galway, and they'll throw you right out of the Rangers." But he turned serious again, calm. "If Alice Parker tries to stick her nose back into the McGarrity case or come after you—"

"We'll find out. She's not stupid. She knows she has to put this behind her and move on." Jack started back toward the family room, clapping one hand on the younger Ranger's shoulder. "You're just looking for things to think about so you won't have to eat any more watercress sandwiches."

"Not me. You're the one who needs distracting. Susanna was down here for New Year's last year. Bet last night was a long one for you." Sam laughed, then said out of the blue, "It's cold in Boston, you know. High of twenty today. Wind chill's below zero."

"Good."

"If that was my wife, I'd go fetch her." Sam's black eyes flashed. "I'd bring my cuffs."

"Sam—"

He held up a hand. "I know. None of my business." He sauntered into the family room and gave the girls more grief about the guy from *Die Hard.*

"His name is Alan Rickman," Maggie said coolly.

Sam shook his head. "You and Ellen have been up north too long. You're starting to sound like Teddy Kennedy."

Jack smiled from the doorway, listening to his daughters give as good as they got from a Texas Ranger more than fifteen years their senior. They weren't shrinking violets. Neither was their mother, although sometimes Jack thought his life would be easier if Susanna would be a little more of a shrinking violet, at least once in a while.

Not long after Alice Parker was arrested, it became apparent that Beau McGarrity wouldn't be charged for his wife's murder anytime soon. People were even starting to feel sympathy for him, believing he was innocent, the victim of police corruption and a rush to judgment.

Jack felt the familiar mix of anger and frustration assault every muscle, every inch of him. His entire body stiffened. He was mad at Susanna, mad at himself—but he knew what he had to do. One of these days, he and his wife were going to have to have a talk about Beau McGarrity.

Maggie and Ellen joined him on his run the next morning. They all did five miles before Maggie pooped out, declared she was on vacation and flagged down a neighbor to drive her home. Ellen would have hung in for the full ten miles, but Jack wasn't up to it himself and veered off on a shortcut that took them back home, settling for a solid seven-mile run.

After lunch, the girls did their laundry and started packing for their trip back to Boston in the morning. They sat folding clothes in the family room, the Weather Channel detailing the frigid temperatures still gripping the northeast.

Ellen plopped a laundry basket on the floor and sat down cross-legged, pulling out a rugby jersey to fold. "Dad," she said, "Maggie and I have been talking, and we've decided—well, we haven't said much about you and Mom…"

"We've tried to stay out of it," Maggie added.

Here it comes, Jack thought. He eased onto a chair, still feeling the seven miles in his calf muscles. Thus far, his daughters had generally avoided lecturing him on his relationship with their mother. But he knew they had opinions. He could at least listen to what they had to say. "Go on," he told them.

Ellen took a breath, as if she were about to confess to something awful or embarrassing. "We think Mom wants to be wooed."

"Wooed?" Jack nearly choked. This was a million

miles from what he'd expected. "How many Jane Austen movies did you watch yesterday?"

"We're *serious,* Dad," Ellen said.

Maggie was sorting through a stack of her vintage clothes. She and Ellen and their friends had combed through every secondhand store in San Antonio, raving over sacks of clothes they'd picked up for a few dollars. Most looked like rags to Jack. "We know Mom's independent and supercompetent and makes *tons* of money and all that," Maggie said, "and she'll watch football with you and talk murder and stuff—"

"But she needs *romance* once in a while," Ellen finished.

"Wooing," Maggie added with a glint in her eye that said she wasn't as intensely serious about this conclusion as her sister was.

Jack shoved a hand through his hair. It was dark, more flecked with gray than it used to be, and not, he decided, just because he was forty. Life with three females had taken its toll. When the girls headed off to college, he was getting a dog. A big, ugly, mean, *male* dog.

"Girls," he said, "your mother and I have known each other since we were college students."

Ellen pounced. "Exactly! Dad, nobody likes to be taken for granted."

"What does that mean?"

She groaned, shaking her head as if her father was the thickest man on the planet. She was in shorts and a rugby shirt, the bruises on her legs finally faded. The San Antonio sun had brought freckles out on her nose and cheeks, lightened her chestnut hair. As far as Jack knew, neither she nor Maggie had any long-term boyfriends. Fine with him. He was in no hurry to see guys "wooing" his daughters.

Maggie folded a pair of old-man striped golf pants, circa 1975, one of her favorites. "Everyone wants to feel they're special."

"This isn't about blame," Ellen said. "It's not about who did what wrong. It's about how you can take the bull by the horns and...and..."

"Woo your mother back," Jack supplied, deadpan.

Ellen frowned up at him. *"Yes."*

Maggie sank back against the couch. "This isn't a double standard. We're not expecting you to take on the wooing because you're a man, but because it's so obviously what Mom wants, and it's so—Dad, come on. It's so *simple.*"

Nothing involving Susanna Dunning Galway had ever been simple. Jack shook his head. "What kind of classes have you two been taking up in Boston?"

Neither girl was backing down. Ellen said, "You were distracted in the weeks before we moved north. Remember? You had that police corruption case. You hate corruption cases, you didn't want to talk about it, and I think it affected you more than you or Mom realized at the time."

Jack couldn't believe he was having a conversation with his daughters about the ramifications of his work on his relationship with his wife. "I liked you two better when I could stick you in a playpen. My work and my family life are separate. There's a fire wall between them."

"There! You said it!" Ellen pointed at him in victory. "You keep a part of yourself walled off from Mom. You don't talk to her."

Who was the one still pretending she wasn't worth millions? He got to his feet. He should have ended this conversation the minute they'd said "woo." It could go nowhere he wanted to go. He started for the kitchen. "Your mother knows the score with me and my work. I don't need to tell her. She knows where she stands."

"Yeah," Maggie said half under her breath, "she sure does."

His spine stiffened, but he decided to pretend he hadn't heard that one, if only because he was putting his daughters on a plane in less than twenty-four hours. They'd be off on their own soon enough. They weren't kids—they were young women. He couldn't control their every word, thought and deed. Sometimes he wished he could. Like now.

At least their instinct was to defend their mother. Even if he were willing to fall on his sword over the problems in their marriage, take the blame for her move to Boston, say everything was his fault, it wouldn't solve anything. It was going to take a hell of a lot more than lavender sachets and fresh roses to repair what they'd had.

He stormed out to the patio and kicked a chair. "A little goddamn honesty wouldn't hurt."

And he knew where it would begin—with his wife, not himself.

He could be stubborn, too.

Wooing Susanna. Taking her for granted. What did that mean? Susanna was about as unsentimental and unromantic as he was. What would she do if he started writing her poetry? He stared up at the clear south Texas sky and thought about Boston and its high today of eighteen degrees.

Maybe he didn't get it.

He was still thinking about kicking more chairs when Maggie and Ellen headed out to the mall with a couple of their friends. Two minutes after they pulled out of the driveway, Alice Parker showed up at his front door. He'd forgotten how small she was. It was a wonder she'd made it through the police academy. She looked pale and tentative—the effects of her months in prison. Her blond hair was longer, pulled back in a prosaic ponytail, and she wore a white T-shirt, jeans and a lot of inexpensive gold jewelry.

"Afternoon, Miss Parker," Jack said, his voice steady, formal. "If you have something to say to me, it can wait until I'm on duty. Not now. I don't want you at my house."

"I know—I know. I tried calling you, but they said you were off today." Some of the tentativeness went out of her gray eyes. She was attractive—cute—but she looked tired, even drained. She met his eye. "I served my time, Lieutenant."

"All right. What do you want?"

"To apologize." She breathed in, her jaw set hard, as if the words were hard to get out. "I shouldn't have asked you to look the other way. That was out of line."

"Apology accepted." He didn't ask about the rest of it—the trampling of evidence, the witness tampering, the sense he had that she was still holding back on him. A murder remained unsolved at least partially because of her actions. "Get yourself a job, Miss Parker. Move on. Rebuild your life."

"Beau McGarrity—he's still a free man."

Jack said nothing.

"I guess I'll have to live with that. My police department—they're not going to solve the case. You know that, sir. They don't want it to be Beau, they don't want to stir things up again. You know, people think I tried to frame him."

"Miss Parker—"

"I'm thinking about moving to Australia."

"Good luck."

She smiled bitterly. "You don't mean that. What do you hate worse, Lieutenant, that I paid a guy to lie about seeing Beau in the azaleas—or that I'm a royal fuck-up?"

"What I hate is seeing Rachel McGarrity's murder go unsolved." Jack narrowed his eyes on the younger woman. "There's nothing else you want to tell me, Miss Parker?"

"Like what?"

"Why did the anonymous call to check out the McGarrity ranch come to you that night? And your relationship with Rachel McGarrity. I think you two were better friends than you've let on. Her murder isn't my case, but you still haven't told the whole story as far as I'm concerned."

"Like you said, some things you just have to live with. See you around, Lieutenant."

"Stay away from my house," he said. "I don't want you near my family."

She shrugged. "Understood, sir."

She left.

Jack decided it might be just as well that the girls were heading back to Boston in the morning. That Susanna was there. Alice Parker obviously hadn't put Rachel McGarrity's murder behind her. She'd had a year in prison to stew. Now she was free, and if she wanted to knock on his door on a warm January afternoon, she could do it. It didn't break any laws.

Three

She couldn't breathe.

Alice Parker had to pull over and concentrate on the breathing exercises she'd learned in prison to stop her panic attacks. She hated being cooped up. Even as a little kid, she couldn't stand sleeping with the door to her room shut.

Ranger Jack scared the living shit out of her. He always had. She remembered the day he'd shown up to ask her a few questions. She'd known her goose was cooked. He was a hard man.

He'd never forgive her. She didn't even want his forgiveness—she didn't know what had possessed her to go out to his house. She just wanted money. A chance to start over in Australia and forget who she was, a little screw-up cop who'd made sure a murderer walked. Beau McGarrity had killed her friend and mentor, and he'd never be brought to justice for it.

Yeah, learn to live with it. Forget that. She planned to get some money off the murdering son of a bitch.

Feeling better, Alice drove to the small town

where she'd spent all her life, except for her year in prison. She was driving a rusted little tank of a car that she'd bought from a fellow inmate's mother for seven hundred dollars. She had to watch her finances. She'd been out of prison three days, and she'd already plowed through a good chunk of her savings. She had a job waiting tables downtown, but that was more for show than real income—it sure as hell wasn't going to get her to Australia.

She gripped the steering wheel with both hands, feeling the familiar tightness in her chest, the physical longing, whenever she thought about Australia. She'd gotten as many books out of the prison library as she could on Australia and dreamed of it every night from the moment she'd decided that was where she wanted to be, where she wanted to start over. Sidney, Melbourne, Perth, Adelaide—any city would do. They'd talked to her in prison about setting attainable goals. Australia seemed attainable to her. She just needed the money to get there and get started.

The McGarrity ranch was out of town. It hadn't changed in the past year. There were still the pecan and cypress trees, the live oaks, the huge azalea bushes in front of the sprawling, one-story house. Alice turned onto the long, paved driveway. Before she'd discovered Australia, she used to dream of living in a place like this and being a Texas Ranger. She'd downloaded the names and pictures of all hundred-plus Texas Rangers off the Internet and memorized them. Rachel McGarrity used to tell her about how, if she wanted something, she needed to visu-

.alize it, make it real to her. Then it was more likely to come to be.

Alice wasn't so sure about that anymore. She'd never visualized herself in prison, but she'd sat in a cell for a year. The stink of it was still on her, and her skin was still gray and pasty. She hadn't curled her hair or done her nails in months.

She parked in the spot where Rachel had parked the night she died and started to hyperventilate. She shut her eyes, controlling her breathing the way she'd learned from her yoga books and prison classes. She'd done everything she could to better herself in prison. She hadn't wasted a minute. Her grandma would have been proud of her for that part, but at least she wasn't alive for the other parts—the humiliation of her arrest, the cowardice of her plea bargain, the defeat of seeing Beau McGarrity remain a free man. Grandma had missed all that.

Rachel had loved it in south Texas. She said it was so different from the rich neighborhood in Philadelphia where she grew up. She'd been drawn to the romance of Texas, marrying a Texan—it blinded her to what she was really getting. A mean, crazy bastard who'd shoot her in the back and try to frame her best friend for her murder.

Best friend might be a stretch. Alice sighed, remembering how they'd only met because she'd stopped Rachel for a broken headlight. She'd invited Alice to meet her for coffee. Alice thought that was kind of weird, but she'd agreed. Rachel had slipped into the coffee shop like she was working for the CIA, and she'd talked about flowers and antiques until she finally got to the point—she wanted Alice to do some private investigative work for her.

Rachel was so fine-mannered and naive, so sincere, that Alice went against her better judgment and said sure, she'd do what she could. They met almost every day after that, for a month, and Alice was never too clear on what it was she was investigating—just that it involved Susanna Galway somehow. Rachel had all the pieces, the big picture, and it all seemed to evaporate when she was killed. Alice hadn't ever told Ranger Jack about it. No one else mentioned anything, so she didn't. It seemed like an invasion of privacy.

And she'd been afraid she'd end up dead if she said too much. Damn afraid. She remembered her horror when she'd spotted her change purse in a pool of Rachel's blood on the driveway. It was monogrammed with her initials. Her grandma had given it to her for Christmas one year.

Her only thought had been to get rid of the change purse and scour the crime scene for any other incriminating evidence. Let people say she was a moron cop—she didn't care.

Later, she'd realized that was what Beau had expected her to do. Panic and contaminate the crime scene, make it impossible for the evidence to lead investigators to him. Alice had felt stupid, like an unwitting co-conspirator. In the midst of her self-loathing, she'd come up with the idea of her bogus eyewitness. Beau hadn't expected that—she remembered the edge of panic in his voice that day in Susanna Galway's kitchen, when he'd tried to get Susanna to intervene with her husband on his behalf.

But that wasn't the only reason he'd gone to see Susanna. She had some connection to what all had gone on, but Alice didn't know what.

In any case, her fabricated eyewitness hadn't worked out. Jack Galway had seen to that.

Alice took the curving rock walk to the front door, which opened just as she got to the steps. Beau McGarrity came out. It was a clear, cool afternoon, squirrels chattering in nearby trees. In summer, there'd be a field of sunflowers out back, although Beau leased out most of his land to working ranchers. He just owned the place for show. Rachel had bought into the rugged image he wanted to project. He was a tall man with neat, gray hair, a square jaw and blue eyes. He had the broad shoulders and build that had served him well as a college football player. He and Rachel were married within weeks of meeting while she was in Austin on business. She was his second wife. His first wife, his high school sweetheart, had died of cancer three years earlier. She was a saint, a hard act to follow. No kids.

"Miss Parker," Beau McGarrity said in his deep, twangy accent, "if you don't leave at once, I'll call the police."

He didn't like her coming around anymore than Jack Galway had. "Relax, Mr. Beau, I'm not here for a little vigilante justice. I have a proposition for you."

"Miss Parker, there's nothing you can offer that would be of any interest to me whatsoever."

Alice shrugged. She felt tiny and pale next to him, isolated out here on his precious ranch, but not vulnerable—not like that night when she'd found Rachel out here in the dark. She remembered screaming like a damn fool, crouching behind Rachel's car, expecting a bullet in her back, before she realized Beau needed her alive. As Rachel's murderer.

"Susanna Galway taped you that day you showed up in her kitchen."

His eyes narrowed on her, but he said nothing.

"Her daughters had one of those little digital tape recorders, and Susanna saw it and hit the record button." Alice was matter-of-fact. "I'm surprised you didn't notice."

"This is ridiculous. You're making this up."

"No, sir, Mr. Beau, I am not making this up. I am telling you the flat-out truth. It's not a regular cassette tape. It's a digital audiotape, about three inches by three inches. I've listened to it. You know all that sympathy you've been building up this past year? All these people who're thinking, oh, poor Mr. Beau, he's the innocent victim of police corruption and incompetence—well, let them hear you threatening a Texas Ranger's wife."

"I didn't threaten her."

"You were subtle," Alice said, "but not that subtle."

"Get off my property. You're trying to set me up again. I've been under suspicion for months of killing my own wife—"

"You did kill your own wife, Mr. Beau. You killed her because you're paranoid and crazy. Not twenty-four hours before I found her dead out here, I told you that if I were her, I'd smother you with a pillow while you slept, and you killed her—"

"I'm calling the police." He turned to go back inside.

She held up a hand, breathing hard. "No, wait. I'm sorry. That's all over with. Let me finish."

He said nothing, but he stayed put.

Alice went on. "I happened to show up at the Galway house right after you left—I was hoping to catch Ranger Jack and plead my case to him. It was just a few hours before I was arrested, and here's Mrs. Jack Galway, all pale and scared, telling me how you'd just walked into her kitchen and she'd taped you. I assumed she'd give the tape to her husband, but she never did, probably because everything was such a big mess by then. Why drag herself into it?"

Beau straightened, recovering a bit from his shock. "This tape. You believe Mrs. Galway still has it in her possession?"

This was the tricky part. Alice remembered how Rachel had often warned her against making things too complicated. But she couldn't tell Beau that Susanna Galway had thrust the tape at her that day at her front door—Susanna obviously had thought Alice was still on Rachel's murder investigation and wanted to be rid of the damn thing. "I don't know if it's any good," she'd said, "but, please, take it."

Alice had gone out and bought a tape recorder and listened to the DAT herself. There was nothing on it that would pull her own hide out of the fire, nothing a prosecutor would bother with as far as Beau went. The Texas Rangers wouldn't like it, a murder suspect trying to get under the skin of the wife of one of their lieutenants. Jack Galway really wouldn't like it. But, too bad.

She'd expected Jack to get around to asking her about it when he'd come to arrest her, but he never did. Alice didn't volunteer. Let the Texas Rangers work for every damn thing they got out of her. Her world had crashed in on her while Beau McGarrity got away with murder, everything.

She'd put the tape out of her mind. It was worthless. Irrelevant.

Then, in prison, she'd started dreaming of Australia.

She still had the tape, and she was betting Beau would want it. It wasn't enough to nail him for murder, but it was plenty to ruin his chances of any kind of political comeback—provided no one realized Alice Parker, corrupt cop, had had it all this time. If he knew that, Beau would never pay. He wouldn't have to. He'd just say she was back to her old tricks, tampering with another bit of "evidence."

She shifted away from him, looking out at the sprawling, shaded lawn. She loved the smells. "I happen to know Susanna still has the tape. That's why I'm here. I can get it for you."

"Miss Parker, you managed to get yourself thrown in prison because of your own incompetence and your zeal to pin my wife's murder on me. Why should I believe anything's changed? Why shouldn't I believe this is just a ploy on your part to entrap me, frame me for something I didn't do?"

"You can quit professing your innocence, Mr. Beau. You already got away with murder. There's nothing I can do about that—I don't even care any-

more. It's time I looked after my own interests."
Alice shifted back to him, squinting, noting that she
wasn't even slightly nervous. "I want fifty thousand
dollars to start a new life."

He scoffed. "Do you actually think I'd pay you
fifty thousand dollars for *anything?*"

"Not just anything. For a tape of you creeping out
Susanna Galway in her kitchen."

"If there's anything on this tape that should concern me—if it even exists—why wouldn't Mrs. Galway have given it to her husband by now?"

"Probably because you scared her shitless that
day. I don't know." Alice paused, shrugging. "Look,
Beau, I know you, and you're going to chew on this
until you can't stand it. The idea of that tape being
out there, out of your control, is going to drive you
crazy."

"She could have made copies."

"Unlikely. I think she just wants to forget it exists."

"Then why not destroy it?"

"She's the wife of a Texas Ranger. She's not going to destroy potential evidence, even if she doesn't
believe it'll amount to anything. If she has, end of
story. I only get the money if I produce the tape and
no copies of it turn up within a reasonable period of
time."

He tilted his head back, staring down at her in that
superior way of his. At first, Rachel had said, she'd
thought it was confidence—she hadn't seen the truth
until later. Her husband was one cold, arrogant son
of a bitch. He'd put his first wife on a pedestal after
she died, then tried to put Rachel on one, too, but

she could never measure up. She was real. His dead wife was a mirage.

"Miss Parker—"

It used to be Officer Parker. She remembered that. She knew everyone in town, and they'd all called her Officer Parker. "Think about it," she said. "I'll call you in a few days."

"This is extortion. Blackmail. You can't—"

"I'll be in touch, Mr. Beau." She started down the walk, breathing in the fresh smells of his yard. She'd grown up in this country. It was home. But she could get used to Australia. She wanted the chance. She glanced back at Beau McGarrity, still standing on his front steps, probably thinking about where he could bury her out back if he decided to wring her neck. Just as well he didn't know she had Susanna's tape in her glove compartment. "Now, you aren't going to tell the Texas Rangers about our visit, are you?" she called back over her shoulder.

"Get out."

She smiled sweetly. "I didn't think so."

A nor'easter was blowing up the coast, promising to dump up to a foot of snow in Boston. Susanna noticed the first fat, wet flakes as she walked back to Gran's from her subway stop. With a full schedule of client meetings, she'd avoided taking her car into the city. It had been a good day. Helping people sort out their finances and set up goals was one of the real pleasures of her work. It wasn't just about money, numbers, calculations—it was about people and their lives. She had clients saving for their kids' college, a first home, a year off to volunteer for something like Doctors Without Borders. One client was digging herself out of debt after a cancer scare and a deep depression that had nearly caused her to pull the plug on her life. Now she was excited, eager to knock off one credit card debt after another.

Susanna wasn't as good at following her own advice. She always told couples to talk about money. What did it mean to them? What positives and negatives did they associate with money from their childhoods? What did they want it to do for them, individually, as a couple?

She and Jack had stopped talking about money beyond the absolute basics. If the bills were paid and they had walking-around money, Jack didn't care about the rest. "Accumulating wealth" fell somewhere after "watching gum surgery" on his list of things he was excited about in his life.

Some days Susanna thought he wouldn't care that she'd invested her money and a chunk of his money, and, now, together, they had a net worth of ten million.

Some days she thought he'd care a lot. And wouldn't like it. That he especially wouldn't like that she hadn't told him. Not that he'd asked. Not that he'd shown any interest whatsoever.

In the months before she'd headed north to join Maggie and Ellen, he'd talked very little about his own work. Things hadn't been right between them even before Beau McGarrity had walked into her kitchen.

The wind picked up, slapping her in the face as if to get her attention. Maggie and Ellen had been back five days, still filled with tales of friends, vintage clothing scores, Jane Austen, and Dad this and Dad that. Susanna was pleased they'd enjoyed their visit home, and they'd had the grace to say they'd missed her. She wondered if they'd be happy about the snow.

She turned up Gran's narrow street of mostly big, multifamily homes built in the late nineteenth and early twentieth century. Iris Dunning had managed to buy one of the few single-family houses on the street, an 1896 two-story stucco with a glassed-in front porch, an open back porch and a detached one-car garage, not that common in crowded Somerville. She'd planted flowering trees and perennial gardens, battling skunks, cats, raccoons and the occasional neighborhood miscreant.

Susanna kicked off her boots in the front hall and found her daughters doing their homework in the dining room. Gran was already off to Jim's Place for clam chowder. She never missed chowder night.

"Dad called," Maggie said. She was wrapped in a 1950s shawl she'd found in Gran's attic and had on fingerless Bob Cratchit gloves. Drama, Susanna thought. Gran liked to keep the house cool, but not that cool. "He wants you to call him back. He said to call him on his cell phone."

Ellen looked up from her laptop. "We told him about the snow. Mom, can you believe less than a week ago we were in south Texas and now it's *snowing?* I hope they cancel school."

Susanna smiled. "Be careful what you wish for. Gran'll put you to work shoveling."

She grabbed the portable phone off the clunky dining room table and sat in a chair badly in need of refinishing. It was a comfortable, lived-in room with its dark woodwork and flowered wallpaper. Her parents liked to tease Gran about coming in and redoing the place, stripping the wallpaper, tearing up the rugs, getting rid of all her tacky artwork, but she paid no attention. She was happy with her house just the way it was. As long as the roof didn't leak, she didn't plan to change a thing.

Susanna dialed Jack's number, and he answered on the first ring. "I'm on the patio," he said, laying on his slow, deep Texas drawl. "It's a beautiful night."

"Liar. It's in the fifties and raining."

"Ah. You checked."

"Only because we're tracking a nor'easter. Thank God it didn't blow in last week when the girls were flying. What's up?"

"I wanted you to know Alice Parker is out of prison. She took a room in San Antonio for a few days. Now she's gone. Her friends in prison say she was obsessed with Australia. Maybe she's headed in that direction."

His voice was businesslike, but not matter-of-fact. Susanna glanced at the girls, both pretending not to be listening. Maggie was frowning over her math homework, Ellen tapping keys on her laptop.

"She'd need a passport, money—" Susanna took a breath, noticing that Maggie and Ellen were no longer making any pretense of studying. "Jack, are you worried she'll come after you? You investigated her. She thinks it's your fault no one's ever been charged in Rachel McGarrity's murder."

"Alice Parker isn't required to tell me or anyone

else where she is or what she's doing. Provided she doesn't break the law, she can do whatever she wants."

Susanna frowned. "Then why tell me she was released from prison?"

He didn't answer at once. "No particular reason."

What was that supposed to mean? Jack Galway didn't do anything for no reason. Everything he did and said had a purpose. He was the most deliberate man Susanna knew. She felt hot, jittery, as if he had her in an interrogation room and she was lying to a Texas Ranger, not just having an ordinary conversation with her husband. "Well, I hope Alice Parker gets her life back on track. Do you want to talk to the girls?"

"Sure," he said, his tone impossible to read. "Put them on."

She handed the phone to Ellen and ran into the kitchen, diving into the half-bathroom. She splashed her face with cold water. Her eyes were hot with tears. She was shaking, her reflection pale in the small oval mirror. She touched her lips with wet fingers and could almost imagine it was Jack touching her. She'd loved him so hard, so long. What had happened?

Susanna, Susanna…you don't believe I killed my wife.

Beau McGarrity. She could still hear his cajoling, hurt voice that day in her kitchen. He'd never made an overt threat against her or her children. It was in his gesture, his tone, the fact that he had walked into her kitchen from her patio, without knocking. She'd been doing a tai chi tape in the family room. The girls were at theater and soccer practice. She hadn't thought to lock the patio door.

She'd started the recorder, not knowing what he meant to do or say. At first, she didn't even know who he was, except that she'd spotted him twice before that week, once in town, once at the school. Susanna had told herself it was coincidence and chided herself for starting to think like a jaded law enforcement officer, taking the routine oddities of life and turning them into something potentially sinister.

She hadn't known Alice Parker was being investigated—or that Jack would arrest her that afternoon. Giving her the tape when she showed up at her front door had made sense at the time.

Saying nothing to Jack about Beau McGarrity's visit had, too.

When he came home that evening and told her about Alice's arrest and never mentioned the tape, Susanna assumed the tape was no good, completely irrelevant—and that Alice hadn't mentioned it to him. Why should she? She was on her way to prison, her career ruined. If there'd been anything useful on the tape, she'd have turned it over, if only to nail Beau McGarrity and prove herself right.

Jack had been so taciturn that night, even more uncommunicative than usual. He was glad to have the Alice Parker investigation over with. The local police department would continue with the investigation into Rachel McGarrity's murder. He'd opened a beer, took a long drink and laid back his head, shutting his eyes.

All Susanna could think about was how he'd react if she'd told him Beau McGarrity had been to their house. His work had never touched his family this way. Never. They were both accustomed to her being afraid for him. But not for herself, not for their daughters.

She'd found herself unable to tell him what had happened. She didn't know what he'd do.

Her own fear was irrational, visceral. Just pretend everything was okay and go to Boston with the girls, let the dust settle, clear her head…then tell him.

Now Alice Parker was out of prison, and Susanna still hadn't told her husband what had happened on that hot, confused day over a year ago.

But she loved him.

Oh, God, she loved him.

"Mom!" It was Ellen yelling. "Dad wants to talk to you!"

Susanna dried her face and hands and slipped out of the bathroom. The girls were in the kitchen, and Ellen handed her the phone, whispering, "We told him about the cabin. We thought he knew."

"He's *pissed,*" Maggie added, more as a point of fact than a warning.

Susanna nodded and ducked back into the half-bath. She wanted total privacy for this conversation. "A cabin in the Adirondacks," she said cheerfully. "Sounds wonderful, doesn't it?"

"When were you going to tell me?"

There was nothing calm, professional or deliberate about him now. This was Jack Galway at his stoniest. "I don't know. I hadn't even thought about it." But that was an outright lie, and when she caught her reflection in the mirror, she saw the guilt. "I'm sorry.

It was a spur of the moment thing, but I should have told you—''

"Don't be sorry. I don't give a damn what you do.''

He hung up.

Susanna stared at the dead phone. Then she hit redial. He let his voice mail take the call. She hit redial again. More voice mail. On her third redial, he picked up, but didn't speak. She did. "Damn it, Jack, did you hang up on me?''

"Yes, and I'm going to hang up on you again.''

"And I'm going to keep calling you until you knock it off!''

"That's harassment. I'll have you arrested, even up in Boston.''

No one could get under her skin the way he could. "Just try.'' She took a quick breath, decided not to fight fire with fire. This once, she could be reasonable. "I can see how you'd look at the cabin as a thumb in your eye, but that's not what I was thinking when I bought it. Truthfully, I wasn't thinking—it was like it was meant to be. I couldn't resist. It's in the most beautiful spot, right on Blackwater Lake. Gran grew up there. You'll have to see it.''

"Why?''

"Why?'' she repeated dumbly. The man drove her mad. He knew the worst, most awkward, most difficult and probing questions to ask her. But he was a trained interrogator. He could get people to confess to murder, never mind to why they'd bought a cabin in the Adirondacks.

"Yes. Why do I have to see it?''

"I don't know—it makes sense. You're my husband."

"It's an open invitation?"

She licked her lips. He had her off-balance, and he knew it. "I suppose so. Sure."

"You know what Sam says, don't you?" His voice lowered, deepened. "He says I should go up there, cuff you and haul you back to Texas."

Susanna nearly dropped the damn phone in the sink.

"I knew that'd leave you speechless," her husband said. "Good night, darlin'. Enjoy your cabin."

He hung up on her again.

This time, she didn't call him back.

When she returned to the kitchen, Gran was back, heating up a quart of Jim Haviland's famous clam chowder on the stove. The girls were setting the table. It was a comfortable scene, three generations of women in Gran's simple, clean kitchen with its tall ceilings, old painted cabinets and framed samplers from her cross-stitch craze fifteen years ago. Even at eighty-two, Iris Dunning retained her tall, graceful build. Susanna could picture her grandmother as an Adirondack guide in her youth. People assumed she was a widow when she moved to Boston, but that wasn't true. She'd never married. Now she was in her sunset years, her hair white and wispy, her skin translucent and wrinkled. But her mind was sharp, and she stayed active and socially engaged—she was taking tai chi at her senior center. Before her granddaughter and great-granddaughters had moved in, she'd rented rooms in the house to university students to supplement her income and give her company.

Susanna sank onto a chair at the table. Her knees were wobbly from her talk with her husband.

Gran glanced back at her from the stove. "Jimmy Haviland says you're avoiding him."

"I've been busy," Susanna said. But that wasn't entirely true. Busy, yes, but the last two times she'd stopped at Jim's Place, its opinionated owner had asked her if she'd told Jack about her stalker. He would keep asking her until she said yes. He wouldn't squeal to Gran. That wasn't Jim Haviland's style. He might to Jack, though.

Ellen set a sturdy white bowl in front of her. "Mom, we're sorry we told Dad about the cabin—"

"No, no, that's not your fault. I was going to tell him. It just slipped my mind."

Maggie shot her mother a dubious frown, but said nothing. Ellen sighed. "We tried to talk to him while we were home. We told him he should try to be more romantic."

"Romantic? Your father?" Susanna smiled, shaking her head with affection for her two clueless daughters. "He just threatened to handcuff me and drag me back to Texas."

Gran set the steaming soup tourine of chowder in the middle of the table. "I don't know," she said, a mischievous gleam in her very green eyes. "I think it's a start."

Four

~~~~~

After thirty years of running a neighborhood pub, Jim Haviland considered himself a good judge of character. It came down to experience and survival—they'd honed his instincts about people. Still, he had to admit that the woman at the bar had him stumped. He guessed she was in her late twenties. Slightly built, short, curly, dyed red hair and pale skin, almost pasty looking. She wore a lot of makeup and about a half ton of gold jewelry. Dangling earrings, rings on both hands, bracelets, a thin gold necklace with a tiny heart pendant and a thicker chain necklace. He wouldn't want all that metal on him in a nor'easter. But the snow had finally stopped, and the cleanup was in full force. The plow guys would be showing up later for the beef stew special.

The woman's clothes made her stick out in this neighborhood, too. She had on a close-fitting baby blue ribbed V-neck sweater, tight western-cut jeans and leather boots that would land her on her ass on an icy sidewalk. She played up her femininity, but there was a hardness to her, a toughness that Jim couldn't reconcile with the jewelry, the clothes, the painted nails. He wouldn't be surprised if she had a .22 strapped to her ankle.

After making sure he didn't use a mix, she'd ordered a margarita. Her accent wasn't local, but Jim was no good at placing accents outside of New England. He drew a couple of drafts for two firefighters who'd come in, complaining about the hazards of space heaters and overtaxed extension cords. Davey Ahearn, on his stool at the end of the bar, was listening in, nursing a beer and keeping an eye on the woman with the makeup and the margarita.

"New in town?" Jim asked her.

"Two days. It's that easy to tell?"

"With that accent?" Jim smiled at her. "Where you from?"

"Texas. A little bitty town outside Houston."

"Hope you brought a good winter coat with you."

She gestured toward the coat rack next to the door, gold bangles sliding down her slender wrist. "No, sir, but I bought one on sale this morning. They said it's a basic parka. I never knew there was anything but. I bought a winter hat and gloves, too. I think mittens would drive me batty." She raised her gray eyes at him. "I'm holding off on the long underwear."

She had an engaging manner, whoever she was. "That's one thing about owning a bar," Jim said. "I can get through a Boston winter without long underwear. You'll like it here in the spring. Are you planning to stick around that long?"

"I'm hoping to relocate here, but have you checked out the rents lately? Whoa. They're sky-high.'' She sipped more of her margarita, looking as if she relished every drop. ''I don't know why you put up with it. Aren't you the folks who dumped the tea in the harbor?''

''That we are. You have a job lined up?''

''More or less, yes, sir.''

''What's your name?''

''Audrey,'' she said. ''Audrey Melbourne.''

Jim studied her a moment, noticing she didn't flinch under his frank scrutiny. Definitely a tough streak. ''What are you running from, Audrey Melbourne?''

She shrugged. ''What do any of us run from?''

''The law and husbands,'' Jim said. Davey Ahearn glanced down the bar, not saying a word, but Jim knew his friend's suspicions were on full alert.

''No, sir, I don't believe that's the case at all.'' Audrey Melbourne slid off her stool, looking even smaller. ''Mostly we run from ourselves.''

She walked over to the coatrack and put on her new parka, hat and gloves as if they might have been a space suit. She left without looking back.

Davey breathed out a long sigh. ''Sure. I hope she comes back real soon. That pretty little number is trouble.''

One of the firefighters snorted. ''All women are trouble.''

Two female Tufts graduate students took exception to this comment, and the argument was on. Jim didn't intervene. The Bruins and the Celtics were having a lousy year, the Patriots hadn't made the playoffs, and pitchers and catchers didn't report for weeks yet. People needed something to do. Maybe he needed to wonder about a redheaded Texan coming into his bar. It happened now and again, a stranger popping in for a drink. He doubted Audrey Melbourne would be back.

An icy gust bit at Alice Parker's face as she climbed over a blackened, frozen, eighteen-inch snowbank to get to her car. The Texas tags were a dead giveaway, but what the hell—so was her Texas accent. She'd arrived in Boston in the middle of a damn blizzard, and now it was so cold her cheeks ached and her eyeballs felt as if they were frozen in their sockets. Her chest hurt from breathing in the dry, frigid air.

"I should have bought the damn Everest parka," she muttered, picking her way over an ice patch. Even sanded, it was slippery. She supposed she'd need new boots if she ended up staying more than a few days. Damned if she'd move up here on a permanent basis. She'd rather sit in prison.

She did not understand why Susanna Galway was living here on an old, crowded street in a working-class neighborhood, with the salt and sand and soot making everything even uglier. She had a nice house in San Antonio. A Texas Ranger husband. What the hell was wrong with her?

Alice tried fishing her keys out of her pocket with a gloved hand, decided that wouldn't work and peeled off the glove. Winter was complicated. She couldn't believe she'd driven a couple thousand miles in her crappy car to track down Susanna, just so Beau could think she still had the tape. Not that he was biting—he kept telling her she could go to hell and threatening to turn her in for blackmail and extortion. She was calling his bluff. He'd pay her to steal the tape and hush up about it. She knew he would. Things worked on his nerves. He was paranoid and dramatic. She'd made that one little remark about Rachel smothering him in his sleep, and less than a day later, her friend was dead.

Alice was confident he'd come around. He deserved to pay for something.

Of course, he could decide to shoot her in the back and go after the tape himself, but that was extreme. Even Beau couldn't think he'd get away with two murders. He'd let her do his dirty work for him. And pay her.

If he did end up shooting her, Jack Galway and Sam Temple could catch him. At least he'd go to prison for her murder, if not Rachel's.

An old woman pushed open the porch door to the stucco house just up the street. She had on pants stuffed into fur-trimmed ankle boots, a dark wool car coat, a red scarf, a red knit hat and red knit gloves.

It had to be Iris Dunning. Susanna's grandmother.

Alice had found out from Beau that Susanna Galway was living up north with her daughters and grandmother. He'd obviously expected this information would make Alice give up on her plan. She'd thought about it. It was kind of nuts, traveling two thousand miles, taking the risk of breaking into Susanna's house to steal something that wasn't there.

But what else was she supposed to do? She had the tape. Beau would not be pleased if he found out she'd had it all along—for one, he'd never pay her the fifty grand. For another, he'd probably shoot her.

He was balking as it was. If this was going to work, Alice knew she had to go through the motions.

She climbed back over the snowbank. "Mrs. Dunning?" Alice stepped carefully onto the sidewalk, not wanting to slip. "Excuse me, ma'am, I didn't mean to startle you. My name's Audrey Melbourne—I'm new in town. Someone mentioned you might have a room for rent." No one had, but Alice decided it was a good way to launch a conversation.

The old woman's clear green eyes cinched it for Alice. They were just like Susanna's. She had to be Iris Dunning. "I'm sorry, I'm not renting rooms at the moment. Are you a student?"

Alice shook her head. "No, I'm in the process of moving to Boston. This seems like a nice neighborhood."

"It is," Iris said. "I've lived here for years and have never been robbed."

That would probably change, Alice thought, if she had to stage a robbery to convince Beau she'd gotten the tape off Susanna. "Well, ma'am, I don't want to keep you out in the cold—"

"Have you had supper yet? Jimmy Haviland makes good, hearty food. His clam chowder's the best in the city, but tonight's not chowder night."

Alice hated even the thought of clams. They had to be slimy. "I know—I was just in there. I think he's serving beef stew tonight."

"Come on, then, I'll buy you a bowl." Iris Dunning seemed ready to take Alice by the arm and walk her into the pub. "I was new in town and all alone once. My granddaughter and daughters are out for the evening. I'd like the company."

"Ma'am, I don't want to impose—"

"You're not imposing, and you can stop calling me 'ma'am.' Iris will be fine."

Alice was taken aback. No wonder Susanna had ended up here—her grandmother was a good soul who'd take in anyone. "I'd love a bowl of stew, Iris, but I'll pay my way."

They entered the bar together, and Alice immediately noticed the obvious suspicion of the owner and his friend with the handlebar mustache. If Iris noticed, she didn't care. She headed to a back table. Alice smiled self-consciously at the two men, who continued to frown at her. Well, that was a good sign. At least Iris Dunning had people who looked after her. She was the sort of person people could easily take advantage of.

"Now, Jimmy," she said when the owner came over to take their order, "don't start lecturing me about strangers. I can have stew with anyone I want. Miss Melbourne is new in town."

"Audrey," Alice corrected with a smile.

"I'd never lecture you, Iris," Jimmy said. "What are you drinking with your stew?"

"I think I'll have merlot tonight. I haven't had wine in ages. Alice, what about you?"

"Oh, no, ma'am, I don't drink. I'll just have a Coke."

"And don't skimp on the beef when you dip up my stew, Jimmy. I had a low-fat lunch."

He still didn't seem too happy.

Iris sighed at him, her green eyes vibrant. "Jimmy, I know about women on their own. They're either widowed, divorced, broke, on the run or ex-cons."

She turned her bright gaze to her new friend. "Am I right, Audrey?"

Alice laughed. "One or more of the above."

"*There*. I knew it. I guess that's better than 'all of the above.'"

Tess Haviland sank into the soft leather couch that Susanna had bought when Tess had moved out of their shared office space the summer before. She still had the remnants of her tan from her holiday in Disney World with Andrew Thorne, her architect husband, and seven-year-old Dolly. Harley Beckett, Dolly's reclusive baby-sitter, had stayed home and worked on Tess's nineteenth-century carriage house. She took possession of it last May and promptly found a skeleton in the cellar—something that hadn't sat well with Jack Galway, Texas Ranger. Not that Susanna had told him about her involvement. The girls had let it slip. She remembered his call. "You and Tess Haviland crawled around in a dirt cellar looking for a body?"

"We didn't find it."

Small consolation.

Tess's move to the North Shore, her marriage and new family seemed to agree with her. Her blond hair was longer these days, her dedication to her graphic design work still high but not as all-consuming. She'd hired an assistant. She had balance in her life. She also had strong opinions, which made her more like her pub-owner father and plumber godfather than she would ever admit to.

She'd brought her own latte, Susanna's coffee-making abilities the only source of conflict between them. She had on her business-in-the-city clothes. "I like the leather," she said, sweeping a critical glance over the conversation area Susanna had set up in Tess's vacated half of the office. A contemporary leather couch and chairs, an antique coffee table and three orchids painstakingly chosen for their forgiving natures. Tess smoothed one hand over the soft leather. "I didn't think I would. I really wanted you to go with a Texas theme. At least it's not stuffy."

Given that her office was on the fourth floor of a late nineteenth-century building overlooking Boston's oldest cemetery, Susanna had rejected a Texas theme. She hadn't bothered to confront her friend on her ideas of what a Texas theme would entail—all spurs and Lone Stars, probably.

"Susanna, do you mind if I speak frankly?"

Susanna sat on one of the chairs, the sky outside her tall windows gray and gloomy. She'd worked at her computer most of the day. She smiled at Tess. "Since when would it make any difference if I minded?"

Tess didn't return her smile. "Your computer's dusty," she said.

"That's what you wanted to tell me?"

"It's part of a larger pattern." Tess leaned forward, holding her latte in both hands. "It's like your brain's gone inside your computer and won't come out. It can't. It's all filled up with numbers and money things."

"Money things?"

"Investments, annual reports, interest rates, bond prices—God only knows what. I'll bet you know to the penny what each of your clients is worth."

Susanna took no offense. "That is my job, Tess."

She shook her head, adamant. "You go beyond what the average financial planner would do."

"Good. I'd hate to be an 'average' financial planner." Susanna glanced over at her desk, her monitor filled with numbers, which was probably what had unnerved Tess. "I want to be very above average."

"You see? You're driven. You're a perfectionist. It's causing you to lose perspective on the rest of your life." Tess set her jaw, aggravated now. "Damn it, I'm making a good point here. Your life is out of balance."

Susanna slid to her feet and walked over to the table where she had her coffeemaker, a tin of butter cookies, pretty little napkins and real pottery mugs for herself and her clients. "I've hired a part-time assistant," she said. "She comes in two mornings a week."

"You should have at least two people working full-time for you. You told me so yourself last fall."

"Did I?"

"Yes, you did."

Susanna poured herself a half cup of stale, grayish coffee and turned back to her friend. "All right, I'll dust my computer. Promise."

Tess groaned. "You are so *thick*."

"Hey, that's my line. That's what I tell Jack—"

"There. Jack." Tess set her latte on an antique table Susanna had picked up at an auction, a nice contrast with the more contemporary pieces. Balance, she thought. If Tess approved, she didn't say. She narrowed her blue eyes on Susanna. "You haven't told him how much you're worth, have you?"

"Why would I? He pays attention to money even less than you do."

"Susanna, you have to tell him!"

Susanna returned to her desk, feeling stubborn now that they were talking about her husband. "Why?"

"He's going to find out, you know. That's what you're afraid of, isn't it? He's a guy's guy. He might not like having his wife sneaking around making millions."

"It's his money, too."

"Uh-huh. And he's a Texas Ranger. You've always said it's all he's ever wanted to do, even when he was at Harvard. Suppose he'll think you'll want him to quit?"

Susanna frowned. "I'd never tell him what to do, anymore than he'd tell me."

"Yeah, what about all the other Texas Rangers? What will they think if one of their own's suddenly worth eight million?"

"Ten," Susanna corrected.

"Ten million? Damn, Susanna. Maybe it's time to hire bodyguards—or make peace with your husband. Talk about armed and dangerous."

"Nobody knows how much I'm worth. You, my accountant and my attorney." Susanna could feel her heart pounding, but she kept her tone breezy, as if none of this really bothered her. She knew Tess wasn't fooled. "It's not as if I've radically changed my lifestyle."

"Moving to Boston, buying a cabin in the Adirondacks. That's not radically changing your lifestyle?"

Susanna dropped onto her chair in front of at her computer. "I was only worth five million when I left San Antonio."

Tess swooped to her feet. "God, you're impossible. If you get kidnapped and held for ransom, don't expect me to come here and figure out how to fork over the money." She hoisted her microfiber satchel onto her shoulder. "I've got to run. I have one more devil of a client meeting." She sighed, shaking her head. "Susanna, please—you'll think about what I said?"

"Tess, you know I will—I appreciate your concern. Thanks for stopping by."

"Come up sometime. Bring the girls. I know it's winter, but the ocean's still beautiful."

After Tess left, Susanna stood at the tall, arched windows overlooking historic Old Granary Burial Ground, snow drifting against its thin, centuries-old tombstones. No radical changes in her life. Who was she kidding?

Tess was right.

As if to prove her point, the doorman buzzed her and announced Destin Wright was there to see her. Susanna dropped back onto her desk chair and felt an instant headache coming on. She'd been putting Destin off for days. She sighed. How could telling her husband about ten million dollars and a murder suspect showing up in their kitchen be any harder than dealing with Destin Wright? She said into the intercom, "Send him up."

He would take the old elevator, she knew, not the stairs, and he'd find a way to irritate her within twenty seconds of arriving in her office. She got up and unlocked the door, just so she wouldn't have to let him in.

He didn't knock. He pushed open the translucent glass door and grinned at her. "Yo, Susanna. How's it going? Was that Tess I just saw leaving the building?"

"Yes, she stopped in for a visit—"

"I wasn't invited to her wedding, you know."

Susanna felt the blood pulse behind her eyes. "Destin, you and Tess aren't even friends."

"What? We grew up together."

"You're ten years older than she is."

"So?"

Susanna gave up. Destin Wright had grown up on the next street over from her grandmother's house, never, apparently, making a secret of his desire to get out of the neighborhood at his first opportunity. He was in his mid-forties and fit the stereotype of the preppy Harvard grad with his blond good looks, except he'd quit a local junior college after one semester. He'd started an Internet company a few years ago and made millions, then went broke almost overnight. He'd had a fun idea, but no real business plan, no profits—and wildly expensive tastes. Now he wanted to start over. With Susanna's help.

"Destin…"

He held up a hand. "No, wait. Hang on. I'm not here to pester you about money." He grinned sheepishly, as if he'd known he'd pushed her too far with his various comeback schemes. He was charming, energetic and incredibly self-centered, with a sense of entitlement that knew no bounds. He had on an expensive camel coat left over from his high-on-the-hog days. "I just wanted to tell you I followed your advice and wrote up a business plan. The whole nine yards."

"Good for you, Destin."

He scratched the back of his neck, eyeing her. "I was thinking you could take a look at it. As a favor."

Susanna shook her head, adamant. "You know I'm not getting involved in this project. I've told you. This isn't what I do, even if I thought it was a good idea to help out someone from Gran's neighborhood."

"One little look?"

"No. I'm sorry. I can recommend people—"

"I can't pay anyone. Come on, Suze, you know the score. I need to do a deal, barter a little. I've downsized as much as I can. Hell, I'm about to have my BMW repossessed."

How he'd ever pulled together the attention span and backing to start a company in the first place was beyond Susanna. Luck, guts, flare, charisma, just enough skill. If he'd come to her sooner, she might have been able to help him save some of his personal wealth when the dot-com craze came crashing back to earth, but the same relentless optimism that had drawn Destin Wright into starting a risky business made him stick with it too long. He just hadn't seen the bottom coming. When he hit, he hit hard.

"I just need some angel money," he said, unable to resist.

"If you have a good idea, you'll get it. But not from me."

"A hundred grand would get me off the ground—"

"Not a dime, Destin." She'd learned from hard experience that she had to be very clear and very straight with him. Subtle didn't work with Destin. "I'm not changing my mind."

"You could be a founding partner. Suze, you're bored, you know you are. This'd be exciting, a new company, your business experience and smarts hooked up with my ideas and energy." He paused, obviously waiting to see if his words were having any impact on her. When they didn't, he sighed. "Okay, okay. You've got a full well, and you don't want me dipping in my rusting, leaking bucket. I understand." He was remarkably good-humored for a man who'd been told no for at least the fourth time. He grinned suddenly. "I'll just have to work harder to convince you. If you could take two seconds and peek at my business plan—"

"I can offer you cookies and a cup of bad coffee," Susanna said. "That's it."

He dropped a shiny black folder on her desk. "If you get a chance," he said, leaving it at that. He started for the door. "I'll see you around the neighborhood. You know, people are starting to talk about how much money you have. I heard one guy say he thought it was at least five million."

"People like to talk."

"If you're worth five million, you wouldn't miss a hundred grand, even if you threw it down the toilet, and I'd—"

"*Destin.*" She shook her head, unable to suppress a laugh. "Look, I'll talk to some people. If this idea doesn't work out, another one will. You'll be okay."

But he barely heard her. He hadn't come for a pep

talk from her. He wanted free advice and money. He headed out, and Susanna sank back against her chair, wrung out. Destin never knew when to quit—and sometimes she wondered if she quit too soon.

She thought of Jack, what he might be doing late on a Thursday afternoon. Would he quit on her? Had she already quit on him?

Her eyes filled with sudden tears, and she quickly shut down her computer and packed up her briefcase, turned off the coffeepot. It had been a lousy day, but at least tonight was chowder night at Jim's Place.

Five

~~~ co ~~~

Jack unlocked the door to his empty house and stood in the kitchen, staring at a picture of Maggie and Ellen on the refrigerator. He'd taken it over the holidays. They had their midwinter break coming up, but they were spending it in the Adirondacks at Susanna's new cabin. Snowshoeing. Cross-country skiing. "Freezing our butts off," Maggie had said less than enthusiastically in their last conversation.

He could join them. He had that open invitation from his wife to see the cabin.

He smiled, thinking of what Susanna would do if he turned up out of the blue with a pair of snowshoes strapped to his back. He'd made it clear it was up to her to come home and figure things out here, not up to him to go there. It wasn't just a matter of digging in his heels and forcing her to toe the line—it made sense. Maggie, Ellen and Iris would all be distractions. He and Susanna needed time alone, on familiar turf.

So far, that strategy wasn't working. Whatever time they'd managed to have alone during this endless stalemate, they'd spent in bed. That suited him, but it wasn't getting the job done—Susanna was still living with her grandmother in Boston. And he had to admit he was using his work to distract himself, taking the hardest cases, working the longest hours.

He got a beer from the refrigerator and went out onto the patio and found a spot in the late afternoon sun. There'd been nothing on Alice Parker since she'd cleared out of San Antonio a month ago. Her former police chief boss said he hadn't heard from her. She had no family left in the area. Her parents were drug addict transients who hadn't been heard from in years. They'd abandoned Alice to the care of her paternal grandmother when she was twelve, a good woman by all accounts, but she died five years ago.

"She's probably feeding the kangaroos in Australia by now," the chief had told Jack.

He wasn't so sure. Alice Parker had unfinished business in south Texas, and he'd be happier knowing where she was.

Jack stared up at the vibrant, golden sunset. He supposed he should get some supper, but he didn't want to move. He wanted to sit here a while and think about the Rachel McGarrity murder investigation, Beau McGarrity, Alice Parker, a contaminated crime scene, a fabricated witness and his wife.

He had a mind to check with a travel agent in the morning and see about flying into the Adirondacks. What was the closest airport? Albany? Montreal? Burlington, Vermont? He'd rent a car, and he'd drive out to Blackwater Lake, find this damn cabin and surprise the hell out of one Susanna Dunning Galway.

Susanna slid onto a stool at Jim Haviland's bar and ordered a bowl of clam chowder. The girls were with friends, and Gran had already been in and was home watching a game show, still trying to decide whether she'd come up to Blackwater Lake with them on Saturday.

"Destin was in earlier asking for you," Jim said, setting the steaming chowder in front of Susanna.

She groaned. "I hope you told him I never come in here anymore. He's driving me nuts. I'm tempted to invest in this new idea of his just to shut him up."

"Is it a good idea?"

"I don't know. I won't let him tell me about it. Jim, I just can't give him the kind of money he's asking for—"

He held up a big hand. "Hey, you don't have to explain to me."

She sighed. "Destin's not a bad guy."

"He's an asshole," Davey Ahearn blurted from the other end of the bar. He shrugged, apologetic, when Susanna looked at him. "Excuse my language. Ask Destin how much he gave back to the neighborhood when he made it big. See what he says. You're rich, Suzie-cue. You give back."

She tried her chowder, which was thick and creamy—perfect. "What makes you think I'm rich?"

Davey grinned. "I'm a plumber, remember? I hear things. I know what you pay for your office in town, and I know what you gave to the family of that firefighter who got killed over Christmas."

She frowned at him. "That was supposed to be an anonymous gift."

"One or two less zeroes in it, it might have stayed anonymous."

Jim Haviland tossed a white bar towel over his shoulder. "Tess told me she stopped by your office a few weeks ago and gave you a lecture. She called this morning. Says she hasn't seen you and asked if I saw signs it was taking."

Susanna ground pepper into her soup, carefully avoiding Jim's critical look. "What did you tell her?"

"I told her hell, no, it wasn't taking. Look at you. Head to toe in black."

She glanced down at her black sweater and black jeans. "I like black."

"Wicked Witch of the East," Davey said, humming a few measures of "Ding Dong the Witch is Dead."

"We never got to see the Wicked Witch of the East." Susanna kept her voice steady, determined not to let these two men get the better of her. "Just her legs and her ruby slippers. Maybe she wore red."

Davey shook his head. "Nope. Black. All black."

Jim waited on one of the tables, then came back behind the bar. There was always a crowd on chowder night, not that it changed his pace of operations. "You haven't been coming around much lately," he told Susanna.

"I've been swamped."

"All that money," Davey said. "Must be time-consuming adding it up."

"I'm ignoring you, Davey Ahearn."

"It won't work. That's why you haven't been coming around much. You know we're not going to leave you alone about that guy who killed his wife."

Her stomach twisted, and she stared at her chowder, suddenly no longer hungry. "Davey, for God's sake..."

"You still haven't told Jack," Jim said gently.

She shook her head. "I told you, there's no point. It's been over a year. The woman who screwed up the investigation is out of prison, and Jack—I don't know, he's chasing escaped convicts or something. This thing's over. Whatever happened to me is irrelevant." She believed that, even if Jack would want the final word—even if Rachel McGarrity's murder remained an open case. She added stubbornly, "Whether I say anything or not won't make a difference."

Jim dumped ice into a glass, working on drinks for his customers. "It would to your husband."

"Don't you think a wife deserves to have some secrets from her husband?"

Davey snorted. "Only about the occasional trip on the sly to the dog track."

"When are you heading to the mountains?" Jim asked her, mercifully changing the subject.

"Saturday morning." Susanna dipped her spoon into her soup and smiled. "I'm taking black pants, black shirts, black socks—"

"Black underwear?" Davey asked without missing a beat.

She couldn't suppress a laugh, but said to Jim, "Can I throw my soup at him?"

"No way. I gave you extra clams." He then

shifted from one foot to the other in a rare show of discomfort. "Look, Susanna, before you go, especially if Iris is staying behind—you might want to meet her new friend."

"Ah. Audrey. I've been meaning to. Gran says they eat together here once in a while."

"Two, three times a week. She's from Texas, you know. Houston."

Susanna set her spoon down carefully, not wanting her shock to show. "No, I didn't know. Gran's never said, and I never thought to ask. Tell me more."

"I don't know much more," Jim said. "Audrey Melbourne, from Houston, small, curly red hair, lots of makeup and jewelry. She turned up not long after New Year's saying she was thinking about relocating to Boston but didn't like the high rents. She found a place to live a few blocks from here, says it's temporary. I'll admit, I didn't think she'd come back in here after that first night, but she and Iris have kicked up this friendship…" He trailed off, eyeing Susanna. "You okay?"

"Melbourne…" She almost couldn't get it out. She was shaking visibly now, unable to contain her shock. Davey eased off his stool, obviously ready to come to her aid. She tossed her head back a little, trying to rally. "The next time this woman comes in, will you call me? You have my cell phone number? I want to meet her."

"Susanna." Jim's blue eyes drilled into her, and she remembered he had long experience with his own daughter and her half-truths, including her recent dissembling about her haunted carriage house and the dead body in the cellar. He set the finished drink he'd been making on a tray and pulled her soup bowl away, dumping it into a dishpan to bring out back. "If there's something I need to know about Audrey Melbourne, you need to tell me. Now. No screwing around."

"She—I don't want her near my grandmother."

"That goes for Maggie and Ellen as well?"

Susanna stared at him dully, unable to think. "What?"

"The twins. They had soup with Iris and Audrey a few nights ago, when you were at your tai chi class."

"Oh, my God."

Before she knew what was happening, Susanna had fallen off the stool, but Davey Ahearn was there instantly, bracing her with a muscular, tattooed arm. "Easy, kid," he said.

"I don't usually come apart like this." But her daughters. Maggie and Ellen. Gran. Susanna placed a shaking hand on her temple, as if that somehow would help her organize a coherent thought. *"Damn it.* I could be wrong—I hope so. I've been living with a Texas Ranger for so long…" She looked at Davey, managing a weak, unconvincing smile. "It's because of Jack I could tell Tess about decomposing bodies."

Davey continued his iron grip on her arm. "Susanna, who is Audrey Melbourne?"

She didn't answer him, instead turning to Jim. "Do you know where she lives?"

"No," he said, "and I wouldn't tell you if I did. You'd go over there and get yourself into trouble. I can see it in your eyes. Then I'd have to call Jack and tell him." He picked up his drinks tray, straightening. "Answer Davey's question, Susanna. Who is this woman?"

"I'm not positive—really, I could be wrong. The woman I'm thinking of is blond—"

"The red's a dye job," Davey said, not letting up on his grip.

Some of the adrenaline oozed out of her, some of the tension in her muscles released. They deserved to know. This was their neighborhood, Iris was their friend. "The man I told you about who killed his wife," she said, pausing for a breath, feeling the clam chowder churning in her stomach. Davey remained at her side, steady, not interrupting for once. She tried again. "The local police officer who found her—the wife—ended up in prison for official misconduct. Witness tampering. She got out on New Year's Eve. She took off a few days later. She was obsessed with Australia, and everyone thought—"

"Melbourne," Jim said. "That's in Australia."

Davey released his grip now that Susanna was steadier on her feet. "I knew that was a phony name." He gave her a hard look. "Are you going to call Jack, or do you want to leave that to me and Jimmy?"

Meaning Jack would get called, one way or the other. "I'll call him," she said. "Just first let me make sure I'm right about this woman."

Alice knew something was wrong the minute she walked into Jim's Place. It was chowder night, and she deliberately arrived after Iris would have come and gone. Alice didn't want to draw too much attention to their friendship and tried to stagger their visits, not make it obvious the old woman was her focus.

With freezing rain forecast for the evening, the bar was relatively quiet, the television tuned to a repeat of an old Red Sox game. Davey Ahearn was staring up at it, his broad back to Alice as she eased onto a stool at the bar. Jim Haviland put a bowl of chowder in front of her even before she'd ordered it.

Definitely, something was up.

She'd never had particularly good instincts, but prison had taught her to tune in to her environment, notice the undercurrents, see trouble before it happened—not wait to get her ass kicked. She'd been trying to show her best side in Boston. She found herself wanting Iris Dunning to think well of her. It was as if she were adopting the new persona she would use in Australia—letting her real self out. That was what she used to tell herself about her parents. When they were sober and straight, that was their real selves. That was who they really were. Not perfect, but decent, interested in her.

When they were drunk or high on drugs, they weren't their real selves. Her grandma said it was the devil, but Alice didn't believe that. She could never see the devil in her mother and father, even when they were passed out in their own vomit. They weren't mean, just a couple of no-accounts.

She wasn't like them.

Her real self was pleasant, optimistic, empathetic, kind to old people and not one to hold a grudge. Sure, she was still trying her damnedest to extort fifty thousand dollars from a murderer, but she'd also learned in prison that she had to be practical, use

what she had. Attainable goals. She hated to involve
Iris and the Galway women in her scheme, but that
just couldn't be avoided.

If she had to sit in judgment of herself—well,
she'd opt for forgiveness. She'd see a woman who'd
been through a lot and was just trying to get to a
point where she could make a fresh start, maybe put
the screws to a murderer who was otherwise getting
off scot-free. That wasn't so bad.

Beau was still dragging his heels—but he'd crack.
He was getting close. He asked questions about Susanna Galway. He repeated things he'd said to her in
the kitchen that day, insisting he hadn't said anything
bad. But he wasn't sure—he wanted to hear what was
on that tape.

Every week, Alice told herself, okay, one more
week. She had to stick to her guns, because it wasn't
a good idea to waffle with Beau. She couldn't give
up too soon or he'd wonder, and that'd make him
dangerous. He'd wondered what she and Rachel were
up to, wondered if they were plotting to kill him and
get his money—wondered about Alice's remark
about smothering him.

Boom. Next thing, Rachel was dead, and Alice's
monogrammed change purse was floating in her
blood.

What Beau needed was some encouragement—
maybe she just needed to get on with it, break in to
Iris's house, search Susanna's room and pretend
she'd found the tape. Then tell Beau she was bringing it to him or the Texas Rangers, either one. Maybe
the media. Something that'd rattle his cage.

She was dillydallying, she knew, because of Iris

and clam chowder nights at Jim's Place, fooling herself into thinking she could start over here, in Boston, and maybe not have to go all the way to Australia. That was her greatest weakness, always looking for the easy way out. She'd fall short of her goals and say it was good enough. Why be a Texas Ranger when she could be a small-town cop? Rachel McGarrity used to tell her to recognize that tendency and fight it. If she wanted to be a small-town cop, great—mission accomplished. If not, then go after what she wanted.

Alice hadn't touched her soup. The pat of butter had already melted. She tore open her packet of oyster crackers. She had the most awful feeling of foreboding. She tried smiling at Davey Ahearn, but he wasn't looking at her.

"I didn't want to believe it."

Alice recognized Susanna Galway's voice and felt a little like she did that day Lieutenant Galway had pulled her aside to ask her a few questions about the Rachel McGarrity investigation. A Texas Ranger, on her case. She knew it'd only be a matter of time before she was charged with official misconduct, or worse.

But this time, Alice didn't bother trying to hide what she'd done. "Mrs. Galway, please, I know this looks bad." Alice kept her voice respectful, but wondered if her cheeks were red or pale, revealing anything about how frightened and awful she felt. "I don't mean you or your family any harm."

Susanna tilted her head, her long black hair hanging down her back, her green eyes half-closed, but

Alice could see she was rattled, scared. "You used a false name."

"I'm in the process of legally changing my name to Audrey Melbourne. I want a fresh start."

"Here? You didn't just happen to show up in the same neighborhood as the family of the Texas Ranger who put you in prison—"

"Lieutenant Galway didn't put me in prison," Alice said. "I put myself there through my own actions."

Jack Galway's wife inhaled sharply. She was so tall and limber—Alice felt tiny next to her. She'd always wanted to be more of an *über*-girl. She almost didn't make it as a police officer because of her size. People liked to tell her she was cute. She didn't have Susanna Galway's dramatic good looks.

"If you wanted a fresh start," Susanna went on tightly, "you wouldn't be here in Boston, in my neighborhood. That just doesn't wash, Miss Parker."

"I know." She spoke quietly, respectfully, aware of Jim Haviland and Davey Ahearn watching her, listening, ready to act if she did anything stupid. She had rehearsed this moment a thousand times in the past few weeks. "I came up here because I wanted to make up for any damage I'd done. I heard you'd left your husband after I got arrested—"

"That had nothing to do with you," Susanna said stonily.

Alice wasn't so sure about that, but she nodded anyway. "I can see that now. I probably knew it even before I got here."

"But you stayed."

"Where else was I supposed to go? I'm saving for

Australia. Did Iris tell you that? I like her a lot, Mrs. Galway. I'd never do anything to hurt her. I mean, if I were up here to get revenge, I've had weeks.''

Susanna went slightly pale at Alice's last words.

"Please believe me," Alice said quietly, earnestly.

"It doesn't matter what I believe or don't believe." Susanna stuffed her hands into her coat pockets, everything about her rigid, serious, determined. And scared, Alice thought. Susanna Galway wasn't one who liked admitting she was scared. "I don't want you anywhere near my grandmother or my daughters."

Alice nodded. "All right. I understand."

But her tone didn't come out quite right, and she could see that Susanna had read her words the way Alice had really meant them—defiant and in-your-face defensive. She didn't have to stay away from anybody. She was a free woman. She hadn't threatened Iris or Maggie and Ellen Galway. She hadn't stalked them. She hadn't broken the law. Her presence in Susanna's neighborhood was provocative, yes. But it wasn't illegal.

"Stay away from my family," Susanna said.

Alice didn't argue, although she couldn't imagine not seeing Iris again—at least to explain who she was, why she'd lied to her. She didn't want Iris to think badly of her. She didn't know why, but the old woman's opinion mattered to her.

Susanna swept out of the bar, and Alice looked up at Jim Haviland, feeling her eyes fill with tears. "I suppose you think I'm pretty awful."

"I think you're scaring the shit out of Susanna Galway and used an innocent old woman—"

"I'd never hurt Iris. Never. I consider her a friend."

But she could see she wasn't getting anywhere with him, and down the bar, Davey Ahearn looked ready to take her out and shove her face into a snowbank. She jumped off her stool and tossed money on the bar, next to her barely touched bowl of chowder. She mostly choked down the clams, anyway. She couldn't understand why New Englanders had clam chowder contests. It wasn't even in the same universe as a good bowl of chili.

She sniffled, knowing she wasn't eliciting an ounce of sympathy from either man. "I'm a free woman," she said. "I can come and go as I please."

"Then go," Davey Ahearn said with an edge of sarcasm. "Please."

She did, grabbing her parka but not bothering to put it on. One of them would call Jack Galway. Jim, Davey, Susanna. Jack wouldn't stand by while a woman he'd put in prison, a corrupt fellow officer of the law, slipped into the neighborhood where his wife and daughters were living. It didn't matter what was going on between him and Susanna. He'd be on the next plane out of San Antonio the minute he found out.

Alice pushed out the door into the cold night. There was a time when she'd wanted to stick it to Jack Galway for what he'd done to her, when she'd have been happy to think he was worried sick about his family because of her.

That wasn't what this was about, she told herself. Revenge was pointless. This was about money for Australia and her new beginning.

Not that it'd make any difference to Jack Galway, Texas Ranger, but it did to her. She had a higher purpose in mind.

If he was about to find out she was up here with his wife and daughters, Alice couldn't fool herself. There were no two ways about it. The squeeze was on, and she was running out of time.

Six

On the drive to the San Antonio airport, Sam Temple tried to talk Jack into calling Susanna and telling her he was on his way. "She's the crack of dawn type," Sam said. "She'll be up."

Jack shook his head. "I'm not arguing with her."

They were in Sam's slick car, the beautiful early morning doing nothing to improve either man's mood. "You don't argue," Sam said. "You say, 'Suze, babe, I'm coming to Boston whether you like it or not.'"

"That'd work," Jack said dryly.

"I'm not talking about going Neanderthal on her." Sam was driving fast, as alert at six o'clock in the morning as any other time of the day or night. Nothing seemed to affect him. "Women don't like men popping up out of nowhere."

"Susanna's my wife. I've known her since she was a skinny college kid with a calculator brain."

Sam grinned at him. He was dressed for work, wearing a suit and the white cowboy hat that was customary among Texas Rangers. His Oakley sunglasses were not. "It wasn't her calculator brain that caught your attention."

Jack said nothing. He'd been thinking about his wife since he'd checked his voice mail an hour ago and got her message. It had taken him exactly fifteen minutes to book a flight to Boston, call Sam and pack his bag. He'd been up early for his run, which meant he could catch one of the first flights out of town and be in Massachusetts before it would occur to Susanna that she'd pushed the wrong buttons with him and he might just be on his way.

She knew what she was doing last night when she'd left that message. Susanna always knew what she was doing.

"Jack? I thought I'd catch you." That was bullshit. She'd deliberately called his cell phone number because she knew it was midnight and he was home in bed, next to their home phone. *"I wanted to let you know that Alice Parker has turned up in Boston. Well, in Somerville. She and Gran have become pretty good friends over the past few weeks, which is unnerving, I know, but I spoke to her tonight—Alice, I mean."*

This last comment had gone right up his spine, because it meant Susanna had jumped in and confronted Alice Parker without first calling him and asking his advice on how to handle her. Or, more specifically, on what in hell not to do.

"She's changed her name to Audrey Melbourne. She assured me she means us no harm. She came up here to make amends and basically ended up sticking around longer than she meant to. The situation's under control. I'm just telling you because I know you

were concerned about her. If you have any questions, call me. Bye.''

If he had any questions. Hell, he had no questions at all. He knew what he was going to do—fly to Boston and throttle his wife. Then he'd see about Alice Parker, aka Audrey Melbourne.

"You're going unarmed?" Sam asked.

Jack nodded. He wasn't on official business. This was strictly personal. He had to follow Massachusetts gun laws just like anyone else. He wasn't a law enforcement officer anywhere but Texas.

"Not me," Sam said. "I'd go armed to the teeth."

"And you'd be fired."

They arrived at the airport. Jack got his bag from the back seat and started out, but Sam tried one more time. "You want me to call her?"

"Sure. You call her."

Sam grinned. "She can't hurt me over the phone." But he added in a more serious tone, "I'll keep an eye on things down here, maybe take a ride out and see what Beau McGarrity's been up to."

"Thanks."

"Alice Parker isn't in your wife's neighborhood to make amends or any damn thing. You know that, don't you, Jack?" Sam gripped the wheel with both hands. "She thinks it's your fault Beau's still a free man. Susanna has a point—if Alice planned to hurt any of them, she'd have done it by now. She's got something else up her sleeve."

Jack agreed. Alice had careened into committing a felony and landing herself in prison for a year—he could see her careening into revenge, getting in over her head again, with the law, or, even worse, with

Beau McGarrity. She'd risked everything to nail McGarrity for murder and lost. What was to stop her from trying again? "I should have bought her a damn ticket to Australia the day she was at my house. If I hit on anything up north—anything at all—I'll notify the local police and bring her in. Keep me posted on what's going on down here."

"Will do."

Jack climbed out and shut the door. His stomach tightened at the thought of seeing Susanna again. None of the intensity of his feelings for her had lessened in twenty years, whether he was loving her or so mad at her he couldn't see straight—like now.

"Hey, Lieutenant."

Sam Temple had gotten out of his car and was looking out over the roof. Jack could feel the warm morning sun on his back. "What is it?"

Sam grinned. "They have telephones on planes nowadays. You can still call her."

Susanna treated herself to professionally brewed coffee and a fresh almond biscotti at Fanueil Hall Marketplace. It was the sort of mid-February day that made Bostonians rhapsodic—highs in the forties, bright sun, melting snow. Even the potholes forming in the streets didn't sour their mood. As far as they were concerned, there was a whiff of spring in the air. But Susanna had lived in south Texas too long to consider forty-four degrees spring, especially when she knew it wouldn't last. There was already talk of more snow that weekend, but not before she and the girls were on their way to the mountains. Gran was leaning toward joining them. The revelation that her new friend was an ex-convict Susanna's husband had put in prison didn't sit well with her.

"I feel like an old fool," she'd told Susanna the previous night.

"Don't, Gran. Alice has been here for weeks, and none of us had any idea. Come up to the mountains with us. The change of scenery will do us all some good."

Iris admitted it probably would, but her ambivalence about the trip surprised Susanna. She was beginning to wonder if there was more to Gran's past on Blackwater Lake than she'd ever let on. Going back was obviously harder for her than Susanna had anticipated, not the adventure she'd wanted it to be.

She'd sell the cabin and never set foot near Blackwater Lake again if that was what Gran wanted.

Maggie and Ellen had taken the news about Alice in stride, much more so than Susanna had. They had grown up with a Texas Ranger as their father and were determined not to overreact now that his work had spilled over into their lives.

When they found out their mother had left him a message on his voice mail, they saw right through her. Maggie had grinned. "Gee, Mom, why don't you just poke him with a sharp stick?"

Ellen was appalled. "I don't know, Mom, you might have really stepped in it this time. You haven't seen Dad in a while. You don't know what he's like these days."

"Ellen's right," Maggie said. "He's a lot edgier."

But Susanna didn't need her daughters telling her what her husband was like. She knew. Edgier or not, he wouldn't take well to her midnight voice mail—

he'd take even less well to Alice Parker cozying up to Gran and the girls. He would see dire motives, conspiracies, all the awful, deadly, nasty possibilities, because that was his training and his nature.

No, she thought, because that was what circumstances would lead anyone to think. She was thinking the same thing, and she hated it. If nothing else, it meant that fleeing to Boston with her daughters hadn't made her safe—Alice Parker was *here*.

She'd tossed and turned most of last night, considering the same motives, conspiracies and possibilities Jack would—and maybe then some. She didn't care what Alice said, or how small and cute she was with her newly dyed hair and feminine look. The woman had no business showing up in Somerville.

Susanna dumped the last of her coffee and ducked into an upscale sporting goods store. She hoped when they all returned from their week in the Adirondacks, they'd discover Alice Parker had moved on.

She debated buying snowshoe poles for a few minutes, then gave up and headed back to her office. She enjoyed the walk through the crowded marketplace, through Government Center and onto Beacon Street, heading up toward Boston Common and the gold-domed Massachusetts State House.

Despite the longer days and moderating temperatures, it was still very much winter. She wore her black cashmere coat, black gloves and boots, but, because of Jim Haviland and Davey Ahearn's comments about the Wicked Witch of the East, she'd bought herself a deep scarlet scarf. She was unapologetic about her black gabardine wool pantsuit. She was a professional in a conservative business—people trusted her with their money. She couldn't wear bangles and tight little pastel sweaters like Alice Parker.

She paused at a store window, pulling her scarf over her head as a sharp gust of wind hit her. She glanced up the street out of the corner of her eye, and her breath caught. She spun around, convinced she'd made a mistake, but she hadn't.

Jack stood at the entrance to her nineteenth-century building with his hand on the head of one of the marble gargoyles.

Susanna didn't move. His dark eyes were on her. He had on his white cowboy hat, a suede jacket, jeans and cowboy boots, and she thought he was the sexiest man on the planet.

But she fought a visceral, inexplicable urge to bolt. Not that she'd get far if her husband meant to talk to her, but this was her office, her city, her space. His presence felt like an invasion—yet it was what she'd wanted. For months, she'd dreamed of him coming to Boston, telling her he wanted her back in his life. Wooing her, Maggie and Ellen would call it. But that wasn't it. She wanted to know she mattered to him. She wanted him to tell her. She wanted him to ask her to tell him all her secrets, one by one, to understand all of them. To admit his own fears and secrets, finally, she thought. To talk.

Well, sometimes that was what she wanted. Other times she didn't have a clue, except a certainty that something had gone wrong between her and the man she loved.

Of course, none of that was why Jack was here.

He was here because of her phone call last night. Because of Alice Parker.

Susanna made sure her legs were steady under her before she resumed walking up the street. She peeled off her gloves, stuffing them in her coat pockets. "Hello, Jack," she said calmly. "Have you been waiting long?"

"Thirty minutes." His Texas drawl was slow and not at all casual, curling up her spine, oozing in like smoke. She felt self-conscious, aware. He kept his gaze pinned on her, revealing nothing of what he felt. "Your doorman wouldn't let me in."

"Smart doorman."

"An unarmed doorman and a couple of ugly gargoyles. That's not much security."

"I don't need much security."

He moved off from the gargoyle. If she wanted to get into her building, she'd have to go around him, not just past him. Her opportunity to do an about-face and get out of there had evaporated, if it had ever existed. He tilted his head, taking her in with those trained eyes, more Texas Ranger right now than husband. But then he said, "Your nose is red."

"I've been out walking." She pulled off her scarlet scarf, aware of him watching her hair fall. "I had meetings this morning. I was taking a break."

"Sam said I should tell you he tried to get me to call ahead."

"I've always liked Sam." The wind gusted again, but it didn't feel as cold this time. "You're here because of Alice Parker."

He kept any reaction tightly under control. "I'm here because of you."

"Because you're annoyed at me."

He took a step closer, close enough that she could feel the heat and warmth of him. "Very."

"I've wondered what it would take to get you on a plane." She cleared her throat, wishing she could control her response to him. Twenty years of sleeping with him hadn't done a thing to dampen her desire for him. And it had been so long since she'd had him next to her, loving her. "Um—there's a coffee shop down the street. We can talk there."

He smiled knowingly. "What's the matter, Susanna, you don't want to be alone with me?" He skimmed a finger across her cold cheek and along the curve of her jaw, sending warm currents through her. "It doesn't matter. I can kiss you right out here on Beacon Street."

"Jesus, Jack," she breathed, "you could be more neutral."

His dark gaze stayed on her. "Not where you're concerned."

"All right," she said briskly, furious with herself for wanting him to kiss her—right now, right there on a cold, busy street in downtown Boston. "We can go up to my office. It's on the fourth floor."

"I'd like to see it," he said simply, and her throat caught, because maybe it was true. Maybe he did want to see her office.

The lobby was small, elegant with its marble floors, brass trim and dark, rich woods. A curving staircase led up to the second floor. There was a tiny, cramped, old elevator, but Susanna had a sudden image of it getting stuck between floors with just her and Jack in there. She started up the stairs, leading the way, feeling his eyes on her as she moved quickly, unbuttoning her coat. She was hot, self-conscious, trying to regroup. He'd had time to get used to the idea of seeing her—to plot his strategy, the approach he'd take. She'd been caught off guard. It was her own damn fault. She should have known that message would get him on a plane.

She took off her coat on the second flight and slung it over one arm, her scarf falling on the step. Jack scooped it up, tucking it back in with her coat. Every nerve ending she had seemed to be on fire. She picked up her pace, rushing up the third flight of stairs. She could hear his boots click as he maintained a steady pace behind her.

She couldn't get a decent breath. She staggered down the hall to her office, disgusted with herself. She did the stairs all the time. She ran, she lifted weights, she did yoga and tai chi. She was in good shape. It wasn't the exertion that had left her breathless—it was having her husband on her heels.

"This is it," she said, as casually as she could manage, and unlocked her office door, pushing it open. She motioned for him to go in ahead of her. "After you."

He gave her one of his quick, professional scans, but the twitch at the corners of his mouth was disconcertingly unprofessional. He was reading her breathlessness for what it was—him. But there was something else in his eyes, a hardness she hadn't noticed before. He walked into her office, and she shut the door behind her. It was quiet, everything in place. Tess Haviland could come in here and notice that her friend's life was out of balance, but Jack wouldn't. He wouldn't know what to look for, not here.

"I can take your coat," Susanna said.

"No." He looked back at her. "I won't be staying long."

He was angry. She could see it now. On the one hand, she felt guilty because, really, she shouldn't have left that message last night. On the other hand— an angry Jack wouldn't want to tear her clothes off and make love to her on her new leather couch.

Not necessarily, anyway.

She groaned silently at herself. What was the *matter* with her? She flung her coat over a chair and adjusted her suit jacket, making sure her blouse wasn't askew or her lacy silk camisole showing.

Jack set his bag on the wood floor, placed his hat on top of it and walked over to the windows. He glanced down at the cemetery. "You like working with a bunch of dead people at your feet?"

"John Hancock's buried down there. You know, hero of the American Revolution, former governor of Massachusetts. Paul Revere, Sam Adams. Benjamin Franklin's parents are down there, too. The victims of the Boston Massacre." She pushed her hair back with both hands, finally catching her breath. "Mother Goose."

"You and I visited Old Granary when we were in college." He glanced back at her, nothing about his expression softening. "In the fall."

"I remember. And we took the girls when they were in kindergarten and we were up visiting Gran over spring break."

He didn't respond. She wondered if he was remembering that day with the girls skipping out ahead of them amidst the shaded gravestones, or an earlier day, when they were students, madly in love—or neither day. Maybe he was just seething over her midnight call about Alice Parker.

"I didn't want to wake you," she said, knowing he'd follow her train of thought. "That's why I left a message on your voice mail. It was late—"

"When did you find out about Alice?"

"Last night. Jack, I called you as soon as I could—"

"What time?"

She walked over to her desk and sat at her computer. It was in sleep mode, the screen blank. She hit the space bar. "Before midnight. It took a while for it all to sink in. Alice Parker has been here for weeks. I imagine she got here around the time you told me she'd been released. She and Gran have seen each other two or three times a week—Gran had her over to the house one morning." Susanna watched her monitor come to life. "I had no idea. I was stunned. It was a lot to absorb, and I had to talk to her and the girls."

Jack wasn't relenting. "Did you?"

She nodded, still not looking back at him. "I told them to stay away from Alice Parker."

"And Alice?"

"I told her to stay away from all of us."

"So that's it," he said. "It's done as far as you're concerned. You've handled it."

"That's not what I meant."

She swiveled around to face him, calmer now that she'd had a little time to adjust to his presence. But she couldn't fathom what had possessed her not to call him at home. Had she known, deep down, it would bring him to Boston? Had she wanted it to?

No. She'd wanted to avoid having to tell him about Beau McGarrity and Alice, about that day in her kitchen. Having him guess. Was that why Alice had come to Boston? Because of McGarrity? Susanna felt a rush of panic, wondering if she'd missed something that day with Beau McGarrity. Something Jack would have caught if she'd told him.

She was so sure there was nothing he or Alice, the prosecutors, *anyone* could use to help them solve Rachel McGarrity's murder. But what if she was wrong?

"I'm sorry, Jack," Susanna said simply. "It was asinine to leave that message last night. I knew what I was doing."

"You always know what you're doing."

She eased to her feet and stood next to him at the window. "You must have been really ticked off to jump on a plane first thing this morning."

His eyes softened for half an instant. "Stick to the present tense."

"Okay, so you're still mad." She sighed, staring down at the snow-covered graveyard. "I didn't think about your voice mail giving the bloody time I called."

"Susanna…"

"I should have been more vigilant. You warned me about Alice. I should have investigated when Gran told me she had a new friend at the pub." She drew a shallow breath, swallowing as she felt him leaning in close to her. She kept her gaze on the gravestones. "I didn't want to believe it was Alice Parker."

"I know."

He took her hand, and she let her fingers intertwine with his, then turned to him as he drew her closer. He touched her lips, threaded his fingers through her hair, his dark eyes on her, the hardness gone, the fury dissipated. She didn't know what he saw in her eyes, but he kissed her softly, lightly, as if anything more would be too much after so many months apart. "It's good to see you," he whispered.

She placed her palm flat on his chest and sank her forehead against his shoulder, feeling his arms come around her. Tears welled in her eyes, and she thought of Alice Parker changing her name and befriending her eighty-two-year-old grandmother. There was no escaping that Jack's work had touched their lives in a new way. Susanna didn't know what to do. Didn't know what he'd do if he thought his family was threatened by anyone, never mind by someone he'd put in prison.

"Let me help," he said softly.

He wasn't ordering her, and he never pleaded. He was, Susanna knew, simply telling her what he could do. He was a lieutenant with the Texas Rangers. He could help. He wanted to help. She lifted her head off his shoulder and saw his self-control drop into place, the experienced law enforcement officer back on the case. "Jack, it's us this time—Gran, the girls, me. We're the ones with the creepy stuff going on. I hope it won't amount to anything and that Alice was honest with me, but it's not just you this time. It's not strangers."

His eyes darkened. "Why the hell do you think I'm here?"

She stepped back from his embrace. "How long do you plan to stay?" she asked, fighting for a little self-control of her own.

"I have time coming to me. I can stay as long as I need to."

"We're leaving for the Adirondacks in the morning—"

He managed a half smile. "What about my open invitation?"

Her heartbeat quickened. She pictured him up there in the mountains with her. Was that what she wanted? "Jack, I really think I can handle this situation myself. I don't want to mess up your vacation time."

His expression was unreadable, whatever he was feeling tamped down somewhere deep and inaccessible. "I'm not here because I don't think you can't handle the situation. You have local law enforcement you can call. I'm here because I want to help."

"The hell you are," she said abruptly, dropping onto her chair, studying this intelligent, independent man she'd loved for half her life. "This is payback for me trying to do an end run on you."

"Whatever it is, Susanna, I'm here, and I'm not going anywhere until I've talked to Alice Parker myself. Make the best of it." He grabbed his hat and bag and started for the door, stopping halfway and turning back to her. His eyes were very dark. She tended to forget how intimidating he could look—except she'd never been intimidated by Jack Galway. Never. He pointed his hat at her. "If you'd called me at six o'clock this morning, I'd still have come. Alice Parker has no business being anywhere near my family."

"I know that, but you said yourself there's not a damn thing either of us can do about it unless she breaks the law—"

"Susanna," he said, "tell me you're not relieved I'm here."

Her mouth snapped shut. She couldn't say a word.

He grinned as if he had his answer and pulled open the door. He gave her office another appraising scan. "It's nice. You've done well for yourself."

"Thanks." Her throat was still tight, her nerves frayed from seeing him. No one could see through her defenses to her vulnerabilities better than her husband could. She tried to take in a decent breath. "Where are you going now?"

"Subway station."

In other words, he had no intention of answering to her. He'd do as he damn well pleased. Relieved. Oh, yeah, she was relieved he was here.

But part of her *was* relieved, and that just added to her jumble of emotions.

She tilted back in her chair, raking both hands through her hair, and she gave him as casual a look she could manage. "Should I expect you for dinner? Um—should I make up the bed in the guest room?"

"Now we get to the crux of matter. Where does the husband sleep tonight?" He put on his cowboy hat and winked at her, sexily. "Don't worry, darlin'. I'll let you know."

He left, shutting the door softly behind him—as if to tell her he was in total control of what he was doing. Susanna banged a few keys on her computer and counted to ten. Or tried to. She got to seven and jumped up, charging across her office and out into the hall.

She leaned over the stair rail. He was on the bottom step.

"Don't you think you've put me on the defensive," she yelled down to him, "because you haven't. I want you to keep me informed. I won't have you tearing around in my city—"

He kept walking, his footsteps echoing in the stairwell. She thought of the other people in the building, wondered if they thought she was a lunatic. Most didn't know she was married to a Texas Ranger. That didn't fit their profile of a successful Boston financial planner.

"Jack!" She pounded the railing in frustration. He knew every way there was to get under her skin.

Still no answer.

"Fine," she muttered. "Have it your way, Lieutenant Galway."

She swooped back into her office, slammed the door and flopped onto her leather couch. She touched her lips where he'd kissed her and swore silently, not because of the kiss, but because of her reaction to it. He was an overwhelming presence, her husband. It would be so easy to sit back and let him take control of everything, except she'd never done any such thing in all the years they'd been together. He wouldn't respect her if she did. But it would be so easy.

Well, he was *not* coming to the Adirondacks. She'd only bought snowshoes for herself and the girls. She didn't have room for him. There was no guest room in her cabin, not if Gran came, and with Alice Parker in town, Susanna had no intention of leaving her grandmother alone.

As she calmed down, she realized she was getting way ahead of herself. Jack had come to Boston because of Alice Parker. Never mind that he wasn't wearing his badge and carrying his weapon, he was here because of his work.

It was something she needed to remember.

Seven

᎒᎒᎒᎒

Alice stood outside Jim's Place, debating whether she should go in and find Iris and apologize to her for lying. It didn't seem like a good idea. Jim Haviland and Davey Ahearn were mad at her, and they and Susanna Galway would regard any contact with Iris Dunning as an affront.

Then there was Jack Galway. Alice suspected he was in Boston by now, if Susanna had told him a corrupt cop he'd put in prison had moved into his wife's neighborhood under an assumed name.

Alice knew she was feeling sorry for herself. She'd been feeling sorry for herself since Susanna had read her the riot act the night before. Her words still stung. Then again, Alice had lasted up here longer than she'd ever meant to. Lying to an old woman. Getting her to talk about her life. Iris had gone on about Blackwater Lake and the man she'd loved up there so long ago, and Alice had sat there, choking down clam chowder, listening.

Goddamn snake in the grass was what she was.

She didn't want Iris to hate her.

Alice swore silently and turned to leave, running right into Destin Wright. He grabbed her by the shoulders and steadied her. "Hey, hey, hey, you're like the Whirling Dervish. What's going on?"

He was the last person she wanted to see while she was sitting on the pity pot. Destin Wright always felt sorry for himself. Even when he was worth millions, he'd probably felt sorry for himself. No matter how much he had, it was never enough. He was a self-absorbed ass, and Alice couldn't stand listening to him. Over the past few weeks, since she'd arrived in Boston, they met at Jim's Place on nights she was trying not to bump into Iris. She liked Iris but knew she was pushing her luck getting too close to her. Nobody else seemed to like Destin, either, although they tolerated him, sometimes egging him on when he started talking and wouldn't stop. It was as if he thought the world spun for him and no one else.

"I hate Boston," Alice blurted. "I can see why people clear out and move to the Sun Belt. I don't know why I ever left Texas."

He shrugged. "Everybody hates Boston in February."

"I'd hate it anytime of the year. I don't give a damn about all the history and old buildings, I hate riding the subway, and why the hell do I care about Harvard and MIT? You can have them."

"Not me. Harvard rejected me."

Everything was about him. She tucked her hands into the pockets of her parka. She wasn't wearing gloves. She hated gloves. "I lied to people about who I am."

That perked his interest. "No kidding? Who are you?"

"My name's not Audrey Melbourne, at least not yet. Not legally. It's Alice Parker. I was a police officer in Texas, and I screwed up a murder investigation and served time for witness tampering."

"Ouch."

"Susanna Galway—" Alice squinted up at the streetlight, dark still coming too soon for her tastes. She looked back at Destin, knowing he'd lose his interest in listening to her pretty soon. "She's the wife of the Texas Ranger who arrested me."

"Jack arrested you?" Destin laughed, impressed. "No shit. He's a hard-ass."

"Yes, he is."

Destin shifted, looking handsome and Harvard-like in his camel cashmere coat and black scarf and gloves. Rich, Alice thought, although she knew he was dead broke, almost as broke as she was. "Maybe that's why Susanna's been so distracted," he said, "and won't take a look at my business plan, because she's been worried about you. I know she'd go for this idea. It's hot."

Alice resisted rolling her eyes. She knew the conversation would eventually boomerang back to him and his scheme to start a new company. As far as she could see, begging a hundred thousand dollars from Susanna Galway was no better than Alice extorting fifty thousand off Beau McGarrity. At least Beau would get something in return. Susanna would just get Destin off her back.

"I'm not asking for charity," he said for the thousandth time since they'd met. "This is such a no-brainer. I just want someone to—to—"

"To recognize your brilliance," Alice finished for him.

He settled back on his heels and nodded. "Yeah. Yeah, this is one fucking brilliant idea. A hundred thousand in angel money. It's not that much to ask."

"Susanna has that kind of money?"

"Shit, a hundred grand's pin money for her."

Alice could feel the cold from the sidewalk seeping up through her boots. She'd bought winter boots on sale, but they were ugly and clunky. She had on her cowboy boots tonight. They were cheap. If she'd become a Texas Ranger, she'd have bought herself good boots. But that wasn't going to happen now, and even Australia was slipping away.

"There has to be a way to get Susanna to loosen up her purse strings," Destin said.

"How much do you think she's worth?"

"Oh, five million easy. Maybe even ten mil by now. She's got some of the best instincts I've ever seen. She's an investor and financial planner, not an entrepreneur—that's where I come in."

He was getting to the point where he'd strangle his own grandmother for another chance at the brass ring. Alice could see it in his handsome blue eyes, hear it in his deep voice. Suppose she was looking in the wrong place for her ticket to Australia and her new life. Should she forget Beau and instead think about prying a few grand off multimillionaire Susanna Galway?

Except Beau might not let her forget Beau.

And then there was the Galway who was a Texas Ranger.

Destin started toward Jim's Place, but Alice touched his arm. "I'm kind of persona non grata there right now. I don't think anyone believes I'm here to make amends for what I did—I think I'm at least part of the reason Susanna and Jack are on the skids. I feel bad about that. Anyway, I'd like to talk to you. Do you mind if we go somewhere else?"

He looked at her a moment, the charming facade dropping off, telling her she was right about him. This was the Destin Wright who lacked empathy for others, who thought the world owed him. He was smart and ambitious, and he'd do anything. Any scruples he had were pretense, for show, a means to an end. He did what he had to do to fit in and get what he wanted.

"No problem," he said. "Let's go somewhere and talk, Miss Alice Parker Audrey Melbourne."

If not for the translucent door and thoughts of John Hancock and Benjamin Franklin's dead parents—Mother Goose, for God's sake—Jack figured he'd be making love to his wife on her leather couch instead of walking in the cold February wind.

The temperature had dropped with the sun. As he walked by, a trio of construction workers entered Jim's Place, followed by what were obviously university students. The pub hadn't changed much since Jack was a student. Neighborhood protocol, however, dictated that he pay a visit to Iris Dunning before stopping in for a chat with Jim Haviland about his new regular from Texas.

He rang the doorbell on Iris's glassed-in porch. At first she wouldn't let him in. "I thought you were a hoodlum," she said when she finally opened the door.

Jack smiled and kissed her cheek. "Hoodlums don't wear white cowboy hats."

"Nobody wears white cowboy hats up here."

He laughed. "I don't know, Iris. Things change."

She had on stretch pants and a fuzzy pink sweater that made her look like a sweeter old lady than Jack knew his wife's grandmother to be. This was a woman who'd lived most of her life on her own, raised a son alone, made a place for herself in a strange city. She looked life square in the eye, and seldom did anyone underestimate her a second time.

He followed her inside, where little had changed since he'd first come here at twenty, so in love with green-eyed Susanna Dunning he couldn't see straight. The house was the same—so was his love. He felt an emotional tug, an urge to protect Iris, his wife and his daughters, yet knowing all four of them were the type who liked to run out into the street.

He noticed the three pairs of snowshoes lined up in the front hall. They still had their tags. The cabin in the Adirondacks. It definitely rankled.

Iris went into the living room and sat on an over-stuffed chair, its back covered with one of her crocheted afghans. "I suppose you're here about Audrey," she said when Jack joined her. "Or should I call her Alice? Jack, I'll tell you—I haven't been taken in like that in a long, long time."

"She never should have come up here. She knows that. I'm sorry, Iris."

"Oh, it's not your fault. Audrey comes across so genuine and sweet, you find yourself wanting to like her. She has a very engaging personality. But you say she's a former police officer?"

As if being genuine, sweet and engaging was antithetical to being in law enforcement. Jack smiled, familiar with Iris's prejudices. "She was a small-town police officer I investigated for official misconduct and witness tampering."

"She fouled up a murder investigation, I understand."

He nodded, taking in the signs his wife and daughters lived there. Books they were reading, videos, scented candles and hand lotion. Maggie and Ellen had clamored to spend a year with their great-grandmother in Boston—or on their own in Paris. That Jack understood. But Susanna—she should be in Texas with him. It was that simple.

"Do you have any idea where Alice Parker—Audrey—lives?" he asked.

"Not far from here, I know that much. She says she has a job, but I don't know if that's true." Iris looked up at him, her green eyes intelligent, alert. "Does Susanna know you're here?"

"Yes." He left it at that. "Where are the girls?"

"They're at the grocery. They don't want to get to the mountains and find out there's nothing there to eat. You'd think we were taking off for the moon, the way they act. It's not *that* remote up there." She sank back in her chair, smiling as if at a distant memory. Then she focused again on Jack. "I'm going. Susanna won't want to leave me here alone until she's figured out what this Alice Parker woman is up to.''

"Susanna's not figuring anything out. You all are staying away from Alice." But he realized how dictatorial he sounded and softened his tone. "Iris, this is serious business. A woman was murdered. Alice spent a year in prison."

Iris nodded. "I know, Jack. So does Susanna. She understands her limits." She paused, studying him, and added quietly, "Trust her."

Jack wasn't going there, not with Iris Dunning. "I don't know why you all are trekking up to the Adirondacks when you can come down to San Antonio for the week." He knew he was goading her. Iris didn't like to travel, and she especially didn't like Texas. That her only son and granddaughter had both taken up residence there galled her. "It's a lot prettier there in February than it is here in the frozen north."

"I'm not fond of Texas." She pursed her lips, certain of her opinions. "I was there in August that summer when Maggie and Ellen were born, and it was like being in hell. And you're always executing people."

Arguing politics and Texas weather with Iris Dunning was to jump headfirst into quicksand. There was no winning, only getting back out onto firm ground again. Jack had learned that a long time ago, not that he always resisted. "That's pure prejudice, Iris. Texas is a big state with a diverse population—"

"It's too big."

"Good. Let's carve it up. We can have Texas A, B, C and D, each with its own two senators—"

She waved a hand at him, biting back a smile. "You're incorrigible. You always have been." But Iris's mischievous mood didn't last, and she shook her head, looking disgusted with herself and very old. "I'm afraid I told Audrey—Alice—too much. She's so easy to talk to, and I just yammered on about the neighborhood, Kevin and Eva, you and Susanna, how proud I am of Maggie and Ellen heading off to college. Oh, Jack. I never thought I'd turn into an old fool."

He scooped up her hands, brown with age spots and lined with prominent veins, but her fingers were still long and graceful, reminding him of the old pictures of her in the dining room with her chestnut hair and youthful smile. She had worked at Tufts University for years, then took in students after she retired. She maintained her house, volunteered, had a wide circle of friends. That Alice Parker had undermined an elderly woman's confidence in her own good judgment didn't sit well with him.

"Iris, listen to me," he said as gently as he could manage through his anger. "I don't want you worrying about whatever you told Alice. You thought she was your friend. Your openness and kindness have helped you far more in your life than they've hurt. Susanna and the girls will be fine."

"They're why you're here?"

"You all are." At least Iris recognized that he was here because of them, not just his work. He patted her thin hands. "I don't want you blaming yourself. You did nothing wrong."

"I saw myself in her," she said. "That was wrong."

"That was human, not wrong." He winked at her, adding, "Susanna telling me this whole story on voice mail—now, that was wrong."

He released her hands, and she shook her head. "You two. This separation of yours has gone on long enough, you know."

"I know."

Her green eyes twinkled. "I think that other Texas Ranger's idea about the handcuffs was a good one."

Jack laughed. "I'll tell Sam you approve." He glanced at his watch. Almost six o'clock. He needed to get busy. "Do me a favor, Iris. Tell Susanna to meet me at Jim's Place at seven-thirty."

"Of course, I'll tell her. Where are you going?"

"Just checking out the lay of the land." Jack started into the hall, glancing back at Iris through the open doorway. "And tell Susanna it's not a good night to make me hunt her down."

Susanna slid onto her favorite stool at Jim's Place with a full hour to go before she was to meet her husband—something she had no intention of doing. Gran had already told her she was being pig-headed for ignoring Jack's summons, and maybe she was. She couldn't seem to stop herself. Events were careening out of control, and she didn't know what else to do.

"Jim, has my grandmother ever called you pig-headed?"

He was getting her a Coke. "About once a month."

"It's kind of an old-fashioned word, don't you think? Pigheaded."

"It works. Why, is that what you are?"

"That's what I'm being," she corrected. "It's not what I am."

"Why are you being pigheaded?" Jim asked, setting the frosty glass in front of her.

"I can't seem to help myself." She knew what Jack would do if she waited around until seven-thirty. He would read her the riot act. She, Maggie, Ellen and Gran would all need to stick as close to him as possible until he decided that Alice Parker truly meant them no harm. When he was satisfied, then they could all do what they wanted. He might even nix their trip to the cabin. Susanna sipped her Coke, aware of Jim and Davey Ahearn both watching her, Davey on his stool at the opposite end of the bar. "You'd recognize my husband, wouldn't you?"

"Jack? Of course. Big guy. Texas Ranger."

"White cowboy hat," Davey chimed in.

"He's a serious professional," Susanna said.

Davey shrugged. "So am I, and I have to make sure I keep my pants pulled up."

"What does that have to do with anything?"

"We all have our stereotypes to fight," he replied loftily.

Jim stepped into the conversation again, shaking his head. "Ignore him, Susanna. Jack turned up after you called him about this Alice character, didn't he?"

She drank more of her soda. "Yes, he did."

"Did you tell him about the stalker while you were at it?" Jim asked.

She could tell from his tone that he knew she hadn't, but she shook her head anyway, confirming his worst suspicions. "Not yet. I will, though. Don't you and Davey go jumping the gun."

"Suzie-cue and the lieutenant," Davey said, apparently addressing no one in particular. He turned to Susanna, rubbing one finger on his carefully groomed handlebar mustache. "You're a couple of lifers. I think this whole separation thing is just a way to spice up your sex lives."

"Davey!" She almost fell off her stool. "My God, no wonder your last three dates have stormed out on you. Jim—" She stopped abruptly, noticing that Jim Haviland was wiping down his bar, which was spotless, putting effort into the job, concentrating on it. Then she knew. "Oh, I see. Jack's been here already. You and Davey just weren't going to tell me. You were going to distract me for an hour with speculations about my sex life and—" She could feel heat rushing to her cheeks. "Well, damn if men don't stick together."

Davey snorted. "Like women don't?"

"He was here a little while ago," Jim said. "I learned more about what's going on in talking to him for five minutes than I have in over a goddamn year from you."

Susanna could feel herself going pale. "Jim, you didn't tell him what I said on New Year's Eve—about the stalker—the man who killed his wife—"

He shook his head, and Davey said, "That goes against Jimmy's code of conduct. It doesn't go against mine, but he'd throw me out if I opened my big mouth. Jimmy thinks a wife should tell her husband about stalkers."

"I do, too," Susanna said, "under normal circumstances."

"There are no normal circumstances when it comes to stalkers," Davey said.

"I told you—it wasn't like he was a real stalker. He didn't break any laws. I just..."

"He scared the blue blazes out of you." Davey's voice was soft, and she wondered if he understood.

She wasn't going to answer Jack's summons. She didn't care if she was being pigheaded. Right now, she didn't even care if she made any sense. She knew she couldn't explain her reasoning.

She was the one who'd been sleeping with Jack for twenty years. No one else had to understand her reasoning.

Her heart was racing, her head was throbbing, and all she could think about was getting out of there, as far from Alice Parker as possible—and Jack, now that he was in full investigation mode, all his training and experience not focused on strangers but on his own family. It unnerved her. It scared the hell out of her. She felt exposed, raw, vulnerable.

She didn't want to think about Rachel McGarrity shot dead in her own driveway, or Beau McGarrity pushing open her patio door and walking into her kitchen.

She wanted to go up to the mountains and snowshoe, build a fire in the fireplace and enjoy this last winter vacation before Maggie and Ellen went off to college.

She threw a couple of dollars onto the bar. "I can see I'm doomed." She tried to be good-natured about it. "Jim, can you dip me up a quart of tonight's soup? I don't want to cook."

"It's corn chowder," Davey said, "but Jimmy put curry in it. Tastes like shit. He's trying to please the vegetarian graduate students."

Jim sighed. "I tried a new recipe. God forbid." He turned to Susanna. "What time you leaving in the morning?"

She grabbed her soda and took a sip, hoisting her handbag higher onto her shoulder, pretending not to be paying attention.

Davey wasn't fooled. "Well, well, Jimmy. Our Suzie-cue is skipping out on Jack Galway, Texas Ranger." He clicked his tongue behind his teeth. "I'll be damned, Suzie, I never took you for a coward."

"Never mind the soup," Susanna said, pushing her still half-full glass toward Jim Haviland. "I'll pick up fast food on the road." She slid off the bar stool, her knees faintly weak under her. "You can tell Jack whatever you want to tell him."

"Don't tell him a damn thing, Jimmy," Davey said. "He might shoot up the place."

Susanna buttoned her coat. She'd never taken it off, which probably had clued Jim and Davey in that she planned to deliver her message and sneak out, not chance having Jack show up early. "For once," she said, "Davey has a point. Jack won't shoot up the place, but I have no right to ask you to do my dirty work for me. Don't tell him anything. He can find out on his own."

Davey glanced over at her, his big handlebar

twitching as he shook his head at her. "You know, kid, sometimes discretion's the better part of valor."

"You mean I should give in and do as Jack says, meet him here?"

"Oh, horse hockey, Susanna, you know damn well this has nothing to do with getting your back up because your husband asked you to meet him here. This is about you not wanting to confess."

"Confess? Well, there you go. That says it all. Like he's the interrogator and I'm the guilty perpetrator—"

Davey shrugged. "Yeah, that's it."

No, it wasn't it, Susanna thought. She was rattled by Alice Parker's presence in her neighborhood—her subterfuge—and completely and totally undone by Jack showing up in Boston. She couldn't think straight. She was so rational in every other area of her life. When it came to the safety of Gran and her daughters and her relationship with Jack, sometimes she had to act on basic survival instinct. Or thought she did. Maybe Davey had a point.

"Come on, Davey," she said, struggling to smile, "you know I can't stay."

"Why not?" He picked up his beer glass, his bowl of curried corn chowder still full. "What have you got to lose?"

Jim grunted knowingly. "An hour's head start."

Eight

⚬⚬⚬

Alice was sweating inside her parka, hat and gloves. Destin had already shut off the heat in her car, which didn't work that well, anyway. She pulled off her gloves, aware of Destin fidgeting next to her. They'd cooked up a hell of a scheme, but so far he hadn't gotten cold feet.

They were parked across the street from Iris's house. Susanna had just left with Iris and the girls, off to the mountains for a week. Iris had talked to Alice about whether she should go or not go—she hadn't been back to Blackwater Lake since she left with her son over fifty years ago.

"We can't just go into this blind," Alice said, not looking at Destin. "We have to have good information. Susanna'll blow us off if we screw up one little thing."

Their plan was sketchy at best. Now that Susanna, her grandmother and daughters were safely out of town, Alice figured she and Destin could sneak into their house and have a look around. They could plow through Susanna's financial records. Destin would know what to look for, and then they could decide on the best approach to take with her—and how much they could squeeze out of her and still have her think it'd be easier to give them the money instead of going to the authorities. The pain had to be enough, but not too much. Destin wanted to know what "leverage" they'd use with Susanna, but Alice figured she'd think of something once they had more information.

The car was cold again, and Destin started fiddling with the heat. He had already complained about not being able to buy a new car because he couldn't afford to replace his BMW. "You don't know what it's like to have a BMW repossessed," he said.

"No, Destin, I do not," Alice told him. "That's for darn sure."

"I mean, you watch your stock go into the tank and all those zeroes in your net worth disappear—but getting your Beemer repossessed, that's reality. That's concrete."

The man was making her head throb. A locked cell was reality, Alice thought. A year in the slammer as a corrupt police officer was concrete.

He banged the heat controls. "I fucking hate winter! A year ago, I could pop down to the islands for a weekend and get a break. Now—" He slumped against his seat. "I have to put everything into getting back on my feet."

"That's right, Destin. Let's focus on that."

Her cell phone rang, and she fished it out of her parka, knowing it was Beau McGarrity. No one else had the number. Her throat tightened, and she could feel her hands getting clammy, the fear gnawing at her insides. She couldn't let Destin see it. He needed to believe she was tough and in control, up for the course they were setting out on. She couldn't afford to have him weasel out or, even worse, think he needed to run things.

"I've decided you're not going away," Beau said.

Alice licked her lips, chapped from the cold and the dry heat in her old car. "I wouldn't say that. Once I get the money, I plan to go all the way to Australia."

"Jack Galway left for Boston today. You're in Boston. I've got Sam Temple, another Texas Ranger, sniffing around." Beau's tone was matter-of-fact, but Alice knew better than to think this was a casual call. "If you're trying to trick me—"

Alice stiffened. "You're one to be talking. You tried to pin a murder on me, Mr. Beau. I don't appreciate that. I'm willing to let bygones be bygones—"

"For fifty grand."

"That's right."

He paused, not saying anything for three whole seconds. Alice counted. She thought the connection had cut out, but then he said, almost distracted, "I've never trusted Susanna Galway."

Alice could feel the car heat blowing hot on her face, drying her skin, her nostrils. Destin was still fidgeting, tapping his kneecaps and staring out the window. She'd rubbed snow and dirt on her Texas tags, in case Jack Galway walked down the street. She'd spotted him earlier knocking on Iris's door.

"Look," she said, "maybe it was a bad idea, me

stopping at your place that day. I was fresh out of the joint, and I wasn't thinking—''

"Get the tape." Beau's voice was steady, thoughtful. "I want to know why Mrs. Galway didn't destroy it or give it to her husband. I want to know why she kept it."

"Answers aren't part of the deal. Look, Mr. Beau—" Alice tried to sound cheerful, full of bluster and self-confidence. "You don't owe me a thing until I produce on my end." She didn't want to say she was after a tape, in case Destin was actually listening for once. He usually didn't tune in to a conversation unless it was about him. She hadn't told him about Beau and the tape—she didn't want to scare him off. Destin could be her way out of this mess. "For all I know, she did get rid of it, and this has all been a waste of my time. But I'll find out for sure, okay?"

"You do that."

He clicked off, and Alice breathed out, the sweat trickling down her back. She shut off the car heat. She wondered how long she had before Beau McGarrity took matters in his own hands now that Jack Galway was here on her trail. She glanced at Destin. "I don't know if we can wait until Susanna's back from the mountains. We might have to go on up there and press our case. Time's getting critical. You've got your monkeys on your back, and I've got mine."

Destin nodded, excited. "The Adirondacks are awesome. I thought about buying a place in Lake Placid, but I opted for a condo in the White Mountains instead—I had to sell it to raise cash. Took a loss. What I want's Aspen."

What Alice wanted was to belt the guy. "Iris gave me a key to her house. I was supposed to water the plants and bring in the mail while she was gone. She must have forgotten I have it. She didn't ask for it back."

"Oh, yeah, so that's good." He grinned, looking less and less as if he would bolt any second. "We can just unlock the door and walk in. It wouldn't even be breaking and entering."

Well, it would be if they tossed the place, but Alice kept that to herself. "You game?"

Destin didn't even hesitate. "You bet."

Even before he entered Jim's Place, Jack knew he'd made a tactical error with Susanna. Several, in fact. He hadn't called ahead to tell her he was on his way to Boston, he hadn't made love to her in her office, and he'd given her that order to meet him. All of which, together, had to have her head spinning and her defenses on overdrive.

He did know his wife.

He stood at the bar. "She gave me the slip?"

"I'm afraid so," Jim Haviland said.

Davey Ahearn shifted on his stool at the end of the bar. Jack thought the plumber had been sitting in that same spot twenty years ago, when he'd first checked out the neighborhood. Davey ate most of his suppers there but never seemed to have more than one beer a night. That he and Jim Haviland remained pals with Kevin Dunning, Susanna's artsy father, amazed Jack.

"I saw her tear out of here about forty-five minutes ago," Davey said. "Iris up front with her,

Maggie and Ellen in the back seat, the car loaded. They must have packed in record time.''

"Do you know where this cabin of hers is?" Jack asked, tight-lipped.

"Blackwater Lake," Jim said. "That's all we know."

Jack nodded and left the bar without another word. On his way out, he thought he heard Davey Ahearn sigh in relief.

The temperature had dropped precipitously with nightfall, but he didn't notice the cold. He walked up to Iris's house and used his key in the front door. He should have waited with Iris until Susanna and the girls came back, then gone about his business. Instead, he'd stopped briefly at the bar, checked with the local police to see if they had anything on Alice Parker or Audrey Melbourne and called Sam Temple.

The house was quiet and cold, the heat turned down while they were out of town. Jack turned on the hall light and headed up the carpeted stairs, figuring he'd start with Susanna's bedroom in his search for information on her cabin. He wanted an address, a number, a sense that his family was safe on Blackwater Lake. Then he'd decide if he needed to go to up there himself, or if he needed to stay here and find Alice Parker.

He hadn't even seen his daughters yet.

He paused on the landing and dialed Susanna's cell phone, but got a recording that she wasn't available. Bullshit. She'd turned it off.

She had the front room down the hall, where they always stayed on their visits north. He wondered if she lay alone in the double bed, thinking of the times they'd made love there, quietly, whispering in the dark, believing nothing would ever get in the way of their love for each other—not work, not money, not kids. Nothing.

What the hell had happened?

He eased into the bedroom doorway. The shades were pulled, little of the dim downstairs hall light reaching into the room. He felt along the wall for the light switch.

He heard a sharp intake of breath and knew he was too late. He turned in a defensive move, automatically, deflecting the blow slightly as he was struck behind his left ear. Pain erupted in his head, spreading into his jaw and down his neck. Acting on training and instinct, he shot out one arm and snatched the weapon before his attacker could strike again.

It was a stick, a pole, something long and thin. He jerked it hard, trying to knock his attacker off balance, but whoever it was had already made off down the hall.

There were panicked footsteps on the stairs.

Jack sank forward onto his knees, fighting to stay conscious.

He could smell lavender in the dark bedroom. He recognized it because it was Susanna's favorite scent.

Voices now. Whispers in the front hall.

He stifled a wave of nausea and staggered to his feet, finding the switch for the overhead. The light was another blow. His face tingled, and he saw black spots, his head throbbing.

He'd been hit with one of Iris's walking sticks— that was what he'd snatched from his attacker. He still hung on to it. Burglars, taking advantage of an empty house? They could have seen Susanna, Iris, Maggie and Ellen pack up and leave and decided to seize the moment. Plausible, but unlikely.

He felt along his hairline, behind his ear. Some blood. A nasty lump.

He took the walking stick and made his way down the stairs, through the hall to the back of the house.

Ahead of him, he heard a door shut hard. He pushed back the pain and nausea and moved quickly into the kitchen, then out onto the small, open porch.

The winter cold slapped him in the face. He could hear a dog barking in the neighborhood, music playing, cars out on the street. The yard was quiet, lights from nearby houses creating eerie shadows on the drifting snow.

The sharp pain in his head settled into a persistent, pounding ache. He ignored it and followed the sanded, shoveled walk out to the front of Iris Dunning's old house.

Nothing. Whoever he'd come upon upstairs had gotten the hell out of there.

Jack scooped up a handful of snow, placed it on the lump on his head and retraced his steps to the kitchen. He put a couple of ice cubes in a plastic sandwich bag and noticed the stack of college handbooks on the table. His wife and daughters and eighty-two-year-old Iris Dunning were on the road alone.

He placed the ice on his head and checked the house, quickly and efficiently, room by room. Nothing was obviously missing, ransacked, searched or vandalized.

That could mean anything. They'd known where to find whatever they were looking for and didn't need to wreck the place. They weren't after anything concrete. He'd interrupted them before they could finish.

Jack didn't take the time to do a thorough search of Susanna's room. He'd find Blackwater Lake and her cabin on his own. He didn't need precise directions.

He locked up and headed down the street to Jim's Place.

It was crowded, an argument raging between Davey Ahearn and a group of construction workers about the Red Sox chances this year. Jack didn't take a seat. He briefly told Jim what had happened at Iris's house. "Blackwater Lake. Can you give me a general idea where it is?"

"High Peaks Region," Jim said. "You want an ice pack for that head?"

"That'd be good. Thanks."

Jim took Jack's sandwich bag of melting ice cubes out back and returned a half minute later with a proper ice pack. "I can call the police," he said.

"I don't want to get delayed. I'll call once I'm on my way. They won't like it." Jack placed the ice pack on his lump and gritted his teeth in disgust. "I never saw the hit coming. Damn. There was no forced entry. The windows and doors checked out. Who else has a key?"

"To Iris's place? The world."

Jack nodded, which he regretted immediately, pain spreading into his teeth, pounding behind his eyes. "Audrey Melbourne?"

"I don't know. She and Iris have been tight the past few weeks. Maybe Iris asked Audrey to look after the house while she was in the mountains, before Susanna found out about her." Jim Haviland spooned curried corn chowder into a heavy bowl and shoved it across the bar. "You'll need to eat something before you hit the road. I'd pour you a shot of whiskey, but it's a long drive up to the Adirondacks."

"She's not an easy woman," Jack said.

Jim seemed to know he meant Susanna. "No, she's not."

"That's a goddamn understatement," Davey Ahearn said. He lumbered over with a map, spreading it out on the bar next to Jack's soup. He thumped a callused finger on upstate New York. "In summer you could take the ferry across Lake Champlain. Can't in February."

"I know. My in-laws have a place on the New York side of the lake.

"Kev." Davey shook his head, sighing in commiseration. "I hope he never hears about this little escapade. Susanna's always given him fits. I guess none of us'd like her if she were too easy. Anyway, I'd take I-93 to New Hampshire and pick up I-89, then go across Vermont on Route 4. When you hit New York, pick up the Northway in Fort Ticonderoga."

"Nah. That's too complicated this time of night," Jim said. "He'll end up in Montreal or Maine or some damn thing." He pulled out a red ballpoint and put on his reading glasses, examining the map. "I'd take the Mass Pike and pick up the Northway in Albany.'' He drew a red line along his preferred route.

"Which route is the one Susanna most likely took?'' Jack asked.

Davey sighed. "The Pike,'' he acknowledged.

Jim continued his red line north into upstate New York. "Get off at the exit for Lake Place, Keene Valley and Saranac Lake. It'll be another forty-five minutes, minimum, out to Blackwater Lake from the interstate. I haven't been up that way in years, but I doubt it's changed. Darker than the pits of hell, twisting roads. At night when you're tired—''

"I won't be tired,'' Jack said.

"You might have a concussion.''

Jack said nothing.

Jim and Davey both seemed to know arguing was futile. In his shoes, they'd do the same. "The adrenaline'll keep you alert,'' Davey said, returning to his stool.

The soup was spicy and hot, but it turned Jack's stomach. He ate all the crackers as he studied his route. The Pike, the Northway, Blackwater Lake. He could do it without passing out.

"Watch for moose up there at night,'' Davey said. "You hit them in the legs, they fall onto your windshield and crush you to death.''

Moose. Hell. "Thanks for the warning.'' Jack folded the map neatly and tucked it into his jacket pocket. "I'll need to rent a car.''

Davey waved a hand in dismissal. "No problem there. Transportation I've got. I bought a new truck—I'm still trying to unload the old one. It's yours for as long as you need it.'' He dug the keys out of his pants pockets, grinning over at Jack. "Sometimes I think if I'd chased after an ex-wife or two instead of saying the hell with it, I might not be sitting here every night."

Jim Haviland shook his head in mock despair. "He's deluding himself, Jack. Davey's wives chased him off. They were glad to be rid of him and vice versa. Married life doesn't suit him. His truck's in good shape. He's charging an arm and a leg for it, which is why it's still available."

"I'm asking a fair price," Davey said.

The construction workers, who'd apparently checked out the truck themselves, hooted in protest from their table, and a fresh argument was on. Jack managed to get the keys and a sense of where the truck was parked, then left.

The puddles from the melting snow and ice had frozen over, creating treacherous patches of black ice. The houses and streetlights glowed brightly in the cold. Jack made his way across the street. Susanna had to be really pissed to have left tonight.

And scared. Except she never liked to admit when she was scared, tried not even to acknowledge it to herself. Better to be angry and stubborn, to keep secrets. To run.

Davey Ahearn's truck smelled like cigarettes but otherwise was immaculate. The engine started on the first try. It seemed to run fine.

Susanna would calculate the projected return on her investments down to the last damn dime, but she wouldn't think to calculate what would happen if she stood him up in a Boston bar and took off for the wilderness without telling him.

And now he'd been hit on the head.

It was a five- to six-hour drive to the Adirondacks, but Jack doubted he'd be in a better mood when he got there.

Susanna paid the toll at the end of the Massachusetts Turnpike and continued west into New York State. She'd turned her cell phone back on, and she'd told Maggie and Ellen about their father turning up in Boston.

Ellen sighed from the back seat. "We told him not to go all tight-lipped Texas Ranger on you. He knows it makes you mad."

"I was mad," Susanna admitted. "I'm not so mad now."

"No," Maggie said, "because *he* is. That's a phenomenon we studied in psychology class."

One semester of psychology, and she was an expert. Susanna glanced over at Gran, who was staring out her window at the dark landscape, removing herself from this discussion.

"I can't believe you stood him up," Ellen said in amazement. "Geez, Mom."

"I wasn't trying to goad him." Susanna sighed, not sure she could explain her motives to herself, never mind her daughters. "This wasn't just about him showing up unannounced. Frankly, I'm unnerved about this Alice Parker thing."

Ellen didn't get it. "But, Mom, Dad *is* a Texas Ranger. He can help figure out what's going on, why she's here, why she lied to us. He's the one who put her in prison."

"Ellen has a point," Maggie said sagely. "Alice

Parker is Dad's responsibility. If this were about money or one of your clients, you'd want him to listen to your advice and respect your expertise."

"This doesn't just involve you father," Susanna said steadily, ignoring the twist of fear in her gut. "It involves all of us. Normally his work doesn't affect our lives this way. Look, your dad and I will work this out." She smiled into the rearview mirror at both girls. "Don't you two worry about it. Let's concentrate on having a good time in the mountains."

They stopped for gas just north of Albany. While Iris and the girls fanned out to the rest room and snack shelves, Susanna ducked into a corner with her cell phone and dialed Jack's number.

He answered on the second ring, and she took a sharp breath at the sound of his voice. Even his hello didn't sound pleased or patient. In his place, she supposed hers wouldn't, either. "It's me," she said. "We're at a quick-stop about ten miles north of Albany."

"Not too far ahead of me."

"What?"

"Davey Ahearn loaned me a truck."

"Jack, there's no reason for you to come to the Adirondacks with us. Alice Parker is in Boston—"

"I have directions to the lake, not to the cabin. Are you going to tell me how to get there or do I have to figure it out for myself?"

Susanna opened a glass door and pulled out a bottle of cold water, her knees shaking under her. Something was wrong. She could hear it in his voice. He wasn't just short-tempered and irritated with her for bolting—he wasn't following her for payback. There was an edge. Worry, not just frustration with her for sneaking out on him. "Has something happened? Jack—"

"I'm losing the signal. We can talk later."

She quickly gave him directions. "Jack—"

"I'll see you in a few hours."

The connection went dead, and Susanna grabbed a bag of chips and joined Gran, Maggie and Ellen at the checkout counter. "Did you reach Dad?" Ellen asked.

"Yes, he's on his way."

Ellen laughed. "You mean he's following us to Blackwater Lake? Oh, cool. I can't wait to see him on snowshoes."

Maggie narrowed her dark eyes on her mother. "Mom, is everything okay?"

"As far as I know, yes, everything's fine."

Gran was plainly suspicious, but said nothing. They all heaped their snacks onto the counter, Susanna paid and they piled back into the car, the temperature noticeably colder, the night very dark. As they headed further north, the highway narrowed to two northbound lanes, and the ambient light from nearby towns and cities disappeared, leaving only the stars, a sliver of a moon and their headlights to guide them.

For long stretches, theirs was the only car on the road. Gran, Maggie and Ellen drifted off to sleep, and Susanna stayed focused on her driving, trying not to think about Jack somewhere on the road behind her. Huge outcroppings of rock and tall evergreens showed up on the edges of her headlights, and she was on alert for moose and deer, ice patches, sleepiness. All in all, she should have stuck to her plan and waited until morning.

Three hours north of Albany, she finally turned off on their exit, taking the winding, narrow road into the village of Keene Valley. This was the High Peaks region of the Adirondack State Park, a preserve of six million acres of state and private land in the northern reaches of New York state. It was the largest wilderness area in the continental United States, bigger than Yosemite, Yellowstone, the Grand Tetons—thirty thousand miles of rivers and streams, more than two thousand lakes and ponds, with forty mountains over twenty-five hundred feet.

Blackwater Lake was deep, cold and acidic, located near the resort villages of Saranac Lake and Lake Placid.

Iris roused, as if she sensed they were close to her childhood home. "The air's different here. Can you tell?"

"I can, actually." Susanna smiled at her grandmother. "It's a hell of a lot colder."

Gran nodded. "People believed the air helped relieve their tuberculosis. Saranac Lake was a health resort for people who suffered from tuberculosis. Before antibiotics, thousands came here, rich and poor alike, for the mountain cure. They were required to be out in the air for eight to ten hours a day, four seasons a year. It didn't matter if it was twenty below."

"And it worked?"

"For many," Gran said quietly.

They came to Blackwater Inn, a rambling lakefront

house that Gran's parents had owned when she was a child. The Dunnings had come to the Adirondacks in the early nineteenth century as trappers. The rugged mountains and the harsh, inhospitable climate generally kept permanent settlers away, even the native Iroquois who hunted and traveled the waterways but seldom stayed.

Susanna made her way up along the lake and turned off the main road onto a narrow, frozen dirt road. The girls jerked awake as the car began to bounce over the hard ruts. "Oh, man," Maggie breathed, "it's so dark up here."

"How cold is it?" Ellen asked. "It has to be below zero. Dad's going to croak when he gets here."

Susanna could hear the eagerness in her daughter's voice. Despite the circumstances, she and Maggie were both excited to see their father. Intellectually, they understood their parents' stalemate had nothing to do with them—they'd done nothing wrong. But they loved and missed their father.

The dirt road fingered off into three driveways, and Susanna took the left-most, which lead straight to the back door of her cabin. There was no garage. She parked and turned off the engine, feeling the silence around her. Maggie leaned forward in the back seat and whispered, "Gran, I can't believe you grew up here. It's *creepy*."

"That's because you're not used to it," Gran said. "I thought Boston was creepy when I first arrived. All those buildings and people, all that light blocking out the stars." She drew a deep breath, pushing open her door and peering up at the starlit sky. "It's just as I remember."

Susanna had more prosaic concerns. She jumped out into the cold, very dry air and unlocked the back of her all-wheel drive wagon, starting the girls on unloading. The cabin was open, her property manager having seen to cleaning and stocking the cupboards.

Maggie shivered in the still, frigid air. Susanna shook her head. "You'd be warmer if you weren't wearing a coat from 1957."

"Don't worry, I brought all my winter jock clothes. I don't plan to freeze to death up here." Maggie grabbed a backpack and hoisted it on one shoulder, then grabbed another. "This is going to take a million trips."

Ellen swooped in and loaded up as much as she could in one trip. "Let's get inside and turn on some lights."

She and Maggie rushed toward the back door, Gran following at a slower pace. There was no wind, no sound coming from the nearby dark woods or the expanse of snow-covered lake.

Lights came on in the cabin, and the girls whooped in pleasure—Susanna could hear them running around, checking out the big kitchen, the stone fireplace in the living room, the windows overlooking Blackwater Lake, the downstairs bedroom. They pounded upstairs to the loft and the two bedrooms there. Susanna followed her grandmother through the mud room, into the kitchen with its warm colors. "Why don't you go on to bed, Gran? We can unpack in the morning. You can take the downstairs bedroom—"

Iris shook her head. She had on her red knit hat,

but looked tired after their long trip, showing all of her eighty-two years. "No, I'll sleep upstairs. You and Jack might want your privacy."

"Gran—"

She smiled. "I said 'might.'"

Maggie and Ellen banged back down the stairs. "Mom, this place is great," Ellen said. "I can't wait to build a fire. Look at this fireplace! When you said it was a cabin, I though you meant *Little House on the Prairie* or Daniel Boone. The pictures don't do it justice."

"It's really beautiful here," Maggie said, more restrained but, Susanna could see, equally pleased with her mother's choice.

They'd heaped most of the stuff from the car on the kitchen floor. They grabbed their backpacks out of the mess, looking tired after their long trip. Ellen scooped up Gran's suitcase, and Maggie took her grandmother's arm. "I'll spot you on the stairs. You wouldn't want to fall your first night here. They'd probably have to airlift you to a hospital."

"There's a hospital right in Saranac Lake," Gran said.

Ellen started across the living room, but turned back to her mother. "Should we wait up for Dad?"

Susanna shook her head. "No, you all go on up to bed," she said. "I'll wait for your father."

Nine

While she waited for Jack, Susanna dragged her suitcase into the downstairs bedroom and unpacked everything into the oak dresser and closet. The queen-sized bed was already made, with an electric blanket and a fluffy down comforter folded at its foot. There was an adjoining full bathroom with sage-colored towels and woodsy scented candles. She laid out her toiletries and debated whether she had time for a bath. She decided, though, it wouldn't be smart, having Jack find her in the tub when he still had up a good head of steam.

She pushed the image aside and ignored the jolt of desire, concentrating instead on relaxing into her cabin. She could come up for a stretch in the summer and paint and replace rugs, buy new furniture—make it her own. Her parents would be over on Lake Champlain.

Thinking that far ahead was difficult, a toe in the water to see what her life might be like in four or five or six months. What did she want it to be like?

She heard the rattle of a truck engine, and headlights sliced into her bedroom window. She quickly slipped back into the kitchen and looked out the window over the sink. Davey Ahearn's truck came to a hard stop behind her car. The driver's door opened and banged shut.

She could see Jack's tall silhouette as he walked toward the cabin.

He didn't knock. The mud room door creaked open and thudded shut, and he materialized in the kitchen doorway. No coat, no hat, no gloves, every muscle in his body rigid—but he was pale.

Susanna took a step toward him. "Jack, what is it?"

He held up a hand, stopping her. Without a word, he went to the sink and heaved. Not a lot, but with violence.

She swore under her breath and ran back through her bedroom into the bathroom, wetting a face cloth with cold water. Her own stomach felt a little queasy.

When she returned to the kitchen, he had the sink rinsed out and his head under the faucet, cold water running over his hair and face. He took five gulps of water in a row, rinsing out his mouth. "Fucking curried corn chowder. I should have known it'd come back up."

He pulled his head out from under the faucet and sank against the counter, taking the face cloth from her and putting it behind his ear, holding it there while water dripped from his dark hair, down his neck, into the collar of his denim shirt.

"Jack...Jesus, what happened?" Susanna saw the caked blood on his fingers and touched the face cloth, easing it back, wincing at the one-inch gash and nasty lump. "You drove like this? You could have a concussion. You should have gone to the emergency room."

"I should have paid better attention." His eyes, pain-racked and very dark, drilled into her. "I was thinking about you instead."

"Cursing me, you mean. Do you want ice?"

"No." And he added, without softening, "But thanks."

Susanna dropped her hand, but stayed close. "Was it Alice?"

"I don't know. I was hit from behind, the hall was dark—I didn't get a description. By the time I got to my feet, whoever it was had cleared out."

"Where did this happen?"

"Your bedroom."

She could feel her own face pale. "At Gran's? You were attacked—"

"Yes. I was attacked in Iris's house. I went over there when you didn't show at Jim's Place. Someone was upstairs—two people, from what I could tell." He dropped the face cloth in the sink. His face had more color after the dunk under the faucet. "They got out before I could catch them."

"Did you call the police?"

"On my way out of town. They're not happy with me for clearing out, but they'll get over it. They won't find anything. For all I know, I walked in on a couple of Iris's friends and they took me for the intruder."

"But you don't believe that," Susanna said, stiffening so she wouldn't start shaking.

"No."

"I should have been there. I feel so guilty—"

His gaze burned into her. "Good."

She nodded. "I deserved that."

"Damn right." But this time, his voice softened, if not his eyes. "Don't you ever consider consequences?"

"All the time. Day in and day out in my work, with Maggie and Ellen, Gran. Just not with you."

And that did it.

He hooked an arm around her middle and pulled her to him, using his free hand to trace her mouth. "Susanna…damn…" A gleam came into his eyes. "I suppose I shouldn't have said I'd hunt you down. Iris told you?"

"Oh, yes. She told me every word you said. It was a provocative comment, but—" She stopped, gulping in a shallow breath when he threaded his fingers into her hair, then cupped the back of her head with his palm. "Don't you have a concussion?"

"Probably."

He spoke into her mouth, drawing her against him. She could feel that he was fully aroused already, within minutes of walking into her kitchen and throwing up in her sink. He kissed her, a hard, deep, hungry kiss. He tasted of spring water now, and as she responded to him, she had to contain a moan of pleasure. After so many years together, he knew all her responses, all her defenses. He knew just how to kiss her, just how to touch her.

"We shouldn't…" she whispered. "Your head…"

"It's pounding. It's been pounding for three hundred and fifty miles as I thought about what I'd do when I got to you.''

''Was this it?''

''This was just the start.'' He curved both hands over her hips and drew her against him, thrusting, as if he were inside her. His eyes were impenetrable, and if he were in any pain from the lump on his head, he wasn't paying any attention to it. ''Where's your bed?''

''Jack…we should…''

But he wasn't listening, and she pointed to her bedroom, shaky with desire. This was what she'd wanted since the minute she saw him leaned up against the gargoyle in front of her building. He was her husband, the only man she'd ever loved, and she wanted him to make love to her.

He positioned one arm around her middle and half carried her into her bedroom. She could have said no, they needed to wait and talk in the morning— talk *now*. She could have thought twice, even, about what they were doing. But she'd been thinking about this moment for the entire long, dark drive into the mountains once she knew he was coming after her.

He laid her on the bed, dispatching just with her pants, then with his own. No niceties. No romance. No ''wooing.'' He didn't have the patience for it, and neither did she.

''Damn it, Susanna,'' he said under his breath, ''you know how to drive me out of my mind.''

They came together furiously, and suddenly it was as if he were a stranger, not her lover of twenty years, not the man she'd married just out of college. Susanna thought of what her daughters had said, that he'd changed, that there was an edge to him.

The thought vanished, obliterated by the feel of him inside her, then the suddenness of her own release. She hadn't seen it coming, and she quaked as he stayed with her, matching her rhythm, her need, not letting up until his own release came.

"I'd like to lock us in here for three days straight," he said, still inside her, his face lost in the dark shadows, "and get things settled between us."

She placed a hand on his firm, warm skin. "This isn't one of our problem areas."

He lowered his mouth to hers, as if to confirm her words. "We're either going to be married or not married." He parted her lips with his tongue. "I'm not going to fly two thousand miles and drive off into the mountains to have sex with my wife."

"That's not why you're here."

"Isn't it?"

He raised himself slightly off her, pushing up her sweater and unclasping her bra. He took one nipple into his mouth, and she thought she'd melt into the blankets, turn completely to liquid. She took his hips and pulled him back inside her, memorizing the feel of him, as if this had never happened before and might never happen again. She lost herself in their movements, and this time when she came, she was aware of him watching her, as if this was the image that had sustained him during his long, hard, painful drive to Blackwater Lake.

But before she realized what was happening, he was back on his feet, grabbing his pants. He slipped into them, then bent down and kissed her lightly. "Hell of a cure for a lump on the head."

She eyed him in the dark. "I feel downright wanton. My God, I didn't even wait to get undressed all the way." She smiled. "Consequences?"

"You knew this would happen when you decided to sneak out on me. The knock on my head was the only surprise." He grinned at her. "I had you a little worried there when I pitched my cookies."

"If you're suggesting I plotted this—that I *wanted* you to drive up here and pounce—" She didn't finish. There was absolutely no way she'd win this one, not after what they'd just done. "There's a sofa bed in the loft at the top of the stairs." This was why she was living with Gran, she thought. Who could think straight with Jack Galway too close? "If you die in your sleep, it serves you right."

"At least I'll sleep," he said, laughing softly, knowingly, as he shut her door on his way out.

When Maggie and Ellen woke up and started making noise in the next room, Jack reminded himself that they didn't know he had a raging headache. They didn't know he'd been knocked on the head and threw up curried corn chowder and nearly killed himself making love to their mother. Or that he'd lay awake half the night, his head pounding, thinking he should at least have properly undressed her. That would have been more romantic. There was every chance, however, that he'd have passed out before he finished, and he'd been very intent on the lovemaking part.

So had she, as he recalled.

There was also the matter of not freezing to death. Shivering made his head hurt even more. He only had a couple of thin blankets, and if the place had heat, the loft wasn't getting any.

"*Dad!*"

"*You made it!*"

The girls' voices reverberated in his head, producing sharp arrows of pain that sliced into the backs of his eyes, which were shut. He wanted to go back to sleep. Desperately. A couple of aspirin and warm clothes would help, but he could manage just with silence and sleep.

His daughters plopped on the edge of his sofa bed. "You're awake, aren't you?" Ellen's voice was cheerful, even perky. "The sun's up. Mom wants to take us snowshoeing. It's about four degrees out, but she's determined. You should come with us."

"You can rent a pair at the local inn," Maggie said. "But you'll need warm clothes. You can't go out in jeans and a cowboy hat. You'd freeze."

He had to open his eyes. There was no choice. They'd sit here all morning until he acknowledged their presence. "Hey, kids." He managed what he hoped would pass as a smile. "Do you see me on snowshoes?"

"Sure, Dad." Ellen's chestnut hair caught a ray of light from a window somewhere. It was like a hot needle in his eye. She grinned at him. "We see you on cross-country skis, too."

They were both devils, Jack thought.

Maggie slid to her feet. She had on a sparkly turquoise robe that Rosalind Russell might have worn in *Mame*. "Do you want coffee?"

"I'll get up." He managed to ease onto an elbow with no sign of nausea. That was good. "Just give me a minute."

They pounded down the wooden stairs, making far more noise than seemed necessary. He threw back the skinny covers and staggered out of bed, pulling on his pants. He should have slept in them, it was so damn cold. He shrugged on his shirt, leaving it unbuttoned as another arrow of pain stabbed both eyes. He hadn't packed aspirin. No gun, no aspirin. A hot shower and fresh clothes would help put him back fully on his feet.

He looked out the loft window at the impressive landscape of snow-covered lake and mountains. The sky was clear blue, no clouds. He could feel the cold seeping through the glass. How the hell had he ended up here? He'd learned a long time ago that with green-eyed, black-haired Susanna Dunning Galway, his life didn't always go as he planned. She liked curves and side trips, surprises and secrets.

But not telling him about Beau McGarrity was irrational. Even dangerous. Bolting last night—the same. He didn't care if it was an instinctive reaction to having murder—his work—affect their lives this directly.

Of course, he hadn't confronted her about McGarrity. He'd found out by accident, talking to his neighbor a few days after Susanna had run off to Boston. *Wasn't that Beau McGarrity at his door last week? Wow, that must have pissed you off.*

Susanna apparently had gotten rid of McGarrity as fast as possible, and Jack knew she'd have told him if Beau had said or done anything the detectives conducting Rachel McGarrity's murder investigation could use. She had been in Boston, safe. Maggie and Ellen were with her, safe. Alice Parker was on her way to prison, and Jack knew—everyone knew—she'd made a complete mess of the Rachel McGarrity murder investigation. It would have been a hard enough case to unravel without her incompetence at the crime scene and subsequent misconduct.

Still, he was madder at Susanna for her silence than he was at himself for his silence. Easier that way. Sometimes he wondered what he'd have done if she'd told him about McGarrity that rotten day he'd confronted Alice with the evidence against her, told her police chief, arrested her. If he'd come home and found out then that Beau McGarrity had scared the hell out of his wife, what would he have done?

Not that he for one moment thought Susanna had kept her silence just to spare him.

He shoved such thinking to the back of his mind and made it downstairs without falling on his face. Maggie glanced up from her spot in front of the fire-place. "Mom and Gran got up early and built the fire."

"Where is she now?"

"Mom? She went into town for some things she forgot."

"She said not to wait for her if you have stuff to do," Ellen added.

"Uh-huh."

"Gran's out on the porch looking at the lake," Maggie said.

Jack went into the kitchen. There was coffee made. A plate of muffins on the counter. He found a mug in a cupboard and poured himself coffee, sinking onto a chair at the big oak table. There was a window with a view of the driveway and the woods and a lot of snow.

Iris came in from the porch and sat with the girls in front of the fire, discussing possible snowshoe routes. She glanced over at him, and Jack guessed from her serious expression that Susanna had told her grandmother about the intruder. But Iris would give him a chance to have a cup of coffee before she asked him about last night.

Alice Parker. The intruders in Iris's house. The walking stick to the head. Beau McGarrity and his murdered wife, Rachel Tucker McGarrity. Jack reminded himself those were his reasons for being up north. Not sex with his wife, regardless of what he'd said and done last night. Not vacationing with his daughters and Iris. This was Susanna's cabin—her space. First things first.

The coffee humanized him. He refilled his mug and grabbed a blueberry muffin.

Iris joined him at the table. ''How's your head this morning?''

''I'll be fine. I might have cracked your walking stick.''

She waved a thin hand. ''Oh, I have a dozen of those things. The students I used to take in all loved to give me walking sticks as presents.'' She took a chunk of his muffin and began tearing it apart with her fingertips, staring at a fat, juicy blueberry. ''There's something you should know, Jack. I didn't think of it until this morning when Susanna told me what happened. I gave Audrey—Alice Parker—a key to my house the other day.''

Jack said nothing, drinking his coffee, watching her tear apart her bit of muffin. There were crumbs all over the table.

''I asked if she could look after the house for me while we were up here,'' Iris said. ''I hemmed and hawed about whether I would come. You know how I am about traveling.''

''Jim Haviland said a lot of people have keys to your house.''

''That's because I've rented to so many students. It's never been a problem.'' She raised her vibrant eyes to him. ''I hate to think it was Audrey who snuck up on you, that I was the cause—''

''You're not the cause of any of this, Iris. Alice Parker is responsible for the choices she makes. You aren't.''

''I thought she was my friend.''

''We've all been fooled by people at one time or another.''

Iris shook her head. ''This time it was dangerous. What if you'd been killed last night?''

''I wasn't.''

She smiled weakly, trying to rally. ''Can you imagine, a Texas Ranger killed with an old woman's walking stick in his wife's bedroom in Massachusetts? Do you think your pals back in Texas would put together a posse and invade?''

''Iris…''

But her eyes gleamed with mischief, and he remembered this woman was a survivor. She was absorbing the blow of who her new friend had turned out to be. "You're no fun at all, Jack Galway. I suppose you're here for answers?"

He thought of Alice Parker. His wife. "Oh, yes. And that's just for starters."

He'd seemed familiar, even that first day she'd spotted him in downtown San Antonio, probably because of his notoriety as a real estate developer and a murder suspect.

Now, Susanna wasn't sure about any of the assumptions she'd made about Beau McGarrity. She wasn't sure about anything.

She'd pulled into a scenic overlook on the river not far from her cabin. A snowbank kept her from getting too close to the fence above the waterfall with its massive ice formations and rush of clear, cold water. It was a natural waterfall, not one of the dams left over from the industrial revolution that still choked rivers and streams all over the northeast. Here, the river tumbled freely out of the mountains, carving its way through rock and earth.

She didn't feel the cold. As Iris maintained, the air was different in the High Peaks. Susanna had bundled up in her north country layers. Moisture-resistant long underwear and leggings, wind pants, fleece vest, heavy duty anorak, hat, gloves, socks, boots. The high-tech fabrics and design kept everything from weighing a ton. Gran still preferred wool.

On the day Beau McGarrity had walked into her kitchen, Susanna would never have imagined herself here in the mountains of upstate New York, in the dead of winter.

She remembered how absorbed she'd been in her

tai chi tape, doing the movements, the breathing, the concentration and balance. She'd knocked off work early, the girls were at school and Jack was out on an investigation. Police corruption. He hated corruption cases, and she knew few of the details about this one. He had been more silent and uncommunicative than usual in recent weeks. She was preoccupied with how she'd tell him about their growing net worth, not with stories of the terrible murder of a woman in a small town not far from San Antonio.

While she'd practiced her tai chi—she wasn't very good—she didn't think about anything that bothered her. She didn't worry about how money could change her relationship with her husband, if he'd resent her because the millions were her doing—if the money might affect his work when word got out. He was a Texas Ranger. It was all he'd ever wanted to be.

Oddly enough, it was her parents who'd helped her make her first big investment, when they'd introduced her to a woman who'd just bought artwork from their gallery and owned an Austin computer firm. Jack knew about that investment. But Susanna hadn't told him how well it had done, providing the bulk of the ten million they were now worth. She'd also timed her entrance into and her exit out of technology stocks well. Not all luck, but a lot of it.

None of that was on her mind while she was doing her tai chi.

The sound of the patio door opening and shutting had broken her concentration. She assumed it was Jack or the girls coming in early and hit the pause button on the VCR to go check.

The tall, gray-haired man she'd seen downtown and then again the other day at the high school was standing in her kitchen, on the other side of the table with its vase of small sunflowers. She'd tried to tell herself he hadn't actually followed her. She hadn't mentioned him to Jack, because she knew she was just being paranoid. Of *course,* he wasn't following her. Who would follow her? Now he was in her kitchen.

She'd managed a quick smile. "Just a sec," she said, as if he were a neighbor who'd stopped in for a chat, and slipped into the family room. She spotted Maggie's tape recorder and set it on a bookcase on her way back to the kitchen, hitting the record button. She'd considered running out the front door, but it, she knew, was locked. She didn't think she had enough time—she needed to stay calm.

At least if this man did anything to her, her husband would have it on tape.

"You don't recognize me," he said.

"No, I'm afraid I don't. Look—"

"I'm not going to hurt you." He had a twang to his accent, making him seem folksier than he was. He ran a finger over the back of a chair. "I didn't knock because I wasn't sure you'd let me in, and I need to talk to you."

"Why? What do you want?"

"Your husband has to know I didn't kill my wife. I'm being framed by an overzealous police officer."

Suddenly Susanna knew who he was. Beau McGarrity, the wealthy real estate developer and political aspirant whose wife had just been shot to death in their driveway.

No wonder she'd thought she'd seen him before.

"You have to make him understand."

"I'm sorry," she told him carefully, "I don't get involved in my husband's work."

"Of course you do. You provide comfort to him. You make it possible for him to give his work the focus and attention it requires to be done well." McGarrity stepped around the table, coming toward her. "Your husband couldn't make the lives of the criminals in this state a living hell without your cooperation."

"Jack's a Texas Ranger. He follows the law. He's not out to make anyone's life a living hell. Mr. McGarrity—that's who you are, isn't it? Beau McGarrity? I want you to leave. It's really not a good idea for you to be here."

His gaze was steady, absolutely determined. "The witness against me is lying. Your husband needs to understand that."

"All right. I'll give him your message—"

"As if dealing with Rachel's death weren't enough—" Some of the fierceness went out of his expression, and he ran a hand through his gray hair, as if he were suddenly tired. "Susanna, Susanna... you don't believe I killed my wife."

Her instincts—her fear—told her not to make a move for the knife rack or do anything that might provoke him to violence. He had size and position on her. The smartest course of action was to get rid of him as fast as she could.

She remembered what she told her clients about money. Listen to your fear. Your fear can protect you if you let it.

"I'll talk to Jack. I promise."

McGarrity smiled in approval, perhaps a touch of relief. "I know I must sound desperate. There's no need for your husband to know I was here." His tone was controlled now, self-assured, that of a man convinced of his rightful place in the world. "Do you understand?"

She nodded. "I do."

He stood back on his heels, watching her through half-closed eyes. He said casually, as if it were a non sequitur, "Your daughters finish up play practice in ten minutes."

Susanna stopped breathing. He knew their schedules. He knew where they were.

Beau McGarrity touched her then, a feathery brush across her chin. "You should be running along to pick them up. You're a good mother. That's what good mothers do. I know," he added, "I've seen you."

He slipped out the patio door, and Susanna popped the DAT out of the recorder, her hands shaking. She was reaching for the phone to call Jack when a police officer knocked on her front door. Alice Parker. She introduced herself as the officer working on Rachel McGarrity's murder and asked if Jack was there.

Susanna told her about Beau McGarrity and gave her the tape.

Then Maggie and Ellen came home, and Susanna didn't tell them anything. She decided to wait for Jack, but he came home late, short-tempered and obviously distressed. Alice Parker had been arrested for witness tampering. She'd screwed up the crime scene. The Rachel McGarrity murder investigation was a mess. There wasn't a damn thing anyone could do about it now. His role in the whole business was over.

When he didn't mention the tape, Susanna assumed it was worthless. Alice Parker wanted to nail Beau McGarrity for murder to the point of fabricating a witness. If there'd been anything on that tape they could have used against Beau, surely she'd have given it to Jack, at least to prove to the world McGarrity was a threat and she wasn't so awful for having tried to make sure he was caught for his wife's murder.

Not that anyone would have believed anything, coming from a corrupt police officer.

With or without the tape, prosecutors wouldn't have touched Susanna's tale of possible stalking and veiled threats. A good defense lawyer would say it only proved Beau McGarrity had been so upset by Alice Parker's conduct that he'd inadvertently scared the hell out of the wife of a Texas Ranger.

Even if Susanna couldn't prove it, Beau McGarrity had followed her *twice*. He'd walked into her *kitchen*.

She didn't know what Jack would do if he found out. He was a professional, but his work had never come this close to his family.

She'd never felt so completely paralyzed.

It was simpler to say nothing. Simpler for him, as well, that she did nothing. So, that was what she did. And for that and a thousand other reasons that seemed to make sense at the time, she'd packed up and joined her daughters heading north.

A few weeks to clear her head had turned into

months, and now she'd bought a cabin in the mountains.

But it was beautiful here, she thought. Stunning and invigorating, and she meant to enjoy her week here. With any luck, Alice Parker had cleared out and last night was just an innocent mistake, Jack stumbling across a burglar or one of Iris's legion of friends.

"Yeah, right," she muttered, turning back to her car. "Who do you think you're kidding?"

Ten

It had been a very close call with Ranger Jack.

Alice tried not to think about how she'd almost hyperventilated into passing out when she'd sneaked up behind him with Iris's walking stick and whacked him. He'd come within a hairsbreadth of grabbing her, and his defensive move had kept her from knocking him out.

Once he had the walking stick, she'd grabbed Destin and cleared out.

Now they were almost at Blackwater Lake, driving right back into the lion's mouth. Well, what else could they do? Alice couldn't think of anything that'd get Jack Galway and Beau McGarrity off her tail, put her on the road to Australia and stop Destin from whining about his repossessed BMW and the lousy heat in her car. The man needed a hundred grand. The world would be a happier place if Destin Wright had money in the bank again.

He'd panicked when she'd hit Jack Galway. *You attacked a Texas Ranger? Shit!*

He'd also wanted to go back and explain, tell Lieutenant Galway they'd just been checking on the house for Iris and mistook him for a burglar. Alice had asked him how they'd explain the papers he'd pulled out of Susanna's files and the directions they'd found to her place in the Adirondacks. Jack would want to know what they were doing with those. Destin had seen the light.

He was riding shotgun, navigating. He had a map they'd picked up at a gas station in New Hampshire spread out on his lap. Driving across New Hampshire and Vermont had been his bright idea. They'd spent the night in a fleabag roadside hotel, sharing a room but not a bed. He had no interest, and Alice sure as hell didn't.

The bright sun hitting the pristine snow and ice hurt her eyes, but she had to admit the scenery was stunning. Destin told her to turn down a steep, unpaved driveway that led to the Blackwater Inn, a rambling old building with slate gray clapboards, white trim and burgundy doors. Iris Dunning had grown up here, fallen in love, known tragedy. She'd told Alice about skinny-dipping all alone on a hot summer night.

Alice didn't want to think about how she'd betrayed and manipulated an old woman and now was trying to figure out how to pry a hundred grand off her granddaughter.

The inn was owned by a young couple who introduced themselves as Paul and Sarah Johnson and looked as if they spent a lot of time trekking up and down mountains. Alice asked for separate rooms. Destin muttered something about money, but she shot him a look and he shut up.

Both rooms were on the second floor overlooking the lake. Alice's was decorated with country quilts that reminded her of her grandma's house back in Texas, although the four-poster bed and cherry dresser were more expensive than anything her grandmother could ever afford.

Destin lingered in the doorway. "We can get some lunch and settle in, but I want to get this show on the road."

"I'm not hungry. You go on."

She dumped her battered suitcase on the floor and looked back at him. He seemed to be waiting for her to tell him what to do next. This was what she wanted, but it was unnerving, too, because she wasn't sure she knew what to do next—and she didn't want to screw up his life right along with her own. Not that he wasn't making his own decisions. She couldn't let his blond, preppy good looks throw her off. He wanted a hundred thousand dollars and a fresh start. He'd helped her sneak into Iris's house last night. He was ready to put the squeeze on Susanna, however Alice saw fit. He seemed to see Susanna as his savior, Alice as his smart and equally desperate cohort.

Except she knew she wasn't that smart. She'd learned that the night Beau McGarrity had tried to frame her for his wife's murder. She was probably going to learn it all over again, using the likes of Beau and Destin to fund her new life in Australia.

"I don't want to drive over to Susanna's cabin with my Texas tags," Alice said. "You'll have to hike in."

Action appealed to him. "Great. I can snowshoe

or cross-country ski—I can break a trail if I need to. I did a lot of winter sports before I had to give up my condo.''

And I did a lot of things before I had a criminal record, Alice thought. ''Life's a bitch. Make Susanna feel your urgency this time, not just hear your desperation. Trust me. This is just the first step, but maybe it'll work—maybe we won't have to ratchet up the pressure. Just don't panic, okay? We'll get the money out of her.''

He grinned. ''Damn right.''

They just had to keep Jack Galway from catching them and Beau McGarrity from figuring out she'd tried to double-cross him about the tape.

Destin left, shutting the door softly behind him, and Alice flopped onto the bed with its soft, pretty quilt. All in all, manipulating Susanna Galway into giving them a hundred thousand dollars was the easy part. If she had a hundred grand, Alice thought, she'd give it to Destin herself, just to shut him up. Well, she'd give him ninety grand. Ten she'd keep for herself and Australia. She could make do with ten just fine. She didn't need Beau's fifty.

Susanna's fantasies of her week in the Adirondacks with her daughters took another blow when they tried out their new snowshoes. She'd rented snowshoes over the Christmas break and had little trouble getting hers on, but Maggie and Ellen were having fits with theirs, both losing patience with the labyrinthine traditional bindings and fine adjustments. The cold air didn't help. With the sharp cleats, Susanna didn't want them using the mud room.

Jack was watching them, sipping a cup of coffee at the mud room door.

"I've got snow all over these *stupid* straps," Maggie muttered, bent over her snowshoe as she tried to shove her boot in tighter, fussing with the bindings in increasing frustration. Finally, she jerked up straight and gave her foot a good kick. The snowshoe flew off and buried itself in the snow. "Good. It can stay there and *rust*."

Ellen had one glove in her teeth and was following one strap across the toe of her boot with her bare hand, figuring out how the bindings worked. "Ah-ha! I get it!"

Susanna retrieved Maggie's snowshoe and handed it to her. "Do you want me to help?"

"No. I'm going to freeze to death before I figure this out. What are the signs of hypothermia?"

"Maggie," Susanna said, reining in her own impatience, "you're making this harder than it is."

Jack stepped out onto the shoveled walk. "God forbid you girls should read the directions."

Maggie scowled at him. "It's not as easy as it looks."

"And you're making it ten times harder."

Ellen had managed to get one snowshoe on properly and tested it, gently kicking out her foot. When it didn't come flying off, she let out a victorious whoop, which only drew another scowl from Maggie. Ellen ignored her and started on her other snowshoe, getting it on within seconds now that she had the hang of it.

"I hate you, Ellen," Maggie said, deadpan, "I really do."

Jack dumped his coffee in the snow and squatted down to help her. "You've got everything all out of whack."

"How do you know? You're a Texan, too. You don't snowshoe."

He glanced up at her. "I read the directions."

Both girls, at least, Susanna thought, were dressed properly for the winter conditions, although Maggie had added a 1940s purple orchid pin to her jacket. Jack secured her left snowshoe, and when she realized what she'd been doing wrong, she tackled the right one herself. She tested them in the driveway. "Oh, this is so cool!" She laughed, tramping after her sister toward the lake. "I love it! Dad, you'll have to get a pair!"

He hadn't told them about the lump on his head. "That's okay," he said.

Susanna watched Maggie make her way along Ellen's broken trail and felt a sudden wave of affection for her twin daughters. "They're not so different than when they were six."

Jack stood next to her. If he was cold in his suede jacket and cowboy boots, he didn't show it. "Maggie threw her bike the first time she tried to ride it, remember?"

"You were patient with her then, too."

He glanced at her, his eyes very dark against the snow and blue sky. "I'm not as patient as I used to be." His voice was low and intense, but he shifted, squinting out at the girls' trail to the lake. "You'd better go. You'll get cold standing here."

But Susanna couldn't yet bring herself to move. She thought about earlier, staring out at the waterfall, replaying that day with Beau McGarrity in her kitchen. She'd bit back tears on her way back to the cabin, and Jack must have noticed her red eyes. But he'd said nothing, and now she had on snowshoes and wasn't saying anything, either. She cleared her throat. "Gran's making hot chocolate for when we get back. She feels terrible about Alice—"

"It's not her fault."

"You mean it's mine."

He shifted his gaze back to her, expressionless. "No. Mine."

"Jack—"

"Go snowshoeing, Susanna. Enjoy your vacation. I'll figure out what to do about Alice Parker."

She decided not to argue about who'd do what, not now. She could feel the cold against her face, and although there was very little breeze, she knew she needed to get moving to stay warm. "If anything had happened to Gran—if Alice—"

"Nothing happened." He took her by the arm, his eyes serious but with a warmth that hadn't been there since he'd arrived in Boston. There'd been a lot of heat last night, but not much warmth. "Nothing will."

Susanna managed a quick smile. "And you with a big fat lump on your head."

He shrugged. "The lump's gone down. It's just a cut now."

"Another scar."

He winked at her. "You like my scars."

"Jack, for God's sake." But he'd made her laugh, and she started along Maggie and Ellen's trail, glancing back at him. "If you're planning to stick around, you can go into town and buy yourself some winter clothes."

"Good. I'll put them on your credit card."

"I can't believe Gran grew up here," Maggie said when they stopped at a fallen tree above Blackwater Lake. "She's such a city person now."

Ellen stared down the steep embankment at the icy lake. "I keep imagining her at our age, clomping around out here in the wilderness. She just had those big old fur-trapper snowshoes in those days."

"Gran's pretty amazing," Susanna said. They'd set off on a snow-covered path along the lake, moving easily on their snowshoes among the tall pine and spruce trees, their branches drooping with snow. "She wants to go snowshoeing one day while we're here."

"Do you think she can?" Maggie asked.

"I don't know," Susanna said. "The snow's fairly deep, but maybe if we break a good trail, she can make it."

"She and Dad could go together." Ellen laughed at her idea, shaking a clump of snow off her snowshoe. "Can you see *him* out here?"

"Snowshoeing falls under the 'any idiot' category," Maggie said. "I mean, the hardest part's getting the things on your feet." She grinned. "Listen to me, the expert after thirty minutes."

Susanna didn't tell them she had no idea if Jack was staying or leaving. He would do what he wanted to do. He might discuss his decision with her—he might not. He was in just that sort of mood.

The path looped back through the woods, away

from the lake, and Susanna let the girls swoop on ahead of her. They were almost eighteen, strong and agile. She thought of Gran out here at eighteen, alone, unmarried and pregnant. She couldn't just pull a cell phone out of her pocket and dial 911. She'd endured hardships and moved to Boston, alone with a young son, absorbing the changes in her life and ultimately thriving.

Susanna took in the snow drifting against the naked beeches and birches, the clouds hovering over the mountains in the distance. She couldn't stay stuck in neutral, she thought. It wasn't fair to Maggie and Ellen, it wasn't fair to Jack—or even to herself. She had to move forward before the standstill in her marriage solved matters on its own, like the old, rotten tree that all at once crumbled, without any wind, any axe, anything at all to spur it on.

The truck Jack had borrowed from Davey Ahearn was gone when she tramped back down the hill, through the woods, to the cabin. He might have left a note inside saying where he'd gone—to town for winter gear, back to Boston, after Alice Parker—but Susanna didn't count on it. She peeled off her snowshoes and sank onto the bench in the mudroom. The twins had gone in ahead of her and their snowshoes were leaning up against the rough-board wall, the clumps of snow melting onto the floor. Their wet socks and gloves were scattered, their boots stood in muddy pools.

Susanna didn't blame them for leaving a mess. She was dead tired herself. She eased off her boots, still caked with snow, and pulled off her outer layers. Her nose was running, her hair was crackling with static electricity and, impossibly, she was sweating.

She couldn't wait to go out again.

"Hey, there. Anybody home?"

"Destin!" Susanna jumped up, landing in a cold puddle in her stockings as she stared at Destin Wright in the mud room doorway. "What are you doing here?"

He brushed snow off his cashmere coat, grinning, his cheeks red from the cold. "Man, it's cold. I thought hiking'd warm me up, but I'm still freezing."

"That's because you're not dressed properly. Destin—"

"Relax, Susanna. Don't go getting your nose out of joint. I'm checking out the Winter Olympics training facilities in Lake Placid. I want to try the luge and bobsledding, maybe try the ski jump. I haven't skied Whiteface in a while. Hell of a mountain."

"How did you find me?"

He shrugged. "It wasn't hard. I heard people talking at Jimmy's, figured it out." He frowned at his pants, wet from the knees down. "Hope they don't freeze solid on my way back."

"On your way back where? Destin, you're not staying on the lake—"

"What?" He didn't seemed prepared to give her an answer. "Hey, look, I've got a life. I can come up here the same time as you if I want."

Susanna eyed him as the cold water seeped into her socks and the cold air blew in from the open door. If she asked Destin to shut the door, he might think he was invited in. She didn't want that. "You must know I don't believe you," she said. "I think you're here to try to get me to give you money."

He licked his lips, his expression—a mix of panic and irritation—telling her she was right. "My window of opportunity's closing, Suze. I have to do something. I can't—it's a great idea. If you'd just look at the damn business plan. I worked my ass off to do one up after you told me I needed one."

"You don't need me, Destin. If your idea is as good as you think it is, take it to venture capitalists, network, work your contacts. It'll fly."

"You'll regret this," he said.

There was an edge to his tone that drove her back on her heels. "Destin, are you *threatening* me?"

"What? Nah, I'm just telling it like it is. You know this is a once-in-a-lifetime opportunity, Suze. It'll make your ten million look like petty cash—"

"My ten million?" She stared at him coolly, but her mouth had gone dry with tension. "What makes you think I have ten million?"

He gave her a sheepish smile. "It's what everybody says at Jimmy's."

She didn't believe him.

"I don't know what happened," he said. "I had buckets of money. Buckets. And people crawling all over me, wanting to invest in anything I came up with. Now it's all disappeared." He lowered his gaze to her, the edge still there. "What would you do if you lost everything?"

"By 'everything' I assume you mean all my money. Well, for starters I'd hope I wouldn't alienate everyone who cares about me. I'd look to the constants in my life for emotional support—family, friends.'' She thought of Jack, who'd been there in the lean times when they were first starting out, at her side when she delivered twin babies—through everything she'd done since she was nineteen years old. But she pushed the thought aside, focusing instead on Destin. ''You have to get a grip, Destin. Money isn't who I am. It's not who you are.''

''Easy to say when you're sitting at the end of the rainbow with your pot of gold. I'm in the red zone. I liked me better when I had dough. Shit, I'm lucky they haven't come for the fillings in my teeth.''

Susanna had started to shiver from the cold. ''Did you break into Gran's house last night?''

''Hell, no. Jesus—Susanna, you don't think I—''

''You know Audrey Melbourne, the new woman who's been hanging around at Jim's Place, don't you? Redhead, small, Texas accent.''

''Maybe I should go.''

She heard Davey Ahearn's truck rattle into her driveway. Destin turned, going pale at the sight of Jack climbing out. Susanna said, ''Audrey is actually a former police officer from south Texas named Alice Parker. Jack investigated her for official misconduct, and she ended up serving a year in prison. She got out on New Year's Eve.''

''I wouldn't know anything about that.''

''That's why Jack's up here.'' She tilted her head back, feeling less anxious, either because her husband was here or she had Destin on the defensive. Or both. ''He ran into an intruder at Gran's last night. He's not happy about it.''

Destin licked his lips, glancing outside. ''Holy shit,'' he said with a fake laugh, ''he just gets bigger and meaner looking, doesn't he?'' But his gaze shifted back to Susanna, his blue eyes intense as he added in a low voice, ''Suze, you have to help me. This is my last shot. I can't—it's only a hundred grand. I'll never bother you again. Promise.''

Jack walked into the mud room, and Destin flew around, grinning awkwardly. ''Hey, there. Jack, right? The Texas Ranger? I'm Destin Wright, a friend of your wife's. I'm up here doing some bob-sledding, thought I'd drop by and say hi.''

''You hiked in?'' Jack asked, tight-lipped.

''Yeah, I went down the wrong driveway, decided I'd just tromp along the lake. Wish I'd brought my snowshoes with me. The ones I have back home, I could climb Everest in them.''

Jack unbuttoned the top button of his suede jacket. ''Do you want a ride back to your car?''

Destin quickly shook his head. ''No, no, that's okay. I don't want to interrupt your vacation. It's nice out—kind of cold, but that's what we're up here for, right? The snow and the cold?'' He grinned un-easily, taking a step toward the door, which Jack was still blocking. He looked back at Susanna. ''I'll see you around.''

Jack stepped out of the way, deliberately, and Des-tin shot past him. Jack shut the door and turned to Susanna. ''You want to tell me about this guy?''

''He's a pest.'' She was shivering, her socks soaked, her feet half-frozen. ''He wants me to invest in a new company he's starting. I said no, and he thinks if he keeps asking me, I'll change my mind.''

''What about coming up here?''

"It's vintage Destin. He has no sense of bound-
aries."

Jack unbuttoned the last of his coat, and it fell
open, his broad chest reminding her of last night. But
he was still on Destin. "He's broke?"

Susanna nodded. "He made a fortune in a dot-com
company he cooked up a few years ago, then lost it
all. He's even had his car repossessed. I'm not getting involved. He's a black hole. He has a huge sense
of entitlement—" She stopped, shaking her head.
"He's not getting a dime out of me."

But Jack was frowning at her, and suddenly he
took two long steps over to her and grabbed her by
the waist with both hands, lifting her off her feet.

"Jack? What are you doing?"

He sat her on the wooden bench in the middle of
the mud room. "Your lips are blue." He squatted
down in front of her and pulled off her wet socks
one at a time. Then he took one foot in each of his
hands and massaged them, easing his thumbs over
the sensitive skin of her arches. He looked up at her,
a spark in his dark eyes. "You don't want to get
hypothermia."

That was impossible now. "Jack…"

"This guy, Destin," he said, caressing her ankles,.
sending heat up through her calves, higher, deeper.
"How desperate is he?"

"As desperate as he thinks he is. Um, Jack…"

He smiled innocently, although he couldn't quite
manage to make his eyes look even remotely innocent. "What, Susanna?"

She loved him then. At that moment she wanted
to melt into him and stay with him forever. But there

were her secrets, her fears, her questions and the dangers that came with loving a man like Jack Galway as much as she did. He was hard, strong, protective, kind and completely relentless in everything he did.

"I should go in and change clothes," she said quietly, a little hoarse.

"Do you want me to carry you over the puddles?"

She groaned, then laughed. "You don't let up for a second, do you?"

He eased to his feet. "Not my style."

She jumped up, right into an icy blob of snow from his boot. She managed to stifle a yell at the shock of the cold water on her now warm feet and navigated the rest of the pools, the clumps of unmelted snow, the wet socks, the wet gloves. When she was at the kitchen, she glanced back at the mess. "I'll tell Maggie and Ellen to get in here with the mop."

But he said nothing, his jaw set hard, his body rigid, and her own body responded almost automatically. Last night hadn't been enough, and not just for him.

She turned quickly, making a beeline for her bedroom and warm, dry clothes.

Eleven

Jack dumped his winter gear on the kitchen table and cut off the tags with his pocket knife. Maggie and Ellen had finished mopping the mud room and joined Iris at a card table in front of the fire to work on an old jigsaw puzzle she'd found. He knew he was here for the duration today, but he had no intention of putting together an English countryside castle. At least the lump on his head had gone down.

He'd bought insulated wind pants, insulated boots, insulated gloves and a knit hat the girls said was cool. He figured he'd hang in with his jacket, socks and shirts and didn't need long underwear. How cold could it get? He wasn't sure how long he'd stay. Right now, through the night at least—perhaps until he learned more about this Destin Wright character.

A lot depended on Susanna.

He'd also bought snowshoes. Having learned from his daughters' machinations, he had opted for spring-loaded bindings. They were more expensive, but he didn't care.

He'd put everything on his own damn card. By the

time he got to town, he was frustrated he was picking out wind pants instead of finding out what Alice Parker was up to, why she'd moved to Boston and befriended his wife's grandmother.

And he was pissed as hell at his wife and all her millions.

Then he spotted Destin Wright in her damn cabin in the woods, and all he could think about was making sure no one touched her.

Hell of a thing, being married to Susanna. But even after their months of living apart, he couldn't imagine life without her. If only roses and lavender sachets would do the trick. He suspected, however, it was going to take more—like confronting her about what she was hiding from him. *Talking* to her. He'd let his work preoccupy him in the months before she'd left. He knew it. Maggie and Ellen had a point about the fire wall he'd put up between his home life and his work. It extended to Susanna's work, too.

He scooped up his snowshoes. "You girls want to go out and help me break in my new snowshoes?"

They were unenthusiastic. "Do you hear the wind howling?" Maggie asked, shuddering. "The wind chill must be below zero."

"But it's a dry cold," her great-grandmother said. "It doesn't penetrate into your bones the way a damp cold does."

Maggie sighed at her. "Frozen solid is frozen solid, Gran. I don't care if it's a dry or damp cold."

Ellen had about twenty puzzle pieces laid out on the palm of her hand and up her wrist. She was deep into her puzzle-building, staring at a stretch of rose garden she was putting together. "Maybe Mom will go with you."

Jack doubted it. Susanna was still hiding in her bedroom after her foot massage. Maybe she was dreading the long hours of silence and darkness that lay ahead of them. There was no television, no VCR, no computer, no regular telephone, spotty cellular reception. Maggie and Ellen each had a Walkman, and there was an old radio on top of the refrigerator. There were no neighbors. No city lights. With snow in the forecast, they wouldn't want to head into town and find a movie theater or a restaurant.

If not for his presence, it'd be Susanna's idea of heaven. But he liked complicating her life. He needed to complicate it more often, the way he had last night.

"We're starting a Scrabble tournament after we put in a few more pieces of this puzzle," Maggie said. "Do you want us to wait for you, Dad?"

Scrabble.

"No," Jack said. "Don't wait."

He didn't know how he'd last until morning. He headed out through the mud room and dumped his snowshoes on the driveway. Clouds had moved in from the west. The landscape was soft grays and whites now, making everything seem closer, more intimate.

He put on his snowshoes without a hitch and tramped down to the lake. Easy. Just like walking with Bozo shoes. He left the trail and broke through the fresh snow, moving along the edge of several fir trees above the lake, toward a granite outcropping. Darkness came early this far north, but it wasn't here yet, the last of the daylight slowly easing out. Snow flurries seemed to hover midair.

When he came to the outcropping, he started up a short, steep incline, hit rock and ice and fell on his ass. No warning, just down he went.

Behind him, Susanna sputtered into laughter.

He leaned against the boulder and untangled his snowshoes, an awkward maneuver that she seemed to enjoy watching. She was about two yards from him, up to her knees in snow. She wasn't wearing snowshoes, which gave him a definite advantage if he decided to go after her.

He didn't move to get up. "What if I broke an ankle?"

"You'd swear louder." She walked up to him, lifting her legs high in the deep snow. She had on a headband, not a hat, her dark hair hanging down her back, dotted with melting snow. She had on close-fitting pants that emphasized her long, slim legs, even with her coat covering her hips and upper thighs. She settled her green eyes on him. "Need a hand?"

"Nope. Just thought I'd sit here and watch you wonder if I'm going to pull you down into the snow." But he got to his feet, his lower half covered in fluffy snow. "You want to help me brush off?"

"No."

He grinned at her. "You're blushing."

"You think so, huh?"

"Why else would your cheeks be red?"

She bit back a smile. "Because it's eleven degrees out."

"I don't think so." He pulled off a glove and touched his fingers to her cheek, lingering on the warm, smooth skin. "Doesn't feel cold to me." He leaned in close, letting his fingers trail across her mouth. "You blushed the first time I saw you naked."

Her eyes sparked, and this time there was no way she could deny what she was thinking, feeling. "I don't care where all you grew up, I think you still have a little repressed Yankee in you," he said, kissing her then, for no reason, which he used to do all the time. He wanted to let the kiss last, deepen it, but he took a step back from her and looked out at the quiet lake. The mountains were lost in the clouds now, as if they weren't there. "Susanna, we can't go on like this forever."

"I know." Her voice choked a bit, telling him she was still recovering from their kiss. "The status quo isn't easy on either of us."

"Although when you only have sex every few months, it gets damn hot." He cut a glance at her. "Blushing again, Mrs. Galway?"

"It's not like it's once every few months, not if you count the number of times in each—well, never mind."

He laughed. "You and that calculator mind." He moved back in close to her, tucking a finger inside her headband and adjusting it over her ear. He could feel the heat of her skin, the softness of her hair. "You don't have a boyfriend?"

"What?" Her face lost its color instantly, becoming almost ashen. "Jack, no—absolutely not. Never. That wouldn't be the status quo. We're still married. I wouldn't—" She took a small breath. "Do you? Have someone else, I mean?"

"No."

He ran his fingers along the edge of her jaw and across her lips. "If it weren't so damn cold, Susanna, I'd make love to you right here, right now. We could camp out here all the night, leave the cabin to Iris and the girls." But he let his hand drop, and he put his glove back on, because he could see the way her eyes darkened and widened, how she'd stiffened and set her jaw. He knew what was coming next. He'd been waiting months for it.

"Jack—" She took in another shallow breath, her eyes fixed on him. "I should tell you about Beau McGarrity."

He straightened. "Yes, you should."

She shot back a step, startled. "Goddamn it. You know?"

He realized there was no humor in him now. None. He felt his gaze harden on her, this generous, stubborn woman he'd loved for half his life. "That's what you forgot, Susanna. I always know."

"*Damn* it."

She kicked snow at him and flew around, skidding back down the steep incline, catching the limb of a fir tree, which dumped snow on her. She swore, sinking halfway to her knees in snow, then kicking her way out of it down to the trail she and the girls had made earlier with their snowshoes.

She was furious. Jack didn't care. She should have said something a year ago.

He should have, too.

She spun around at him, snow on her hair, her shoulders. "You don't scare me, Lieutenant Galway." She ripped off her snow-covered headband, the snow coming down now in fat flakes that filled the sky. "I'm not one of your damn suspects. I'm your *wife*."

"Exactly."

His voice was stone, but it had no effect on her. "This isn't one of your investigations. This isn't an interrogation. I didn't marry a man with a badge."

"You've always looked life square in the eye, Susanna. Why not this time?"

"I *did*," she said, "and it scared the hell out of me."

The tightness in his jaw eased, and he moved down the slope toward her, leaning hard into his heel cleats. If he fell on his ass again, it'd be all over. She'd have the opening she needed, and she'd be out of there, off to the cabin, Iris and the girls. They'd never get back here again, to the heart of the misery and secrets that had oozed into their marriage. Murder, corruption, fear—and silence. They'd eroded the trust between them, drove them apart before they'd realized what had happened.

He'd vowed never to let his work come between them. And it had.

He stood as close to her as he could manage without kicking her with one of his snowshoes. "Half the reason I fell in love with you was because you had the strength and the backbone to take me on, on my good days and my bad. I couldn't just roll over you." He lowered his voice, tried to soften it. "That works the other way, too. You're no picnic, either, darlin'."

"I couldn't tell you."

He said nothing, the snow gathering on his new

winter gear, the lake and the trees—everything absolutely silent.

"I didn't want murder…your work…" She hesitated, groping for the words she must have known she'd have to tell him for months now. She shut her eyes, squeezing back tears. "I didn't want your work to infect our lives. Not that way."

"You mean a murder suspect walking into our house."

"He came into the kitchen. He didn't knock." She opened her eyes again, but her face was white, as if she were back on that day over a year ago. "I spotted him a couple of times before that day."

"When?"

"That same week. He showed up in town and then again at the school. I didn't know who he was. I hadn't paid enough attention to the news reports— he must have seemed familiar to me, or I wouldn't have noticed him."

"Christ," Jack whispered. "I didn't know about the two other incidents."

She tightened her gloved hands into fists. "I wasn't in denial. I knew what I was doing when I didn't tell you."

"At the house," Jack said. "What did McGarrity say to you?"

"He was oblique—very careful."

And she told him word for word, as if they were back on that day and he'd come home and found her in the kitchen staring at a cold cup of tea—and instead of telling her about Alice Parker, he'd first asked her what was wrong, and she'd confided in him. But he'd missed it all—how terrified she was, for herself, for their daughters, for him. He'd missed it, and she'd run away.

He could see that so clearly now.

When she finished, she cleared her throat. "That's it," she said quietly. "That's everything."

It wasn't. He could tell, but he waited.

The snow continued, the flakes smaller, coming faster. One hit her cheek and melted on contact. She brushed at her face, her gloves covered in snow. "Everything except for the tape," she said.

With anyone else, he would have kept quiet and let the silence work to his advantage, but not with his wife. "Goddamn it, Susanna, what tape?"

Her eyes flashed, the fight coming back in her. "I taped my conversation with Beau McGarrity."

Her conversation.

"Maggie and Ellen's tape recorder was right under my nose. It seemed like the thing to do."

Jack stiffened. "What the hell would you have done if he'd caught you?"

"He didn't." She wasn't backing down. "It's what you'd have done. You know damn well it is. It wouldn't have mattered if you were a Texas Ranger or a plumber—you'd have taped the bastard."

"But I *am* a Texas Ranger."

"Yes, and if he'd slit my throat in the kitchen, you'd have had the evidence you needed—"

"Jesus Christ," he breathed, realizing the depth of her fear that day. Even now.

"It was one of those little digital audio tapes," she went on. "Alice Parker showed up not long after McGarrity left, and I gave it to her. I didn't think twice. I thought she was working on the murder investigation. Jack, that tape must be worthless. Alice was in such a frenzy to nail McGarrity, if it had been any good, she'd have given it to you—''

"Not necessarily."

Susanna frowned. "Why wouldn't she?"

"She didn't like being arrested, Susanna. She clammed up."

"Then what did she do with it?"

He could feel the bile rise up in his throat, the past months of frustration and stalemate crashing in on him. "That'll be harder to find out now, won't it?"

"Give me a break, Jack. I've been married to a law enforcement officer for a long time. Tell me you could have used that tape. Tell me you think there's a damn thing on it—''

"You should have told me what happened that day."

She turned away from him and stared out into the snow, toward the lake. He could see tears shining in her vivid eyes, mixing with the snow melting on her cheeks, and he knew she'd get out of there before she let him see her cry. "I went to call you, even before Alice showed up." He saw her swallow and knew she was fighting to keep herself together. "It was my first instinct."

"Why didn't you?"

"I don't know. I guess I wanted the whole thing not to have happened. I'm used to you dealing with violence and crime and all that—it's your duty. You have the training. You made that commitment. But Maggie and Ellen—''

"And you. None of you signed up to put yourselves in the line of fire."

She took a shallow breath, not looking at him. "I wanted not to feel something really had happened where I needed you to protect me—to protect the girls. I wanted there not to be this murderer and stalker who'd walked right into our kitchen and made veiled threats, not because of anything I'd done, but because I was married to a Texas Ranger—"

"You wanted not to be my wife."

That was it. The tears came, and she took off.

Jim Haviland had burned the meringue on two pies in a row. He'd give them to Davey Ahearn and a bunch of the construction workers who were regulars. He was distracted because his daughter had just come in and announced she was expecting a baby. His Tess, who'd been scared of kids since she was six and had lost her own mother to cancer.

"We're all thrilled," Tess said, sitting on a stool at the bar. "Dolly says she doesn't care if it's a baby sister or a baby brother."

"She'll be a good big sister," Jim said. "Andrew? He's excited?"

She beamed. "Oh, yes."

"He's a good father."

"What about me? I'm a great mum. Dolly says so."

"Dolly's seven," Davey contributed from down the bar. He was Tess's godfather, and Jim had been listening to the two of them for years. "What does she know?"

"I *am* a great mother."

"Scared?" Jim asked her.

She didn't look a bit scared. "I'm too green at the gills most of the time to be scared."

"No puking at the bar," Davey said.

Tess ignored him. "I can't wait to tell Susanna. Do you have her number in the Adirondacks? I'm not getting through on her cell phone."

"Probably the mountains," Jim said. "I don't think she has a regular phone up there yet."

"Blackwater Lake." Davey shook his head. "It's as deep in the boonies as it sounds. Hard to believe Iris grew up that far out into the wilds."

Just then Andrew and little Dolly swooped into the pub, and Jim congratulated them, knowing he had a tendency to sound awkward and repressed when he was talking about things like his daughter being pregnant. He didn't give a damn.

Davey got down off his stool and gave Tess a big hug. "Don't think I'm going to be godfather to any new little ones. Being your godfather's been pain in the ass enough."

Jim gave Dolly a present he'd been saving, a new stuffed animal he'd picked up at the New England Aquarium. She was a cute kid, wanted to be a marine biologist these days. But who knew? Last year it was a princess.

After Tess left with her family, Davey plopped back down at his place at the bar. "You going to start knitting booties, Jimmy?"

But Jim's attention was on a man coming over from a back table and taking the stool Tess had vacated. He set an empty beer glass on the bar. He'd been nursing it for almost an hour. He was gray-haired, distinguished-looking, wearing an expensive business suit. He had on a college football ring, and he spoke in a twangy Southern accent.

He asked what he owed for the beer.

Jim told him. "Where you from?"

"Not here, I'm afraid." He wasn't snotty, but he wasn't friendly, either. Used to people waiting on him. He added, "I'm in town on business."

"We don't get too many out-of-town businessmen in here. We're mostly a local place."

"That's what I like about it," the man said. "A friend recommended it. I overheard what your daughter said. Congratulations."

Jim didn't know why, but the man's words didn't sit well with him. He glanced at Davey and saw his friend had the same reaction. "Thanks," Jim said. "Where you staying?"

"Hotel in town."

That could be anywhere. He didn't order anything else, just paid for his beer and left.

Davey half turned on his stool and looked out at the door as it shut. "Think I should follow him?"

"Jesus, Davey, no. Why would you do that?"

"You look suspicious, Jimmy."

"You think that was a Texas accent?"

"Hell if I know. If it was, we've got too damn many Texans showing up here, if you ask me."

"Yeah." Jim frowned, staring at the closed door. "Cops were in earlier, asking about Jack Galway and last night at Iris's place."

Davey nodded grimly. "Maybe you should give them a buzz."

"Why, because a man with a Texas accent ordered

a beer and congratulated my daughter on expecting a baby? That's thin.''

"Jack leave you his cell phone number?"

"No, and I didn't ask for it."

"Three Texans in a row. The ex-con, the Ranger, and now this guy with the ring. I don't know, Jimmy. I'm starting to think you should tack a Lone Star on the front door."

Jim ignored him and put another pie in the oven, but he ended up burning the meringue on this one, too.

Twelve

~~~~~

Susanna splashed her face with cold water in her little cabin bathroom and recovered her composure. In all the months she'd pictured herself telling Jack about her encounter with Beau McGarrity, she'd said to herself—for God's sake, don't cry. Just tell him straight up and let him get all official and try to tell her he should arrest her for withholding evidence. She'd be objective, calm and reasonable, understanding of the anger and sense of betrayal he might feel at her long silence.

That plan had gone to hell when she found out he'd known about Beau McGarrity practically all along.

In hindsight, she should have told Jack what had happened. It had been her first instinct, and she should have followed it. But clarity was so much easier now when he was here. She wasn't dealing with the reality of a stranger in her kitchen. There'd been so much at stake. The Rachel McGarrity murder investigation. Maggie and Ellen's safety. Her own. Once Jack told her about Alice Parker, it had seemed safer, simpler, better for all concerned for her just to say nothing.

She noticed in the mirror that her eyes were red-rimmed and puffy. Tough to blame that on the snow, the cold, the face wash. Damn, she'd held back on that cry for far too long.

Jack was right. That moment she'd decided not to tell him about Beau McGarrity, she hadn't wanted to be married to a Texas Ranger. She'd have taken an accountant, a social studies teacher, a construction worker—except she knew better. Violence could strike anyone, anytime. She'd learned that in her years married to Jack Galway. And she loved him.

She'd seen him cry once, at his mother's grave in San Antonio. She was killed in a car accident when he was fifteen and his younger sister was just nine. His father worked two jobs and pushed both his son and daughter to excel, to open up their world and possibilities. Jack had gone to Harvard, Kara to Yale—and both had come home to Texas, although Kara only recently. Bill Galway had remarried and moved to Corpus Christi, satisfied to spend his retirement fishing and telling people he had one kid who was a Texas Ranger, another who was a lawyer, so between the two of them, no matter what happened, he was all set.

The Galways were a tough lot, that was for sure.

Susanna splashed her face once more, dried off and headed back into the kitchen. Jack and the girls were making dinner—spaghetti, salad, garlic bread. He glanced at her but said nothing, and she could tell his mood was definitely dark. At least with her. He seemed fine with Maggie and Ellen.

She joined Gran at the puzzle table. "We should go to England," Gran said, "and look up this castle."

Susanna smiled. "I thought you didn't like to travel."

"Well, England might be nice." She glanced up at her granddaughter and whispered, "You told him?"

"He already knew."

"Ah."

Gran was aware some of the details about what had happened with Beau McGarrity, but not all of them. If she knew everything, she'd have likely gone to Jack herself long before now. Susanna didn't know how she'd managed to keep any secrets, much less a few big ones, given the Dunning propensity for getting everything out in the open. Her work had taught her how to keep confidences—so had Jack's. But that was professional, not personal, and a confidence was different from a secret.

Susanna put in a couple of pieces of the rose garden before Maggie called them to the table.

During dinner, they talked about snowshoeing, the weather and food, and Susanna could feel the isolation of her cabin with nightfall, the quiet all around them. There were no street noises, no city lights—in summer, the windows would be open, with crickets and owls to listen to, but now, there was just the occasional whistling of the wind as the snow fell. Jack sat next to Gran at the other end of the table, and Susanna managed not to make eye contact with him through dinner. Afterward, she ran everyone out of the kitchen and cleaned up the dishes.

Gran, Maggie and Ellen resumed their Scrabble tournament once the table was cleared. Jack brought in wood, one load after another, until the wood box was overflowing. Susanna knew he was climbing the walls.

"You could go out and look for moose tracks in the dark," she said as he started out for another load.

He gave her a short, intense look, and she knew he had two things on his mind. One was Alice Parker, Beau McGarrity and the missing tape. The other was her. Neither made hanging around a mountain cabin easy to do.

"Mom," Ellen said from the table, "you should join our Scrabble tournament. We can have four players."

"It's too late to add a new player," Maggie said.

Gran drew her wool shawl around her thin shoulders. "Susanna can take my place."

Ellen shook her head. "No way. You can't quit while you're ahead. You're winning, Gran."

"I made a seven-letter word," she told Susanna, pleased with herself.

"She did, Mom," Maggie said. "*Avenues*. Can you believe it? It's such a city word for up here."

Susanna let them play their game and retreated to the couch in front of a fire, trying to concentrate on a book. Jack dumped his last load of wood and tried working the puzzle. He put in one piece and gave up. "I never did like puzzles."

"Not if they don't involve criminals." Susanna didn't think there was an edge to her voice, but he shot her a look as if he thought he'd heard one. She shrugged under her warm fleece blanket. "You are a Texas Ranger."

"Am I?"

He wasn't back to neutral. He was still in interrogation mode. Still angry with her—and himself. An ex-convict he'd put in prison had insinuated herself into his family's life for *weeks,* he'd been hit on the head and he hadn't known about the tape. There was still an unsolved murder in Texas. His professional and personal lives had collided, and Susanna knew he didn't like it. Neither did she. But instead of facing it, she'd fled. It wasn't her style, which made reconciling herself to the past months even more difficult.

That didn't mean she liked having the professional Jack Galway turned loose on her. Intellectually, she understood her culpability in their current standoff. Emotionally, she was still raw and hurt and furious with him. He'd *known* about Beau McGarrity.

Under the circumstances, she felt no obligation to tell him about the ten million. Not yet. Maybe not until his lawyers came hunting for it.

But the thought of divorce brought an instant tightness to her throat, and she could feel the tears brimming again. She was exhausted, wrung out from the turmoil of her emotions, lack of sleep, snowshoeing, the cold air—just the edge of having her husband back in her life.

She flipped a page in her book, not that she was able to absorb a single word she read. Jack bit off a sigh and abruptly headed for the kitchen. "Where are you going?" she asked.

"Star gazing."

"It's snowing. The stars won't be out."

"Then I'll count snowflakes."

She heard the mud room door shut hard and pulled her fleece blanket up to her chin, debating whether to go out and offer to count snowflakes with him. Maybe not, she thought, and flipped another page while Maggie and Ellen groaned when their great-grandmother put the *Q* on a triple-letter score.

Alice wrapped her damp hair in a soft, warm towel and sank onto her bed in her room at the Blackwater Inn. She could live in this room for the rest of her life. Never mind Australia. Just give her maid service, pretty-smelling soaps and a beautiful view right here in the Adirondacks. She'd be fine.

Her skin was plump and wrinkled from her long, scented bath. She'd snuggled up in the natural cotton terry-cloth robe that came with her room, feeling pampered and special. They had a fire in the living room downstairs, but she was content staying up here in her room, enjoying the quiet and a few minutes of freedom from Destin.

Jack Galway was up here. That wasn't good news.

"He scares the hell out of me," Destin had told her when he'd come in from his excursion out to Susanna's cabin.

But if Jack's presence put more pressure on her and Destin, Alice thought, maybe it put more pressure on Susanna, too. It could work to their advantage.

Destin was down in the living room, yapping with the innkeepers. Alice stared at the shifting shadows on her ceiling, the swirling plaster strokes. She remembered Rachel McGarrity telling her that the best part of being rich was always having quality. She'd loved fine linens. Egyptian cotton towels, 300-count cotton sheets, Anachini bedspreads, merino and cashmere blankets. Alice tried to learn what the best brands and fabrics were. She wasn't jealous, just curious. Rachel never lorded her wealth over anyone. She was born with a silver spoon in her mouth but had been raised to be gracious and kind. Alice's grandma had always set stock on good manners as the true tell of character.

Rachel wasn't perfect, but never pretended to be, not that Alice had seen. Beau hadn't wanted to know about her imperfections, just as he hadn't wanted to know about his first wife's cancer, like it was her fault—a character flaw.

Philadelphia blueblood or not, Rachel Tucker McGarrity had bled like anyone else. The medical examiner said she'd died within a minute. She probably hadn't suffered.

But had she known what was happening to her? Did she know she'd been shot, even if she didn't really feel it? Did she know her husband had just killed her?

Did she know Alice had inadvertently provoked him?

Alice knew there were things Rachel had never told her. Why her interest in Susanna Galway, what she was working on. They were getting to that— she'd promised Alice more answers, soon.

Had she thought as she died, *I should have told Alice more?*

Alice shut her eyes, trying to block out the unwanted thoughts and images. She didn't know what the mind could absorb in the last seconds before death. Had Rachel seen Alice's change purse on the driveway and thought it was her friend who'd killed her? Was Beau that evil to have wanted Rachel to believe it was Alice who'd killed her, not him? Would that have given him some kind of sick satisfaction?

Alice knew she should have secured the crime scene and let the investigative team figure out that her change purse was planted. Instead she'd grabbed it—she'd had to move Rachel's arm—and scoured the area for other evidence that would lead the detectives back to her, trampling evidence in the process.

What a mess.

She got up and walked over to the mirror above her dresser, letting her towel drape over her shoulders. She liked her red hair. She might keep it. She'd never really expected the slight changes in her appearance to keep Ranger Jack at bay. Maybe they were simply a start to adopting a new identity. Leaving behind Alice Parker of Loserville, Texas.

Her cell phone trilled. She grimaced, knowing it was Beau.

She grabbed her phone from the night stand where it was recharging. "Hey, Mr. Beau—that you?"

"You're in the Adirondacks," he said. "You followed Susanna after you searched Iris Dunning's house last night."

His words took Alice by surprise. She shivered, suddenly cold. "Are you in Boston?"

"Did you find the tape?"

If she said yes, she had no reason to be in the

Adirondacks. Nothing to keep him from tracking her down and beating her to death. She sat on the edge of the bed. Her damp towel had turned cold. She dropped it on the floor and tucked her bare feet up under her, folding her bathrobe over them. She couldn't let her teeth shatter. He'd assume it was nerves.

He wouldn't take well to her shenanigans with Destin Wright.

"No," she said. "I have reason to believe she keeps it with her. That's why I'm up here." A lie, she thought. A dangerous lie.

"It's not in San Antonio."

Alice's heart seemed to stop beating, then start up again with a jolt, rushing blood through her system so fast and hard it hurt. Her fingertips were purple and cold now, no longer warm from her bath. She furrowed her brow, making herself concentrate. "Beau, Jesus, what are you doing? You broke into the Galway house in San Antonio? Are you *nuts?* You said Sam Temple's keeping an eye on you—"

"Not that close an eye. You don't need to worry about me." He paused, a tactic, she knew, to ratchet up the tension. His voice never changed, making it impossible to read him, whether he was dead serious or just testing the waters. "Not in that way."

"You're supposed to stay home and trim your roses and let me do the dirty work. That's what you're paying me for."

"Miss Parker, if you have presumed in any way to play me for a fool—"

"Now, don't be silly, Mr. Beau."

But she thought of the tape sitting in her battered

suitcase and Destin Wright down in front of the fire, probably yammering to the innkeepers about how he had a hundred grand in the bag to start over. His angel money.

Beau would probably consider both of these playing him for a fool.

"You're the smartest man I know," she told him. "You got away with murder. I'd never try to trick you."

"I'll be in touch," he said, clicking off.

Alice pulled the quilt up over her and sat crosslegged in the middle of the bed. Now what? Susanna Galway was a sane woman with a perfectly good ten million in her name, and here Alice was, messing with a murderous sociopath for a lousy fifty grand. Probably half that. Beau'd never pay her full asking price.

It was too late to backtrack on her deal with him now. If he found out she'd lied to him, never mind what he'd pay. She'd be lucky if he didn't chop through the ice on Blackwater Lake and heave her in.

She wanted Australia. In Australia, she would know only nice people.

Susanna had shut her book and was staring at the fire, heat radiating out to her from its orange flames. Maggie and Ellen had gone upstairs to take turns reading *Pride and Prejudice* aloud to each other. It was how desperate they were, they'd said. Susanna didn't think so. She could tell they were enjoying this time together, away from the distractions of their lives in either Boston or San Antonio.

Gran had gone up to her room, too. Susanna had asked if there was anywhere she wanted to go, anything she wanted to see while they were on Blackwater Lake. "The cemetery," she'd said.

Susanna hadn't argued. "Okay, Gran. I'll take you to the cemetery in the morning."

She imagined her grandmother in her room, thinking about the people whose graves she'd visit tomorrow.

She tucked her blanket around her. The fire crackled, and she bit back sudden tears. She didn't know what was wrong with her. Her family was right there with her, and yet she'd never felt so alone.

Jack came in from the mud room, brushing melting snow off his hair. "It's coming down hard now." He walked over to the fire, and Susanna could feel the cold coming off him. "Where is everyone?"

"Upstairs. I think they're making themselves scarce."

He glanced back at her, his dark eyes narrowed. "Good."

He sat next to her on the couch and took a corner of her blanket, scooting closer. She loosened her grip on the blanket and gave him more of it. "Your hands are freezing," she said, taking one and sandwiching it between her palms, sharing some of her body heat. She noticed they both still wore their wedding rings. They'd been so broke when they'd bought them. They were simple white gold bands, inscribed with their initials and the date of their wedding.

"If I'm going to sleep in the loft," he said, "I'll need another damn blanket."

"You can use the electric blanket from my bed."

"You have an electric blanket?"

She smiled at him. "I'm not surprised you didn't notice last night."

He grabbed one of her hands, circling his fingers around hers. "You have an electric blanket *and* a down comforter?"

"Nice, huh? That way I can warm up the bed with the electric blanket before I get in." She tossed her head back, cutting her eyes at him, having fun. "I don't like a cold bed."

"Holding out on me on a stalker is one thing, but holding out on an electric blanket—" He dropped her hand and slipped both arms around her, drawing her against him, his cool fingertips reaching the bare, hot skin of her lower back. "There's no forgiving and no forgetting on that one. You let me freeze last night."

"Well, you weren't exactly freezing when you left me."

He leaned into her, his mouth finding hers as he whispered, "You didn't need either your electric blanket or your comforter last night, did you?"

Her answer was lost in their kiss, a long, slow, deep kiss that made her forget she'd ever felt alone in her life, never mind a few minutes ago. He eased one hand from her lower back to her front, moving his palm up her stomach, until he reached her breast.

"I know you think I can handle anything, Susanna," he said, "but I can't. I can't handle being alone in San Antonio."

"I never meant to stay in Boston—"

"You were scared and confused. So was I." His tone was matter-of-fact, as if he was used to admitting to fear and confusion. "If we'd tried to deal with this sooner—well, who knows."

"I know this is going to sound weird, but it's like these past months, this cabin—all of it's part of my destiny, somehow, something I had to go through. We did. I don't know. Maybe it's just that a part of me knew I needed these months with Gran, and this hasn't all been just about us and that son of a bitch Beau McGarrity."

But Jack wasn't listening, not really. He was letting his hand drift down her abdomen, and he pulled back the stretchy fabric of her pants, easing his hand lower, until he was between her legs, touching her in ways only he ever had. It had been so long, she almost moaned with pleasure, then remembered her family upstairs. But he knew, and he probed deeper, not stopping when she couldn't get a decent breath, when she shut her eyes in an effort to maintain this moment, prolong it.

"Come to bed with me," she said in a ragged whisper.

"Not yet."

He stayed with her, letting her quake silently against him, not stopping until she collapsed onto his chest and breathed in the scent of him. "Jack, I swear—no electric blanket," she said, her face buried in his shirt. "You don't deserve one."

"I don't know about that." He gave a low, deliberate laugh. "I'd say I've earned a lot more than an electric blanket."

"Bastard."

He laughed again.

But she didn't lift her head from his chest, feeling

an unexpected wave of embarrassment, as if this was the first time they'd done something like this and she'd gotten ahead of herself.

She quickly pulled away from him, avoiding his eyes as she took as much of the blanket with her as she could, wrapping it around herself. "It's this stretchy high-tech fabric. It's a danger. These pants are comfortable, but—" She didn't finish, letting it go at that.

Jack was clearly not the least bit embarrassed, even for her sake. She snuck a sideways glance at him, but his dark gaze gave her no break whatsoever. He was, she thought, decidedly amused.

She swept to her feet with her blanket around her, as if that might stop him from guessing she was aroused all over again. He was obviously aroused. Not that he cared a whit if she saw.

She muttered good-night and headed for her bedroom, hoping to make it without tripping over the ends of her blanket and falling on her face. Damn near forty years old, married forever, two kids on their way to college, a super-successful financial planner worth ten million last she checked—and she was feeling self-conscious over a spontaneous romantic encounter with her husband.

Except she didn't think it was spontaneous. She thought he'd planned it.

"Counting snowflakes—ha!"

She thought of him back on the couch in front of the fire and ducked into her bedroom, turning her electric blanket to the highest setting. She shot into the bathroom, tearing off her clothes and jumping into the shower, still not able to get a proper breath.

If Jack wanted his chance, she'd handily left the next move up to him. She didn't know how wise that was. He had her off-balance, thoroughly aware of his physical presence—of her own.

She lathered herself with lavender soap, leaving her hair dry when she rinsed off. She stepped out of the shower, dried off with a big towel and put on her full-length blue plaid flannel nightshirt. She looked like a mountain woman.

The wind had picked up, slapping snow against the window, steamy from the heat of her shower.

When she returned to her bedroom, she immediately noticed that the thermostat on her electric blanket was off. She assumed it must have heated up and some kind of safety feature had kicked in, but when she rubbed her hand over the blanket, her bed was ice cold.

From a dark corner, Jack said, "I figured we should start out with a cold bed. It'll give us a fighting chance not to get too hot."

He had already taken off his clothes, and he walked over to her bed and pulled back the covers, sliding between the sheets as if it were the most natural thing in the world.

Susanna knelt on her side of the bed. "Jack, are you sure this is what you want?"

"You have no idea how sure."

"We should probably talk some more—"

"Not a chance," he said. "Not tonight." He looked up at her, his eyes as hot as the fire in the other room, a sexy half smile destroying the last shreds of her self-control. "Are you going to run me out?"

He knew the answer already, but she shook her head, smiling. "Not a chance."

She lifted her nightgown over her head, but before she could cast it to the floor, he was there, smoothing his hands up over her hot skin, following with his mouth, his tongue, his teeth. He eased the nightshirt off and tossed it, lowering her to the bed. She eased her legs apart, feeling the hard length of him, but he didn't come into her right away, and she knew tonight would be different from the other times they'd made love during their long months apart.

He kissed her, a kiss that seemed meant to imprint on her everything she loved about him. Every touch, every stroke, every taste and shudder reached deep into her mind, body and soul. When he came into her, there was none of last night's fury, although his passion was just as deep, his need as insatiable. And her own. He set the pace, as if he were bringing her to the edge and making her look over and see what was on the other side, where she would be in one year, five years, ten years, if she didn't figure out how she fit into this man's life, how he fit into hers.

They came at the same time, free-falling off the edge of the world together.

They cooled down in each other's arms, and when Susanna gave a small shiver, he pulled the comforter over them. She could feel herself drifting to sleep, her head on his shoulder. For that moment, it was if she'd never left him and had told him long ago about Beau McGarrity and Alice—and wasn't still keeping any secrets from him.

Thirteen

Jack awoke at dawn, reached over and switched on the electric blanket. He wasn't cold. He was taking the down comforter and thought it'd be decent to make sure Susanna didn't get cold. He grabbed the comforter off the bed, pulled on his pants and gathered up the rest of his clothes, heading for the bedroom door.

He knew Susanna. Never mind that she was his wife and Iris, Maggie and Ellen had all seen them wake up in bed together—this was different. Easier for Susanna to have him wake up in the loft. Less complicated, less explaining, less trying to pretend she didn't care that they all knew what she'd been up to in the dead of night.

He glanced back at her, asleep in the gray light. He felt a rush of emotion, a tightness in his chest. He knew her love for him had enriched her life, and there was no question his love for her was soul deep. But this was his breaking point. He wasn't going back to San Antonio with matters between them unresolved. There'd be no more status quo.

He crept through the kitchen and past the fireplace in the living room, over to the stairs and up them as quietly as he could. The sofa bed in the loft was still made up with its scrawny blankets. He climbed in, pulling the comforter over him and shivering for a few minutes until the bed warmed up.

In the morning, he discovered it was Iris who kept turning down the heat. If an old lady could take it, so could he. She said it was because of tuberculosis. She was drinking coffee at the table while the girls were making whole-grain pancakes.

"Tuberculosis was the scourge of the late nineteenth and early twentieth century," she said. "We forget nowadays. They called it the White Plague. In the 1870s, a doctor by the name of Edward Livingston Trudeau came to Saranac Lake when he thought he was dying of tuberculosis, but he ended up being 'cured.' He credited a strict regimen of mountain air, rest, good food, light exercise and a lack of stress. He was convinced it would cure other sufferers, and he helped turn Saranac Lake into a health resort. Thousands upon thousands came until antibiotics were discovered in the late 1940s and 1950s. They'd stay weeks, months, even years, until they were well enough to leave. They called it 'curing,' although the disease didn't actually go away—it went into a kind of remission, as I understand."

Jack poured himself a mug of coffee, said good-morning to the girls and sat at the table across from their great-grandmother. "This cure involved a cold house?"

Iris ignored his teasing tone. "Patients were required to spend eight to ten hours outside. It didn't matter the time of year. When you drive into Saranac, you'll see many of the older homes have porches—upstairs, downstairs, the front of the house, the back. Wherever they could stick one. The porches gave the patients a place to sit or lie down while they did their outdoor curing. They call them 'cure cottages.'"

"Amazing," Jack said, meaning it.

"My mother was a nurse at a cure cottage when she was young. My father took her away from that life and brought her up here to Blackwater Lake. But she never lost her belief in the restorative powers of the mountain air."

Jack drank some of his coffee. "Iris, it's ten degrees out."

She smiled, not too sweetly. "It's supposed to get into the upper twenties today. That's not bad for the Adirondacks this time of year." She adjusted her shawl, and if she was cold, Jack knew she'd never admit it. "The Trudeau cure was remarkably effective. Tuberculosis tends to run in cycles of wellness and sickness—patients often had to return for another round of curing."

Maggie swung over with a platter of hot pancakes. She was wearing a brightly striped top from about 1976. "Yuck. I'm never taking antibiotics for granted again."

"They ended Saranac's days as a health resort. For years, *everyone* came up here. Actors, writers, politicians, bankers, war veterans, European royalty, circus people. There were curing places for the rich and the poor. But I don't remember it as a sad place at all. People had hope—they didn't come to die. They came to cure.''

"Then why are you going to the cemetery?'' Ellen asked, setting a pitcher of hot syrup on the table.

Jack grimaced at her frank question, but Iris took it in stride. "Because I'm an old woman,'' she said. "Most of the people I knew when I was a girl are dead.''

"Oh,'' Ellen said. "*Duh*. Sorry, Gran.''

Jack helped get plates, forks and napkins on the table, making no comment about Susanna's absence. He remembered the taste of her, and almost spilled the hot syrup.

While he was distracted, Maggie and Ellen cooked up a plan for him to take them cross-country skiing while their mother and Iris went and looked at old tombstones.

Many of their friends in Texas skied in Colorado and Utah, but he'd never been big on winter sports. He preferred his ten-mile runs, the weight room and his heavy bag. But he was cornered, and he knew it. Cross-country skiing. He'd gone a few times when he was at Harvard. Fell a lot.

He'd planned to check out Destin Wright, then track down Alice Parker and figure out who'd slipped into Iris's house the other night and hit him on the head. Destin was a possibility. It wasn't as if he was after Susanna for pizza money.

But he said, "Sure, I'll take you cross-country skiing.''

Susanna finally wandered out of her bedroom, looking as if she'd done some lovemaking last night—but Jack thought only he would notice. She was dressed for tramping in a northern cemetery in the winter cold. A heavy, expensive Norwegian sweater in a black-and-white geometric print and slim black pants. Hair pulled back. Very sexy.

She didn't say good-morning to anyone until she'd got a mug from the cabinet and poured herself coffee. Then she turned, leaning against the counter, her eyes meeting his for an instant before she smiled. "Gran, you ready?" she asked.

Maggie frowned. "Aren't you going to eat? Ellen and I made pancakes."

"They smell wonderful. I'll take a couple and eat them on my way."

"Cold? With no butter and syrup?" Ellen shuddered. "Yuck."

She and her sister headed upstairs, Gran behind them, to get ready for their excursions. Jack cleared the table, aware that Susanna was on edge, maybe a little tired and testy. He came up next to her, touched the hair at her ear. "Mad I climbed into bed with you—or mad I climbed out?"

A smile tried to develop. "You stole my down comforter."

"Ah."

"And I'm not mad. Preoccupied."

Probably because she still had to tell him about the ten million. He'd told her he always knew everything, but she hadn't seemed to take that as an indication he knew about the money. Well, he was in a fine mood. His head didn't hurt anymore, and he'd made love to his wife last night. Find Alice Parker and figure out who got the jump on him the other night, and he'd be a charmed man. He didn't even mind cross-country skiing for a couple of hours.

"We can talk at lunch," he said. "I need to make a couple of calls."

She nodded, but he could see she had a lot on her mind. *And* she was tired. He could have gone easier on her last night, but she hadn't seemed to want that—and their second bout of lovemaking had been at her instigation. Not that he objected.

He started for the mud room, but she caught the tips of his fingers. "Jack—no regrets about last night?" she asked softly. "That's not why you left?"

"No, that was to spare you the knowing looks this morning."

But she didn't smile. "It wasn't the fire we let go out, you know. It was the light."

"What?"

Now she did smile, shaking her head. "Nothing. Go make your calls. We'll talk later."

To get a better signal, he went outside and stood in the driveway in half a foot of fresh snow. The sun was out, sparkling on the white drifts, and it was very cold. Fortunately, Sam Temple picked up on the first ring.

"I've got two minutes before hypothermia sets in," Jack said. "Any news?"

"Yes." Sam was all business. "I tried to get through to you last night—I left a message on your voice mail. McGarrity took off."

Jack went very still, focusing on a nearby pine tree, its branches arced almost to the ground with snow. Wind gusted suddenly up from the lake, dumping some of the snow off a branch, spraying it in his face. "Where?"

"His cleaning lady said hunting. I don't believe it. He took his truck."

"Have you checked with the airport and airlines?"

"Nothing yet. There's more, Jack. The cleaning woman overheard McGarrity talking to Alice Parker way the hell back in January. Her English isn't great, but it's better than McGarrity thinks."

Jack's Spanish was decent, but Sam was fluent, moving between Spanish and English with ease. "What's your schedule like?" Jack asked him.

"Already talked to the captain. I'm on my way to the airport now. My flight leaves for Boston in an hour."

"How much time does McGarrity have on us?"

"A day. The cleaning woman said he went alone. No hunting buddies."

"I'm missing something," Jack said. "I've been missing it all along."

"I'll call you when I get to Boston." Sam's tone lightened, static creeping into their cell signal. "What about you and Susanna? Has she come clean about being rich?"

"No."

"Just going to let her agonize and think you don't have a clue?"

"Susanna doesn't agonize."

"You know, if I had a rich wife, I'd be happier than you are."

"If you had a rich wife, you'd turn in your badge and run for governor." Jack could feel his jaw set hard, the cold seeping into him. Sam had found out about Susanna's money on his own, from coming around the house and talking to her. Jack hadn't told him. "We need to find McGarrity."

Jack didn't need to tell Sam Temple to watch his back. He knew. He was a professional, but he'd also seen the crime scene pictures of Rachel McGarrity.

He turned to head back into the cabin, but Maggie was there, shivering in the snow, her arms crossed on her chest. She wasn't wearing a coat. "I came out to ask you what time you want to leave." Her dark eyes leveled on him, wide and scared, with a touch of her mother's grit. "Dad....do you mean Beau McGarrity, the man they think shot his wife?"

"Maggie—"

"Is he after Mom?" she asked quietly.

Jack settled back on his heels. When she was a little girl, Maggie had wanted to be a Texas Ranger. Now she was talking about anthropology. He moved toward her, noticed she hadn't changed into a warm high-tech shirt. She still had on that one from the 1970s. "Why would McGarrity be after your mother?"

She shook her head. "I don't know anything, if that's what you're thinking. God forbid anybody tells me anything. You were talking to Sam, right?"

Jack didn't like one thing about this conversation. "Sergeant Temple, yes."

"Dad. I'm not stupid. If you're here and this guy McGarrity has disappeared—"

"No one said he's disappeared."

She snorted. "You asked if Sam—Sergeant Temple—checked the airports and airlines. That sounds like disappearing."

"He said he went hunting."

Maggie's teeth were chattering now, partly with the cold, but also anger. "Why don't you just tell me to mind my own business? I wouldn't mind that as much as you acting as if you're telling me something when you're really not telling me anything."

Jack tried to keep himself from glaring at her. Why the hell couldn't his wife and daughters be *easier*? "I don't want you or your sister to worry about Beau McGarrity or Alice Parker."

"Why, because we're not Texas Rangers? Is that what you tell Mom? Don't worry, let me handle it, I'm the big Texas Ranger."

"You know, Maggie—"

She didn't back down, not half an inch. "That's the thing, Dad. You can't protect Ellen and me from worrying—you can't protect us from anything." She thrust her chin up at him, defiant even with chattering teeth. "Not anymore."

He fought an urge to march her back inside and lecture her about who'd trained at Quantico and who hadn't. But he ached, because he knew that wasn't the answer. He had no answers. Maybe that was why his family was in Boston and he was in Texas. He fucking *didn't* get it.

"Dad," she said, fighting back tears from the cold wind, nerves, indignation—and fear.

He loved this kid. He loved her twin sister. And their mother. He remembered the night his daughters were born, how helpless he'd felt at the pain Susanna was in. He remembered holding Maggie and Ellen as they slept, bundled tightly in their baby blankets.

They weren't babies or preschoolers or even

twelve-year-olds—those days were over. His daughters were strong, independent young women, and they were looking for their father to recognize them as such.

He sighed, feeling the cold now himself. "I never thought I'd say my life was easier when you and Ellen were two. Maggie, do you know anything about Beau McGarrity? Anything at all?"

She shook her head. "No. Why?"

"He's never come to you, tried to follow you—"

"God, Dad." Her cheeks were pale now. *"No."*

"Ellen?"

"She's never said anything. I mean, she would have. You know Ellen."

Ellen didn't keep secrets. It was one of the few things Jack still knew for sure about his family. Ellen didn't keep secrets, and Maggie did. He slung an arm over her shoulders. "Come on, before you freeze solid. Let's go inside and warm up." And he forced himself to add, "We'll talk about Beau McGarrity."

Alice dreamed about Rachel McGarrity all through the night and woke up exhausted, wrung out. She'd stumbled down to breakfast, but couldn't eat. A piece of toast, juice. She brought a cup of coffee back to her room with her. She hadn't run into Destin. That was something.

A quiet knock on her door pulled her out of her thoughts. "Alice? Alice, open up. It's me, Destin."

Lie down with dogs, Alice, honey, and don't be surprised when you come up with fleas.

She should have listened to her grandma. She had been an uncomplicated woman with a clear sense of right and wrong. Would *she* ever have befriended Rachel? Done work for her on the sly? Would her grandma have cut corners to save her own neck and bring Rachel's murderer to justice?

No. Grandma never would have become a police officer in the first place. She thought there was only a hair's difference between a cop and a thug. Work hard, keep your head low, save your money. Don't gamble, don't drink, don't smoke. Pick one man, and make sure he's a good one. Then treat him right.

Most of her grandma's advice Alice hadn't followed very well.

"Come on, let me in."

Destin spoke in a panicked whisper, but that was Destin. He was highly emotional with a sense of entitlement he'd use to justify anything, provided he got what he was after. Everyone in the world was supposed to realize what he wanted was all important. He didn't care how they got the money off Susanna. Honest was good. Dishonest was good. So long as he got what he wanted.

Then again, he wasn't a killer. He'd balk at killing. He might put a knife to Susanna's throat, but he'd never cut it.

He preferred to get his money the easy way—for Susanna to recognize his brilliance and give it to him.

Alice had learned a lot about Destin Wright in the past couple of days.

She dragged herself to the door and opened it for him. He slipped in like he had the Gestapo on his tail and quickly shut the door behind him, raking a hand through his blond hair as he paced. *"Jesus."*

He stopped a second, catching his breath. "Susanna and Iris are here."

Alice pulled the tie on her robe tight. She doubted Destin even noticed she was naked underneath it. He had a one-track mind, and it was on his hundred grand. "Here at the inn?" she asked, staying calm.

"They're talking old times downstairs with the owners."

"I suppose it makes sense if Iris grew up here. We should have picked a different place to stay, but this is the closest to Susanna's cabin." Alice realized Destin was too agitated to listen. "Do you think they saw my car?"

"I don't know. We hid it pretty well. If Jack finds out I'm up here with you—" He shook his head. "I don't know what made me think I could do this shit. Damn."

Cold feet. Just what she needed. "You believe in yourself, don't you? You believe in your company. How bad do you want that money?"

"Susanna's just being selfish and short-sighted. If we can just make her see, give her the right jolt—"

"Fear'll do that to you," Alice said. "Give you a jolt."

He made a face. "Damn right. I've been scared for weeks. Hell, once they took my BMW—that was a jolt."

Alice didn't want to think about it. He was willing to put the screws to Susanna over a repossessed BMW. That was what had tripped his switch from pleading with Susanna to hooking up with an ex-con and following her to the Adirondacks. Alice's own reasons wouldn't have passed muster with her grandma, she knew, but at least she was trying to get to a place where she wouldn't have to resort to cutting corners. She would lead a good life once she got to Australia.

She didn't want to *hurt* Susanna, just get some money off her. Alice knew she was damn near to popping up on Beau McGarrity's hit list. That lent more urgency to her mission with Destin. Get the money and clear out before McGarrity caught up to her. Susanna would probably understand, if she knew the truth. A hundred grand for an idiot like Destin— Alice could see Susanna not going for that. But for herself? For a woman who'd only tried to do good and now just needed cash for a fresh start? Susanna had to understand that.

Ranger Jack wouldn't. No way. Alice would be in handcuffs and on her way back to prison.

"What're we going to do?" Destin asked.

"Ratchet up the pressure."

She sat on the edge of her bed, trying to think fast. She'd learned to juggle options and pieces of information faster in prison—it was a matter of survival. But she was still a plodder. It was in all her fitness reports. *Alice Parker needs to think faster on her feet.* If she were better at it, she probably wouldn't have made such a mess of the crime scene when she'd seen her monogrammed change purse in Rachel's blood and realized Beau was trying to frame her.

Destin resumed his pacing, occasionally raking both hands through his hair and pausing at the mirror above her dresser to sigh at his reflection.

"What if you go back to Susanna's cabin?" she said.

He turned around and shook his head. "I didn't make any headway with her out there yesterday. She just said no, no, no." He sounded like a three-year-old. "Then Jack showed up. Man, that guy scares me. He did *not* like me being there."

Alice stood up and took him by the arm, squeezing it. "*Listen* to me, damn it. You need to go on over there and toss the place, make it look as if somebody went through there looking for something. Make it look purposeful, but leave scars. You know, enough of a mess so they know someone was there."

"What the hell for? We found out what we needed to know at Iris's place. We *know* Susanna's worth ten million—"

"This isn't for information. This is for effect."

"For Christ's sake, if I get caught—"

"You're Susanna's friend. You've known Iris all your life. You grew up in her neighborhood. If you get caught, you just say you stopped by for a visit, heard a noise and came in to check it out, and here's the place tossed. You fall back on your friendship."

He breathed out, still uncertain. "Do you think this'll work?"

"Yes, but I can't explain why. Susanna's up here for a reason, and we can use it to our advantage. She doesn't like to be afraid, let me put it that way." Alice wasn't sure she was making any sense, but she couldn't think of another option that would both put pressure on Susanna and convince Beau that Susanna did indeed still have the tape and Alice had gotten it from her. "You're the one who said we need to get under her skin. Once she realizes it's just easier to give you the money than have you pestering her—"

"Not give," Destin said. "She's investing in a company that'll turn her lousy hundred thousand into millions. She'll get back every dime and then some."

"Right." And her eyewitness was going to put Beau McGarrity on death row, not land her own butt in state prison. "I think this can work, Destin. At least let's give it a shot."

"It's not risk-free, but if I do it right—well, it's about as close to being risk-free as anything I can think of that'd get to Susanna. She'll bite. I know it. We'll work things out between us, too. This'll prove how committed I am to this idea."

It'd prove what a greedy jackass he was, but Susanna probably already knew that.

"I have to do something dramatic to convince her," he went on. "I know she thinks I'm a has-been."

Alice had known people like him in prison. Blaming everybody else for why they were serving time. Their lawyers, the judge, society, the system. At least she didn't blame anyone but herself. She'd made mistakes the night she found Rachel McGarrity, and because of them, she'd gone to prison and Beau McGarrity was still a free man.

"You don't have to steal anything," she told Destin. "That'd put you in real trouble with the law. You'd never be able to explain swiping petty cash off the kitchen table."

He eyed her, rubbing the back of his neck. "I hear you."

"It's a beautiful day. Everyone at breakfast was excited about the fresh snow. Iris and Susanna are obviously seeing the sights, but I bet Jack and the twins are out, too. You want to be careful, though, and make sure he didn't head out on his own and leave Maggie and Ellen back at the cabin.''

''Right.''

Destin was with the program, serious now, seeing the possibilities as his optimism and entitlement started working together again. Alice was also feeling better. ''We should clear out of here. I'll check us out after you leave. You can hike into the cabin again—I don't know, say you're investigating the ice-fishing if someone asks.''

''We'll need to meet somewhere.''

Alice nodded. She'd already thought of this. ''The north end of Blackwater Lake is owned by a rich family that never comes up here anymore. Iris told me about them. Anyway, there's a geological survey map of the lake on the wall by the front desk downstairs. Take a look at it on your way out. There's a house up there, not right on the shore but close—it's marked on the map.''

Destin frowned. ''You expect me to hike out to Susanna's cabin, then all the way up to the north end of the lake?''

''It's not as far as you might think. It's shorter, actually, to go on foot along the lake than to drive. You'll see when you look at the map. I can park at the house and hike down to the lake—there's a little teahouse on the shore where we can meet.'' She smiled, trying to encourage him. ''I'll bring you hot coffee.''

''I don't know—''

''Destin, if anything happens, no one will think to look for us there. It'll buy us time to get out of town." She sighed. "Look, it's the best I can do. If you have a better idea, now's the time."

"No—no, this'll work. I thought about training for Everest, you know, back when I had money, so the snow and the cold won't bother me."

Because he'd *thought* about training for Everest. Alice didn't say a word.

He headed for the door, his eyes shining again with enthusiasm. "I think Susanna'll go for half a million."

Alice resisted rolling her eyes. She no longer felt so smart for having hooked up with Destin Wright, ex-millionaire. But there was more bounce in his step when he left, checking up and down the hall before he darted out into the hall, like the Nazis were still after him.

She flopped on her bed and stared up at the ceiling, the bright morning light doing nothing for her mood. She didn't know if her plan made any real sense— after all, how well had she done when she'd found Rachel dead? She thought she'd done some good thinking then, too.

She had come to at least one conclusion. Beau McGarrity was a bigger problem for her than Jack Galway. Jack would toss her back in prison if she crossed the line. Beau would kill her.

She sighed at the ceiling. "I am no good at this shit."

Then she jumped up off the bed and grabbed some clothes. Damn northern winters. She was freezing.

Fourteen

❧⟨❧⟩❧

Susanna waited with Gran in a small, cozy sitting room off the wide hall where Paul and Sarah Johnson, the young couple who owned Blackwater Inn, had set up their reception desk. They'd decorated the room in warm tones of deep green and honey, and it had a bay window that looked onto the lake. Gran stared out at the snow-covered landscape. "This is the room where my mother died," she said quietly.

"Gran, if you want to leave—"

"No, let's wait for Audrey...Alice."

Susanna sat on an elegant upholstered chair. She and Gran had decided to stop at the inn first, before going to the cemetery. The Johnsons had greeted Gran as if she were a living legend. In a way, she was. She was Iris Dunning, the daughter of renowned Adirondack guide John Dunning, a famous guide in her own right. The Johnsons proudly showed off the wall of old pictures they'd collected and framed of the inn's early days. Gran couldn't bring herself even to look at them.

Embarrassed by their enthusiasm, Sarah Johnson

had pulled Susanna aside and apologized. "It's easy for us to forget your grandmother experienced terrible tragedy here. Sixty years seems like such a long time to us, but for her—it must be like the blink of an eye."

"She's never said much about her past here," Susanna said simply. It was an understatement. Gran *never* talked about her life on Blackwater Lake.

Paul Johnson added, "Nobody around here thinks of the scandal anymore."

"No," his wife said, "absolutely not."

He nodded. "We all think of Iris Dunning as a truly remarkable woman in the history of this region."

Gran had made a noise, turning to the young couple. "That sounds like an epitaph. You'd think I've been dead all these years instead of living a few hours away in Boston."

That was when Susanna had decided to ask about Destin Wright. Jack would no doubt consider this treading on his turf, but at this point she didn't care—she'd needed a change in subject. Eager to make amends, the Johnsons told her that Destin had checked into the inn with Audrey Melbourne the day before. They were both in. Did Susanna want to see them?

They'd called up and Audrey—Alice—was on her way down now. They hadn't been able to reach Destin and assumed he must have gone out.

Susanna glanced at her grandmother after the Johnsons excused themselves. What tragedy? What scandal? She knew only the bare outlines of her grandmother's life before she'd moved to Boston.

Susanna admitted she was madly curious, but Gran's reaction to the innkeepers' innocent missteps encouraged caution. She didn't want to push for details her grandmother might be reluctant to share with her—or thought were none of her damn business. This was Gran's *life* they were talking about.

"I told Alice about this place," Gran said. "That viper. She made herself so easy to talk to, pretending to be interested in my life—"

"Maybe she was interested, Gran. People are complicated."

She waved a hand, impatient. "I was indulging myself. I thought she wanted to know what I'd been through to help her sort out her own life."

"Don't beat up yourself—"

"I'm not. I'm merely stating the facts." She shook her head, her eyes never leaving the beautiful view of the lake. "Jimmy Haviland will never let me hear the end of this one. He was suspicious of her from the start."

"Not so suspicious that he told me about her right away," Susanna said. "He waited several weeks before he said anything."

Alice Parker entered the room with a snap to her step and no indication she'd done anything wrong by turning up on Blackwater Lake. She wasn't taking any pains to pretend she was here for the winter outdoor sports. She wore tight jeans, a close-fitting rib-knit teal sweater, western boots and lots of gold jewelry. "Hello, ma'am," she said politely to Iris, then nodded at Susanna. "Mrs. Galway."

Iris spoke first. "You lied to me, Miss Parker."

"About some things, ma'am, yes, I did." Her tone

was apologetic if not contrite. "But I didn't lie about everything. Not most things."

"Your name. Why you were in Boston. You never mentioned that my granddaughter's husband investigated you."

Alice fiddled with one of her rings. "I am truly sorry, Ms. Dunning. I never meant to upset you. This inn—this country up here—" she paused, but went on again in that same sincere but steady tone "—it's all as pretty as you said."

"I never lied to you," Iris said.

"No, ma'am, you didn't."

Gran eased onto the window seat, sitting sideways on the honey-and-green brocade cushion, her back to Susanna and Alice, as if they'd both offended her. With a pang of regret, Susanna wondered if buying her cabin on Blackwater Lake was more of an intrusion into her grandmother's life than she'd realized. In hindsight, she should have consulted Gran first, instead of acting on impulse. But it was as if she'd been moved along by a force greater than herself. Once she saw the lake, the cabin, the snow-covered mountains, she wasn't sure she'd had any choice at all.

"You came here with Destin Wright," Susanna said.

Alice nodded. "Yes, we struck up a friendship at Jim's Place."

"Did he tell you he's after me for money?"

"Well, we talked about the new company he's working on." She shrugged her slender shoulders, tossing back her red curls. "I don't know much about business, I'm afraid. He said he needs—what does he call it? Some kind of money.''

"Angel money," Susanna supplied, her tone neutral.

"That's right. I'm not involved in any of that. I just wanted to see the Adirondacks and get out of town, figure out what to do now that I was persona non grata in your neighborhood." She smiled matter-of-factly. "I have to tell you, after being in prison all those months, I don't even mind the cold up here."

Susanna refused to let herself get distracted, either by Alice shifting the subject or trying to charm her. It couldn't have been easy for Jack to investigate her. "Did Destin tell you that Jack is here?"

"Your husband. Yes, Destin told me. I guess Lieutenant Galway would think it a provocation, me showing up right down the street from you."

"That's what we all think, Alice," Susanna said calmly. She supposed Jack would want her to stop here, leave and tell him that Alice was at the inn—not let her irritation and concern get the better of her. "He ran into someone at Gran's house the other night and got hit on the head."

"Lieutenant Galway?" Alice looked surprised—or did a good job of it. "Do I look as if I could get the jump on him? I'll bet you I'm not even half his size."

"You're an experienced police officer."

"And he's a Texas Ranger. I'm sorry he got hit, and I can see how you all might think I had something to do with it. Well, I didn't. So, you either prove I did, or you leave me alone. I've served my time. I'm not on parole. I can come and go as I please, provided I don't break the law.''

She was right, and Susanna sighed reluctantly and nodded. "Fair enough. Do you know where Destin is? I'd like to talk to him."

"He wanted to try bobsledding. I think he might have hitched a ride with someone. I don't really know." Alice shrugged, losing interest. "We're just here for a good time."

"It was his idea?"

"I don't know, we just got to talking about you all coming up here, and how I was curious about it, after what Miss Iris had told me—" She stopped, frowning. "How many more questions do you have for me, Mrs. Galway?"

Susanna didn't answer. Gran turned from the lake and got slowly to her feet. "Alice, I think you should talk to Jack, before you get in over your head and do something you regret."

Alice's mouth snapped shut. She seemed insulted. "How stupid do you think I am?"

"How did you land up in prison?" Gran went on, her eyes vivid and alive now, relentless. "You got in over your head, and you did something you regretted. No doubt it all seemed to make sense at the time, but in retrospect, I suspect not. We tend to repeat our mistakes, you know, until we learn from them."

Alice was breathing rapidly, a flush spreading from her face down her neck. She seemed taken aback at Iris's straightforward words—her insight. But she said nothing, and Susanna remembered her brief conversation with Jack before they'd left for

Blackwater Inn. Sam Temple was on his way to Boston.

"Beau McGarrity," Susanna said, before she could stop herself. "Do you know where he is?"

"No, but he worries me."

"If you still have the tape I gave to you, I'd like you to give it to Jack and let him listen to it. I've assumed all this time it's irrelevant, but—I'm not making any more assumptions."

Alice stood in front of Susanna and touched her shoulder, her fingers ice-cold even through Susanna's heavy sweater. Her gray eyes were intense, and she said in a low voice, "There's nothing on that tape anyone can use against Beau. I'd have given it to your husband if I'd thought it would have made a difference."

"But you still have it?"

She shrugged, evasive. "Mrs. Galway, Ms. Dunning—you don't have to believe me, but I just did what I thought was right, no matter how it turned out."

The sunlight caught the wrinkles in Gran's face, but they didn't make her look drawn and ancient— they made her look very alive, a woman who'd lived a full life. She didn't know anything about the tape, but wouldn't ask Susanna about it in front of a friend who'd betrayed her. "If you hadn't lied to us, Alice, we might give you more credit now."

"There's so much you all don't know." Alice flopped onto a second love seat, looking petulant and stubborn and very young, not at all like a small-town Texas police officer or an ex-convict. "Rachel McGarrity—she and I were friends. That's why Beau called me that night to find her body. I know it was him. I can't *prove* it, but I know. And you, Miss Susanna. You think he started following you after he killed his wife. Well, that's not true.''

Susanna jumped to her feet and stared at her, aware she was giving Alice the shocked reaction she wanted. ''What do you mean?''

''I mean Mr. Beau looked you up *before* Rachel was killed.''

''When?'' Her voice was choked, and she only just managed to stay on her feet. ''I never saw him before Jack started investigating you. How do you know?''

''Rachel was interested in you and your folks in Austin. She wanted me to do some investigative work for her on the side, but I never got much of it done—she never clued me in to the big picture. Beau must have got wind of what she was up to and followed you. After Rachel died, we—the police didn't find anything that linked back up to you. I don't know, maybe there was nothing, or maybe Beau got rid of it before he killed her.''

Susanna couldn't speak.

Alice raised her eyes, and they were cool now, with a slight gleam of victory. ''I followed Beau right to your door.''

''When?''

''A week or so before Rachel's murder. Your daughters were still at school. You were out front working in the garden. He parked across the street, got out of his car and watched you for about five or ten minutes. Never said a word. And you didn't look at him. When you went around back, he got into his car and drove away.'' She sank back against the soft cushions in the attractive sunroom. ''He did pretty much the same thing a couple days later, except this time you got in your car. He followed you while you picked up your daughters at school.''

''Did you know who I was, that my husband's a Texas Ranger?''

She nodded. ''I imagine we both did.''

''Why didn't you say something?''

She shrugged, without arrogance or defensiveness now that she had Susanna reeling. ''I told Rachel. We were still trying to figure out what was going on when she was killed. You have to understand, Mrs. Galway, we had no idea Beau was going to do what he did. Not a clue in the world. Rachel was a very private woman, but I think she'd have gotten around to telling me everything. She just didn't live that long.''

''Alice,'' Susanna said, her voice hoarse from tension, ''please tell me the truth. Did you tell the detectives on the murder investigation, your chief of police, my husband—*anyone*—about Beau McGarrity following me? About Rachel McGarrity's interest in me?''

She shook her head. ''No. I didn't want anyone to know I was friends with Rachel. It would have complicated everything. Maybe if I'd had proof.'' She lifted her small shoulders and let them drop, sighing. ''I was up against someone smarter and meaner than I am.''

Susanna said nothing. She was reeling, her mind flooded with thoughts and images and a thousand different questions.

Alice didn't move from the love seat. "Maybe you can see now why I came to Boston. I was worried Beau McGarrity might come after you. I thought maybe that's why you were up here—because you were afraid of him." She swallowed. "I guess none of that matters now."

"You know I'm going to tell Jack everything."

"That's what I've always assumed," Alice said, her eyes bright, a little smug. "That you'd tell Lieutenant Galway everything."

Susanna ignored the jibe. "He'll want to talk to you."

"Fine. Let him talk to me."

"Come on, Gran," Susanna said. "I promised to take you to the cemetery. Let's go."

They left Alice Parker on the love seat, gazing out at the Adirondack view. Susanna briefly debated calling the local police and asking them to sit on Alice until she could get Jack out here, but Alice seemed willing to wait—and talk.

Susanna followed Gran out into the hall, feeling hot and breathless, as if she'd been running up and down the inn's stairs instead of chatting in a slightly cool sunroom. Her great-grandmother had died in there. Gran's mum. Suddenly she was overwhelmed, wondering what Rose Dunning must have been like, how they'd all ended up here so many decades after her death—her daughter, Susanna, Alice Parker, Destin Wright.

They said goodbye to the Johnsons, and Gran added that she thought their inn was wonderful. They seemed pleased, and even a little relieved.

When they reached the parking lot, Gran said, "Her parents are alcoholics."

"Whose? Alice's?"

"'Total no-accounts,' she called them." Gran half smiled, pulling open the car door. "She has an engaging manner when she isn't so focused on how all her good intentions have never amounted to anything."

Susanna felt bile rise up in her throat. Alice Parker had never told Jack or her or *anyone* that Beau McGarrity followed her before his wife was killed. That was a serious omission. It was more than good intentions gone awry.

"She told me she always wanted to be a Texas Ranger," Gran said, seemingly oblivious to the February cold. The bright sun caught her face, making her eyes seem less vivid, more serious somehow. "She's the type who's always living her life in the future, never in the present. That's the easiest way of all to lie to yourself, I think, by not looking in the mirror and being honest with yourself about who you are."

Susanna touched her grandmother's thin shoulder. Maybe the trip to the inn had been too much for her—the memories, Alice Parker, the talk of murder and stalking. "Gran, are you okay?"

She smiled gently, covering Susanna's hand with hers for a moment. "I'm just fine. What about you, love? Are *you* okay?"

"I have to talk to Jack."

"Yes, you do. You've had to talk to him for a long time."

* * *

Susanna followed her grandmother to the far end of the snow-covered cemetery, to the Dunning family plot, a dozen or so graves enclosed within a low stone wall. Gran climbed over the stone wall unaided, seemingly oblivious to the cold wind and knee-deep snow that drifted up against the tombstones. She had her red knit hat pulled tightly down over her ears, but her pants were more suited to a trip to her senior center in Somerville than trekking in an Adirondack cemetery.

A biting gust of wind rocked Susanna back on her heels, but Gran didn't seem to notice. She came to a pair of simple, matching headstones and sank onto her knees, brushing the snow off the stones with her gloved hands. Susanna stood behind her, worried that the winter conditions were too hard on her grandmother. Perhaps they should have waited until summer.

The graves were of her parents, Rose and John Dunning.

"No one believed my father would die an ordinary death," Gran said. "He was a risk-taker, he loved the mountains. He respected their dangers, but he never let fear stop him from doing what he wanted to do. And what he wanted to do was spend as much time as he could in the mountains."

"How did he die?" Susanna asked.

"Bee sting. He got stung while he was working on the dock in front of the inn and was dead in fifteen minutes."

Susanna looked at the dates and did the math. He was forty-eight when he died, Gran just twenty. Her mother died a year later.

"Everyone thought he'd die on a mountain," Gran went on quietly, "or out on the lake rescuing someone in a storm. Or he'd live to be a very old man, and when he was done, he'd walk into the wilderness and go to sleep. He was an extraordinary man. He taught me as much as he could about these mountains."

"I'm sorry I never knew him," Susanna said.

"My mother was hard-working, forbidding in many ways. She kept the inn running and the family in food and clothes. That wasn't my father. But she loved it here as much as he did, and she loved him. She was devastated when he died." Gran stood up slowly, balancing herself with one hand on her mother's tombstone. "Those were difficult years."

"Dad was just a baby when you lost both your parents."

"Yes, he was all that kept me going." She gestured at some of the other graves. "Those are two of Father's cousins and several people Mother knew from her nursing days in Saranac, former tuberculosis patients who came to work for us at the inn."

She lifted her leg high and stepped into a deep drift of snow, pushing forward to another headstone in the opposite corner of the plot. Susanna, worried about her grandmother now, stayed with her, ready to catch her if she stumbled.

"Here we are," Gran said under her breath, stumbling in front of a pink granite marker. "Oh, Jared…"

Susanna put her arm around her grandmother. "Gran, you're freezing. I don't want to rush you, but we can always come back here when it's warmer—"

"I'm fine." She glanced up at Susanna, her eyes shining. "This is your grandfather." She pulled off a glove and ran her fingertips over the name carved in stone. *Jared Rutherford Herrington.* "He had the bluest eyes. He was a preppy, square-jawed Princeton graduate from a very wealthy family. They still own most of the north end of Blackwater Lake."

Susanna had never known her grandfather's name. She wasn't even sure her father knew it. "Why is he buried here?" she asked.

"Because of me."

"Gran…"

"I took my father's place as Jared's guide on a day hike up Whiteface Mountain. He was twenty-five, and I was eighteen—we fell in love on our way up the mountain. I can remember—" She shut her eyes tightly and smiled. "All of it. Every minute we had together."

Susanna tried to picture her grandmother at eighteen, madly in love with a handsome Ivy Leaguer. "What was he like?"

"He was smart, charming, well-traveled, much better read than I. He used to write me poetry. I knew the mountains, every inch of Blackwater Lake, and I was down to earth—we were so in love. But there was a problem," she said, looking up at the blue sky, as if she could see him. "He was married."

Susanna remained silent, sensing what it cost her grandmother to talk about her past.

"He had a son," Gran went on. "He loved his little boy very much, and I think but for him—well, those were different times. It was an unhappy marriage, for both of them. He'd asked for a divorce, but agreed to come up here for a few months separation. He was supposed to be hiking and canoeing, not carrying on with a girl guide. But when he told me he had a wife—I was furious.'' She tucked her hand into Susanna's, pulling herself to her feet, wisps of white hair coming loose out of her hat. ''He left her late that summer and asked me to marry him as soon as the divorce was final. We never had that chance.''

''My God, Gran.'' Susanna could feel the tears in her eyes. She'd seen the date on her grandfather's grave. A few months before her father was born. ''I'm so sorry.''

''He went out one day on the lake, alone. And he never came back. I found him that winter, five months later. I was snowshoeing on my own, debating whether I should fling myself off a cliff or cut a circle in the ice and jump in.''

Susanna held back her shock. ''Because you were pregnant?''

''Pregnant, alone, despairing of ever finding happiness again. I was thinking about whether I'd freeze to death or drown first if I went into the water when suddenly here at my feet was this man I loved. He must have tripped over a rock or a tree root and hit his head. Just like that, and it was over.'' A sudden strength came into her step, and she pushed through the snow toward the stonewall. ''I knew then that I had to carry on.''

''Your parents—''

''They accepted what had happened, and your father was such a charming baby—how could they not accept him? Then my father died, and my mother came down with a sudden, virulent case of tuberculosis, of all things. It took her so quickly. There was no chance for her to cure.''

"You lost everyone you loved in such a short time. Gran, my God, I don't know how you survived.''

"Because I didn't lose everyone.'' She smiled up at Susanna. "I had Kevin. I had Jared's son. *My* son. I sold the inn and worked as a guide for as long as I could. I'd strap Kevin on my back, and off we'd go. But those were hard years, and I knew I couldn't stay here. So, I moved to the city and started over.''

A breeze floated through the evergreens, whistling slightly, almost eerily, as they climbed over the low stone wall.

Gran wasn't even breathing hard. "I've had a good life, Susanna, if not always a happy one.''

"I think I understand.''

"Oh, you don't understand a thing.'' She spoke without any edge or condescension, simply stating a fact that was obvious to her. "Life brings with it hardship and loneliness from time to time. I learned to move forward from where I am, not to keep insisting I ought to be where I once was, not to keep dreaming about where I might be one day. To truly embrace where I am.''

Susanna sensed where her grandmother was headed and smiled, trying to veer her off subject. "Did you learn to talk this way in your seniors' yoga class?''

But Gran wasn't letting her off the hook. "Do you understand what I'm saying?''

"Sure. Live for today—''

"*No.*'' Gran shook her head, impatient. "Figure

out where you are and move forward from there, that point and no other. That's different from living for today.''

"Gran, if you're talking about Jack—''

"I'm talking about *you*. You can't move forward until you know where you are.''

Susanna gave up. "Okay.''

Her grandmother cast her a sideways glance. "You're a smart-mouth, Susanna Dunning Galway. I can see how you give that husband of yours a run for his money.''

"Most of the time he deserves it, you know.''

"I imagine that's a two-way street.'' They came to the car, and Gran paused, looking out at the cemetery, the snow, the evergreens, the blue sky. "It's lovely here, isn't it?''

"Yes, it is.''

"But I don't want you burying me here. I'll have to put it in my will. I want to be incinerated and my ashes scattered in Florida.''

"Florida?'' Susanna shook her head in disbelief. "You've never even been to Florida!''

"Yes, I have. I went with Muriel in 1963. I remember, because it was right after JFK was assassinated. Her family stuck her in a cold grave in Malden.''

"Gran, are you serious?''

She smiled then, breathing in the cold, dry Adirondack winter air. "Yes, by God, I think I want my ashes scattered on Miami Beach.''

Fifteen

❧⟨✦⟩❧

Jack fell three times cross-country skiing before he figured out he was leaning too far back and throwing off his center of balance. Maggie and Ellen thought it was hysterical to watch him fall. They were on a groomed trail at a cross-country ski center a few miles from the cabin. No lesson. He thought he'd remember enough, and the girls said they could show him what to do. Overreach on both counts. They weren't much better on skinny skis than he was.

They rounded a curve, Maggie and Ellen ahead of him. "I don't laugh when you fall," he commented.

Ellen glanced back at him and grinned. "That's because it's not as funny when it's us."

Probably not.

Their beginner trail looped through an evergreen forest on a rare stretch of flat land. They had to stay far enough apart to keep from crashing into each other, which created a sense of separateness and allowed them to experience their surroundings without having to be out there all alone.

The rhythmic gliding over the snow helped his thoughts settle, simmer, refocus.

The call from Sam Temple had flipped this situation into a higher gear. Alice Parker contacted Beau McGarrity before she moved to Boston, and now he'd left town. Jack had already learned that Alice was a mix of good intentions, guile, loyalty, strong survival instincts and romantic ideas about herself—all of which, together, had landed her in prison.

This was no longer about a nonviolent ex-convict showing up in his wife's neighborhood. However provocative, it wasn't illegal. It was also about an open, if cold, murder investigation.

Beau wouldn't want the tape of him coercing a Texas Ranger's wife to intervene on his behalf to go public. If it wouldn't convict him of murdering Rachel McGarrity, it would certainly reveal him as a desperate man who'd stepped over the line. Public opinion would shift right back against him. He could kiss his social and political comeback goodbye.

Was Alice trying to blackmail him with the tape? Extort money from him to finance her dream of a new life in Australia?

Where the hell did Destin Wright fit in, if anywhere?

And his wife. Where did Susanna fit in? The tape would be more valuable if she'd kept it. It wouldn't be tainted by Alice's misconduct in the Rachel McGarrity investigation. Was Alice trying to make it look as if Susanna had never given her the damn thing?

Shaking down a murder suspect was just the kind of complicated, dramatic, dumb-ass scheme that would appeal to Alice Parker. Jack had investigated her—she was dedicated and well-liked, but law enforcement wasn't a good fit for her personality and abilities. Another woman on the town force described her as drawn to the idea of law enforcement, not its reality.

Jack tucked his poles under his arms and coasted down a long, gentle slope, not feeling the cold after ninety minutes of cross-country skiing. He, Maggie and Ellen made their way to the warming hut, leaning their skis against a rail fence and heading inside for hot cider. The cider was in a big pot on a woodstove, and Jack filled three mugs and brought them back to the small, rickety table where the girls had plopped down, flushed from the exercise and the cold.

"Mom would love this place," Maggie said, blowing on her steaming cider. "She told us we could forget any notions of sitting in the cabin all week, reading books and watching the fire—we were to get out and ski, snowshoe, enjoy the great outdoors."

Jack leaned back in his wooden chair, smiling. "Is that a note of sarcasm I hear?"

She smiled back. "Dad, she bought us *snowshoes.*"

He shrugged. "This vacation means a lot to her."

"I think she fell in love with it up here," Ellen says. "What if she moves up here? I know it's beautiful and everything, but, Dad, she'd go bonkers."

Not with the kind of money she had in the bank, Jack thought. If she got bored, she could afford to do something else—like rent a villa in the south of France for a month. Although he had strong opinions on where his wife should live, he decided a measured response was called for. "Your mother will figure out what she wants to do. We can have our opinions, but we can't do it for her, anymore than she and I can decide for you what college you ought to attend."

"But she's almost forty," Ellen said.

Jack smiled. "And?"

"She should already have her life figured out."

"Maybe it needs refiguring."

Maggie stretched out one leg, wincing as she ran her hand along an obviously stiff muscle. "Do you think Mom's having a midlife crisis?" she asked. "Maybe she got herself in a panic about Ellen and me not being around. Our guidance counselor at school talked to us about how our parents might have problems of their own with us leaving for college. We're not the only ones experiencing change."

"I thought guidance counselors were supposed to talk to you about grades and colleges and not screwing around in the lunch room."

"They do," Maggie said, "but that's not all."

Jack drank some of his hot cider while he debated how to get off this subject. If he said the wrong thing, Susanna would hear about it. If he said the right thing, she'd hear. And this was about Maggie and Ellen's relationship with their mother, not with him, not with both of them. "So what do they do, tell you to keep an eye on your parents in case they get depressed when you go off to school?"

Maggie nodded, stretching her other leg. "It can happen even before we leave. Pre-empty nest syndrome."

He stared at her. "You're serious?"

She and Ellen both nodded.

"Do they do this in Texas, too?" he asked, teasing.

They laughed, but Ellen's laughter didn't last. "Dad," she said, avoiding his eye, "maybe if you'd tell her what you want—if you said you wanted her back—" She let it go at that, leaving the rest to her father to interpret.

His first instinct was to tell Ellen that she'd stepped into territory that was none of her business, but her concern was palpable. Maggie was drinking her cider, pretending not to care as much as her sister did. Jack knew he was on tricky ground. Whatever happened with his marriage, he and Susanna were these girls' parents. This was their immediate family, the four of them. They deserved his care and attention in addressing their concerns.

But he'd rather go through the whole business about Beau McGarrity and Sam Temple heading to Boston than to negotiate this emotional minefield.

"Ellen, I never wanted Susanna to leave." He spoke carefully, thoughtfully. "But it's not her fault she did. It took both of us. Relationships are complicated, and right now ours is probably more complicated than most."

Ellen seemed relieved that he'd treated her question seriously. "Because you're a Texas Ranger and she's a financial planner?"

"That's one reason."

"She's rich, you know," Maggie said.

Ellen nodded. "She won't tell us how much she's worth. She says we have no concept of money."

"She's right," Jack said.

Maggie, who felt she was entitled to know everything, made a face at him. "Do *you* know how much she's worth?"

He'd had enough cider and pushed his mug away. The one-room warming hut was filling up with people, not the best place to have a heart-to-heart family discussion. "We're off the subject."

"You should have called instead of just turning up in Boston," Ellen blurted.

That he didn't regret. His life with Susanna had always had its sparks. He shook his head. "She's still paying for the time she let the air out of my tires when we were in college."

Maggie's eyes lit up. "She *didn't*."

"Why would she do that?" Ellen asked.

Because she'd lost her virginity to him the night before, and when he put it that way to her, she got pissed, said it was old-fashioned and male to say something like that. Which was beside the point. She was in love with him. She knew he'd be a force in her life forever. It scared the hell out of her. So, she let the air out of his tires. He saw it as her way of asserting to him that she was smart, strong, independent and not incapable of sneak attacks.

The minute he saw his tires, he knew she was the guilty party, but it took him months to drag the truth out of her.

No shrinking violet, this love of his life. And now she was rich. *They* were rich.

But he told their teenage daughters, "I guess it seemed like the thing to do at the time."

"Gee, Dad," Ellen said, "Mom's always had guts, hasn't she?"

"Don't you two get any ideas. I could have had her arrested." Except she'd covered her tracks well. But he knew he wasn't finished with this conversation, and after they returned their skis to the rental counter and started back to Davey Ahearn's truck, Jack made himself go on. "Your mother got caught up in one of my cases through no fault of her own, and she ended up fearing for your safety—for her own. It rattled her down deep."

Maggie nodded with understanding. "The classic fight or flight impulse. Normally Mom'd fight— that's always her first impulse. Or she'd resist either impulse and think things through, analyze, choose her next move. That's what she's always telling us what to do. But this time, she fled." She gave her father a small smile. "I took psychology last semester."

"You could be right, Mag, I don't know. But I might have handled things differently if she'd run up to Boston just because she was bored with me—"

"Mom's never bored with you," Ellen said. "She tells us that all the time—*your father's never boring*. But, Dad, be honest, it's not just this Alice Parker thing. It wouldn't hurt if you—well, you know you're about as romantic as a rock."

"Aren't you two being old-fashioned? All this talk of wooing, flowers, fancy soaps—"

Maggie shook her head. "If you needed a break from Mom because *she* was an uncommunicative lunkhead, we'd tell *her* to be more romantic."

"I'd get flowers and fancy soaps?"

"Dad." Ellen smothered a laugh, trying to be serious. "We know Mom's a hardheaded businesswoman. We've had her go MBA on us, just like you go Texas Ranger on us."

Her sister nodded in agreement, and Jack saw their pride in their mother's accomplishments. Ellen said, "We're not being retro. We're just—I mean, who doesn't like to be romanced? You and Mom need more flowers and silk nighties and jewelry and stuff like that going on."

"Less murder and money," Maggie added.

Jack knew he was beat. There was nothing to do now but concede and get the hell off this subject. He was supposed to give Susanna flowers, silk nighties, fancy soaps and jewelry—and he couldn't even get a decent blanket off her.

"Point well taken," he said, neutral.

"If it's any consolation," Maggie said, "whenever Mom calls you a rock-headed son of a bitch, she always apologizes and says she didn't mean it that way."

He cast his daughter a look. "What way do you suppose she did mean it?"

But they all laughed, and he knew it was tough treating Maggie and Ellen like adults—damn tough. Probably would take him a few more years to get used to it.

They piled back into Davey's truck. Maggie made exaggerated gagging noises at the stale smell of cigarettes, as she had when she'd climbed in the first time. Ellen brought up Davey Ahearn, Tess Haviland and the dead body in Tess's dirt cellar last spring, another reminder of Susanna's life without him. Jack remembered she'd called and checked with him about how long it took a body to decompose. He should have known something was up.

When they got back to the cabin, Susanna's car was still gone. All in all, Jack preferred taking Maggie and Ellen cross-country skiing to escorting Iris to a cemetery. As they charged into the cabin, nestled cozily amidst the trees and lake, he could feel the ache, knew he wanted to stay here and break in his new snowshoes, maybe try a little ice-fishing. He wanted to spend time with his family. But he had to check with Sam and see about Beau McGarrity, Alice Parker and, perhaps, Destin Wright.

"Dad! Oh, my God!"

Maggie. Jack ran for the cabin. Ellen was yelling now, panic raising the pitch of her voice. "Dad, Dad—*no, Maggie, don't!* What if they're still here?"

He grabbed a ski pole in the mud room. Ellen, white-faced, burst from the kitchen. She was hyperventilating. "Dad, Maggie went upstairs. Someone— someone's—"

He reached into his pocket for his cell phone. "Call the police."

She was blinking rapidly, gulping in air. Purple and white blotches had broken out on her face. "They took the place apart. Maggie…" Suddenly she was a little girl again, hanging on to his hand. *"Daddy."*

Jack curled her stiff fingers around the cell phone. "911. Go."

She nodded, damn near passing out, and headed outside.

The kitchen was tossed. Cupboards opened, drawers pulled out, towels, food and utensils thrown on the floor. In the living room, the couch cushions were off, the throw blankets scattered, the bookshelves dumped. Half the castle puzzle had ended up on the floor.

"Maggie, where the hell are you?"

"It's okay, Dad." She appeared at the top of the stairs, as pale as her sister, but glaring down at him with a greater, more immediate sense of indignation. She clenched the handrail. "Whatever *bastard* did this is gone."

"Maggie." Jack started up the stairs with his ski pole. "Go outside with Ellen. She's calling the police. Then call your mother. Wait for me." He thrust the truck keys at her. "If anyone but me comes out of this cabin, get out of here."

"Dad, I checked up here—there's no one—"

"Downstairs. Outside. Now, Maggie."

Her mouth snapped shut, and she complied, her feet barely touching the steps as she slid past him. No ski pole for her. She'd done her checking unarmed, which Jack knew was just as well given her inexperience.

Whoever had tossed the place had lost steam by the time they reached the second floor. Given his daughters' level of neatness, Jack couldn't tell what all had been dumped and gone through in their shared bedroom and what they'd done themselves.

In Iris's room, the mattress was askew, and her clothes were hanging out of her dresser drawers, her empty suitcase upended.

The sofa bed in the loft was similarly roughed up.

An amateur. Someone who wanted to make it look as if he'd done a thorough job.

Jack checked Susanna's bedroom downstairs. The same thing.

He went back outside and found the girls in the truck, both doors wide open. Ellen was behind the wheel, calmer now but still shaken. "I got through to the police," she told him. "It took a couple of tries. They're on their way. Dad…"

"Are you two okay?" he asked, standing at the open driver's door.

They nodded. Maggie looked at him, her dark eyes serious, angry and scared, even if she'd never admit to being afraid. She was like her mother in that. "This is about Alice Parker and that murder investigation, why you and Sam are here, isn't it?"

"I don't know what it's about," Jack said. "We can guess, but that won't do any good. It could be a coincidence for all we know."

"Is that what you believe?" Maggie asked.

He shook his head. "No."

Ellen started gulping for air again. "Dad, what about Mom? What if whoever was here went after her?"

"Let's not get ahead of herself. Your mom's with Iris. They're looking at old tombstones. I'm sure they're fine."

Maggie hunched her shoulders. She'd taken off her coat and had to be cold. "Mom and Gran'll be pissed at the mess we have to clean up."

Jack knew both girls would be all right. "Do you two mind if I take a look around out here?"

They shook their heads. Ellen managed a wan smile. "No, Dad, go ahead. Go be a Texas Ranger."

When she arrived at the cabin and found Jack building a snowman, Susanna knew something was wrong. He had the bottom done and was working on the middle, and he didn't stop when she and Gran got out of the car and he told them about the break-in. The local police had been and gone. He'd told them about Alice Parker and Beau McGarrity. And Destin Wright. They were nonetheless inclined to believe it had been a local scrounging for cash, probably thinking the cabin, only recently sold, was still on the market.

Iris, her blood up, retreated inside to help the girls with the cleanup.

Susanna scooped up a handful of snow, which was just wet enough to hold together. "Alice Parker is staying with Destin at the Blackwater Inn," she said. "Gran and I just talked to her. I should have come straight here and told you, but I'd promised to take Gran to the cemetery. It's just as well, I suppose. We could have walked in on this guy tossing the cabin."

Jack remained silent as he carefully patted more snow onto the middle section of his snowman.

"She said Beau McGarrity checked me out before his wife was killed."

Jack stopped then, his dark eyes boring into her. "Jesus, Susanna."

"She never told the detectives. I don't know if she didn't think it mattered—he parked across the street and watched me in the front garden. One day he followed me out to the school."

"And this was before his wife was murdered?"

"That's what Alice said. Jack, I don't know what to believe. I don't know if she's up here to get under my skin, or if she's after McGarrity somehow, thinks I can help convict him of murder. *I don't know.*"

"You don't have to know. It's not your job."

His tone wasn't antagonistic, which somehow only made Susanna feel worse. "And Destin—who knows what he and Alice have cooked up?" She watched a chickadee perch on the very top branch of a spruce tree, then swoop off into the woods. "If I did anything to cause that woman's death—if she died in any way because of me—"

"Tell me everything Alice told you," Jack said.

Susanna nodded. "Gran was there, too. She can help fill in any blanks. Jack—" She added her snow to his snowman-in-progress. "There's something else I haven't told you. I don't know if it has any role in what's been going on—I've told myself a million times that it can't possibly, but...my God, Jack, that man followed me *before* his wife's death."

He slid that hot, dark-eyed gaze at her.

She jumped back, as if she'd been seared. "You already know?"

"I told you. I always know."

"*Damn* it, Jack. You *know?*"

He lifted his snowman's middle off its base, adjusting it, patting the snow smooth. He focused on his work, as if the damn snowman had his full attention. "Ten million dollars isn't that easy to hide."

"I wasn't hiding it—I was just not telling you about it."

"Sam's been guessing five million. I think he has a pool going."

"But you knew?"

He scooped up a palmful of snow and dumped it into a crack in the middle section. "It's an educated guess. I take it I'm not far off?"

"No."

His eyes lifted to her. "Miffed?"

"Miffed. What kind of word is that?" Her throat was tight, and she could feel tears welling. Not this time. She was *not* going to cry this time, not when someone had just ransacked her cabin and scared the hell out of her daughters. She had to stay focused, like Jack on a case. "It trivializes the importance of how I feel."

"Sort of like saying I'd taken your virginity."

"What? Where did *that* come from? We're talking about money—" She took all of him in, this tall, dark-haired, dark-eyed man in his western-cut suede jacket and his new insulated gloves and boots. No hat. He was the only man who'd ever made love to her, the only man she'd ever wanted in bed with her. She didn't know what she'd have done if she'd lost him at nineteen, if he'd gone home to south Texas without her. But she shook off the thought, because he was here, twenty years later. "Forget it, Jack. You're not going to distract me by talking about sex. Why didn't you say something if you knew?"

"You're the one who made this fortune." He took a step back and admired his handiwork, still as if his snowman were all he had on his mind. "You're the one who turned it into a problem for yourself. So, I figured you could be the one to decide when you were ready to tell me about it.''

''But you knew—''

''That's beside the point.''

''Jack, that *is* the point. Damn it, you left me to agonize over how to tell you—''

''As I told Sam this morning, you don't agonize, Susanna.'' He scooped up more snow, building a head for his snowman. ''You strategize. You were waiting for the right strategic moment to tell me, and this was it.''

''Oh, it is, is it? When my cabin's just been ransacked?''

''Apparently so.''

Susanna felt blood rushing to her cheeks. He was being deliberately maddening. ''It's our money. It's not just my money. I invested a chunk of your paycheck every month. You signed things. And we're still married.''

''Yes, we are.''

''Once it started happening, it happened fast.''

He shrugged. ''You're good at what you do.''

She stood still in the snow, aware of the silence around her. She needed to go into the cabin and see what had been done to it, talk to Maggie and Ellen. She didn't know what she and Jack could accomplish now, with the pressure of a break-in and Beau McGarrity's disappearance on them. ''Money's never been the most important thing in my life. I enjoy investing, and I enjoy working with my clients, helping them figure out their relationship with money, what they want it to do for them. People always come first.'' She glanced at her cabin. It was the first big thing she'd done with her money, and the police had just been here. "I didn't follow my own advice. I amassed a fortune without knowing why, what I wanted to do with it. What we wanted."

"Not having money was never a problem for us," he said. "Why should having money be a problem?"

"I don't know." Her eyes connected with his. "You tell me."

"No, ma'am." He held his oversized snowball—his snowman's head—at arm's length in one hand, assessing it. "I'm not the one with the problem. You are. That's why I haven't said anything. I decided you needed the space to work this out for yourself."

"Oh, I see. You were being *nice*."

"Damn nice, I think."

"You know what I think? I think you just didn't want to say out loud that you have a rich wife. I think you didn't want to have to think about what having money might mean to you. I was wrong not to ask you if you wanted to get rich, it was easier for you to ignore what I was up to—"

"You're not the easiest woman to ignore, Miss Susanna." He added more snow to his snowman's head, but the way he patted it suddenly struck her as remarkably sexual. No doubt he intended it that way. He went on, his voice steady, "My life hasn't changed because of the ten million. Yours has. You moved north, you bought a cabin. It wasn't all Beau McGarrity and the tape. It was the money, too." He set his oversized snowball on the middle section of his snowman. "He's kind of a pinhead, isn't he? He needs more snow."

That did it. Susanna shook her head at him. "Oh,

no, you don't. You're not going to do this. I've been working this out on my own for *months,* trying to figure out—"

"Trying to figure out who you are," he said. "Not who I am. I'm the same."

"Only because you're pretending you don't know we have money."

His gaze, very dark against the snow, settled on her. "I'm not in any kind of denial. I know you're rich. I know you haven't told me."

"You haven't asked."

"I know that, too."

"Ten million dollars is a hell of a lot of money."

"I could quit," he said.

Susanna stared at him. "What?"

"I have a rich wife. I could quit." His voice was very quiet now, deadly. "Turn in my badge and go fishing."

"Why would you do that?"

"People would expect it."

"Not me—"

"No?"

"No way. I don't get to tell you what to do with your life. You know you're doing the work you were meant to do. You're good at it."

"But in these last months, haven't you grown to hate it?"

She refused to cry. Alice Parker, the cemetery, the cabin—now him. She knew she was overwhelmed. She fought an urge to grab Gran and the girls, jump in the car and drive away. They could go to Canada and stay there until Jack gave them the all-clear. Easier than standing here having this conversation with her husband.

"Jack, do you really think I'd tell you not to be a Texas Ranger?"

He smiled, not that nicely. "Any more than I'd tell you not to make ten million?"

"You wanted to," she said suddenly. "Didn't you?"

Nothing about him softened. "I thought about breaking into your computer and figuring out ways to get rid of every dime."

"Because you didn't want it affecting what you do, who you are—"

"Who we are," he said.

"The money's what we make of it. Nothing more, nothing less."

"It's not changing me," he said. "I've decided that."

She nodded. He fiddled more with his snowman's head, saying nothing.

"I should kick your snowman to bits," she told him.

"You should."

"Jack, damn it, you *knew*. You knew *everything*."

"Admit it, darlin'." His voice deepened, and he laid on the Texas drawl. "You'd have been disappointed if I hadn't."

She couldn't remember ever being so frustrated— so completely thrown by this man. He set the snowman's head on top of the two larger snowballs and admired his handiwork. Without thinking, Susanna swept the head off with one arm and snatched up a chunk of it, charging Jack, fully intending to stuff it down his neck. But he made one little defensive move, and next thing, she was on her back in a snowdrift, with him on top of her with his own handful of snow.

"I swear, Jack, if you put that snow down my back—"

Too late. Down her front it went, but even as she felt the rush of cold, she reached out with one hand and flipped snow into his face, kicking at his damn snowman.

He responded by bringing his mouth onto hers, which, she realized, was exactly what she wanted. There was no pretending otherwise. His lips were cold, but the wet heat of his tongue made her forget the snow melting on her chest, under her breasts.

"I've spent too much time thinking about the damn money." His voice was low and intent, very calm, but there was no studied self-control in place now. He was holding nothing back, and it made her breath catch. He kissed her again, furiously, then said, "I'm not going to stop loving you if you lose the whole ten million tomorrow, or make another ten million. I don't give a damn."

"You did."

"I'm not going to change on you, Susanna. I am what I am."

"Everything's changing on me," she whispered. "Sometimes I feel I can't keep up. I thought if I moved in with Gran for a little while, I could stop time and catch my breath…" She blinked back tears, even as she felt a surge of love and straightforward, unabashed physical desire for this man kissing her in the snow. "Then a few weeks turned into a few months, then more months, and now Maggie and Ellen are getting ready to hear from collages, and here we are, with you bonked on the head, my cabin ransacked, Alice Parker and Beau McGarrity on the loose—''

"We'll sort it out, Susanna."

"I love you," she said. "I've always loved you."

He touched her mouth, let his fingers trail across her cheek and into her hair. "I know. It'll be all right."

"You're always so sure of everything," she said, caught his fingers in one hand and kissed them. But with her free hand, she grabbed a handful of snow and, catching him off guard for once, shoved it down his neck. "You're a bastard for not telling me you knew about the ten million."

He shot up off her and dug the snow out of his neck. "And what do you think I should do to you for not telling me?"

He tossed a clump of snow at her, and it thudded off her hip as she rolled away, very aware she was at a disadvantage now that he was on his feet—and on his guard—and she was still on her back in a snowdrift.

"I felt guilty," she said, "when here you were, wondering how it'd affect your damn work and your man's man reputation—''

"You wrecked my snowman."

She gave up. They'd talked as much as either of them could manage at this point. "I'll help you rebuild it."

She started to get up, and he offered her a hand. She took it, not sure he wouldn't pop her headfirst into a snowbank—or maybe drag her off somewhere and make love to her. But she could see from his expression it was back to the business at hand.

She brushed the snow off her arms and front, felt it melting into her hair. She breathed up at the sky, the clouds pinkish above the tops of the trees. "Destin wasn't at the inn today with Alice," she said. "It was probably about the time the cabin was broken into."

"I should have known McGarrity followed you before his wife was killed." Jack stepped on a chunk of snow, pressing it down under his boot. "I knew there was more. I knew Alice hadn't told me everything."

"There was nothing you could have done—"

"There was a lot I could have done."

Susanna didn't argue. She wasn't going to make him feel any better.

He took her hand, brushed the last of the snow off her shoulder. "Let's go inside and drink something hot, make sure Gran and the girls are okay. Then I want to hear everything Alice Parker said to you."

Sixteen

Another Texan had come into Jim Haviland's bar. This one sat on a stool and ordered the nightly special. Jim put a plate of vegetarian lasagna in front of him, another new recipe he was trying out. "I'm going to take a wild guess and say you're from Texas."

"Yes, sir, I am." The man was dark and black-eyed, and he eyed the lasagna as if he wasn't sure he wanted it, after all. Then he grinned, and the female Tufts graduate students at one of the tables damn near went into a swoon. "How could you tell?"

"The white hat. The boots." He tilted his head back and stared a moment. The black leather jacket threw him off, but he suspected he was right. "You're a Texas Ranger?"

"Only in Texas. In the great state of Massachusetts, I'm just a regular guy."

Jim didn't think there was anything "regular" about this guy. In addition to the cowboy hat and leather jacket, he was wearing a tie and a holster with a gun in it. "You know Jack Galway?"

"Yes, he's my lieutenant, Mr.—"

"Haviland. Jim Haviland. I own this place."

"Sam Temple. I'm a sergeant with the Texas Rangers. I'm in Massachusetts on official business, duly authorized."

"That's why they let you in armed?"

"I don't do business unarmed, Mr. Haviland."

Jim thought he heard one of the graduate students make a choking sound, but he gave her a warning look. One of her friends was pretending to revive her by waving a cocktail napkin in front of her face. Jim figured they all needed spring to get there. Cabin fever was setting in. He was fairly sure that Sam Temple wouldn't give a damn about a couple of smart-assed eavesdropping anthropology students going ga-ga over him.

Temple produced a color photograph and set it on the bar. "Have you seen this man by any chance?" he asked.

Jim took the picture and frowned at it. "He was here yesterday. Early evening. I remember, because I was burning pies and he commented on my daughter. Didn't say much else. Who is he?"

"Texas real estate developer."

It wasn't a straight answer. Jim could see Davey Ahearn squirm at the other end of the bar. He had the vegetarian lasagna in front of him. He'd already complained about finding a carrot stick. The graduate students had told Jim they wanted to have his baby, they loved his vegetarian lasagna so much. This was the problem with a diverse clientele, but it kept his work interesting. He could probably do without armed Texas Rangers, though.

Davey suspended a forkful of lasagna midair and looked over at Sam Temple. "Is this the son of a bitch who shot his wife and stalked Susanna Galway?"

The Texas Ranger set his fork down. His black eyes settled on Davey, and there was more napkin-waving at the Tufts table. "Susanna told you that Beau McGarrity stalked her?"

"Uh-oh. Me and my big mouth," Davey backtracked, which wasn't his style. Usually when he put his foot in his mouth, he just made things worse. "It was New Year's Eve. She was drinking margaritas. Maybe she was exaggerating."

"Susanna doesn't exaggerate," Sam Temple said.

Jim laid a towel on his shoulder. First, Audrey Melbourne, aka Alice Parker, the ex-con, then Jack Galway, the break-in at Iris's and the guy last night. Now, Sergeant Sam Temple. "You want to tell me what the hell's going on?"

The Ranger paused a beat, and Jim could see he was all business, a total professional. Which meant he wasn't telling anyone anything. "Jack said you know about Alice Parker, the woman who came in here under the name Audrey Melbourne and befriended Susanna's grandmother. Any idea where she's been staying?"

Jim shook his head. "The local police want to talk to her about the break-in the other night."

"I imagine so. I haven't talked to them yet." He smiled. "Thought I'd stop in here first, before they give me a shadow."

The bar was small, and the grad students were noisy—but Jim had a feeling Sam Temple was deliberately including them in what he had to say. If he'd wanted to, he'd have asked to talk in private.

From the table behind him, one of the graduate students said, "I know where Audrey lives." Temple looked around at her. She was an anthropology major Davey liked to tease about doing digs on Lake Titicaca in Bolivia. They all knew he could be an idiot. The kid added, straightforward, "She lives in my building, about two blocks from here. She has a rathole apartment just like mine, except she's on the third floor and I'm on the second."

Sam Temple eased off the bar stool, his lasagna barely touched. "Can you give me directions?"

The grad student had almost stopped breathing, and Jim could see her friends kicking her under the table. Davey scratched the side of his handlebar mustache with his little finger. "I know the building. I can take you over there."

As disciplined as Sam Temple was, Jim could sense the man's intensity. "Much obliged."

Davey swung to his feet, nonchalant. Wyatt Earp could walk into the place, and Davey Ahearn wouldn't give a damn. "I haven't had anything to drink. I've just been trying to choke down this vegetable lasagna. Jimmy, curried corn chowder and now this? Stick to the basics."

Temple stayed focused, not distracted by Davey's wisecracks. He turned to Jim. "Last night when Beau McGarrity was here—did you happen to mention that Susanna Galway had gone to the Adirondacks?"

The Texas Ranger spoke in a measured, steady drawl, but Jim understood every word. He wished he hadn't. He nodded. "He was at one of the tables while I was talking to my daughter. We mentioned Susanna's cabin. Damn.''

"Draw me a map of how to get there, will you, Mr. Haviland?" Temple's manner was pleasant, but no one within five yards of him would miss the underlying sense of urgency. He shifted back to Davey. "I'm ready whenever you are, sir."

For once, Davey Ahearn didn't have a quip. He got his hat and his coat, and he and Sam Temple left.

The door shut, and the Tufts graduate students all slid onto the floor in unison, faking a group swoon. One of the firefighters at another table said, "I bet he eats meat," and the place erupted.

Jack could see it now.

He dumped a load of wood in the wood box and looked at his wife and daughters bundled up under a blanket together on the couch, watching the fire. They had the place picked up, and they'd talked, he and Susanna filling in the gaps of what Maggie, Ellen and Iris knew about Beau McGarrity, Alice Parker, Destin Wright and the unsolved murder of Rachel McGarrity.

Susanna was steady and straightforward, a rock for her elderly grandmother and teenage daughters. And for her husband, Jack thought. He'd never had his work infect his family to the point they were huddled in an isolated cabin in the Adirondacks, frightened and confused.

So much for his fucking fire wall.

But he saw it clearly now—Beau McGarrity walking into their kitchen was the catalyst for Susanna to move north. It wasn't the cause. The dry tinders were there already for McGarrity to ignite. She'd already made millions and started keeping her secrets from him, and he'd already let himself drift into silence.

He hadn't liked the idea of her making so god-damn much money.

He was an enlightened man. Harvard-educated, for God's sake. But he'd let the fact that she'd made millions eat at him, let it undermine Susanna's trust and confidence in him—her satisfaction with a job well done.

The money wouldn't change his life unless he allowed it to. And he had.

Ten million. Damn.

Today he was reminded that his wife had her own hardheaded and unyielding side, a toughness that he sometimes forgot.

Even so, he knew what he had to say. He brushed wood chips off his jacket, still feeling the cold from outside. Destin Wright and Alice Parker had checked out of the Blackwater Inn. No one knew where they were.

"I want you all to come back to San Antonio with me," he said to his wife and daughters. "I can protect you better there until we get this mess figured out."

He hadn't mentioned this idea to Susanna ahead of time. She threw off the blanket, jumped to her feet and stormed into the kitchen, opening cupboards, pulling out food for dinner, generally slamming around in there.

Maggie rolled her eyes at him. *"Dad."*

Iris got up from the table, where she'd been nursing a mug of hot cocoa, and patted his arm. "You go on and help with dinner. The girls and I will work on the puzzle. We'd just gotten the topiary garden put together, but that sneaky bastard this afternoon wrecked it.''

The girls reluctantly followed their great-grandmother's lead and moved to the puzzle table, but they were clearly more interested in telling their father what he'd done wrong. But he knew. He'd told Susanna something she didn't want to hear.

He went to the kitchen counter and took over peeling carrots and chopping onions on a worn wooden cutting board. ''You know I'm right.''

She hacked at chicken on the other side of the sink. ''I have a sharp knife in my hand.''

''Maggie was going to take on the burglar today all by herself,'' Jack said. ''I think she gets that from you.''

''Which? That she's a fighter or doesn't know her limits?''

He chopped off the end of a carrot and smiled at her. ''Both.''

''We're up here on vacation.'' She dragged out a pan for the chicken and smacked it down on the counter. ''The local police are investigating the break-in here. Alice and Destin probably realized they went too far and took off—or Alice just doesn't want to talk to you.''

''Alice has to talk to me,'' he said simply. ''She withheld critical information in a murder investigation.''

Susanna laid the chicken pieces in the pan. ''Ah. Yes. That sums it up. 'She withheld critical information in a murder investigation.' It just happens to involve a rich real estate developer stalking your wife in the days before his wife turned up murdered in their own damn driveway.''

He peeled his carrot, using a cheap paring knife. It was dark outside, the window over the sink reflecting his own image back at him. ''I consider that understood.''

She reeled around at him, her green eyes hot and angry—and scared. ''That's because you're a law enforcement officer. You can distance yourself from what you do. You spend your days rooting around in crime and misery and violence—''

''Do you think that means what I deal with doesn't have an impact?'' He turned on the water and rinsed off his peeled carrot, knowing he meant what he said. ''Susanna, the day I don't hate what I see on the job really is the day I quit.''

She seemed stung. ''I didn't mean it that way. I meant that you're a professional at this and I'm not. Jack, I know you love your work. It's what you do, it's who you are.''

''You're half right. It's what I do—it's not who I am.''

She put the pan of chicken in the oven and washed her hands, tearing off paper towels to dry them. ''You're not thinking of giving it up?''

''Would it shock you if I did give it up?''

She narrowed that smart, incisive gaze on him. ''No,'' she said quietly. ''No, you'd quit if I asked you to. That's one of the things that's had you on the defensive these past months—you were afraid that I *would* ask you, now that we could afford it.

But that would be wrong, just as wrong as if you asked me to give up my ten million.''

He set down his carrot and moved closer to her. ''I thought it was *our* ten million.''

''Well, it is, but you don't pay attention to money.''

Her tone was light, but when he put one hand on the counter on either side of her, he saw her teeth come down on her lower lip, knew what she was thinking—what she wanted. ''That was when we didn't have any money.'' He took another step toward her, pinning her against the counter. Not that she minded. ''Susanna, if we were dealing with a money problem right now, I'd listen to you, because you're the one with the expertise. I wouldn't feel patronized or bossed around or left out because—''

''Fair point.''

He brushed his lips against hers. ''Then what's wrong?''

''If it were just the two of us, if Gran and the girls weren't here. Jack, I feel such a sense of responsibility—''

''I know.''

Her eyes widened slightly, as if he'd said something she hadn't expected, and she nodded. ''You do, don't you?''

He touched her chin. ''You've been carrying this thing with McGarrity on your own for too long. Let me in, Susanna. Let me take some of the load.''

''That makes it serious. If you're not involved, I can pretend—'' But she stopped herself, sighing as she shut her eyes a moment. ''I can't pretend anything, not after the past few days.''

"But you're not going to San Antonio?"

"That's your fight or flight impulse kicking into gear, as Maggie would say. Get us home, under your protection—"

"That's my professional opinion."

"It's your opinion as a husband and a father."

"And a Texas Ranger."

She managed to put up both her palms and shove him in his midsection. "You were doing well there for a minute, Lieutenant Galway, not reminding me of what you do for a living. Here we were, a normal couple having a heart-to-heart discussion—"

"We're not normal, Susanna."

She smiled. "This is true."

He stood back from her and resumed his place at the cutting board, tackling another carrot. He grinned. "I thought I did okay with the heart-to-heart."

"You did," she said softly. "Except for pitching me into a snowbank."

"You deserved it. You should tell Maggie and Ellen I did okay."

"Nope. I like it when they get on your case about not communicating, being more romantic—they get on mine for not cutting you more slack. As if that'd make any difference."

"They think I should buy you silk nighties." Jack picked up the paring knife, watching the color rise in his wife's cheeks. "I might after that getup you had on last night."

"That was my mountain woman nightshirt." She glanced at him, the spots of color deepening. "As I recall, it didn't seem to bother you at the time."

"That's because it ended up on the floor." He winked at her. "Are you blushing again, darlin'? I think you're becoming a bit of a Yankee prude."

She threw a towel at him and ran him out, saying she'd finish a hell of a lot faster without him distracting her. He liked that. He wanted to distract her. But he checked on Iris and the girls and their puzzle building, then headed out to the porch overlooking the lake and tried Sam Temple for the dozenth time.

This time, his call went through. "Can you hear me?" Sam asked through the static.

"Barely. Where are you?"

"Some godforsaken place with mountains and snow. Mass Pike, a few miles past the last toll booth. I got your message." Jack had given Sam everything he'd learned in a succinct, brutal message on his voice mail. "I should warn you—I'm coming after your wife. I'm duly authorized, and I intend to drag her ass back to Texas for withholding evidence in a murder investigation."

"I already considered it. It won't hold up."

"It's a bad sign, a woman not telling her husband about a murder suspect showing up in her kitchen."

"It's our kitchen, not just her kitchen."

"Jesus."

"What do you have?" Jack asked.

"A Somerville apartment rented by our Audrey Melbourne, aka Alice Parker, was broken into and searched. A neighbor called it in earlier today. No leads. I went over to the grandmother's house. Likewise. They went in from the back porch. Really tore up Susanna's room." A little humor crept into his voice. "I know it was her room because there were no pictures of you in it."

"McGarrity."

"Probably looking for the tape. My guess is Alice is blackmailing him with it and told him Susanna still has it. More valuable that way. It's crazy, until you realize this is Beau McGarrity and Alice Parker we're talking about."

"There's more," Jack said. "I just don't know what it is."

"I hear you." But Sam didn't waste time on more speculation. "McGarrity was within earshot when the plumber and the bartender mentioned Susanna was in the mountains. Local law enforcement on the case?"

"More or less."

"McGarrity won't be happy with Alice for lying to him about the tape, shaking him down—if that's what's going on."

Jack knew no comment from him was necessary. "What are you driving?"

"I broke down and rented an SUV."

A huge sacrifice for Sam Temple, who hated most trucks and SUVs and all rentals, period. Their crackle-filled connection worsened. Jack gave him directions to the cabin. "Crank up the heat and don't get lost. It's dipping below zero here tonight."

Sam swore and disconnected.

Jack looked out at the night sky, lit up with stars above the lake. Maybe Susanna was right, and there was something about being here that was meant to be. He shook off the thought, decided the cold air was addling his brain and retreated into the warm cabin.

Iris got up from the puzzle table and stood next to him in front of the big windows that looked out onto the lake. "You look tired, Iris," he said, swinging an arm around her and giving her a hug. She'd never been a frail woman, but he could feel her age. "It's been a long day."

"Blackwater Lake is bad luck for the Dunnings." She stared out into the darkness, past her reflection in the window. Her voice was quiet, calm, convincing. "I hate to think that way because it's so beautiful here, and I have so many wonderful memories. But it's true."

"Because of Jared Herrington?"

She smiled. "Jared Rutherford Herrington. Isn't that a name?" Her smile faded, but there were no tears in her eyes. "I've experienced such tragedy here. I should have warned Susanna not to buy this place—to pick another lake."

"You love this lake," Jack said. "You can't hide that, Iris. You do."

"I'm a part of its past. Almost a century. I've been gone for sixty years. My Lord, when I was in my twenties, I thought I'd be old and shriveled up in sixty years. And look at me. I am!" She patted the hand he still had over her shoulder, hanging on to it. "Yes, Jack, I love Blackwater Lake with all my heart and soul. I should have come back long ago and made my peace with it."

"Gran, that's not what this is about—"

"Yes, it is. On some level, yes, that's exactly what it's about."

She was adamant, and Jack planted a kiss on her white hair, smelling the mountains in it. "I'll bet you were hell in a pair of hiking boots, tramping up these hills, catching trout in your teeth and taking a rich Ivy Leaguer for a lover."

"I was very independent." This time, her smile reached her eyes, reminding him of her granddaughter. "It·was no surprise to me when Susanna ran off with a Texas Ranger."

"I wasn't a Ranger then. I was a Harvard grad. Another Ivy Leaguer."

"Oh, no. You were a Texas Ranger then, too. You just didn't have the badge yet."

When dinner was served, she claimed she wasn't hungry and took a glass of milk up to bed with her. Jack could see the fatigue in her as she mounted the stairs. Susanna watched her grandmother uneasily, and if there was any good in these past months, he thought, it was for these four women he loved—Iris, Susanna, Maggie and Ellen—having this opportunity to be together.

But he wanted it to end. He wanted his family back. And somehow he didn't think Iris would want him under her roof for more than a few days at a time.

Maggie and Ellen fought at the dinner table. They were tired, too. Ellen was mad at herself for "freaking out" when she found the place torn apart, which made her mad at Maggie for charging upstairs to check under the beds—and Maggie obviously thought she was very courageous for having done so.

Jack told them they both had screwed up. Ellen

should have stayed calm, and Maggie should have gotten the hell out of there.

"Gee, Dad," Maggie said, "like you could have taken on an armed burglar with your stupid ski pole."

Before he could articulate who'd been in law enforcement for twenty years and who wasn't even eighteen, Susanna intervened. "We all handle stress in different ways," she said. "What's important is to learn something about yourself from this experience and work on what you want to change." She eyed her husband across the table. "Right, Jack?"

He smiled at her. "Does that mean next time you're stressed, you won't beat up on my snowman?"

Seventeen

Alice pushed through a butt-deep snow drift and came out on the other side of a stand of naked trees, the snow only knee-deep here. She was breathing hard, and it was dark, with only the quarter-moon and the glow of the snow to relieve the blackness. She would come upon the teahouse or run into Destin soon. She had to. Either that or just trip over a rock, hit her head and die a quick, clean death.

She wished she'd brought Destin the damn hot coffee she'd promised. She could drink it herself. Hell, she could warm her hands and feet with it.

She didn't want to freeze to death. She was from south Texas. Fire ants, poisonous snakes, tornadoes, heat stroke all sounded better to her than dropping facefirst in the snow and freezing into a block of ice out here in the northern wilderness.

She hung on to a thin tree trunk and caught her breath. A few bright stars had appeared in the night sky. And Venus. That had to be Venus up there, beaming down at her. When she got to Australia, she'd have to learn all new stars, not that she knew northern hemisphere stars that well.

Right now, she liked the idea of the southern hemisphere. Anything south. Well, maybe not the South Pole.

A gust of wind howled through the woods, scaring her, making her more cold. She wouldn't mind the mountain parka now instead of her basic parka, but it had cost more than she'd paid for her car. A damn coat.

She coughed, then went still, listening for wild animals. What would she do if a big old moose walked up to her? What if she woke a bear up from his winter nap? She'd be pissed herself, waking up to temperatures in the single digits.

At least it'd be an active death, fighting off a bear. This business of freezing to death was so passive. Hypothermia was a danger in Texas, on cold, rainy days when people didn't dress right, let their core temperature drop too low. Sheer stupidity, usually. She'd never seen anyone die of it, but she knew the process—the shivering, the slurred speech, the muscles getting weaker and weaker, not being able to think straight, then lying down, losing consciousness and dying.

If she died of hypothermia out here, who knew when anyone would find her? Someone would be walking around looking for wildflowers or a place to pee, and they'd trip over her dead body, the way Iris Dunning had come upon her rich lover, the father of the baby she was carrying.

Except, Alice thought, nobody who loved her would find her dead body.

More stars came out, and the wind in the trees created eerie shadows on the blanket of snow. She had no flashlight, no food, no water, no sleeping bag. She'd started into the woods before dark, expecting to fetch Destin and clear out. She was late getting to the Herrington place to begin with. After her tête-à-tête with Miss Susanna and Iris, she'd packed up her and Destin, checked out of the inn and tried to take a back way up to the north end of the lake. And got lost. It was her day for getting lost.

With her gas tank practically on empty, she finally came upon the big, boarded-up house. A miracle. She parked at the end of the snow-covered lane that supposedly led to the teahouse and started hiking.

She was still hiking, at least an hour later, maybe close to two hours later now, with the temperature steadily dropping. Destin must have given up and either found proper shelter or hitchhiked into town. He couldn't still be out here waiting for her. She'd called for him quietly a few times, but didn't bother now that it was dark and frigid, and she was so lost and exhausted she could barely keep going.

She lurched from one tree to the next, trying, at least, to keep herself moving in a straight line. She didn't want to wander around in circles. Eventually she had to come to the lake or a road or a summer cottage. Even these thick, dark, remote woods couldn't go on forever.

Above her, barren treetops clicked together in a light breeze. She gasped at the painful numbing in her cheeks and pressed her palms to them, trying to keep off the wind and the cold. The breeze died down, and she pressed on. Her chest was toasty warm, her vital organs at least protected from the frigid air. She remembered nights in prison when she'd ached for an open window, a cool breeze.

Suddenly she couldn't remember what had possessed her to drive out to Beau McGarrity's house that day and offer Susanna's tape in exchange for fifty thousand dollars. And why the hell go all the way to Boston to implement her scheme to make it look as if Susanna had the tape all along? It would have been simpler to tell Beau she'd hid it in the wall or something in her house in San Antonio. Alice could have waited for Jack to head off to work, torn up the place and gone on back to Beau.

Except Beau had needed time to come around, and somehow, Alice knew it required Susanna Galway to be firmly in the picture. Maybe because Beau had followed her, maybe because he had unfinished business with her. Alice was operating more on instincts than information and logic, just as she had the night she found Rachel dead—of course, her instincts that night had landed her in prison.

Rachel had tried to get her to have more faith in herself. "If you want to be a Texas Ranger, Alice, go for it," she'd say. "Apply for a position in the Department of Public Safety, get the training you need. You *won't* be one if you just keep dreaming about it."

"But what if I fail?" Alice remembered asking. "What if it doesn't work out? Then I won't have that dream anymore."

"Then you'll find a new dream."

Australia...

She broke into a halfrun, her eyes tearing with the

cold. She was losing strength. Soon she wouldn't be able to lift her legs high enough to manage the deep snow. Then what? She didn't want to die out here. She almost wished she were back in prison.

She came to a hemlock with low-hanging branches and ducked under them, thinking this would be a good place to rest. What would happen if she sank into the soft snow, leaned against the rough trunk and just went to sleep? *You'll wake up with grandma in heaven...*

Or maybe she'd wake up in the fires of hell.

She needed time to make amends for her mistakes. And Rachel...*I can't die with her murder unsolved.* But blackmailing Beau was about money and Australia, not justice, not avenging Rachel's death. And this scheme she'd fallen into with Destin. It had nothing to do with putting Beau McGarrity into prison for cold-blooded murder.

She burst onto the other side of the hemlock, and the woods opened up, giving way to a rock ledge and the open expanse of Blackwater Lake. She almost cried. Her legs gave way, trembling and weak from pushing through the snow, and she sank to her knees. She'd be okay now. The teahouse, Susanna's cabin, other cabins, the inn, a marina and campsites were all on the lake. She'd come to *something.*

Alice slowly got back onto her feet and leaned against a boulder as tall as she was. She looked out at the lake, the black sky shining with stars now. She could distinguish the outlines of an island just offshore and tried to orient herself, remembering the geological survey map at the inn. She was still on the upper reaches of Blackwater Lake. The jagged shoreline, the rocks and hills and trees—the sheer distance involved—obstructed any view of lights to the south, the more populated end of the lake.

She pushed back a crawling sense of panic at not seeing any lights. She felt very alone in a very big wilderness.

The lake made a deep moaning sound, and her heart raced, even as she told herself it was just the ice. She stood motionless, calling upon the techniques she'd learned in prison to stem what she now recognized as an oncoming panic attack. She thought of Texas, walking across open land with her grandma and breathing the warm spring air, smelling the wildflowers.

The mountains and dark seemed to close in on her, stealing her breath, but she didn't gulp for air—she'd learned not to hyperventilate. Instead, she stayed with that peaceful image. In her mind, the bluebonnets were real, and all her dreams were ahead of her, not laying in shards at her feet.

"Honey, you can do anything if you put your mind to it."

Her grandma had believed in her. And all Alice had wanted, even then as a little girl walking in a field, was to be a Texas Ranger and do good for people. There were women Rangers. Fine ones.

Australia. She reminded herself that was her new dream. It was what she wanted now. She'd tried to do good for people, and it hadn't worked out.

She should find Destin, drop him off in Boston and forget she'd ever gone down this road of trying to get her money the easy way. Get a job. Save.

"So, please, God," she whispered, "please don't let me die out here."

She hoped God wasn't as unforgiving as Jack Galway. She'd known he'd never look the other way when she messed up the crime scene and came up with her phony witness. Jack didn't know about the change purse, but he suspected she hadn't told him everything about her and Rachel McGarrity. He didn't believe it was sheer incompetence that had driven her to contaminate the crime scene, trample on evidence. But when she plea-bargained, playing on everyone else's desire to put a police corruption case behind them, she hadn't left him much room to maneuver.

At least he didn't think she was so stupid as to not follow basic police procedure when coming onto a murder scene. That was something.

But she'd never become a Texas Ranger now, that was for darn sure.

She eased around the boulder, coming to a steep embankment. If she got to the bottom without breaking a leg, it looked as if the going would be easier, and there was a point that jutted out into the lake where she might get a better fix on which direction she should go. She needed to get out of the elements. She'd read about people digging snow caves and surviving that way. She had no idea how she'd even start.

She grabbed hold of a thin sapling, anchoring herself, and edged sideways down the hill, then let go and half scrambled, half tumbled the rest of the way, dropping to her butt for the last few feet.

When she came to a stop, she sat there in the

snow, her feet pressed up against thick lake ice. She was breathing hard, fighting tears. She was hungry. A nice, hot bowl of Jim Haviland's clam chowder would do her fine. She'd even eat the clams.

A light came on further along the shore, about twenty-five yards from her. A flashlight. It bobbed toward her, and Alice got unsteadily to her feet. She sniffled. "Destin?"

She doubted whoever it was could hear her. Destin wasn't the sort to be prepared with something as practical as a flashlight—or to wait for her out in the cold. Maybe it was a winter camper, someone who'd heard her thrashing around. The Johnsons had mentioned that people camped in the Adirondacks year-round.

Alice watched the light moving toward her, unable to make out the dark silhouette of the figure behind it. She could see the snow bright under the arc of light, tree trunks, a stretch of ice and jutting rock, and squinted as the light found her, settled on her. The figure stopped, raising the light to her face, shining it in her eyes. She shielded them, but made out the man's face and immediately thought hypothermia must have set in. "Beau? Is that you?"

"Hello, Alice." His voice was cold, steady. "You've had a tough time out here."

"I sure have. I'm glad to see you—"

"You were supposed to meet Destin Wright."

She tried to lick her lips, but her tongue felt dry. "Have you seen him?"

McGarrity shifted the harsh light off her face. He was properly dressed for the frigid temperatures in a high-end parka, the hood up, and wind-resistant gloves and pants. He didn't look cold at all. "I caught up with him after he broke into Susanna Galway's cabin."

"I sent him after the tape—"

"Alice." Beau's voice was ice. "I have the tape."

The tape was in her suitcase in her car, parked at the rich people's house through the woods. Except Beau had it. "You found my car?"

"Mr. Wright said you two had planned to meet at the teahouse. It made sense you'd leave your car at the main house."

"I got lost."

"Yes, I know." He took a step toward her, his demeanor still calm, but with a menacing undertone that kept her sitting in the snow, unable to move. "Your friend didn't know anything about a tape."

"He wouldn't know he could tell you—"

"Alice, if you haven't seen him since you got lost, how did the tape end up in your bag?"

She cleared her throat, wishing she could think faster. Even warm, she wasn't a fast thinker. "I lied to him."

"No, Alice. You lied to me."

Her entire body convulsed into uncontrollable shivering, and she staggered to her feet, her teeth chattering, her hands shaking. She'd lied to Beau McGarrity. He knew it. He'd shot his wife in the back, and now he'd kill her. She was dead. She'd never see Texas again. She'd never make it to Australia.

And Destin. He was a self-absorbed jerk, and he'd had no idea what he was up against in Beau McGarrity. Alice hadn't warned him.

She didn't want to think about Destin.

She crossed her arms tightly over her chest, but she didn't think she'd ever get warm again.

Beau McGarrity had a gun pointed at her in the hand not holding the flashlight. Destin's Heckler & Koch. It was an expensive gun. He'd showed it to her the other night in the motel in New Hampshire. He was very proud of it, but he barely knew how to hold the thing.

He should have brought it with him when he broke into Susanna's cabin, just so he could have it on him when he'd run into Beau. Instead, he must have left it in his pack, and Beau had found it when he'd searched Alice's car.

"You're a former police officer, Alice," Beau said, almost amused. "You should know not to leave a weapon in an unoccupied vehicle."

"It's Destin's—I don't have a gun."

Not that it mattered. Her brain felt dull and mushy, and she knew she was putting together the pieces of the mess she was in slowly, some floating away before her mind could quite grasp them and put them in place. *Rachel Tucker McGarrity, interior designer, a woman with fine manners, a lover of fine things…her friend…dead…murdered…gone forever…*

"I should have left well enough alone with Destin." Alice spoke absently, hunching her shoulders as her teeth chattered. Her eyelids were heavy. She desperately wanted to sleep. "I'm very cold."

"The teahouse is just up this way."

At least he wouldn't shoot her out here on the ice

and snow. He'd take her inside the teahouse, and shoot her there.

He stood back and motioned with his flashlight, the H&K held steady. "After you, Officer Parker."

He left her in the teahouse.

Alice didn't know where he was. She was alone, huddled into a corner of the crumbling, gazebolike structure on the lake front. He had thrust a sleeping bag at her and told her to climb inside, and she'd thought he meant to smother her. Or maybe he hoped the down feather lining would muffle his gunshot. But once she was inside, Beau handed her a bottle of water and told her to keep it in the sleeping bag with her or it would freeze.

"You'll survive until morning," he told her. "If you don't, you don't—but you will."

"Why won't I crawl out of here and get help?"

"Because you don't have the strength. Because you're desperate. And because you might run into me."

"Destin—"

"He's no help to you. It was a mistake on your part ever to think he would be." He'd stared at her behind that flashlight, so still she thought he might have turned to ice. "I know why my wife was interested in Susanna Galway. I understand the connection now."

"Jesus," Alice breathed, "you don't care about the tape. That's not why you're here. You don't want it to get out to the public, but it's Rachel's interest in Susanna—"

"Sleep well." His tone was without inflection, and

he started out, stopping at the gazebo door and looking back at her, the flashlight pointed at the floor.
"You should have told me the truth. Instead, you
tried to double-cross me."

"We can still do a deal."

"Maybe."

And he'd left her like that. She took a few sips of
water and shoved the bottle to the bottom of her
sleeping bag, and now she was hunkered down deep.
She'd sealed off any gaps where the cold air could
seep in. She could feel her breath hot against the
slick fabric. Freeze or suffocate. What a choice. She
thought of the idiots who climbed Mt. Everest. What
did the women do when they had to pee in the middle
of the night?

Even if she didn't run into Beau, she'd die of exposure if she left the teahouse. She had no flashlight,
no compass, no provisions. She already knew she had
no sense of direction in these woods. And her socks
were wet. She wouldn't get far in wet socks.

Her only hope was to stay alive until morning and
try to work out some kind of deal with Beau.

*I loved my wife, Officer Parker. I loved her very
much.*

She couldn't remember when Beau had said that.
Tonight? The night of Rachel's death?

*It's your fault she's dead. Yours and Susanna Gal-
way's. You're the ones responsible.*

Had he *ever* said that? Alice shut her eyes, her
cheeks and lips burning from the wind and the cold.
If Beau had said that, she should have told Jack Galway.

Maybe Beau hadn't said it. Maybe this was one of

her prison dreams, and she'd wake up on her cot in her cell, sweating and hyperventilating.

She'd never had much luck in life.

She rolled onto her side, trying to get comfortable on the rotting, loose floorboards. She imagined Iris Dunning as a young woman, her chestnut hair flowing, shining in the moonlight as she made passionate love to a rich, married man out here on a hot summer night.

Eighteen

━━━━━∾⟨⟨⟩⟩∾━━━━━

Sam Temple sat at the oak table drinking coffee and eyeing Susanna, who was showered, dressed and accustomed to being in the company of Texas Rangers and therefore not intimidated. Sam, however, had already made it abundantly clear that he was not happy with her. It was morning and a storm was brewing. Clouds had moved in from the west, and the wind was picking up. Susanna pictured them all trapped in the cabin for days on end in a major blizzard. She couldn't imagine Sam building jigsaw puzzles and playing Scrabble.

Jack was in the shower. Maggie and Ellen were in their room taking turns reading *Pride and Prejudice*. They'd rebounded well after yesterday. Gran was on the couch in front of the fire, pensive, uninterested in working the castle puzzle.

"My life would be easier if you'd just come on back to Texas," Sam said.

Susanna leaned back in her chair. "And just how would your life be easier?"

"Well, I wouldn't be up here in the frozen north freezing my ass off."

"That's a stretch, Sam. It was your choice to come up here. I had nothing to do with it."

He shook his head. He was chiseled, dark and very handsome. "You have everything to do with why I'm here. Beau McGarrity turned up in your neighborhood when he told his cleaning woman he was going hunting. I don't like that."

"He's after Alice Parker, not me."

"That's what we regard in my line of work as a leap of logic. There are two detectives back in Boston keeping an eye out for McGarrity, and Jack and I will be talking to the local and state police up here. Mr. McGarrity has some explaining to do."

"You need an articulable reason for picking him up—"

"I know what I need. We have good reason to believe he broke into Alice's apartment and your grandmother's house."

"But it wouldn't matter," Susanna said. "You'd pick him up for having a beer at Jim's Place."

"It's provocative conduct."

"You don't like it."

He almost managed a smile. "That's right, Mrs. Galway. I don't like it. And if McGarrity's after Alice Parker, she has a right to protection, as well."

"Courtesy, service, protection."

He winked. "That's our motto."

Susanna stared out the window at the white and gray landscape. "Sam, I'm sorry. If I'd known Beau McGarrity had hunted me down before his wife was killed—"

"You didn't. I'll give you that one. If we'd known about his visit after his wife's murder, we might have pressed him more, we might have pressed Alice more—but she copped to the witness tampering right off, so who the hell knows?" He shifted in his chair, and if he felt out of place in an Adirondack cabin, he'd never show it. "Never mind McGarrity and Alice Parker. My life'd be easier, period, if you came home. Jack hasn't been in a good mood since you took off to Boston."

"Give me a break, Sam. I was sleeping with Jack when you were in the ninth grade."

His black eyes flashed with amusement. "Sleeping with Jack that tough, is it?"

She gave him a steady look, refusing to let any color creep into her cheeks. "That's not what I meant."

"He loves you, Susanna."

"And I love him." She looked at her hands and absently touched her wedding ring, fighting back tears she hoped Sam wouldn't see. "There are times in a long relationship when that's not enough."

"What else do you need? Clean socks?"

Jack entered the kitchen from the bedroom, where he and Susanna had spent the night together, making love silently, passionately. She could feel herself responding to him all over again, physically, emotionally, as she took in everything that had attracted her to him right from the beginning. His dark eyes, his half smiles, his taut body. His strength and no-nonsense style, and his humor, his tolerance. She remembered how gentle he'd been with Maggie and

Ellen as tots, how haunted he'd been by his first murder investigation.

This time together, she knew, was restoring the physical and emotional bond between them—and messing up her head all over again. Which, of course, wouldn't be the way he or Sam looked at it. They'd say she was coming to her senses. Maybe they had a point.

"What're you two up to?" Jack asked.

"We're discussing laundry," Sam said. "Clean socks. I'd hate to hang out my shorts in this weather. Granny Dunning says she can smell snow in the air."

"You'll see," Gran said from the couch. She hadn't made any comments to Sam about Texas, but she'd given his holstered .357 SIG Sauer a wary look.

"Gran's a legend in these parts," Susanna told him.

He grinned. "I don't doubt it."

Jack didn't even try to follow their back-and-forth conversation. He was all business. He grabbed his jacket. "Sam, I'll check in with the local police and let them know you're in town. I also want to talk with the people at the Blackwater Inn. Unofficially. You'll hang in here?"

"No problem."

Susanna's reaction was automatic, instinctive, visceral—it bypassed all her rational thought processes. She shot to her feet, frustration rising in her throat as she tightened her hands into fists and started for her husband. "You mean you want him to be our protection."

Jack shrugged, but she could see the heat in his eyes. "It's either Sam or me."

"Forget it. We'll pack up and head back to Boston. Gran, the girls and me. We can be on our way in an hour."

Sam muttered, "Jesus, Susanna," over the rim of his coffee mug.

Jack clenched his teeth. "What will you do when Alice Parker and Destin Wright show up in your rearview mirror? Or Beau McGarrity? He shot his wife in the back. What do you think he'll do to you?"

"I have a cell phone. I'll call you and tell you where they are. Then you and Sam can swoop in to the rescue."

Jack took in a sharp breath, his eyes very dark on her now. She knew she wasn't making any sense. She just wanted out of there with her children and her grandmother. She wanted them safe. She didn't want them hurt. Which was Jack's motive, too. But he was including her among those he didn't want hurt, not among those who would do the protecting, and it made her feel helpless—and even more vulnerable.

Sam rocked back in his chair and said calmly, "I was hoping I'd get to try snowshoeing while I was up here. Maybe see a moose."

"You go right ahead." She was on a roll now, unable to stop herself. "Snowshoe, track moose, track criminals. I'll leave you the cabin keys. You and Jack can lock up when you head back to San Antonio."

"It wouldn't work out that way," Sam said calmly.

Susanna instantly knew what he was telling her. "You mean you'd follow me *home?*"

"Sure, all the way back to San Antonio if that's where you want to go." His reference to San Antonio instead of Boston was deliberate, provocative, Sam Temple's way of warning her not to underestimate his resolve. It was understood between the two Texas Rangers that Sam would look after Jack's family, and look after them he would. He took another sip of his coffee, his manner unchanged. "Makes no difference to me."

Jack stood behind Susanna, and she could feel his absolute self-control when he touched her shoulder and said tightly, "Susanna."

She kept her gaze pinned on Sam. "You two cooked this up last night."

Sam shrugged, no sign of remorse. "You were asleep."

"No, I wasn't. I was tossing and turning, trying to figure out how to keep you two from taking over my life. If Beau McGarrity wanted to harm me, he's had the chance. He's had over a year, for God's sake. He had me *alone* in my house, and he didn't touch me. He watched me prune my garden, and he didn't touch me." But she could see she wasn't getting through to either man, maybe not even to herself. "What if he's innocent? What if Alice *is* trying to frame him?"

"Nobody's taking over your life or telling you what to do, Susanna." Jack's tone was still calm, if not gentle. "We're just telling you what we're doing."

"You're not including me in the decision-making."

But he'd had enough. "That's because there are no decisions here for you to make." He started through the kitchen and glanced back at Sam. "A couple hours."

He left without another word, and Susanna kicked a chair and debated picking it up and throwing it out the window.

"I thought he might not wake up so crabby when I got the sofa bed and he didn't." Sam got to his feet and walked to the kitchen, refilling his mug with stale coffee. "What did you do, make him sleep on the floor?"

"Shut up, Sam."

"He has a one-track mind. Right now, he's focused on Alice Parker, this Destin Wright character and Beau McGarrity. He's got me focused on them, and he's going to get local law enforcement focused on them." Sam sat back down with his coffee. "You're just balking and being a pain in the ass because you're scared and pissed off this has happened. That's understandable."

She watched out the window as her husband backed Davey Ahearn's truck out of the driveway. "That's his idea of communicating. *Damn* him."

Sam shrugged. "Well, it's not as if you met him halfway."

"Why should I?"

"Susanna," he said softly, and she knew it was an appeal for common sense.

But she wasn't ready yet, and she swore under her breath and stormed into her bedroom, slamming the door and pacing hard to keep herself from breaking something. Or starting to cry. Worry. Totally freak out.

She'd known last night. Even as she'd felt herself drawn toward him, when Jack slipped into bed with her after plotting her marching orders with Sam, she could feel his remoteness. He was pulling back from her, shutting her out of his worries, his fears, even as he'd slid his hand up her leg. Instead of calling him on it then and there, she'd made love to him, saying nothing.

She splashed her face with cold water and returned to the kitchen. Sam was still drinking his coffee at the table. She dropped into her chair and sighed, if not contrite at least with a little self-awareness. "I know what you're saying, Sam. He's going to be short-tempered and focused until all this gets settled."

"You two are something."

She managed a small smile. "I suppose I don't have to be a horse's ass about him going Texas Ranger on me."

Sam smiled back. "I suppose you don't."

"You used to call me ma'am."

"That was before you turned back into a Yankee."

"I'm not a Yankee. I grew up all over the country, and I've lived almost half my life in Texas—it's home. I love Texas."

"Where were you born?"

"Boston."

"I rest my case." He leaned across the table toward her, his expression intense, reminding her of his intelligence and professionalism. He was not a man to underestimate. "Stop fighting so hard, Susanna. Stop putting all your fears and frustration onto Jack."

"I hate this," she said, her voice choked.

"Sure you do. It makes you feel vulnerable and out of control. It forces you to think about what you usually take for granted. You're mad at Jack because you want it all to go away. Nobody blames you for that."

"If McGarrity was stalking me before his wife's murder—"

"That's not your fault. It's not Jack's fault."

"I didn't see him," Susanna whispered. "Not until that day in my kitchen."

"Don't get ahead of yourself. Alice could have lied about him looking you up before Rachel McGarrity's death."

"You don't think so."

He shook his head, shrugged. "No."

"I keep thinking about it," Susanna said quietly.

"Then you should understand where Jack's coming from."

She nodded. "I do."

Sam settled back in his chair. "You going to cut him some slack?"

"It's not like he's cutting me any—"

"You? Hell, woman, he's cut you more slack than I ever would. I told him. Handcuffs."

"*Sam.*"

He slid to his feet and gave her one of his heart-stopping smiles, adding as if she hadn't spoken, "Ma'am."

Paul and Sarah Johnson greeted Jack warmly, but with a touch of wariness he could understand. The local police had stopped by yesterday looking for Alice Parker and Destin Wright and told them about the break-in at the cabin. Now here he was, a Texas Ranger who wanted to ask them questions. He made sure they understood talking to him was a courtesy.

"We'll tell you anything we can, Lieutenant Galway," Paul Johnson said. They were in a wide hall toward the back of the house, with a fireplace, a roll-top desk, two love seats and a six-foot-tall chainsaw carving of a bear. Another shorter hall led to a back door and out to Blackwater Lake. "Miss Parker checked herself and Mr. Wright out after lunch sometime. I helped her with her luggage, and she paid in cash—and she thanked us, said she loved the inn."

Jack nodded, trying to help the couple relax. "I can see why. It's a nice place."

Sarah Johnson fingered the cording on a love seat. "Mr. Wright left earlier in the day, not long after your wife and her grandmother were here. He was dressed for a hike, but I didn't actually see where he went. He didn't say where he was headed. He made a few comments comparing our inn to other places he's stayed, obviously more expensive. He wasn't obnoxious or rude. I think he just wanted us to know he could afford better than we had to offer."

Not anymore, Jack thought.

But she reddened, embarrassed. "Normally I

wouldn't speak this way about a guest, but under the circumstances—''

Her husband broke in. "If you've met him, I'm sure you understand."

"I've met him." Jack stayed neutral. "Can you tell me anything else he and Alice did or said while they were here?"

"Destin was out a lot," Paul Johnson said, dropping his formality. "He said he was going to Lake Placid to check out the Winter Olympic training facilities, but I don't know if he did. Alice seemed very pleased with her room and spent a great deal of time there. She was an undemanding guest."

Compared to prison, Jack thought, the Blackwater Inn was paradise. He withdrew Sam's photo of Beau McGarrity and laid it on the rolltop desk. "Have you by any chance seen this man?"

Paul picked up the photo and peered at it. His wife came over and looked over his shoulder, gasping suddenly. "Yes! Yes, I've seen him. Paul, you remember, don't you? Not this past summer—the summer before—"

"That's right," Paul said. "Damn. You're right, Sarah. That's the same guy."

"It was August, a year ago this past August," Sarah said with conviction.

Jack remained silent, absorbing the couple's words, containing his reaction. Beau McGarrity had turned up on Blackwater Lake in the Adirondack Mountains two months before his wife's murder in south Texas.

"I remember," Sarah Johnson went on, "because he was so interested in all the old stories about the lake and the inn, which we just love ourselves. He only stayed one night, as I recall. That's unusual. Our guests generally stay for several days at a time.''

''Was he interested in any stories in particular?'' Jack asked.

The couple exchanged glances, and Sarah Johnson went slightly pale. Paul cleared his throat and said, ''He wanted to know all about Iris Dunning.''

Paul Johnson handed Jack the photo, and he slipped it into his jacket, remembering Iris's haunted look last night, her conviction that her past had somehow collided with her granddaughter's life and was doomed to bring tragedy to them all.

It was different, interviewing witnesses when the subject was his family. When they were at the center of violence, lies, obsessions. Murder. He had to fight hard to keep his focus. Yesterday, finding Susanna's cabin tossed, seeing Ellen's panic, Maggie's terrified determination—making love to his wife through the night, desperate to penetrate her fog of fear and vulnerability, her anger at what had infected their lives. He had to call on his training, his professionalism, his ability to distance himself from the raw emotions of the people directly involved in a crime. The victims. He had to stay objective, focused, and as a result, he hadn't been very nice to Susanna that morning.

''Iris Dunning is one of our beloved local legends,'' Sarah said. ''I don't know if she fully realized that yesterday when she was here with your wife. Her affair with Jared Herrington was a scandal at the time, but people don't remember it that way. We think about her finding his body when she was hiking all alone in the dead of winter—''

''She was almost six months' pregnant,'' Paul added.

His wife nodded. ''She was very sick in the early months. We have a picture of the two of them together. I didn't think of it when she was here. Would you like to see it?''

''I would,'' Jack said, and he followed the Johnsons down the short back hall, its papered walls covered in framed pictures.

Paul pointed to a five-by-seven, black-and-white photograph almost in the center of the wall. ''There, that's it.''

Jack leaned in close and studied the old photograph. It was just the two of them, an impossibly young Iris and her rich lover, standing on a rock outcropping above the lake, smiling at the camera as if they didn't have a care in the world. Iris wore her hair in a long, thick braid over one shoulder, and Jack thought she was beautiful in her shorts and camp shirt, her big old hiking boots. He smiled, imagining what she must have been like as a young woman.

Next to her, Jared Herrington was rakishly handsome, right out of the pages of an early twentieth century Princeton yearbook.

Sarah Johnson sighed beside Jack, shaking her head. ''They say Jared was so in love with her. What happened—it's just unbearably sad.''

''Iris has lived a good life,'' Jack said. ''I think it's been a happy one, even if it's not what she envisioned when this picture was taken.''

He read the caption at the bottom of the picture,

handwritten in neat black print. *Iris Dunning, Adirondack guide, and Jared Rutherford Herrington of New Canaan, Connecticut.*

"The Herrington family still owns property on the north end of the lake." Paul spoke quietly, as if he was trying somehow to respect Iris's privacy, acknowledging the tragedy of that time in her life. "They haven't been up here in years. Jared's widow remarried after he died and moved to Philadelphia with their son. Apparently she had nothing more to do with the Herringtons, but I imagine her son inherited the property—"

"Philadelphia?" Jack asked, interrupting. "Are you sure?"

He nodded. "Yes, we've made it a point to learn as much as we can about the history of the lake, the people..." But he stopped, apparently sensing Jack's increased urgency.

Rachel McGarrity was from Philadelphia. A month before she was murdered, her new husband visited the Blackwater Inn in the Adirondack State Park without her and asked the innkeepers about Iris Dunning.

Jack knew he'd missed something. All along, he'd known, but he couldn't grasp it, couldn't figure out the connections. But he'd been looking strictly at Alice Parker, not at his own family. "Thanks for your time," he told the Johnsons.

Sarah inhaled sharply. "If we see this man—"

"His name's Beau McGarrity, and if you see him, call the police."

"Is he dangerous?" Paul Johnson asked.

Jack decided not to screw around with niceties. "Yes."

He was halfway to his borrowed truck when Sarah Johnson ran across the sanded parking lot, clutching the picture of Iris and Jared Herrington. She thrust it at him. "I should have given it to her yesterday. They say this is the only picture of the two of them together." Her face was ashen, and she was near tears. "You get into the history of this place, you hear the stories, and they're so dramatic, so *interesting,* and then an old woman walks into your inn—" Her lips trembled. "I'm sorry."

"You don't have to apologize," Jack said, meaning it. "I'll give Iris the picture."

"Thank you. She's a remarkable woman." She shoved her hands into the pockets of her hiking pants. She hadn't bothered with a coat, but the cold didn't seem to bother her. A fine snow had started to fall, the wind gusting on the frozen lake. "There's something else I remembered, just as you headed out the door. The Herrington teahouse. Alice Parker was very interested in it."

"Where is it?"

She perked up and seemed pleased to be of help. "I have a geological survey map inside. I can show you."

Nineteen

❦

Susanna gathered up two pairs of snowshoes and ski poles while Gran pulled on a pair of insulated gloves she'd borrowed from one of the girls. Sam leaned against the door to the mud room, watching them. "Stay within shouting distance," he said. "Don't go taking off for Greenland."

"Gran just wants to get back on snowshoes." Susanna tucked them under one arm, the poles under the other, wishing she could contain her restlessness now Jack was gone. "She used to do it all the time."

"That was a while ago," Sam said.

"Sixty years since I snowshoed on Blackwater Lake," Gran said. "Just twenty years since I've snowshoed at all."

Susanna glanced at her grandmother, who was less pensive than earlier but still not herself, and smiled at Sam. "We'll stay right around here."

"Don't make me come after you."

She nodded without argument. Sam Temple was committed to being suspicious of everyone and everything, and she'd done nothing to exempt herself.

She had on her ski hat, wind pants, high-tech long underwear, heavy socks and layers of thermal shirt, fleece vest and shell. The snow and the wind had both picked up, Gran's storm starting to move in.

"We'll be fine, Sam" Gran said.

He winked at her. "At your word, Sasquatch. Off you go."

Iris headed outside, and Susanna followed, dumping the snowshoes and poles on the driveway. There was already an inch of fresh snow on the ground, more coming down. Gran strapped on her snowshoes with little difficulty, just needing to hang on to Susanna's arm a few times to maintain her balance. She took the ski poles, beaming as she gazed out at the falling snow. "This is wonderful." She smiled at Susanna, her eyes shining. "These new-styled snowshoes are so light and maneuverable—I could climb Whiteface in them, even at my age."

Susanna laughed, her grandmother's enthusiasm infectious. "I don't think Sam would approve."

She waved a gloved hand in dismissal. "He and that husband of yours have to be careful their law enforcement mindset doesn't squelch their sense of adventure—or other people's." She sighed, a snowflake melting on her nose. "A little rule-breaking is good for the soul."

"Gran?"

"Come with me," she said and set off along the trampled path through the side yard. She moved steadily, rhythmically, if not quickly.

Susanna followed her down to the lake, welcoming the exercise and the brisk air. She assumed Gran would want to tramp around for a while, and then go inside and sit by the fire. But when they came to the lake, she wasn't satisfied staying in the open area in front of the cabin. With a remarkable burst of energy, she shot up the loop path that Susanna, Maggie and Ellen had taken to break in their snowshoes on Saturday morning.

"Let's not get too far afield," Susanna called to her.

Either Gran hadn't heard her over the gusting wind or was ignoring her. Susanna wasn't about to let her grandmother go off on her own, but when she caught up to her, Gran was already detouring off the path, using her poles to help her descend a gentle slope that led to the icy shore of the lake.

Susanna stayed after her. "Gran, what are you doing?"

"There," she said, pointing with her pole. "Do you see it? It's a boot print. I knew it. Destin came this way."

"But the inn is back the other direction—"

"I'm right," Gran said. "It's Destin. Alice checked out by herself yesterday, didn't she?"

"That's what the police said, yes." Susanna frowned. "You're thinking she and Destin had a rendezvous point somewhere."

"I told her stories about the old days out here," Gran said, leaning against her ski pole, staring out at the snow and the frozen lake. "She was so good at acting interested in every word I had to say."

"Gran…we can show Sam and Jack the boot print."

She seemed not to hear. "Most of the places on the lake are seasonal. The Herrington property is

vast. The house is boarded up, and the teahouse
where Jared and I used to meet…'' She trailed off a
moment, as if drifting back in time, but quickly recovered her train of thought. ''I suppose it's not really Herrington property any longer. I suppose it
eventually went to his son—his mother remarried a
few months after I found Jared and buried him. A
Philadelphia businessman. Tucker, his name was.
Brighton Tucker. He adopted little Jared.''

Taken aback, Susanna took her grandmother by
the elbows and held her, turning her away from the
harsh wind. ''Gran—what did you say? Jared's
widow married a man named *Tucker?*''

''Yes, I remember, because I didn't think she
should make little Jared change his name to Tucker.
But she did, and I never said a word. He's your father's half brother, but I—well, Kevin doesn't know
about him. We just didn't put those things out in the
open in those days.'' She anchored her ski pole in
the snow and sank against it, her earlier energy obviously deserting her. ''They had no interest in coming back up here. The property just sat. Oh, that happened even before I left the lake, years and years and
years ago.''

With the snow, the wind and the shock of Gran's
words, Susanna almost couldn't breathe. ''Gran…
Beau McGarrity's wife, the woman who was murdered—her name was Tucker. Rachel Tucker. She
was from Philadelphia.''

''Oh, dear.'' Iris's eyes widened, and the wrinkles
in her face seemed more prominent. But she rallied,
leaning hard on one ski pole, pointing up the lake-
shore with the other. ''Destin's got himself mixed up

in a terrible mess. If you'll just go a few yards down
this path and along the cove, you'll be able to see if
he headed for the teahouse or someplace, or if he
split off and looped back through the woods. At the
rate it's snowing, we could lose his tracks. I should
have thought of this yesterday and checked—'' She
broke off her self-recriminations and set her second
pole back into the snow. "You'll still be within
shouting distance for Sam."

"You go on inside," Susanna said. "Tell him
what you told me."

Her grandmother nodded, but didn't move. She bit
her thin, purplish lower lip, blinking rapidly. "Susanna, I didn't know. This was all so long ago…"

"Let's not get ahead of ourselves, okay?" Susanna managed a smile. "That's what Jack would
say, right? This might just be a coincidence. There
must be a gazillion Tuckers in Philadelphia. Please,
go back to the cabin."

"I'll wait out here for you," she said stubbornly.

Her grandmother was shivering, not so much from
the cold, Susanna realized, as the shock of the possible connection between her lover of more than a
half century ago and a woman murdered in Texas.
"No, it's okay, Gran. Sam's probably chomping at
the bit already. I'll be fine. Trust me, you'll hear me
yell if there's a problem. I'll check to see which way
the tracks go, then I'll hustle back here."

Obviously reluctant to leave her, Gran nonetheless
started retracing her tracks to the cabin, moving
steadily, carefully. Susanna watched her take a few
steps, decided she'd be all right and set off along
Destin's presumed path, staying close to the boot

prints but trying not to obliterate them with her snowshoes. She used her poles to help her pick up speed. She needed to make short work of this little mission. Then she needed to talk to Jack and Sam— and someone needed to find Destin Wright and warn him he'd put his stupid head in the lion's mouth this time.

Rachel McGarrity was a Tucker from Philadelphia...Jared Herrington's widow had married a Tucker from Philadelphia...Beau McGarrity had followed Susanna in the days before his wife turned up murdered in their own driveway.

Susanna pushed the rush of questions and possibilities to the back of her mind and focused on making her way along the trail, the wind slapping snow into her face. She followed the boot prints down to the lake's edge. As Gran had suspected, they didn't veer off into the woods—they stayed right along the shore.

The wind and the now heavy snow had already made the tracks difficult to make out. Susanna picked her way carefully among the rocks and thick, milky white ice that had pushed up onto shore from the lake, rounding a small cove. She'd go out to the point, see what she could make out and then head back.

She used her poles and bore down on her snowshoe cleats to maneuver along the edge of a rock outcropping. It gave way to a treacherous, vertical rock ledge twenty or thirty feet above the lake, but she took a sharp, steep path straight down to the shore. She could barely see in the blinding snow and wind. There was little she could do now but turn around, get local trackers out here to see if these prints amounted to anything. For all Susanna knew, they could be Jack's, from one of his restless bursts outside.

At the end of the path, she realized she'd lost the tracks. Destin must have gone along the top of the ledge, as treacherous as it was, and stayed off the lake, where he'd have been more exposed on the ice.

She was beyond the protection of the trees and rocks now, the wind gusting hard out in the open, slapping into her face, spraying snow against her cheeks and into her eyes. She moaned at the shock of cold, her eyes tearing, blurring. She blinked, clearing her vision, and started back up the steep path that would take her to the cabin.

Then she saw him, just as she turned onto the path, and jumped back, yelling out in horror and shock even as she took in the camel coat, the expensive cream cashmere scarf flapping on the ice.

His body was slumped in the snow and ice three or four yards from her, on the lake, at the base of the vertical ledge.

Destin Wright hadn't made it off Blackwater Lake.

Susanna couldn't take in that he was dead. It refused to register in her numb mind. Maybe there was a chance he was still alive. Maybe he'd just gone to sleep.

She had to get to him. She had to know for sure before she went for help.

She pushed down hard on her ski pole, but it hit ice, throwing her off-balance. The toes of her snowshoes crossed as she tried to adjust, and she fell hard onto one knee, losing one of her ski poles and just managing not to stab herself with the other. She untangled herself and used the one pole to get to her feet, her knee aching, snow down her neck and up her sleeves. She'd dressed for a quick run around the yard with her eighty-two-year-old grandmother.

The wind and snow were fierce on the open lake, blowing straight at her, the snow like tiny ice needles. "Destin," Susanna called, then louder. "Destin, hang on!" And she turned and yelled down the lake toward the cabin. "Sam, help! I need help down here!"

But with the wind and the curve of the shoreline, she doubted he would hear her, and she couldn't wait for him—she had to see if Destin was still alive.

She could feel the lake ice under the snow cover, and even on snowshoes, she moved carefully, as quickly as she could, her stomach twisting when she crouched down at the fringed end of Destin's scarf.

She didn't want to look, but made herself do it.

His skin was bluish white, and snow had collected on his eyelashes. There was ice in his blond hair. Susanna touched the sleeve of his coat, but his arm was like a block of ice.

"Oh, Destin," she whispered, choking on the wind, the cold, her own shock. "Destin—I wish I'd given you your damn angel money. My God."

He could have fallen off the ledge. It was icy, and the trees grew right to the edge of it. He was in boots, a city guy despite his bragging about his winter sports experience. But she didn't know. She didn't know what had happened, and she needed to call the police and get them out here, get back to the cabin and tell Sam, find her husband.

She wanted Jack now. She wanted him here, with her. She knew what she had to do, and she'd do it. But she wanted him at her side.

The simple admission brought her up short, and she stood up, the wind howling out on the lake, whipping more tears out of her eyes. The snow was coming down hard, collecting on her outer layers. Across the frozen lake, she could see nothing but blinding white, obliterating the mountains, the opposite shore. She realized how isolated she was, with poor Destin dead at her feet.

She moved toward the ledge, hoping it would block some of the wind. She was careful not to get too close to the edge, where the ice was rough and difficult to negotiate. Her snowshoes felt heavy now, her knee throbbing and bruised from where she'd fallen. She made her way to the steep, icy path, noticing the displaced snow where she'd fallen. She leaned forward, pressing hard on her toe cleats. If she hit her head on ice or rock, she'd be dead, too.

Two figures materialized at the top of the path, like a mirage. Alice Parker in front, Beau McGarrity in back. Susanna recognized them both even as she stared up at them. Alice's curls were caked with ice and snow, hanging in her face like red icicles.

"Destin's dead," Susanna said, her voice cracking from the cold, the strain. "Did you—"

"That's what Beau wants everyone to think. That I killed Destin. That I killed his wife." Alice's voice was dull and thick, as if she had no strength left in her. She had the ski pole Susanna had lost earlier and leaned heavily on it. Her eyelids were drooping. "He planted something of mine at the crime scene. My change purse. My grandma gave it to me when I graduated high school, and it had my initials on it.''

"Isn't she pathetic? A murderer who wants us all to feel sorry for her." Beau McGarrity shoved Alice from behind, then caught her before she could fall down the icy path. "I didn't want to believe it, Mrs. Galway. Alice Parker befriended my wife. I didn't want to believe she—a police officer—would kill her friend and try to frame me for it."

Susanna decided this was not the time to confront either of them. "I don't know what's going on here, but let's none of us do anything we'll regret later. Jack and Sam Temple are here. They're on the case with the local authorities. It'll all get sorted out."

Alice seemed to want to lick her lips, but couldn't manage the effort. She mouthed words that didn't come out.

"Alice," McGarrity said, and it wasn't a warning—it was a command.

Susanna instinctively took a step backward on the steep path, but she was too late. Alice raised the ski pole and whipped it at her, the sharp tip catching Susanna in the chest as she spun around, diving toward the lake and the cover of the rock ledge.

Her other ski pole flew out of her hand, and she tripped over her snowshoes, tumbling headfirst back down the path. Her shoulder slammed against the icy ledge, and she landed on her hurt knee and pitched forward into the snow. Her left hand plunged through an icy crust, tearing off her glove, scraping her wrist and arm up to her elbow.

She cried out in agony and fell onto her stomach, lying still. With her right hand, she reached for her ski pole, prepared to defend herself against another attack.

But there was silence. Even the wind had died down.

Her heart raced painfully, and she slowly extricated her injured arm from the snow, trying not to add more scrapes as she pulled it back through the crust. It was red and bleeding, aching with the cold. With her uninjured hand, she dug out the glove that had come off and eased it back on, shuddering at the pain.

She got to her feet, unsteady, terrified. Why the hell had Beau ordered Alice to go after her with a damn ski pole if he wanted her to believe Alice was framing him?

"Dead people can't tell tales," she muttered. "That's why."

Or he'd just say Alice seized the moment, and it had nothing to do with him. He was the innocent victim.

Always the innocent victim, Beau McGarrity.

Susanna pushed her questions aside and focused on what to do next. Her left snowshoe had come off. She got it back on, taking off the glove on her good hand to adjust the bindings. They were frozen, covered in snow. She did the best she could. If she had to walk in her boots, she'd walk in her boots. She didn't care. She needed to get to the cabin, to Gran and the girls.

She had no energy left to yell, but she tried. "Sam...Jack..."

Her face was wet with snow, her hair hanging in frozen clumps. She lifted one foot, bringing it down where she'd already mashed down the snow. She didn't look back at Destin Wright. She didn't bother with her one ski pole. She didn't go back up the steep path. She stayed on the edge of the lake, making her way toward her family.

Twenty

Alice trudged through the deep snow with Beau McGarrity right behind her, occasionally shoving Destin's H&K in her back to urge her to pick up her pace. She could hear him breathing hard, as much from the excitement as exertion. His mind must be racing. She figured he had about a dozen different versions of how he could play this out, none of them good.

"You and Rachel were plotting to kill me and get my money," he said.

This was one version. The Paranoia Scenario. Alice shook her head. Or thought she did. She was numb from exhaustion and the cold. Her mind felt dull, but she remembered that someone suffering from hypothermia should try to keep talking. "Rachel didn't care about your money. She had plenty of her own. And I was just her friend. I wanted to be a Texas Ranger." It sounded so romantic now, so pathetically out of reach. She mumbled, not sure McGarrity could hear her, "Ever since I was a little girl, I wanted to be a Texas Ranger."

They were following snowshoe prints on a path that seemed to lead through the woods back to Susanna's cabin. They both had on boots, and Alice wasn't sure when her legs would give out and she wouldn't be able to lift them high enough to take the next step. If not for the snowshoe prints, she'd have collapsed not long after they'd left Susanna on the lake.

"Rachel was writing a book about her grandfather and his affair with Iris Dunning," McGarrity said. "After he died, his own wife wouldn't even take him back home to bury him. Iris found his frozen body out here in the woods and buried him herself. Rachel planned to include that sort of sordid detail in her book for all the world to read."

"That all happened a long time ago—"

"She refused to show me her notes. I had to find them on my own. She planned to write about how bitter her grandmother was, how she and Jared Herrington were estranged long before he took up with his little Adirondack guide."

"I don't think Iris was ever little," Alice said dully. "She's pretty tall by my standards, and I'll bet she was tough in her youth."

"Rachel planned to make contact with Susanna Galway and tell her everything."

"So?"

"She was in the process of turning her life—my life—into a spectacle. I saw her notes. I saw her ideas for publicity and promotion, pictures, magazine spin-off articles about how she'd come to Texas and married the man of her dreams all because she'd wanted to find her father's illegitimate half brother."

Alice tripped on her own feet, and Beau nudged her in the back with the gun. "Don't try anything stupid."

"What, like walking?"

He ignored her. "You knew about the book."

"No, Mr. Beau, I didn't know a damn thing. I wish I had."

"That's why you killed her. Rachel came around at the last minute and promised me she'd burn all her notes and let the past be. You were furious. You saw your chance for the big time slip away. No book, no money for digging around in your new friend's past."

The Paranoia Scenario converged nicely with the Great Savior Scenario. Beau McGarrity as avenger of his wife's death, the man who'd bring her murderer to justice—or just shoot her. It depended, Alice imagined, on what Beau and she did next.

"Okay," Alice said. "That's why I killed her. Why did you kill her?"

He sniffed. "You think you're so clever."

"I'm guessing you two had your fight over the book, and then I pipe up with that comment about smothering you with a pillow—you took it literally. You let your imagination and paranoia take over and got yourself so carried away with what we were up to that you went and shot her."

"You're weak, Alice. You of all people know the power of the bad seed."

She thought of her grandma, her parents when they weren't drinking. They were good people. Alcoholism was a disease. Even as dehydrated and frozen as she was, Alice could feel the tears hot in her eyes.

Her grandma had always told her to watch out for the mean and crazy ones.

Beau was one to talk about bad seeds. He'd murdered an innocent woman. His wife. Rachel, a kind and sweet woman who'd just wanted to write a book about her poor grandfather, a man who'd been dead for more than sixty years. But it wasn't the kind of publicity Beau wanted—it wasn't the kind he could control. And Rachel wasn't the kind of woman he could control. He'd seen it all in those days before he'd hid in the azaleas and shot his wife in the back.

"Susanna Galway knows more than she's letting on," he said. "She has right from the start. Why else wouldn't she tell her husband about our little visit?"

Alice didn't even try to tackle that one, not again.

She prayed Susanna was still alive. She'd expected Beau to go after her, but Susanna had scooted out of reach, using the steep ledge and the harsh conditions to her advantage. He would have had to creep down the treacherous, icy path and climb over poor, dead Destin. Susanna would have had plenty of time to get the jump on him and whack him or trip him with her remaining ski pole.

He hadn't bothered sending Alice. She'd used up the last shreds of her energy swiping at Susanna and knocking her off her feet.

He'd debated trying to shoot her. "We're on a freaking lake," Alice had told him. "Two Texas Rangers are here. The local police are hunting us. Do you really want this place echoing with *gunshots*? Do you want to risk tripping on the ice and shooting yourself? Susanna's probably unconscious. She won't last thirty minutes out here. And I'm already your hostage. Count your blessings.''

He'd backed off. Alice didn't know if her reasoning had convinced him or he'd simply looked at the situation and realized he'd be risking his tactical advantage to go after Susanna Galway. Beau liked to think he only did things for logical reasons.

Mean and crazy. That was Mr. Beau. He wasn't crazy as in a treatable mental illness. Grandma hadn't meant that when she talked about his sort. He was crazy as in he didn't think like other people. No empathy. Lots of rage at the impure. Stuff like that. As far as Alice could see, his favorite scenario was to pin his wife's murder, the break-ins, the mess with the tape, Destin's death, whatever turned out to have happened to Susanna—to pin all of it on her, Alice Parker, the corrupt police officer, the fabricator of an eyewitness against him, the contaminator of evidence in a murder. The nitwit, the loser, the dreamer.

He'd find a way to blame everything on her, and he'd find a way to kill her and make it look as if he'd saved the day.

Poor Rachel. She'd thought he was her knight in shining armor.

''The anonymous call and my change purse. You wanted me to find Rachel and see the evidence you planted to incriminate me. You knew I'd panic and mess up the crime scene. And if you guessed wrong and I was working with a partner that night, you'd still have the change purse. A win-win scenario for you.''

Another nudge with the H&K. ''Keep walking.''

Alice knew her fingers and cheeks were frostbit-

ten. Her toes were numb, dead-feeling, the excruci-
ating pain of frostbite gone now. She could end up
losing couple of them, if Beau didn't kill her first.
She was dehydrated and hungry, dumb with exhaustion.

But suddenly she could smell smoke, assumed it
was from the fireplace at Susanna's cabin, and felt
her heart jump. She had no idea what Beau had in
mind. "You didn't have to kill Destin," she said in
half whisper. "He was just a harmless, self-absorbed
blowhard."

"His greed killed him." Beau's tone was cold,
without remorse or sympathy. "Nothing more, nothing less. He made his choices."

"And you pushed him off a cliff."

He didn't respond, and they descended a long,
sloping hill. She could see the woods open up and
knew they were coming upon the cabin now, that
she'd have to concentrate, anticipate, think, for once
in her life, like a good cop. But the wind and the
snow kept pounding at her, and her mind was numb,
her body aching. She was past shivering. She just
wanted to lie down and sleep. Never mind an active
death. She'd curl up in the snow and go quietly.

"Stop," Beau said, pulling her behind a snow-
laden evergreen. He pressed Destin's gun into her
back and said, his breath hot on her ear, "That's Sam
Temple's vehicle. The truck Lieutenant Galway borrowed from the plumber isn't here."

"What did you do, spend the night scouting?"

"Shh, Alice. You want to live through this, don't
you? You're a survivor. Don't pretend you aren't.

Look at what you let happen to Destin Wright to save your skin with me.''

"That's not fair."

He gave a quiet, cold laugh. "Do as I say, precisely as I tell you to. Do you understand?"

She nodded, her eyelids heavy. What if she just collapsed in the snow?

"I want you to go to the back door," he said. "Draw Sam Temple outside. Tell him you've found Destin and Susanna and you need his help. I'll be watching."

"What're you going to do?"

She could feel his smile. "Stop you."

"You're going to kill me," she said dully. "You're going to be the hero. The great savior." She shook her head—or thought she did. She couldn't tell. "They won't believe you."

"Leave that to me. If you don't do as I say, Alice, I'll kill you right here, right now. Do you understand?"

She nodded. "Yes."

"This path veers off and goes up over the hill out to the Herrington house. It's a shortcut. If you make one wrong move, I will shoot you and get out of here before anyone can do anything about it. There won't be any witnesses. You'll be dead. My prints aren't on this gun. Destin Wright's are."

"Beau, this is crazy—"

He raised the H&K to her temple. "You'll go to the back door. You'll draw Sam Temple out."

He lowered the gun, and Alice knew she had two choices. She could let him shoot her now. Or she could let him shoot her in a few minutes.

She figured she'd have a better chance of surviving with Sam Temple on the scene than up here with just her and Beau. And even if she didn't, it wasn't going to do anyone any good if she let him shoot her now. He was already here. He wasn't leaving. He probably had two or three backup plans, and all of them included shooting somebody.

He couldn't just shoot her in the back the way he had Rachel. He needed a good reason to shoot her, so he could tell Sam Temple "there you go, there's your murderer, I saved you."

Knocking on a door and asking a Texas Ranger for help wasn't a good reason.

Maybe he planned to get Sam Temple to shoot her. Something.

She wished she could think faster.

As she walked toward the cabin, she was vaguely aware that her feet were cold and wet, blistering, and her hands were shaking. Beau had chosen his cover well, a tall evergreen closest to the back door. He was known in south Texas for his excellent marksmanship. If he started shooting, he wouldn't miss.

"Sergeant Temple?" Alice sniffled, her words intelligible and clear, but her voice obviously on the threshold of complete panic. "It's me, Alice Parker. Susanna's in trouble—she needs your help—"

Sam Temple emerged from the cabin with his .357 SIG Sauer drawn and pointed right at her. "Don't move."

She opened her palms in front of him. "I'm not armed. Susanna's hurt." Alice half expected to feel the bullet in her back, pictured Beau crouched in the woods, taking aim with the H&K…Destin's gun.

Would he blame Destin, not her? Destin *and* her? "Oh, my God, Beau's not going to shoot me—Sam, he—"

But Temple had already seen something, sensed something, because he grabbed her, pulling her with him back into the mud room—protecting her—even as she heard the shot.

He kicked the mud room door shut, pinning Alice to the floor, his weapon on her. She knew he'd been hit. She saw his hard grimace as the blood oozed from a wound in his upper thigh.

"I don't know what he's going to do. Give me your gun, sergeant," she said, panicked, "let me go after him—"

"Don't move," Temple said, moving toward the kitchen, the bullet in his leg not stopping him.

A girl screamed.

Iris Dunning appeared in the door to the kitchen. She was pale. Shaken. She sank against the door frame, ghostlike. "Sam—the twins—"

He touched her shoulder, breaking through her shock. "Which way?"

She couldn't seem to focus on what he was saying. "They didn't stay in their rooms like you told them. They ran out onto the porch—I don't know what they were thinking—"

"Iris," Sam said. "Where did McGarrity take them?"

"Off the porch. Up—up into the woods."

"His car—" Alice could barely speak. She felt woozy, and for a second, she thought she might pass out. "It's at the Herrington house. He told me."

"Stay here," Temple said. "Both of you." He glanced at Iris. "Call the police. Get hold of Jack."

He headed outside, and Alice stood frozen in the mud room, noticing the snow melting off her boots. She stared at Iris Dunning. "I'm sorry," Alice whispered. "I didn't know what to do. Susanna—I think she's still alive."

The old woman looked as if she weren't breathing at all. "Can you help Maggie and Ellen?" she asked weakly. "Sam's been shot. That man—"

Alice saw the keys to the SUV on the mud room floor, in a small puddle of water. They must have fallen out of Sam's pocket when he'd pulled her inside, saving both their lives. Beau had meant to shoot them both. She saw that now. He'd had that split second of opportunity, and he'd failed, not because she'd seen it in time—because Sam Temple had.

She should have realized what Beau meant to do sooner. First he'd shoot Temple. Then he'd swoop out of the woods while Alice was still screaming and shoot her at close range. He'd claim she was the one who'd shot Sam Temple and that he'd wrestled the gun from her, shooting her in the process.

Then he'd shoot any witnesses who would tell a different story. Kill everyone if he had to.

But he hadn't managed to kill Sam Temple.

Now he had the Galway twins.

Why hadn't he slipped back through the woods when his plan went awry, while he still had the chance?

The man operated according to a logic and standards all his own. He'd sabotaged his damn automatic garage door-opener, forcing Rachel to get out of the car. So he could shoot her. Why not just trip her in the bathtub, make it look like an accident? Because he wanted to ruin Alice, because she was Rachel's friend, her confidante, because she'd know he'd killed her, no matter how it happened. So, he swiped her change purse, tossed it into his wife's blood and started Alice down this path of misery and lies, as if he'd known everything she'd do.

Australia...

Alice scooped up the SUV keys. It was all she wanted. A new life in Australia. Now Destin Wright was dead, Susanna Galway was out there in the snowstorm, her daughters had been kidnapped— *Jesus, Beau, what were you thinking?*

Iris had out a cell phone, and Alice could hear her talking to the police.

She stepped outside. She saw drops of blood in the snow, Sam Temple on the edge of the driveway with his weapon raised.

Beau was up by the evergreen where he'd taken cover, marching the twins onto the snowshoe path he and Alice had taken. He had a gun to Maggie Galway's head, keeping her in front of him, and he hung on to Ellen Galway, shielding himself with her as he dragged her along, sobbing. Maggie was completely silent.

Temple didn't have a clean shot, and Alice knew he wouldn't fire unless he did. He wouldn't risk killing one of the girls.

She eased open the door to the SUV and slid behind the wheel, breathing in the new car smells. She pulled off her gloves and stuck the key in the ignition, her fingers stiff, frozen. The engine started, and she turned on the windshield wipers, watched them flap off the accumulated snow.

Tears flowed down her frozen cheeks, searing them, streams of hot lava.

Beau McGarrity had just shot one Texas Ranger and taken another Texas Ranger's daughters hostage, and she'd been a part of it. She hadn't stopped it.

Nothing she did ever turned out right. There wasn't one thing more she could do except clear the hell out of there and not cause anymore trouble.

Beau and the Galway girls disappeared into the storm.

Before Sam could turn his SIG onto her, Alice hit the gas and got out of there.

Twenty-one

Jack stepped outside his emotions and listened to Sam Temple run down the facts, his voice steady, professional, but his eyes on fire. Blood dripped into the snow from his wounded leg. They were in the cabin driveway, the snow falling hard, the wind howling out on Blackwater Lake.

Beau McGarrity had Maggie and Ellen.

Susanna was missing, injured if Alice Parker was to be believed.

Jack absorbed the situation piece by piece. Iris had called the police. They were on the way. She sat on the bench in the mud room, her shawl pulled over her thin shoulders. Her lips were a bluish purple. "I told them to send an ambulance." She raised her vivid green eyes to Jack. "This isn't Sam's fault. I never should have let Susanna go alone. The girls— they have minds of their own. Alice...I thought she was my friend."

Sam was having none of it. "Screw that. I was supposed to protect your family. I didn't." He turned to Jack and handed him his SIG. "Go after Mc-Garrity. I'll fill in the locals when they get here."

Jack shoved the weapon into his waistband and squinted out at the snow, trying to concentrate on what he had to do right now, not the images in his head of his daughters being dragged through the woods at gunpoint—of Susanna out on the lake alone, hurt. He glanced at Sam, who gave no sign he was in pain from his leg. "McGarrity went into the woods, not down to the lake?"

Iris looked up from the bench, her lips trembling now. "Alice said he has a car at the Herrington house."

"I was just there," Jack said. "I found her car, too, and checked out the teahouse on the lake. She'd obviously spent the night there." He took a breath, fought to stay focused. "Goddamn it."

Sam hobbled into the mud room and grabbed a scarf off a peg, tied it around his bloody thigh. "McGarrity has an escape plan. He didn't come all the way up here to freeze to death in the woods."

But Jack could see he was losing Iris, and he stepped inside and knelt in front of her, took both her cold hands into his. "Nothing will happen to Susanna or the girls. I won't let it."

Her eyes were haunted. "That's what I said over sixty years ago."

Jack stood up and shifted to Sam. "Get her inside where it's warm."

But Sam's jaw tightened as he looked behind Jack. "Susanna. Jesus."

Jack spun around, and Susanna fell into his arms. "Maggie and Ellen," she said. "Jack…he can't hurt

them…don't let him…'' Her left arm was bloodied
and half-frozen, and she had scrapes on her face that
he doubted she even felt. Her legs were caked with
snow from the knees down. She clawed at his chest,
alert, and he could see her willing herself not to lose
control. ''Destin's dead. His body's not far from
here. I'll show the police.''

She wasn't showing anyone anything. One look at
her, and they'd stick her in an ambulance. ''The police are on their way. Tell them.''

Sam appeared at her side, taking her weight.
''Come on, Susanna. You need to get warm. You
won't be good to anyone with hypothermia.''

She gripped Jack's arm. ''Find our babies, Jack.
Maggie and Ellen—'' Her eyes filled with tears.
''My God, they haven't done anything…''

Iris got up from the bench, her color better as she
took her shawl and put it over her granddaughter.
''You boys go on,'' she said. ''I'll take care of Susanna. Honey, we need to get you out of these cold,
wet clothes, okay? Alice has early stage hypothermia. I don't know how far she'll get before she col-
lapses.''

''I should have shot her,'' Sam said.

Iris cast him a look. ''What good would that have
done? She saved your life. She was unarmed.''

''She created a diversion for McGarrity.'' But he
stopped himself, glancing at Jack. ''You can beat the
shit out of me later.''

Jack nodded. ''Let's go.''

Susanna placed her injured arm in the kitchen sink,
which Gran had filled with lukewarm water and a

heavy sprinkling of baking soda. She winced at the pain. "Just for a minute," Susanna told her as she tried to contain her impatience, her panic. "I don't think we have a lot of time before the police arrive."

Gran nodded. "They'll stick you on a stretcher."

Susanna shuddered at the thought of forced immobility. She'd put on dry pants and socks and was doing all she could to absorb the reality of the situation without letting it overwhelm her. If she did that, she'd be lost, useless, no help to her daughters. But she was so tired, her eyelids heavy and her mind sluggish as the warmth of the cabin penetrated, making her even sleepier.

"I have to go after them," she said. "Jack and Sam can head him off at the Herrington place, and I can come in from behind." The warm water swirled over her cuts and frostbitten skin, but the pain cut through her fog. "In case he lied to Alice or went another direction, or got lost. I can follow their tracks—"

Gran lifted Susanna's arm from the sink and laid it on a dish towel she'd opened on the counter. "If I die," she said, not looking at her granddaughter as she unwrapped gauze from the cabin's medical kit, "I would rather it be out here in these woods, today, searching for Maggie and Ellen than a year or two from now at home in my bed. I want you to know that, in case I'm not as up to hiking these woods in a snowstorm as I think I am."

In the distance, Susanna heard sirens and fought to stem a fresh wave of useless, destructive panic. "Six million acres of wilderness, Gran. They could be anywhere."

"They won't be," she said. "They're here on Blackwater Lake, and we can find them. Susanna, we can't wait. We don't have much time."

She wasn't talking about the sirens and the impending arrival of police cars and ambulances. Susanna wrapped the towel around her arm, foregoing the gauze as she ran into the mud room, taking in Maggie and Ellen's boots, their gloves, their coats, their hats. All their warm clothes.

They'd been in their rooms reading Jane Austen to each other.

Susanna spun around at her grandmother. "Gran—Gran, they'll freeze out there—"

She picked up Maggie's boots and thrust them at Susanna. "You two wear the same size. Hers are dry."

Gran hurried back to the kitchen, throwing water and the medical kit into a hip pack while Susanna pulled on her dry winter gear. The snow hadn't let up. She grabbed Jack's new snowshoes and headed outside, slipping them on easily with their spring-loaded bindings. Gran joined her, thrusting the hip back at her granddaughter and strapping on a pair of snowshoes.

"Gran—"

"I know these woods, Susanna. If I'm no help, I'll turn back. I won't slow you down." She tilted her wrinkled face to the sky. "Help us, Jared. Help us."

Jack drove. The roads were miserable. The plows and sanders hadn't yet reached this isolated north end of Blackwater Lake. He didn't know how fast a small town in the Adirondack wilderness could pull together local and state forces in the midst of a major snowstorm. He knew they'd do their damnedest to get it done as fast as possible.

But he also knew it wouldn't be fast enough.

Neither girl was wearing shoes. Sam had told him. Ellen had on fur-lined L.L. Bean slippers she'd made her mother buy just for this trip, and Maggie had on lime-green sequined slippers from the 1970s.

"Socks?" Jack asked.

"Ellen. Not Maggie. She's wearing pink satin ankle pants and a navy-blue lumberjack shirt. Ellen's wearing a black rugby jersey and leggings."

Jack gripped the wheel. "They'll die of exposure if we don't find them soon."

Sam stared straight ahead. "If I'd had a clean shot—"

"You'd have taken it. Sam, my family—" Jack could feel the tension—the fear—in every muscle in his body. "They're not easy to protect."

Sam said nothing, and Jack turned off the main road onto the rutted, barely maintained dirt road that led down to the Herrington place. It was a huge, lodge-style house, its windows boarded up, its porches sagging, its sprawling, sloping yard obviously overgrown, even with the deep snow. He followed the driveway to a parking area behind the house. Just up ahead, another narrower road—more of a lane—veered off toward the lake.

He nodded toward the lane, ice collecting on the truck's windshield as the snow continued to fall. "Alice left her car just out of sight down that way. The teahouse is about a hundred-fifty yards through the woods, but it's rough going. She and Destin apparently planned to meet there.''

"Destin never made it," Sam said, grim.

"No." Jack shifted, pointing up toward the house. "Beau's driving an SUV. It's parked up there. I decided to check back with you instead of sitting here waiting for him."

"He had Alice. He must have the tape. Why take Maggie and Ellen?"

"His ticket out of here," Jack said. "Revenge. Desperation. It seemed like a good idea at the time. I don't know how this bastard thinks."

"The girls are a win for him no matter what happens. If we catch him, he'll think he can bargain. If we don't catch him—"

"Jesus," Jack said. "He's going to dump them in the woods."

Sam nodded. "That's my guess. He knows how they're dressed. He knows the conditions. He knows we're up here, hunting his ass. He'll leave them, and he'll use them as a bargaining chip."

Jack turned the truck, blocking the road as best he could, but there was still room for an SUV to maneuver around him. He got out of the truck, sinking into six inches of fresh snow. It was still coming down, blowing in their faces out in the open. He drew the SIG, pushing away more images of Maggie and Ellen in the woods in their slippers.

When he met Sam in front of the truck, Jack handed him the weapon. "Unless you think you'll pass out, take it."

"I'm not passing out, but Jack—"

"I'll shoot him, Sam. The second I see him. I

won't think." He could feel the cold through his jacket. "I'm the girls' father."

Sam took the SIG. He was in obvious pain, the light-colored scarf on his leg mostly red with blood now, but his mind was on the task at hand. His eyes narrowed, and he pointed up ahead. "Here he comes."

A black sedan moved out from the cover of a giant spruce up near the Herrington house, Beau McGarrity at the wheel. Sam raised the SIG, pointing it at the car. His aim was steady, no sign of shakiness from pain or loss of blood. "I have a clean shot," he said. "I don't see the girls."

"He sees you," Jack said.

Sam didn't answer, his attention focused on what he was doing.

The sedan slowed. Jack had no idea what was going through the man's mind. Run for it, hope Sam didn't shoot him? Charge into them? Surrender?

Then he heard an engine gun down toward the lane. Jack swore. Alice's car. It barreled through the snow and slammed hard into the back of the sedan, knocking it sideways.

McGarrity never saw her coming. His airbag deployed, and Jack moved in fast, Sam covering him as he tore open the driver door, disarmed McGarrity and dragged him out into the snow. He was dazed from the impact of the airbag, coughing as Jack slammed him against the car. "Where are my daughters?"

McGarrity was covered in snow, ice in his gray hair, and he was breathing hard, panting from exertion—and fear, hatred, righteousness. Jack could see them simmering in McGarrity's blue eyes. He smirked. "They're dying."

"You don't want to go this far, McGarrity." Jack kept his voice steady. "You don't want anything to happen to those girls because of you. Tell me where they are."

"They won't last long enough for you to find them on your own. You need me." He coughed, his nose bleeding. Alice Parker was still in her car, probably stunned from the impact. "I'll call you when I'm free and clear. Then I'll tell you. Not one second before."

"You might want to rethink that," Sam said, falling in behind Jack. "He's those girls' father, and he has your gun. You've already shot me today, and I have my gun. A .357 SIG Sauer pointed at your head."

"Fuck you," McGarrity said. "You won't shoot me without provocation. You have all that Texas Ranger bullshit honor working against you. I don't. I have a passport under a new name, money in an offshore account, a reason to live."

Alice staggered out of her car. She seemed to have trouble walking, and when she spoke, her words were slurred. "That's you, Mr. Beau. You don't do anything the easy way. I think you just like to kill people."

She sniffled, a little hysterical, and Jack realized she was in rough shape from her ordeal. Cold, terrified, guilt-ridden. "Alice, we don't have time—"

"I'm sorry for everything, Lieutenant Galway." She was sobbing now. "He tried to frame me. A stupid change purse my Grandma gave me—he stole it and planted it at the crime scene. I should have told you. Grandma always said I wasn't cut out for the law.'' She shifted back to McGarrity, her eyelids heavy, her skin chalky. ''Beau, honey, you shot a Texas Ranger, and you kidnapped a Texas Ranger's daughters. You're in deep shit.''

''Fuck you,'' McGarrity said.

Alice sighed, turning back to Jack. ''If he's caught, anyway, he's not going to tell you where he left them. He'll let them die. It'll give him satisfaction while he sits in prison. He doesn't think like other people. Rachel and I learned that the hard way. He convinced himself we were going to kill him. That's crazy thinking.''

Sam agreed with her. ''Maggie and Ellen are his trump card.'' He kept the SIG on McGarrity. If his leg was bothering him, no one would ever know. ''Go on, Jack, before this snow covers his tracks. We don't need to waste more time trying to get him to listen to reason. I'm right in thinking you don't want to let him go and give us a call later?''

''Hold him for the locals,'' Jack said. ''If he blinks wrong, shoot him. I'll back you up.''

McGarrity smirked. ''Alice wandered around out here for hours. Destin Wright was out here. Other hikers and snowshoers. You won't be able to tell my tracks from anyone else's—''

''Sure, you will, Lieutenant,'' Alice said. ''His'll be the ones with the forked tail dragging behind them.''

Beau made a move toward her, but Sam cocked his SIG. ''I wouldn't, McGarrity.''

He backed off, but a muscle started working in his

jaw. Jack could see he'd gotten all he was going to get from Beau McGarrity, at least for now.

Alice walked over to Jack's borrowed truck, opened the driver door and climbed in. "I know you boys aren't going to shoot me for stealing a damn truck. Sam, I left your SUV up off the main road. I hiked in here so I wouldn't leave tire tracks. Thought I'd fall on my face and die, but I didn't." Her speech wasn't as slurred, and she sounded more energetic. "Tell Davey Ahearn I'll get him his truck back one day. And Jack—I didn't mean to hurt you the other night."

She shut the door and started the truck, gunning the engine.

Sam kept his eyes on McGarrity. "There are about four thousand state and local cops about to converge on this place. She's bound to run into one of them. Go on, Jack. Go after your daughters."

He could have put a bullet in the engine and stopped Alice Parker, but he looked at the snow-covered ground, thought of Maggie and Ellen. And his wife. "Susanna—"

Sam didn't waver. "You know damn well she and Granny have already gone after them."

And he did, Jack thought. That he did know.

He tucked the Heckler & Koch in the waistband at the small of his back and started through the heavy snow. He picked up Beau McGarrity's trail near the lane to the teahouse and followed it into the woods, moving fast, not daring to think beyond finding the next print, taking the next step.

Susanna leaned forward and forced herself to take another step. She was moving up a steep hill against the wind, the snow blowing in her face, spraying off the low-hanging branches of the evergreens that flanked the trail. The scrapes on her arm hurt. Her legs burned. She kept fighting tears and panic.

Gran had turned back ten yards up the trail. She knew her limits, and this would kill her. "I'll help organize the search parties," she said. "I'll fill them in on what's happened." She'd grabbed Susanna's hands and squeezed them hard, her eyes knowing, frightened. "Maggie and Ellen won't last until nightfall out here. We have to find them. There's a very narrow ravine off the main trail, just over the crest of the hill. If I were looking to stash someone, or protect myself from the brunt of the storm, that's where I'd be."

The wind whistled in the trees, gusting hard, but Susanna was moving well, a fresh surge of adrenaline helping her pick up speed. The prints were disappearing fast in the conditions, but she could still make them out—three sets, leading up Gran's trail.

The hill crested, and even with the limited visibility, Susanna could feel she was high above the lake. The landscape was rugged here, with huge, jagged rock formations and a sense of remoteness and isolation that made her shudder at the thought of what could happen to her daughters. Not here. She couldn't lose everything here.

She could see Maggie and Ellen running to her as four-year-olds, jumping in bed with her and Jack, squealing with laughter as he tickled them and tossed them into the air.

And suddenly she was twenty-two again, picking

them up from their cribs and holding their warm little bodies against her.

If Beau McGarrity still had them, he could take her. He could shoot her, hold her for ransom. She didn't care. Just let her daughters go. This wasn't their fight.

"Bastard."

She let her anger overcome her terror and pressed on, working her way down the other side of the hill. She kept looking for Gran's ravine amidst the boulders, ledges, rises and falls of the land alongside the trail. It descended sharply, then curved to the right, and she wondered if she'd gone too far and stopped abruptly.

There were no prints.

Panic welled up in her, and she looked around wildly. She pulled off her gloves and wiped her eyes with her fingertips, her hair and face dripping with melting snow.

There.

More tracks, off the trail to her right. They moved along the base of a rock ledge, scrubby evergreens clinging to its cracks and crevices, then disappeared around to the other side, where the land swooped sharply down, then straight back up again, creating a deep, narrow V-shaped crevasse in the hillside.

Gran's ravine.

Susanna almost stopped breathing. She didn't want McGarrity to know she was there. She slowly stepped off the trail, following the tracks. There were still very clearly three sets. But as she came to the end of the ledge, where the rock sloped back down toward the trail, she could see one set of tracks rejoining the trail several yards from her. They had to be McGarrity's. He must have dumped the girls and proceeded on his own.

"Mom! Dad!" The voice was faint, exhausted, coming from the other side of the ledge, further off the trail. "Someone..."

Ellen.

Susanna felt a surge of adrenaline so hard, so painful it almost brought her to her knees. She pushed forward around the rock, edging along the steep, downward sloping hill, breaking through fresh snow. The wind was quiet here, blocked by the terrain. Even the snowfall was lighter. But the air was cold, and she yelled out, "Ellen! Maggie!"

"We need help!"

"I'm coming—"

She saw a splash of bright green in the snow. Maggie's sequined slipper. Susanna gulped in a breath, stifled a gasp of panic and picked up her pace, ducking among a stand of birches as she made her way deeper into the ravine. But she lost the tracks and wondered in a moment of sheer terror if she'd only imagined Ellen's cries, Maggie's slipper.

"Maggie! Ellen!"

Her pole hit a rock under the snow, and she almost fell, recovering her balance before she could tumble down the steep hill. Her heart was racing, her pulse pounding in her ears. She was panting, sobbing as she continued on through the snow that had drifted up against a massive, ten-foot boulder.

"Mom..."

It was more a moan than a cry, and very close. Susanna burst around the boulder, immediately sinking to her knees when she saw Maggie and Ellen. "I'm here," she whispered. "I'm here. It's going to be okay."

They were huddled in the snow at the base of the boulder, bungee-corded together at the waist. Ellen was red-faced from the cold, shivering uncontrollably, her hands tucked up in the sleeves of her rugby jersey, wearing just her slippers, no socks.

Maggie was moaning incoherently, her skin very pale, her arms tucked in front of her, against her sister. She had on Ellen's socks.

"I got one cord off," Ellen said through her chattering teeth. "He had it around our knees. I gave Mag my socks. Her slippers came off, but I can't...the other cords...my hands..." Her face screwed up, and she started to cry. *"Mom."*

"Help's on the way," Susanna said. "Gran knew you'd be here. She'll tell the search parties. Look, she packed water and a medical kit. She's our living legend, Gran is, right?"

She kept talking, trying to keep her daughters awake, conscious, fighting their hypothermia as she threw down her poles and pulled off her hat. Ellen grabbed it and stuck it on Maggie's head. Their clothes were soaked from the snow. Susanna got off her gloves and scarf and gave them to Ellen, then quickly peeled off the hip pack and set it against the boulder, unzipping her coat. She slipped it off and draped it over Maggie. With her thinner clothes, she was in worse condition. But Ellen would get there fast if they stayed out here much longer.

Susanna's fleece vest came off next. She wrapped

it around Ellen's shoulders. "Mom," Ellen breathed, "you'll freeze."

"I've been hoofing it up this damn hill." She tried to smile. "I'll be fine."

"Dad…"

"He's coming. You know he is."

She dug in the hip pack, saw that blood from her scraped wrist and forearm had dripped onto her palm. Her fingers were too cold, the muscles too weakened, for her to manage the bungee cord around their waist. The bastard, she thought. The fucking *bastard*.

"Gran packed hot water," she said calmly. "It should still be warm…"

She tried to get Maggie to drink a little first, but only ended up wetting her lips and tongue.

Ellen was sobbing, hanging on to the edges of the fleece vest. Susanna saw she hadn't managed the gloves and dropped down next to her, pulling them onto Ellen's frozen hands. But she gasped, crying harder. "Mom, you're bleeding!"

"It's okay, sweetie. I fell. I'm fine."

"Sam—that man shot him—"

"Sam went with your father. He's not badly injured. Ellen, we're okay, honey. Let's just get you and Maggie warm. Here, try to drink some water."

But Ellen wasn't listening. "Went where? Mom, he has a *gun*. He'll shoot Daddy. He'll kill him. He'll—"

"Ellen, this is what Dad and Sam do." Susanna spoke quietly, as reassuring and as confident as she could be. But she knew what she was saying was true. "Trust them. It'll be all right."

She sank into the snow, gasping at the shock of

cold on her back, and scooted in close to her daughters, trying to reduce their exposure to the elements. She pulled them onto her as much as she could. Maggie was limp, mumbling incoherently, but Susanna kept talking to her, kept Ellen talking as she held both girls close, trying to warm them with her own body heat. Their temperatures had dipped below 98.6 degrees. She could feel it in their bodies, feel the cold seeping deep into her own body.

She heard a man's voice, a curse, and then Jack was there, charging up the ravine toward them.

Susanna found she couldn't speak. He tore off his coat and threw it around Maggie and Ellen, and he sank down against the boulder, pulling them and Susanna onto him, enveloping him with his warmth.

"He was going to shoot us." Ellen gulped in air, talking fast. "Maggie kept talking to him—she stayed calm, Dad. She didn't panic. She told him he'd be better off if he left us out here alive, because we were slowing him down and you were going to come after him. But if he didn't have us, he could negotiate if you caught him. Then he got out these cords and tied us together—" She sobbed into her father's chest, her voice muffled as she continued. "He gagged me with his scarf, but I got it off, and I got off one of the cords and—"

She couldn't go on, and Jack carefully unknotted the last cord that bound the two girls together and tossed it aside. Susanna saw he had tears in his eyes, and she touched his cheek, the tears spilling as he kissed her fingertips.

Twenty-two

~~~⌒⌒⌒~~~

When Susanna finally collapsed onto a chair at her big oak table, Gran and Sam Temple were arguing over a monster pot of chili. Sam wanted to dump in tons of hot peppers. Gran didn't want any at all.

Susanna knew this scene of normality was for her benefit and tried to smile through her exhaustion. The rescue crews had found them not long after Jack had arrived, and she, Maggie and Ellen were all treated and released at the local hospital. The doctors had wanted to keep Maggie overnight, but she refused. Neither she nor Ellen would suffer any permanent damage from their hypothermia and frostbite. But it was a close call. One of Susanna's cuts had required a couple of stitches. Her arm was gooed up and wrapped from wrist to elbow in bandages, and she had pain medication if she needed it.

"Give up, Sam," she said. "They eat their chili with saltine crackers up here."

He looked over at her from the stove, his wooden spoon poised midair. He was on painkillers, too, and had helped himself to one of Gran's walking sticks. "Saltines? No."

Gran sniffed at Susanna. "What do you mean, 'they'?" But she turned back to Sam, resuming their argument. "Davey Ahearn eats crackers with his chili, but I wouldn't make any generalizations of northern behavior based on what he does. I simply don't like hot peppers. There's nothing anti-Texas about it."

Sam handed her the wooden spoon and sank against the counter, his face slightly pale. He was also treated and released, but he'd driven himself to the hospital in his rented SUV, with a New York State Trooper riding shotgun with him. They all spent a long time with the state and local police. They had Beau McGarrity in their custody, arrested on a series of charges, including one count of attempted murder in the first degree for shooting Sam, two counts of attempted murder in the second degree for dumping the twins in the ravine and two counts of kidnapping in the first degree. Jack had done most of the real talking, and he'd made it clear right from the start that he'd do what he could to get Beau returned to Texas for the murder of Rachel Tucker McGarrity.

Alice Parker and Davey Ahearn's truck still hadn't turned up.

"The plumber's not going to be happy about his truck," Sam said.

Gran stirred the bubbling pot of chili. "It'll turn up."

Sam shook his head. "I don't know. Six million acres of wilderness. A foot of fresh snow. Cold. Ice. Mountains. Lakes, rivers and streams. Campsites. Alice can go for a long time before anyone finds her."

"She won't stay up here." Gran set her spoon on the stove, looking tired but remarkably cheerful. "She wants to start a new life in Australia."

Sam shrugged. "She also wanted to be a Texas Ranger."

"I think she'll make it to Australia," Gran said wistfully. "I really do."

"You want her to get away?"

"She thinks she came north for money and revenge for all she lost, but she didn't." Gran nodded, almost to herself, with conviction. "She came for vindication. She came for justice. She served as the catalyst that put Beau McGarrity behind bars."

Sam stared at her, dumbfounded. "Ma'am, I'm not going to argue with you about anything but hot peppers, but you are dead wrong. Alice Parker committed about two dozen different crimes. Breaking and entering, assault, extortion—"

"Yes, but in the end—"

"In the end, she stole a truck."

Jack got up from the castle puzzle. He'd been staring at it for twenty minutes. He was wearing a dark sweater, looking warm but still grim, still digesting, Susanna knew, how close he'd come to losing his family. Really losing it. He'd been upstairs earlier with the girls, making sure they were comfortable. Ellen had said she planned to sleep for a hundred years. Maggie still didn't have the energy to talk. And Susanna knew she couldn't have made it up three steps before she collapsed. Fatigue and shock had left her limp and shaky, and the images of her daughters' bleeding and frostbitten, of Destin's hard, frozen body, tore at her peace of mind.

"Give it up, Sam," Jack said. "Iris isn't changing her mind."

Sam grunted. "When I'm eighty, I'm going to be just as opinionated."

"You're just as opinionated now," Gran informed him.

He kissed her on the top of the head and took her by the shoulders, moving her toward the table. "You, ma'am, are going to sit down and let Jack and me finish this chili. I'll tell you one thing I'm not doing when I'm eighty—I'm not chasing any desperadoes through the goddamn frozen wilderness."

Gran sank onto a chair across from Susanna and sighed up at him. "I did all right today, didn't I?"

"Ma'am, you are something else." Sam got her shawl off the couch and draped it over her shoulders. "I, on the other hand, got my ass kicked today."

"Sam, I'm sorry," Susanna said. "We nearly got you killed."

He looked over at her, and she saw that his eyes were very serious. "That's the other way around. I'm the Texas Ranger who was assigned to keep you warm and safe."

"Uh-huh," she said. "You had your badge and your gun, and you had every reason to think they'd be enough."

He winked at her, seeming to understand she was trying to ease his guilt. "I could poke eyes out with that badge."

"He shot you, Sam," Susanna said quietly. "He meant to kill you. If you hadn't—"

"It worked out."

Jack got two beers from the refrigerator, poured one in a glass and took it to Iris and kept the other for himself. "None for you two," he told Sam and Susanna. "You're on pain medication."

Susanna shook her head. "No, I'm not. I haven't taken any yet."

"Wait'll the adrenaline wears off," Sam said. "You're going to hurt like hell."

"It'll make me drowsy. I don't know if I want to sleep." And an image flashed in her mind of the frost on Destin's eyelids.

Jack brushed a hand gently along her shoulder. "Beer's still not a good idea."

Iris reached across the table and grabbed Susanna's hands, scooping them up into hers as if she could read her granddaughter's mind and see the terrible images that were there. "Destin was in charge of his own destiny." Her green eyes shone with intensity, certainty. "You didn't tell him to become so obsessed with money and himself that he couldn't see anything or anyone else. His death isn't your fault. Or mine."

"*Yours?* No, Gran—"

She cut Susanna off with a curt shake of the head. "I should have told you about Jared years ago. You and Jack might have made his connection to Rachel McGarrity sooner. That was a decision I made a long time ago, before any of you were born. But," she said, lifting her beer glass, "I didn't create Beau McGarrity."

"He's a sick, evil bastard," Susanna said. "To do what he did today—"

"I felt Jared with us today, out here on the lake." Gran's voice was wistful, and she sank back in her chair and sighed softly. "He was with Maggie and Ellen. I know he was."

"Gran…"

She smiled. "I'm fine, Susanna. I truly am."

And she was. Susanna could see it. Her grandmother was fine. They all were, whatever physical and psychological recovery lay ahead. "The police say Destin's death might have been an accident. He could have slipped or tripped. They think the autopsy will show he died when he hit his head on the rock ledge. He wasn't shot—"

"No way was it an accident," Sam said. "There was another set of footprints at the top of the ledge. Beau pushed the poor bastard."

Gran sipped her beer. "Sergeant Temple, you do tend to look at the dark side, don't you?"

"I'm trained—"

"You're trained to look at the facts and the evidence," she said, smug.

Sam grinned at her. "That's it. I'm putting hot peppers in the chili."

But Gran just laughed, and when Sam and Jack served the bowls of steaming chili, the hot peppers were in a small dish on the side. Just to be a smartass, Sam set out a plate of saltine crackers.

Susanna only managed a couple of spoonfuls of chili before she started to slide under the table. Jack caught her firmly around the middle and got her to her feet. "To bed with you," he said.

But when he started to half carry her, half lead her to the downstairs bedroom, she shook her head. "I want to sleep upstairs with Maggie and Ellen, in case they need me during the night."

He didn't argue, and as they went up the stairs together, she felt her feet lift off the floor and let herself sink against his warm chest. He made a bed for her on the floor between the girls' twin beds. Old blankets, throws and quilts from a chest in the hall. Susanna mustered enough energy to grab a pillow from the sofa bed.

She checked on Maggie and Ellen. They were asleep, their cheeks warm to the touch.

"We almost lost them today," Susanna whispered.

Jack touched her hair. "We didn't."

But it had been so close.

She collapsed onto her makeshift bed, and Jack brought her the comforter and laid it over her. She could hear the wind dying down outside, and her mind played through the worst scenes of the day. One after another, over and over. Finding Destin. Coming upon Alice and Beau. Making her way through the storm back to the cabin. Seeing Jack, Sam, Gran and knowing—knowing all of it in that instant, terrible moment of awareness. Beau Mc-Garrity had her daughters. He'd taken them at gunpoint. And they were in mortal danger.

She would replay those images for a long time, for the rest of her life. But that was okay. She could hear Maggie and Ellen's rhythmic breathing above the waning storm outside, and she knew her daughters were safe.

She slept for a while, and later, when she awakened in the dark and almost cried out in panic, she became aware of Jack standing in the doorway, silent, not sleeping.

Twenty-three

Boston was in the middle of a thaw and excited about how the Red Sox looked in spring training down in Florida, a city on the verge of its usual bout of premature pennant fever. Jim Haviland didn't blame them. This was the Red Sox year. Had to be.

And talking baseball beat talking murder and mayhem, hands down. It had been three weeks since Iris Dunning and her family had rolled back down from the Adirondacks. New York and Texas were still sorting out who got to put Beau McGarrity on trial first. Massachusetts was cooperating—they didn't want him.

Alice Parker was still missing. No sign of her since she'd made off with Davey Ahearn's truck in the storm.

Jack Galway and Sam Temple were back in San Antonio, although Jack was spending a lot of time up north, not just because of official business, Jim thought, but because of Susanna. His damn wife was still here. She had her reasons, some of them good, like the girls needing time to recover and get back to their routines—but not all her reasons were good. She had a life here she wasn't so sure she wanted to give up. Jim could feel it. If the past year hadn't changed everything, the past weeks had.

She was at a back table with Tess, who was showing off her plump stomach. "I haven't thrown up in two whole weeks," she said.

Susanna laughed. "Well, I'm glad. I thought I'd never stop throwing up with the twins—"

"Hey," Davey Ahearn said, swinging around on his bar stool to glare at the two women. "I'm trying to eat a bowl of chowder here."

Tess grinned at him. "And I used to think you were tough."

They went back and forth like that for a few minutes, until the two women decided to take a long walk and burn off their two bowls of clam chowder each. It was in the upper fifties, perfect for walking, Susanna said. But Jim had noticed she was doing a lot of walking these days. The weather didn't seem to matter.

"I miss my truck," Davey said when they'd gone.

Jim scowled. He'd been listening to Davey go on about his damn truck for three weeks. "You were trying to sell that truck."

"Yeah, and I was going to get good money for it, too. I wanted to sell it to someone in the neighborhood, so I could see it around. I liked that truck. I got a lot of good miles out of it." It was getting harder and harder, Jim thought, to tell when Davey was making a serious point or just having some fun. "You know, if Destin had gotten over that goddamn

BMW and bought my truck, he might not be dead today.''

"I'm not even going to try to follow that logic," Jim said.

The bar was crowded, but most of the customers were served. And no reporters. That seemed to make everyone happy. They'd had reporters crawling all over the neighborhood for almost a month, scrounging up any tidbit they could on Iris Dunning and the tragic story of her rich, long-dead lover.

Kevin's dad. Jesus, Jim thought. And Iris a bona fide mountain woman.

"He couldn't make his peace with not having money," Davey said philosophically, still on Destin Wright. "And Susanna. She can't make her peace with having money. But, ten million's a hell of pot to find at the end of the rainbow."

"She made the ten million herself. She didn't just find it."

"Even worse," Davey said. "Think Jack's made his peace with it?"

"Yeah. He's figured out what most everyone else already knew. Money's not going to change him."

"He's a goddamn Texas Ranger down to his spurs."

"I don't think they wear spurs." Jim sighed, shaking his head. "Money's not why Susanna's still in Boston."

"No?"

"No."

Davey frowned. "Then why is Susanna still in Boston, Jimmy?"

"Well, there are practical considerations. The girls

need to heal, and they need the stability of their school, their friends up here. They're planning to finish out their senior year. Makes sense.'' Jim drew a couple of drafts for a pair of construction workers who'd just come in. ''I think Susanna's just waiting for that rock-head husband of hers to sweep her off her feet.''

''He's been up here—''

''That's different. By my book, they're still separated.''

Davey gave the matter some thought. ''Nah. Susanna's hard as nails. Jesus, how do you think she ended up being worth ten million? She doesn't care about being swept off her feet. She'd just tell you you're being old-fashioned and dense.''

''Tess would agree,'' Jim said. ''They might be right.''

''Doesn't matter, because Suzie-cue might as well wait for a cold day in hell as wait for Jack Galway to get all mushy and romantic.''

''She had her cold day in hell,'' Jim said quietly.

Davey sighed and nodded. ''Yeah, Jimmy. That she did. They all did.''

Iris Dunning came in, still wearing her red knit hat despite the fifty-seven degree temperature. She hung her winter things on the coatrack and sat up at the bar. ''I ran into Tess and Susanna on my way over. Oh, Jimmy,'' she said. ''Tess looks so good. She's smart and talented, and now she's having a baby. It's amazing how things work out. Do you remember last spring, when she found that body in her cellar?''

Jim did indeed. ''It was a close call.''

"It still gives me nightmares," Davey said. "I hate dirt cellars."

"But good came out of it," Iris said.

Jim put a bowl of chowder in front of her and tended his other customers, noticing when a man he didn't know walked in. He noticed strangers more these days. This one was tall and good-looking, blue-eyed, and when he unbuttoned his overcoat and smiled politely, a little nervously, Jim thought there was something familiar about him. He couldn't say what.

The man walked up to the bar and stopped short, and for a second looked as if he was going to bolt. But he rallied, and he said, "Iris Dunning?"

She turned, and the recognition was instantaneous. "Dear God. You're Jared's son. Jared Herrington—"

"Tucker," he finished. "Jared Herrington Tucker. My mother remarried after my father died, and—" He inhaled, awkward. "I wasn't sure I should come."

"I'm glad you did. Please, sit up here next to me. Oh, my." She seemed to want to touch him, but didn't, and Jim thought he could see something of the girl she'd been in her shining green eyes. "You're so like your father. If he'd lived to be your age…"

Jared Tucker settled onto the stool next to Iris, and Jim noticed the expensive sweater under the overcoat, the expensive watch. Down the bar, Davey mouthed, "Kevin," and Jim saw it now. The man reminded him of Kevin Dunning, Iris's son, Susanna's father, one of Jim and Davey's best friends.

"Rachel was my daughter," Jared Tucker said.

Iris nodded sadly. "I'm so sorry about what happened to her."

"We—my wife and I never thought she was the type to get swept off her feet like that. We only met Beau a few times. I'd like to say we saw through him right from the start, but we didn't." He broke off, leaving Iris to fill in the blanks. "She didn't tell us about her interest in you and your son. I don't know, I think she might have thought we'd be embarrassed."

"She could have been trying to decide what was hers to tell and what wasn't," Iris said.

"We didn't make the connection. We thought she went to Texas on business."

"Nothing she did justified what Beau McGarrity did," Iris said with conviction.

"No. Nothing."

Jim made a move to leave the two of them alone to talk, but Iris touched his hand, held on to it to make him stay. He'd known her since he was a little kid. She was like an aunt to him. He patted her hand and served her and her lover's son bowls of hot chowder.

Jared Tucker stared at his chowder. "My mother told me about your relationship with my father. Often. She was a bitter woman. She did what she could to distance us from what remained of his family. I loved my mother, Miss Dunning, but I wanted you to know—" He looked at her, shadows under his blue eyes. "I'm very glad my father had you in his life."

"I loved him. I loved him with all my heart and

soul.'' She smiled at Jared Tucker, brushed the top of his hand as if he were a little boy. He had to be close to seventy. ''Your dad was there with us on Blackwater Lake, Jared. He wanted us to know the truth about what happened to your daughter. His granddaughter.''

The man's eyes filled with tears, and he grabbed his soup spoon, trying not to cry. ''She came here one day. She never introduced herself. Rachel always tried so hard to do the right thing, always looked for the good in people. She said she watched you have chowder with your friends and decided she didn't want to drag you back to the past. A few months later, she went to Austin.''

''She was an interior designer,'' Iris said softly.

''Yes.''

''My son is an artist.''

He nodded. He set down his spoon, his chowder still untouched. ''My wife and I were supposed to go down and see Rachel the week after she died.'' Jared's tone was steady, laced more with sadness than hatred or bitterness. ''Perhaps we should have done more to find answers to what happened.''

''You were grieving,'' Iris said.

''We still are.''

Jim winced, and at the end of the bar, he could see Davey Ahearn had let his chowder go cold. But he'd obviously heard enough pain and sadness. ''That fucker McGarrity,'' he said.

''Davey!'' Iris shrank back, horrified. ''Jared's daughter—''

''Yeah, I know. It's a bitch, what happened.''

Jared Tucker surprised everyone by sighing instead of throwing his soup bowl at Davey. "That sums it up, doesn't it?" He smiled at Iris. "I can see why you've stayed here all these years."

Davey caught Jim's eye, as if to tell him he knew he'd saved the day with his crack.

Then Jared took in a deep breath and said, "Tell me about my brother," and Jim knew the guy was okay.

Davey shifted on his bar stool, scratching his handlebar mustache with one finger. "Oh, yeah, wait until you meet Kevin and his wife. A white-bread fellow like you. Eva's the wife's name. Artists. Totally daffy. Kevin did a portrait of me once, and I came out looking like Yosemite Sam."

Tucker was silent a moment, and Jim wondered if Davey had gone too far this time. Even he seemed to realize it. But suddenly Jared Herrington Tucker grabbed the pepper grinder and said, "My father— Kevin's and my father—wrote poetry."

They talked, then. Davey, Jim, Iris, Kevin's half brother. After second bowls of chowder and another round of beer, Iris made them move to a table because her back was hurting from sitting on the stool. Jim stayed behind the bar. He felt good. For the first time since Susanna Galway was sipping margaritas at his bar and mumbling about the stalker and murderer she'd left behind in Texas, Jim Haviland could say he felt good.

Then the bar door opened, and Sam Temple, Texas Ranger, walked in. "Doesn't it ever warm up in this damn city?"

"This *is* warm," Jim said.

Temple sat at the bar. No cowboy hat, no badge

and no gun that Jim could see, but he had on the boots and the black leather jacket. The Tufts graduate students had exams. They weren't in.

"I have news about Davey Ahearn's truck," Temple said. "I was going to call it in, but since I feel a certain sense of responsibility for it getting stolen—"

"Over here," Davey said from their table.

The Ranger turned, and when he saw Iris, he smiled. "Evening, ma'am."

She beamed, and Jim wondered if old Iris Dunning had herself a crush on a handsome, black-eyed Texas Ranger.

Davey was getting impatient. "What's this about my truck?"

"It turned up."

"No kidding. Where?"

Sam Temple didn't answer. Instead he shifted back to Jim. "I'm not here on official business. My captain wouldn't authorize me to fly up here just to notify someone about a stolen vehicle. Besides," he added in that slow, deep Texas drawl, "I don't know as the Somerville police and the Massachusetts State Police want to see me back in their state anytime soon. The police in New York even less so, since I never got around to introducing myself before all hell broke loose up on Blackwater Lake."

"You feel bad about that?" Jim asked.

The black eyes flashed. "No, sir, not a whole lot."

"My *truck*," Davey said, growing impatient. "Where the hell is it?"

Sam Temple swiveled around to him and grinned. "San Francisco."

* * *

Alice Parker took an evening flight out of San Francisco. She had a new name, a new birth certificate and a new passport, courtesy of her prison contacts. She liked the name Audrey Melbourne a lot, but she knew the authorities were expecting Audrey to bolt for Australia and would be on guard. She'd decided on Sidney Rutherford. It sounded dignified, and it reminded her of Rachel. And of Iris Dunning.

She had a new look to go with her new name—sort of Old Money Philadelphia with a splash of south Texas. She'd cut her hair real short and dyed it white-blond, and she'd gotten rid of all her jewelry. She just wore the most expensive watch she could afford, which she'd bought from a sidewalk vendor in San Francisco. It was probably a knock-off, but she didn't care. It felt like quality.

Her new identity was the only flat-out dishonest part about her trip, that and being wanted for questioning by the authorities in Texas, Massachusetts and New York.

And her plan to slip into Australia and never, ever leave.

For the first couple of hours, she kept waiting for the captain to walk back to her and tell her she had a phony passport. She hoped he'd just throw her off the plane. She'd rather plunge into the Pacific Ocean than go back to prison. She wouldn't mind having to testify against Beau McGarrity, but they already had him.

Damn, she thought, they did. They had him.

No one came for her, and she stared out the window, seeing only her own reflection. She thought she looked all right. She'd been a police officer and a prison inmate. She'd tramped through a blizzard with a mean, crazy son of a bitch with a gun at her back. She'd helped catch him, and then she'd driven off in a stolen truck—how she'd made it as far as San Francisco, she didn't know. Lucky, maybe, for once. She'd found a seasonal camp with a covered Jeep parked outside and exchanged its New Jersey tags with the Massachusetts tags on the truck. She remembered how her frostbitten fingers had bled, but she hadn't felt it. Not even the warmth of the blood oozing out over her hand.

She'd damn near lost a couple of fingers and toes. Thawing out had nearly killed her. She'd never look at frozen chicken parts the same way.

When she got to San Francisco, she got herself a job at a twenty-four-hour diner in a not-so-great part of the city. She'd worked like a dog these past six weeks, slapping plates of eggs and chipped mugs of coffee in front of bleary-eyed customers and smiling so they'd tip her well. She lived in a cheap, dirty room in a squat, ugly building filled with very nasty people.

It would have been a lot easier if she and Destin had managed to shake loose a hundred grand from Susanna Galway, but that wasn't meant to be. Alice regretted ever making him think it was. She knew she'd regret it to her dying day, no matter how many times she changed her name.

She was making a fresh start, but she would do what Iris had tried so hard to get her to do those first few weeks in Boston, as simple—and as difficult—

as that was. And that was not to lie about who she was.

Except for her name, which was a practical matter.

Rachel had lied to Beau about who she was, and he'd shot her in the back and tried to frame Alice for her murder—but that wasn't Rachel's fault. He'd had no business shooting her, thinking she and Alice were plotting to kill him for his money. Mean, crazy bastard. And getting all obsessed about Susanna and wondering if she was part of the plot to kill him, trying to put a fast one over on him. Alice couldn't recall ever thinking she was the center of everyone's world like that.

But she knew she had much to atone for.

Before she got on her flight, she'd mailed Iris the framed picture of her and Jared Herrington out on Blackwater Lake so long ago. Alice had found it in Davey Ahearn's truck. She hadn't included a note. She couldn't think of what to say.

She drifted off to sleep, and hours and hours later, when the lights came back on in the cabin and the flight attendants started moving around and people popped up their shades, Alice looked out her window. She saw the bridge and the Sidney Opera House, and she started to cry.

She had another chance. One last chance.

Twenty-four

The huge, old trees in Old Granary had sprouted fat, red buds. The grass was turning green, and yesterday Susanna had walked along Commonwealth Avenue to see the famous magnolias and their pink blossoms.

She'd just finished meeting with two clients, a young couple who wanted to get their finances in order before they had children. As they got ready to leave, the woman asked her husband to go on ahead—then told Susanna she was already pregnant, but he didn't know.

"I know we need another year, at least," she'd said.

Susanna had smiled. "Another year for what?"

"To get our finances in order."

"But you're pregnant now," Susanna had said. And she assured the young woman that they could make adjustments in their financial plan. Things change. You start over. Life didn't always go precisely according to one-year, five-year, ten-year plans. In fact, it seldom did.

Did she want the baby? Oh, yes. What about her husband? He'd be thrilled. And the woman saw it herself—there was no problem.

She could see them talking out on the sidewalk in front of the old graveyard, and she would bet a good chunk of change that the husband already knew about the baby. This was the part of her work she loved best, she realized. The people, their hopes and dreams.

She still had many of her original clients from San Antonio—and if she went back, most of her Boston clients would stay with her.

When she went back, she thought.

She hadn't seen Jack in two weeks. It was like an eternity.

He'd been in constant touch with Maggie and Ellen. He wanted to make sure they received proper, thorough post-traumatic care. He was being a good father to them.

This time, she was the one who went emotionally remote on him. She'd felt herself pulling away for reasons she didn't fully comprehend. He didn't push, and she didn't know what that meant. She loved him—he loved her.

But she didn't know if they could put what they'd had back together, before Beau McGarrity, before Alice Parker and Destin Wright and nearly losing Maggie and Ellen on Blackwater Lake. Before learning about Gran and Jared Herrington, and Jared's older son, and his granddaughter, shot to death by her husband in south Texas when he learned she'd lied to him about who she was, believed she was tarnished, out to use him, even kill him.

The money and not telling Jack about Beau McGarrity straight off didn't seem to matter so much.

McGarrity hadn't come into her kitchen that day just to talk her into believing in his innocence, intervening with her husband. He'd come to assure himself she wasn't helping his wife write a book and hadn't been a part of her and Alice's supposed plot to kill him. He'd come because he knew Rachel was Susanna's cousin.

She watched the couple head up Tremont Street, arm in arm, smiling at each other, and thought of herself and Jack twenty years ago when they were students. How could they go back to where they'd been?

The doorman called up, rousing Susanna from her morose thoughts. He had a delivery. Good, she thought. A distraction. She ran out into the hall and met a local florist, a young woman, coming out of the elevator with a huge, white box tied with a pale pink ribbon. Susanna stopped her at once. "You must have the wrong person."

The florist looked at her over the box. "You're not Susanna Galway?"

"No, I am—"

"Then these are for you. Where should I put them?"

Stunned, Susanna mumbled that she'd take them. The florist retreated into the elevator.

Susanna returned to her office and laid the box on the antique table in front of her leather couch. She ran through the list of possibilities as she untied the ribbon. A grateful client? Her parents? It wasn't her birthday, and she hadn't done anything worth celebrating, except survive a murderer—and that was a while ago. Not long enough ago to forget. Never that.

Maybe the flowers were for Maggie and Ellen. They were starting to hear from colleges now.

She lifted the lid on the box, and inside were a dozen long-stemmed pink roses. Each one was perfect. There was a small card. Her hands shook as she tore it open.

"To my darling wife…your loving husband, Jack."

Her heart jumped. Then she shook her head. This was not possible. Jack didn't use words like "darling" and "loving." He'd say "darlin'" in an exaggerated Texas drawl when he was being sarcastic or deliberately sexy, getting under her skin.

Gran and the girls must have talked him into sending flowers. Or goaded him into it. And called in the order themselves and told the florist how to sign the card.

Oh, but they were beautiful roses. Susanna touched their soft petals, then read the card again, feeling her entire body sigh. *Your loving husband, Jack…*

"Look at you," he said from her doorway, as if she'd conjured him. "And I thought you weren't sentimental. I'll have to send you roses more often."

"Jack!"

She swept across the room and jumped into his arms, kissing him as he caught her around the middle. He held her close, letting his hands slide over her hips. He laughed softly. "If I'd known you could be had for a dozen pink rose, I wouldn't have bothered with the rest of it."

She draped her arms over his shoulders. "The rest of what?"

"One thing at a time." He set her down and walked over to her desk, eyeing her computer. "Do you trust me to shut down this baby? Or might I lose a million dollars?"

She couldn't answer. Her throat was too tight, every nerve ending in her body on high alert. He started pressing buttons, and finally she ran over and slipped between him and her keyboard. "I'll do it."

He grinned. "I thought you might." He ran a finger along the back of her neck as she worked, curved it around to her throat. "There's been a plot against you. Nothing you can do but roll with it."

She hit buttons, shutting down her computer, then her printer. "I love you, Jack."

"I know."

"I always have. I never doubted my love for you—"

He placed his hands on her waist and turned her to him. "Susanna, I know."

She licked her lips, feeling slightly dizzy. "I never took your love for granted."

"You didn't? You should, because it's yours, forever." But he smiled, kissing her lightly. "None of this will help you now. Events are already in motion."

"What events?"

He released her and walked around her desk, back to the flower box. "I take it you haven't checked all your bank balances today? Or should I say *our* bank balances?"

"Jack—Jack, I'm not moving another muscle until you tell me what's going on."

He put the top back on the roses and tucked the box under one arm. "Might as well go along with the program, darlin'. If I have to throw you over my shoulder and carry you out of here, I will."

He'd do it. He had that look about him. Over his shoulder, down three flights of stairs with a box of long-stemmed roses. He wouldn't bother with the elevator. More fun taking the stairs. All in a day's work.

"Sam tried to get me to take handcuffs," he said, his eyes very, very dark.

"Jack," Susanna breathed, "this is about the sexiest thing—"

"Romantic," he corrected, and his half smile just about undid her. "I'm wooing you."

She turned off the coffeepot, grabbed her jacket and followed him down to the lobby. A sleek, black car was waiting for them at the curb in front of her building. The driver opened the back door, and she and Jack got in. A few seconds later, they sped off into the city traffic.

"Do I get to know where we're going?" Susanna asked.

"Airport."

She shook her head. "This isn't the way to the airport."

"Small airport west of the city. My plane's there."

"Your *plane?*"

He glanced at her and winked. "If you can buy a cabin in the Adirondacks without telling me, I can buy a plane—"

"But how? How did you get the money?"

"It's in my name, too."

"We don't have that kind of cash in our checking account. You don't have the necessary information and access—"

"I hope Maggie and Ellen put their minds to good use in college," he said, "because if they turn to larceny, we're all in trouble."

Susanna sat back against the leather seat. "I see. They stole my passwords and hacked into my computer."

"Said it was a piece of cake."

"How big a plane?"

"Our daughters are making noises about going to Harvard. They say they can come back to Texas for graduate school and the rest of their lives. That'll mean a lot of flying back and forth, and with your grandmother up here and your folks spending summers on Lake Champlain—"

"Jack?"

He slipped an arm over her shoulder and drew her against him, kissing the top of her head. "It's a damn fine plane, Susanna."

"You're flying it?"

"I am."

"Can I ask where?"

His gaze darkened slightly, and his hold tightened on her. "We need to go back to Blackwater Lake."

Most of the ice had gone from the lake, and the snow had melted in the open areas and along the hillsides that got the most sun. The rivers were full. It was the time of year for ice jams, floods, sap runs and mud, one of the quietest seasons in the Adirondacks, when even many locals liked to get away.

For Jack's purposes, it was the perfect season.

He thought the plane was a damn fine idea. A five-or six-hour drive would have done him in. He'd have had to pull over and make love to his wife on the back seat, and that probably wouldn't meet Maggie and Ellen's basic test for what was romantic and what was not. Although he had the feeling Susanna wouldn't have minded.

He had arranged to have a car waiting at the Lake Placid airport. Susanna was asking about her luggage. "Gran and the girls packed your bag," he told her, then added, "except for what I packed for you."

He heard her small intake of breath and saw the flash of anticipation in her very green eyes, and he knew the flowers and the car and the plane weren't what were getting to her. But, he'd promised Maggie and Ellen he wouldn't skimp on the romance. He'd woo her, good and proper.

They didn't know he'd decided to take her back to Blackwater Lake. That was his idea, not theirs.

When they arrived at the cabin, Susanna shot out of the car and ran down to the lake. He followed, sensing the change in her mood, expecting it. He saw her sink into the soft spots in the wet ground, but she paid no attention, making her way to the lake shore, clambering over rocks. Finally, she stood on a flat boulder, the wind catching her hair, the sun setting in streaks of deep orange and purple that surrounded her, enveloped her. The mountains rose around the lake, still capped in snow.

Jack walked out to her rock, and she turned

abruptly to him, tears shining on her cheeks. "It's beautiful here."

"Yes."

Her hands were balled into tight fists, and she shifted back to the lake. "If I'd told you about Beau McGarrity from the beginning, Alice never would have tried to use the tape to blackmail him. She wouldn't have come north. He'd have stayed out of our lives."

"He was already in our lives, Susanna," Jack said, careful. "And Alice would have found another reason to come up here, because on some instinctive level, she knew this was where she'd find the answers she wanted. Maybe you did, too. And me. Maybe your grandfather pulled us here so we could finally put all the pieces together."

"You don't believe that. You're all facts and hard evidence—"

"There are so many things each of us could have done differently, and probably should have, but you did nothing that endangered anyone. Nothing, Susanna."

"Do you really believe that?"

"Everyone does. I've gone through this entire story in every detail with law enforcement and prosecutors in three states for the past six weeks. Beau McGarrity was an infection in our lives before any of us knew it." Jack tried to keep his voice from getting too hard. "We can both beat ourselves up forever for not seeing it sooner."

"I don't want that," she said.

He touched her cheek. "Then you'll come inside?"

She nodded. "I should put my roses in water."

But once they were inside, Jack made sure she realized she had more to worry about than roses. He'd made a few arrangements ahead of time. Chocolate, champagne, wine and enough food for three days. He'd instructed Gran and the girls not to pack any hiking clothes. This was to be an indoor long weekend.

After she got her flowers into a pitcher of water, he handed her the small bag he'd packed himself. "Take a look."

She sat on the floor in front of the fireplace, and he built a fire while she went through her bag. Lavender soap, bath salts, bubble bath, essential oils whose labels promised an enhanced sense of romance, scented candles and a ring—a very expensive ring he knew his wife would never buy for herself. Davey Ahearn and Jim Haviland had talked him into it. They said she needed more sparkle. She wore too much black.

Jack smiled at her look of pleasure mixed with shock at the ring. "Sam says you'd only be worth five million if you weren't so tight."

"That's a logic all Sam's own. I'd like to dig into his finances—"

"No, you wouldn't. He gives away most of his paycheck." Jack nodded at her. "Keep going. There's more."

She found the scrap of silk he'd picked up at a pricey store and held it up.

"Maggie and Ellen insisted a pretty, romantic silk nightgown was a must."

"This isn't a romantic nightie." Susanna cleared

her throat, and he saw this woman he'd loved for so long blush and smile, almost as if she were nineteen. "Jack, this is a sexy *negligee*."

"Well," he said, unrepentant, "at least it's silk."

She balled it up in her hands, gathered up her goodies and retreated to the bathroom. She didn't stay gone long. When she returned, she smelled of lavender and had on her little scrap of a nightgown, and Jack knew the night was lost. There'd be no candlelit dinner as he'd promised the girls, no champagne, no chocolates. He wouldn't last.

"Susanna..."

"One thing about this pretty, romantic silk nightie," she said, sliding onto him in front of the fire. "It's easy to get off."

But amazingly, he took his time, starting there in front of the fire, exploring every inch of her with his mouth, his tongue, his hands, as if for the first time, until she was liquid and he thought he'd explode. Then he swept her up and carried her into the bedroom, but when he laid her on the bed, she said, "Enough of this torture," and started on his shirt and pants, finally pulling him onto her, into her. "I love you, Jack...I love you so much."

"I want you back," he whispered. "I never want to lose you again."

"You never lost me."

He kissed her long and hard, moving slowly, deeply inside her. "No more secrets."

"No more," she said. "Never again."

They'd have three days of this. Talking and loving, recuperating from the long months of their ordeal…but by his calculations, he had one more secret to drag out of her.

Susanna sat out on her patio in San Antonio on a warm mid-April afternoon, drinking a margarita, easy on the salt. She'd made a pitcher. Jack would be home soon, but right now, she was alone. The south Texas sunset was incredible. It was Maggie and Ellen's April vacation, their last vacation as high school students, and they'd flown down with Gran, who'd insisted on taking a commercial flight because she didn't trust small planes. To prove her point, she recited the details she'd read of small plane crashes she'd heard about in the past few years. One was at least twenty years old.

Jack hadn't let that go and teased her unmercifully. "And I thought you were Iris Dunning, Adirondack Mountains guide, a legend in your own time."

But Gran had held her own. "I don't like guns, and I don't like small planes."

"I'll bet you could take on a bear with nothing but a jackknife."

"I could," she said, sniffing at him, "but that was a long time ago."

She was in Austin now with the twins, visiting her son and daughter-in-law. Jared Tucker had flown in from Philadelphia, and there were discussions of what to do with the Herrington property on Blackwater Lake. Kevin and his older half brother wanted to create a nature preserve and name it after their father and Iris. Gran was opposed. In Jared's name was fine, but she wasn't having anything named after her while she was still alive.

Susanna knew her grandmother was secretly pleased. This visit, the talk of a nature preserve—they were a way for her to integrate the young woman she'd been on Blackwater Lake with the woman she'd become, the woman she was now. They weren't separate. She hadn't just landed into Boston sixty years ago and started from nowhere. She'd carried on. That was the way Maggie and Ellen put it. Carrying on. As if they took some measure of comfort—of inspiration—from what their great-grandmother had done after the tragedies she'd faced on Blackwater Lake.

Jack walked out onto the patio, still dressed for work, tall against the golden sunset. She saw his badge and smiled, thinking that all that was important in their lives was still intact. "It feels good to be home," she told him. "Once the girls graduate, it'll be permanent."

He sipped the beer he'd brought out with him. "Will it?"

She sat up straight, reading his expression, that familiar note in his voice. "You already know, don't you?"

"I have spies everywhere."

She'd spent the day looking at historic houses in downtown San Antonio. "You're a born-and-bred Texan. You've always said you'd like to restore an old Texas house." She stretched out her legs, enjoying the April warmth. Boston was still a little cool for her tastes. "Andrew Thorne's an architect, you know, and Tess said he'd be happy to look at anything we might want to buy, provided it's not too close to when she has the baby."

"That's nice of them."

He seemed to mean it, but he obviously had something else on his mind. Something else he was after. Susanna sipped her margarita. It was her second, and she probably should have had something to eat first. She was beginning to think Jack might have the advantage on her. That she'd missed something after all.

"What else did you do today?" he asked smoothly.

"Damn," she breathed. "You know that, too?"

His dark eyes settled on her, but he said nothing.

He was enjoying this, she thought. But so was she. She'd managed to keep from admitting this one last secret through their three days in the cabin. "I took your plane for a little spin this afternoon." She got up and walked over to him, her world spinning just a little, but not from the margaritas. It was Jack—it was always Jack. She eased onto his lap. "It's better if I confess while you're wearing your badge, isn't it? More official."

"Susanna..."

"My last secret. I have my pilot's license." She smiled as she lowered her mouth to his. "But you knew that already, didn't you?"

His mouth met hers, and he laughed. "I always know."

CRIMES OF

Passion

Sometimes Cupid's aim can be deadly.

This Valentine's Day, Worldwide Mystery brings you
four stories of passionate betrayal and deadly crime
in one gripping anthology.

Crimes of Passion features FIRE AND ICE,
NIGHT FLAMES, ST. VALENTINE'S DIAMOND,
and THE LOVEBIRDS by favorite romance authors
Maggie Price and B.J. Daniels,
and top mystery authors Nancy Means Wright
and Jonathan Harrington.

Where red isn't just for roses.

Available January 2002 at your favorite retail outlet.

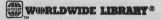

An incredibly gripping novel from bestselling author

DIANE CHAMBERLAIN

When eight-year-old Sophie Donohue fails to return from a camping trip, her frantic parents mount a desperate search...a search made more critical by the fact that Sophie is sick with a serious illness. As her mother, Janine, refuses to give up hope that her daughter is alive, Sophie finds refuge in a remote cabin with a mysterious woman. A woman who holds Sophie's fate in her hands, but who knows doing the right thing for the little girl will mean sacrificing her own daughter.

THE COURAGE TREE

"A suspenseful family drama...this page-turner will please those who like their stories with...many twists and turns."
—*Publishers Weekly* on *The Courage Tree*

On sale January 2002 wherever paperbacks are sold!

MIRA®

CARLA NEGGERS

MIRA®